TUESDAY'S CHILD

Tuesday's child is full of grace . . .

TUESDAY'S CHILD

Louise Bagshawe

BCA

This edition published 2005
by BCA
by arrangement with HEADLINE BOOK PUBLISHING
A division of Hodder Headline

CN 137076

Typeset in Meridien by Avon DataSet Ltd,
Bidford-on-Avon, Warwickshire

Printed and bound in Great Britain by
Mackays of Chatham plc, Chatham, Kent

This book is dedicated to my brother James.

Please visit Louise online at www.louise-bagshawe.com
– and don't forget the dash!

As ever, my thanks are due to my wonderful agent and friend, the peerless Michael Sissons, and to everybody at PFD; James Gill, Fiona Petheram, and Tim Corrie; to Rosie de Courcy; and to the whole team at Headline, including Harriet Evans, Martin Neild, Kerr MacRae, Jane Morpeth, Natalie Higgins, Kate Burke, Catherine Cobain, Barbara Ronan, Emily Kennedy, Julie Manton, Louise Jackson, Lucy Ramsey, Selina Chu, Zoe Carroll and everybody else. I'm very fortunate in my colleagues and I thank you all.

1

'Gooooooooaaaaal!' I scream. 'Gooooooooaaaaaal! Yessss!'

Ha ha ha! Right in the upper left-hand corner. Wooh-hooh! I run up the field like a madwoman and do a quick cartwheel.

'In your face, Ricardo!' I yell.

Paul comes up and hugs me. Yess! Those lads from the Dog and Duck thought they were so hard drafting an actual Italian into their team, been playing since he was five. But I scored! Oh yes.

My boys, the gang from Queen Charlotte, are falling around laughing at them.

'Ha ha ha,' Leo says. 'You got pasted by a girl. Hahahaha!!'

'By a GIRL,' adds Paul, in case they didn't get the point. Mark Stebbins looks askance at Ricardo, who's gone bright purple. This might be the most embarrassing thing that's ever happened to him. He jabs a finger at me.

'Va fancoul'!' he yells. 'Non e ragazza!'

I don't need a translation: 'That's no girl.' I get that a lot. I shrug and blow him a kiss. He kicks a tuffet of grass in front of the goal, aggravated.

'What's that?' says a familiar voice.

I spin round, elated. It's my flatmate, Ollie McCleod. He's also my best friend. Relaxed and funny, a good-looking bastard too. Blond and strapping, like a Viking.

'Lucy scored,' Paul said. 'Beat 'im flat out.' And laughs again.

Ricardo fires off some rapid Italian and stomps away from the goal. If I had to guess, it translates as, 'Fuck it, I'm going for a drink.'

I glance at my watch. Two pounds ninety-nine from a garage five years ago and it still works. Just as well, I have to watch every penny. It's almost noon.

'What are you doing here?' I ask Ollie.

He shrugs, smiles. 'Thought you might like a lift.'

I glance at the lads.

'I'm off home,' Paul says. 'Wife's coming back soon.'

The others have already started walking off the field to the pub. Normally I join the team for the post-mortem and half a cider, but not if Ollie's offering. I'd rather hang out with him, quite frankly.

'All right, see you next week then,' I say. And happily walk off with Ollie towards his BMW.

'Girlfriend around?' I say casually.

'She's working,' he says.

Excellent. He's so much more fun by himself.

'Thought we could order in a curry,' Ollie says. 'Watch the match together, she won't be back till seven. I got some wine in.'

My spirits soar. England–South Africa rugby, a nice curry, and some red wine with Ollie on the couch. And then I might play a bit of *Star Wars Galaxies* this evening, that way I won't have to pay too much attention when Annoying Victoria gets home.

'Sounds good,' I say. I've got a great life, honestly. I'm so lucky.

Ollie opens the door to his BMW for me. He never minds about my muddy boots or anything. 'Should be a good night.' He grins at me, clearly looking forward to it himself. As well he might. Poor Ol. Monday morning, he has to go back to being a lawyer, whereas I get to review, i.e. play, computer games for *PC Games Universe*. He'll be up at seven, I'll lie in till about ten. And all he has to show for it is

2

money, which isn't a very good trade, if you ask me.

Never mind. We'll have a top night. We're best mates and it's going to be fun, which my life is in general most of the time. I settle back against the nice leather seats of his car, so much better than the smelly old bus I generally have to use, and he pulls away into the traffic.

'All right?' he says.

I nod. 'All right.' And I am.

'Fucking hell!' I exclaim.

'What's the matter?' Ollie asks, mildly.

I stare in disgust the screen. 'Fucking bounty hunters. All they want to do is kill Jedi. That's my fourth death this week and I just lost a skill box! Basic Regeneration II, that took me two hundred thousand points.'

'Oh dear,' he says, grinning.

Annoying Victoria looks at me like I'm speaking Swahili.

'It took me weeks grinding that out,' I sigh. 'Just carving up nests of feral gurks and giant spiders . . .'

'Really, Lucy,' she says with icy scorn. 'How fascinating. 'Aren't you a little bit *old* for video games?'

'I'm twenty-four. Fuck,' I say again, with feeling.

'Such language.' She wrinkles her pert little nose.

'Anyway, video games are my job,' I say defensively. 'Remember?'

'If you can call that a job.' Victoria shrugs. 'Reviewing stupid juvenile games for a silly magazine with no readers . . .'

'Victoria,' Ollie warns.

'Well, I'm sorry.' She pouts. 'But it's hardly a job for a young lady.'

I stare at her, daring her to say it. *But then Lucy is hardly a young lady* hangs in the air.

'How's your work going?' I say. I force myself to be nice. Ollie isn't just my mate, he's my landlord, and Victoria *is* his girlfriend. I have to show willing, even though my dearest wish is for her to evaporate in a puff of Anaïs Anaïs.

'Wonderfully.' Victoria tosses her long chestnut hair in that public schoolgirl flick she does so well. Victoria works in magazines too, but that's where the similarity between us ends. She has a high-paying job at *Stylish*, the UK's leading fashion magazine, or so it claims, superbly ignoring *Vogue*, *Elle* and *InStyle*. Victoria is twenty-eight and a polished, thrusting young Turk. She's always getting promoted, and she never turns up at Ollie's without some new, fantastically expensive little dress she snaffled from the samples cupboard, or some perfectly girlie bag.

Vicky doesn't think much of my Doc Martens and Metallica T-shirts.

'Our layout next month is going to be a real winner,' she says, smugly. 'I thought of the theme myself.'

'And what's that?' I ask brightly. I sneak a look at Ollie. I hope he's appreciating all this effort. He's always asking me to be a bit nicer to Victoria.

' "What Is Femininity?",' she says, describing a wide circle in the air with her long, shaped talons. 'We're going to explore the whole question of what's truly feminine. Is it classic? The Birkin bag, the camel-coloured shift? Is it floral? The print dress, the strappy sandals? Or is it modern – LK Bennett shoes, Alexander McQueen, Kate Spade accessories?'

'Mmm,' I say, pretending to be interested. I would imagine 'Jeans and comfy T-shirt' does not count as one of the options.

'And there'll be comment pieces. "Have women today lost sight of what it means to be feminine?"' Vicky adds, giving me a significant look.

'Right,' I say. 'I better get back to my game. My character is stuck in a nest of crystal snakes. And that bounty hunter must DIE!'

'Come on, hon,' says Ollie to Victoria. 'We've got reservations.'

'Going somewhere nice?' I ask encouragingly. I wish they'd leave, I can't concentrate while Victoria's here. It's that cosmetic lens-enhanced stare at the back of my head that puts me off. I know she's doing it even when I can't see.

'Oh, you wouldn't like it,' Victoria says. 'It's the kind of place which uses knives and forks.' She gazes accusingly at the empty McDonald's bag on the floor next to my computer.

'I'm going to clean that up,' I say defensively. 'Just as soon as I'm finished.' Grrr. Can't. Stand. Victoria. 'You guys have a lovely evening!' I add, pasting on my brightest smile.

'Don't worry.' Victoria snakes her slender arm through Ollie's brawny one and gives him her patented Princess-Di-under-the-lashes look. 'We're going to. It's going to be a very *special* night.'

'Bye, mate,' Ollie says to me.

They leave. I wait till I hear the door shut and then breathe an exaggerated sigh of relief. I turn back to *Star Wars Galaxies* and flex my Dark Jedi Apprentice light sabre.

But somehow all the fun has drained out of it.

Curse Victoria Cobham!

'My boosters are going to run out,' I lie to my apprentice Xa-Tu. He's in Australia, plays even more obsessively than I do. 'I'm going to take a break. See you tomorrow.'

'No probs,' he types back. 'U R the best!'

The best. Well, yes, at *Star Wars Galaxies* I am pretty good. In fact not only am I a Dark Jedi Apprentice, rapidly climbing the ranks towards Dark Jedi Knight, I am rich. My net worth is over four million credits. I can buy anything I want . . .

Sadly, this is not the case in real life. I'm quite poor. On the other hand, I'm happy.

Most of the time.

I shut the computer down and push my chair away.

Hmm. I don't know why I suddenly feel a bit gloomy. This is not like me. I'm never down. Who would be if they had this life?

I go into the kitchen and make myself an instant coffee, adding real cream and three sugars. Victoria would disapprove. That makes it all the more pleasurable. She can't understand how I can stuff my face with junk and yet stay a steady eight and a half stone, although I've told her a million times. I like sports. I play five a side with some lads most Sundays, I go for a run every day, even now, in the winter; February isn't the best month of the year, but running cheers me up. And if nobody's about, I dance. I love to dance. Best feeling in the world. Of course I'm sure I look a bit stupid in my DMs and cargo pants, but so what. Nobody's watching.

I pull out my Abba and Madonna CDs from their secret stash hiding place behind all my cool stuff – my collection of eighties' heavy metal and seventies' rock – and bounce around the room like Tigger.

Ollie always says I've got way too much energy.

He's a few years older than me. We met on a tour of Europe, one of those cheap ones where it's two to a coffin-sized room, go everywhere by bus and see the continent in two weeks – total fun. I try to go every year, but usually can't get the money together in time. Every two years, though, without fail. I love travelling. Anyway, he'd graduated from the LSE and I'd dropped out of Durham. I was reading French, but I just got bored. Actually going to France – and Germany, Italy, Spain and Portugal – seemed like a much better bet.

'So are you switching courses when you get back?' he asked me on the second night. He's Scottish, with blond Viking hair and a few freckles, and the body, as I told him, of a prop forward. He told me he wasn't a prop forward, he was a fly half. So he did play rugby! Result. I love rugby.

'Nah.' I tossed my somewhat unkempt blonde hair insouciantly. 'I'm not going back.'

'But why? Are you mad?'

'Not mad. Technically. I just don't want to be tied down.' I sighed. 'Imagine, sitting in a bloody lecture hall listening to a professor for three years. I got enough of that at school.'

'You didn't like school?'

I stare at him. 'Does anybody?'

'I did,' he said mildly. 'Anyway, you can't have done too badly there to have got into Durham, eh?'

'Oh, I'm not thick,' I say hastily.

'I'm sure you're not.'

'And I had Mum and Dad to think of. They wanted me to study and get my A levels and all that.'

'Are you close with them?'

I smiled. 'Oh yeah. Very close.' I have the best parents in the world. And the nicest sisters.'

'Then aren't you going to upset them by dropping out?'

He'd unerringly put his finger on my one problem.

'Ah,' I said triumphantly. 'But I'm not going to tell them. At least, not like that. You see,' I said proudly, 'I've got a job already.'

'Have you?'

'Oh yes. A *great* job. And I'm going to tell them I've been poached.' I waved my hand airily. 'Expanding field, great prospects . . . . you know. That way they won't worry.'

He looked puzzled. 'But you're only . . .'

'Twenty.'

'And you haven't graduated. So what's the field? Law? Translator in the EU? I know it can't be banking, not if you're reading French.'

'Ugh, no,' I told him. 'Nothing like that.' I make a face. 'This is a really *good* job.'

'Let's hear it, then,' he said.

'Reviewer,' I announced proudly.

'Movie reviewer? Book reviewer? Theatre critic?'

'Games reviewer. Computer games.'

Ollie blinked. 'You what?'

'Computer games,' I repeated, slightly annoyed. '*Quake*. *Doom*. You know.'

His face clears. 'Like *Donkey Kong*?'

'*Donkey Kong*,' I said scornfully. 'Um, yeah, if it was about nineteen eighty-three.'

'I'm sorry. I never was one for computer games,' he said humbly.

'Oh well. Takes all sorts,' I told him. 'Anyway, I love them and I sent off a few pieces. And they were impressed, especially because I'm a girl.'

'Girls don't play computer games?'

'Not as many as you'd think. I don't know why.' None of my big sisters ever went near a video games arcade. 'But all the more work for me,' I added cheerfully.

'So what's the magazine?'

'*PC Games Universe*.'

'Never heard of it.'

'Well, you wouldn't have.'

'That's true.'

To be honest, I don't read it either. It's one of the smaller ones. But so what? Everybody has to start somewhere.

'It's my dream job,' I told him. 'Can you imagine? Other people are accountants and estate agents. Or *lawyers*. And I'm going to get paid to sit around playing computer games! And get all my games for free.'

'Sounds great.'

'So what do you?' I asked him, feeling a bit guilty. Ollie would not have a cool job like games reviewer lined up, would he?

'I'm going to be a lawyer.'

'Oh.' I blush. 'I'm awfully sorry.'

'Don't worry.' He winks at me. 'I actually want to be a lawyer.'

'That's great then,' I say, unconvincingly.

After that we got on brilliantly. As I said, I love rugby, all kinds of rugby. Ollie was amazed. He'd never been able to have a conversation about the British Lions with a woman before. And despite the fact that he was a bit strange, not liking computer games, and wanting to spend his life hunched over law books, I thought he was great. Friendly and open-minded.

Not to mention easy on the eye.

By the end of the tour he offered me a place in his flat, for a very reasonable rent. Three hundred a month. And it was a nice flat in Swiss Cottage, although I'd have been happy to bunk up with him in darkest Zone 5. Getting a decent flatmate is vital. How can you enjoy life if you have to live with some miserable sod who puts up cleaning rotas?

It was just as well, for my dream job has one disadvantage. It doesn't actually pay very well. I've been there for four years now, got my name on the masthead and everything: 'Contributing Editor'. Sounds very important, doesn't it? I even have business cards. 'Lucy Evans, Contributing Editor, *PC Games Universe*.' They were great for showing to my dad, he was so proud.

The salary, however. Well, you could call it peanuts, but that might not be fair to peanuts. Put it this way; four years of my absolute best work and I'm currently making twelve grand a year.

I take a sip of my sweet coffee. Is that what I'm depressed about? That I can't usually afford restaurants with knives and forks?

I shiver and blow off the cobwebs. I don't think so; after all, money's never worried me before. There's more to life than money, isn't there? Because of Ollie I live in a great flat. And we go out for pasta at least once a month. Besides, I can cook when I want to, I just usually don't want to. Sandwiches are cheap and they're my favourites. Running doesn't cost anything, and I get all my CDs at flea markets.

My games come free, and so does my computer, in fact they give me a new one every year to keep up with Microsoft.

I live quite nicely, thank you. And I have a piggy bank to save up for the cheap tours of Europe. What else is there to pay for? Food and booze, I suppose. I get a new pair of DMs once a year and there's one set of low heels that I never, ever wear mouldering in the cupboard. Clothes don't interest me. I'm the same size I was at college and most of my clothes date back that far. They're comfortable enough. It's not as if a games reviewer needs a jacket and tie, as I remind Victoria when she looks in my room and sneers.

And then it comes to me.

Victoria. Annoying Victoria. She's the reason I'm feeling down. Why does Ollie have to like her so much? She's *awful*. She comes into our nice flat and ruins everything by complaining about how I do up my room, how I keep my collected back issues of *Kerrang!* magazine . . .

Last month she offered to 'help' me.

'Come on, Lucy,' she said with that bright smile I can't stand. I bet she was the leading light in her Brownie pack and loved to chant 'Brown Owl dib dib dib' or whatever. 'You can't go on like this. Can she, Ollie?'

'Like what?' I asked, aggrieved.

'Like *this*.' Her manicured hands waved disdainfully around my room. 'It's *ridiculous*.'

'I like it,' I told her in what I hoped was a firm tone.

'Oh, really.' She laughed in that disparaging way of hers. 'You like these movie posters?'

'Movie posters are classic decor.'

'Of *Die Hard* and *Predator*?'

'Classics,' I responded firmly.

'And what on earth is this?' Her carefully shaped nails tapped the ratty piece of white paper covered in black marker writing that hangs in pride of place over my bed.

'Ah, that's a set list. From Oasis. Actually, it's really early.

Ninety-five. From the Astoria,' I told her, with (I think you'll agree) justified pride.

'What's a set list?'

'You're not serious.' Now it was my turn to look scornful. 'A list of songs the band is going to play. The roadies tape it to the stage in case they forget the order.'

Victoria's thin lips curled. She's not very pretty, if you ask me, although she is polished. She makes the most of what she has, if you like that sort of thing. You know, lipstick and matching eyeshadow, little pink dresses and teensy cardigans, painful-looking shoes with straps on them . . .

'And why would you want to keep that?' she asks.

'It's early Oasis. It's rock history.'

'Rock history!' She gives a delicate little snort. 'Now come on, Lucy. We can fix this. Rip down all this nonsense, and I can get you some wonderful Laura Ashley wallpaper, it has the *tiniest* burgundy sprigs. You're good at DIY, I'm sure it would only take you and Ollie a day to put up.' She doesn't offer to help herself. Of course. 'And we'll throw away all these old magazines.' She picks up a classic issue from eighty-seven with Axl Rose on the front cover, holding it between her thumb and forefinger as if it's contagious. 'Clutter,' she pronounces, 'is bad for the soul. You need some pretty cream rugs and more space in here. You don't even have a mirror!'

There's so much wrong with this I hardly know where to start.

'Why would I need a mirror?'

'To look at yourself,' she says very slowly, as though I'm a moron.

I shrug. 'I know what I look like, thanks.'

Ollie snorts with laughter. He has been hanging on every word, the traitor!

Victoria says acidly, 'I wonder.'

I tug at my hair. I hope it hasn't gone all ratty again.

'Help me out here, darling,' she wheedles to Ollie in that breathy little-girl voice of hers. Her eyelashes are fluttering away madly. 'Persuade Lucy she just *has* to do something about this . . . room.'

Victoria makes 'room' sound like 'pit'.

'Don't drag me into it, sweetheart,' Ollie says in that lazy way of his. 'It's Lucy's room, she can do what she likes in it.'

This made Vicky pout, but she left me alone after that. She always lets Ollie have his way and never contradicts him.

I wonder if that's why he likes her so much?

I briefly consider what would have happened if *I* always let Ollie have his way. If I didn't tease him mercilessly for weeks after Scotland lost to Italy in the Six Nations, though he got me back when we went down to France, the straw-haired git.

Victoria never teases Ollie, unless it's along the lines of, 'Ooh, look at those biceps,' or 'I read you won another case, darling, they're going to make you a judge soon.'

Whereas I say things like, 'How can you stand that bloody boring job?'

I'm not *jealous* of Victoria, you understand. At least not romantically. When I first moved in I had a heart-to-heart with Ollie. I said, 'Look, mate, don't try it on because I don't get involved with mates.' Which he said was short and to the point.

It's a rule of mine. Dating your mates is always disastrous. I should know; I've always dated my mates and it's always been disastrous.

But you know, if he was interested he would have said something. All my other boyfriends did and I gave them the same speech.

So, I admit, the first six months I was slightly put out. I was sort of expecting the odd kiss after we'd shared a bottle of wine. Or something.

But then I wised up. OK, he's not interested. You can't go around moping after blokes. And for once I'd half meant what I'd said. If you date a friend and it doesn't work out – make that *when* it doesn't work out – what have you lost? Well, a friend. And let's face it, you can always get more of those. But if I'd dated Ollie and it hadn't worked out, I would have mucked up something really special. Because he is my absolute best mate, like, ever. And almost as importantly, I would have lost my flat in Zone 2.

It's a wonderful flat. My room has a great window onto the street and overlooks a huge chestnut tree, so spring and summer I wake up to broad green leaves. And there's even a small – OK, tiny – square of garden, but it's really nice to sit out there when the weather's good and eat a Strawberry Mivvi or drink a cold bottle of Woodpecker.

Besides, I'm not the type to sit around being glum – except maybe tonight. I know the sort of girl Ollie's attracted to and it isn't me. Before Annoying Victoria there were Annoying Rhiannon and Annoying Fay. I'm sure he ordered them all from the same shop: mid-length hair, shiny and sleek, skinny with no muscles, predilection for itsy-bitsy dresses and heels, always do their nails, think he's wonderful.

Actually, this reflection cheers me up. It's been a long time with Annoying Victoria, I'd say too long. Ollie is fairly predictable, and changes his girlfriends with the seasons, once every four months. It's the end of February. Spring is just around the corner. So soon he'll be coming home with another annoying Jemima Khan-a-like, but she's bound to be at least a slight improvement on Victoria.

I smile. Yes, that's it. I've just reached the end of my Victoria tether. And she'll soon be gone, and my life will go back to normal.

Which, I'm glad to say, is pretty much perfect.

* * *

13

'Lucy.'

'No,' I lie. 'She's not here.'

'Lucy.' Ollie's gently but insistently shaking my shoulder.

I grudgingly open the corner of one eye. He's holding a cup of tea, but this only slightly mollifies me. I got a bit carried away with the old *Star Wars Galaxies* last night and stayed up till 2 a.m.

'Did I oversleep?' I grunt. I am vaguely supposed to be in the office by ten.

'You're fine.' He smiles reassuringly. 'It's only seven fifteen.'

'Seven fifteen?' I'm so outraged I sit bolt upright. 'Seven fifteen? Why are you waking me in the middle of the night?'

Ollie knows perfectly well I don't get up till nine, not a minute earlier.

'I'm sorry.'

'I bet you are. A manky cup of tea is no consolation either,' I say grumpily.

'Shall I take it away then?' asks Ollie, threatening to remove it.

'Certainly not.' Aggrieved, I swipe it from him.

'It's just that I have to be in the office early today. Big case.'

'You do have my sympathies,' I say. 'But being a lawyer is your own fault, as I've told you before.'

'Indeed you have.'

'And you really don't need to wake me up to say goodbye.'

'It wasn't that.' Ollie pushes a few copies of *Kerrang!* out of the way and settles down on a bare patch of my carpet. 'I've got something to tell you.'

I take a sip of the tea. 'Good news?'

'Yes,' he says carefully. 'Very good. But there's a bad side to it.'

I smile at him, unafraid. 'Well, let's have it, then.'

Ollie looks awkward, but musters a big smile.

'I'm getting married!' he says.

I don't drop the tea, for which I mentally award myself ten million skill points and create myself an instant Dark Jedi Master.

'That's great!' I lie. 'To . . . Victoria?'

'Of course to Victoria,' he says. 'What, you think I have some kind of James Bond double life?'

'Do you?' I ask, interested.

'No,' he says.

'Oh. Well, that's fantastic. You asked her last night, then?' And never said a word to me, I don't add. Thanks for showing me the ring and all that.

'Actually, she asked me.' Ollie smiles modestly.

'She asked you?' For a second I am shocked out of my misery. That's not like Victoria at all. She would never do anything untraditional or daring like that.

'Yes,' he says. 'It was February the twenty-ninth yesterday. Leap year, remember?'

Oh yes. So it was. Joy.

'Anyway, she asked me, got down on one knee and everything.'

'And you said yes.'

'I did.' He confirms the sorry truth.

'Well, congratulations.' I set the tea aside and give him an awkward hug. 'I'm thrilled for you both.' I try for a caring, Tony-Blair-style smile. 'Will Vicky be moving in with us?'

His face darkens.

'That's the bad news,' he says.

'Oh. She won't be, for a bit? Well, that's a shame,' I say brightly.

'No, no. She is going to move in. Us getting married and all, this is going to be our home.' He squeezes my shoulder. 'I'm awfully sorry about it, mate, really I am. But I'm going to have to ask you to move out.'

* * *

As soon as he leaves I pull on my tracksuit bottoms and my sweatshirt and go for a run. I can't think of anything else to do.

I select some really nasty, grinding music. Slayer. Something seriously depressing. Matches the grey sky and, not coincidentally, my mood.

Move out.

Move out!

I run up the hill towards the tube, trying to block everything out with sheer physical effort. After that I'm going up another hill, up to Hampstead. A really punishing run. Something which doesn't leave you much space to think.

Of course, I think anyway. You can't help it, even if you do have Kerry King wailing out another blistering solo in your ear, and your lungs are burning and there's lactic acid in every muscle.

Why Victoria? He was meant to dump her, not marry her. I can't spend five minutes with the girl, and Ollie wants to spend his whole life with her?

OK, well. I don't own my friends. Got to remember that. It takes all sorts and all that. It's just so disappointing because I thought he was different. But apparently not. Ollie wants to marry a girlie girl who waves using only the tips of her fingers.

Grrr. Annoying Victoria's itsy-bitsy waggle . . .

I stop and bend over, heaving for breath, and catch my reflection in the window of Costa Coffee. Oh dear. All red-faced and sweaty, with my hair plastered to my head. Victoria would never look like this, would she?

'Come on, Vicky,' I said to her once. This was a few months back when she was new on the scene and I thought, you know, she might like to be friends. 'I have a guest slot at my kickboxing class. Want to work up a sweat?'

'I don't *sweat*,' she replied with a fake smile. 'You know

16

the old saying, Lucy, horses sweat, gentlemen perspire, ladies merely glow.'

Come to think of it, that might have been when I decided to hate her.

And now she'll be 'merely glowing' as she rips down all my treasured posters and re-does my entire room in Laura Ashley burgundy sprig.

My digital watch says it's nine. Time to head back and shower. I suppose I can't be late into work today, can I?

I need the money.

2

PC Games Universe doesn't have offices that match its name. More like *PC Games Three Rooms and Share a Loo*. One reason I've never really complained about the peanuts – well, apart from loving the job – is that there's clearly no cash for anybody. We're an independent little mag, very fan-based, surviving on subscriptions and the miraculous good will of W.H. Smith.

In theory this means we are the indie kings of gaming. Bill Gates and Electronic Arts don't scare us!

In practice it means we rent a so-called 'suite' of three rooms in the Oval, south London, above a dingy pub with an old and desperate clientele, and next to a sweatshop where even more desperate women spend all day hunched over sewing machines and not speaking to us. The paint is peeling, the loo has no window, and there's not much space.

Ken, the owner, has a perpetually harassed look on his face and bites his fingernails worse than I do. I feel too bad for him to bother him much for a raise. It's not as if he lunches at Quaglino's with Rupert Murdoch. He's always on the phone trying to scare up new advertising, or get our suppliers to wait for payment. I feel sorry for him. His name's on the masthead but he doesn't have a good time like we do. No time to review any cool games or write interesting previews of the upcoming big releases.

But this morning I'm going to have to. Bug him for a raise, I mean. It has been four years, after all, and everybody likes my reviews best. I did my sums on the way over, crammed into the stinking sardine tin that is the Northern Line anywhere near rush hour; I mean I can't get *anywhere* to live in London on what he's paying me. Even a flat share!

Poor Ken. I try out different ways of asking him in my head. But I'll make it up to him, I'll work doubly hard. I could even offer to help call advertisers. Or something.

That's reasonable, isn't it?

I get out of the tube at Kennington and emerge from the lift into the grey, cloudy mid-morning. It's wet but at least it's mild. I'm borrowing Ollie's umbrella and wearing one of my smartest outfits, my newest jeans and a vintage long-sleeved Bon Jovi T-shirt from 1986 with 'Slippery When Wet' on it, which, let's face it, is a classic. I polished my DMs with some of that instant shine stuff and I even chose my best black scrunchie to tie back my ponytail. It's made out of velvet. Now you can't say fairer than that, can you?

I'm sure I look businesslike, in a media sort of way.

Here we are. The narrow alley round the side of the Admiral Lord Nelson looks particularly grimy today. I square my shoulders and press the buzzer.

'Hello?' he says brightly.

'It's Lucy.'

Ken doesn't say anything, just buzzes me up. But he sounds unusually chipper. Perhaps this won't be so difficult after all.

I stomp upstairs, past the sweatshop which is humming with its normal wretched activity, and enter our cramped offices.

Ken is sitting in his chair by his dirty and cracked window pane. He's wearing a stained sweatshirt and a big smile.

I glance around. Nobody else is here. Brilliant!

'Wotcher,' I say to Ken in my friendliest manner.

'How are you, Lucy?' he beams at me. 'It's a great day, isn't it?'

I look uncertainly at the drizzle that has started to fall into the alley, the louring clouds overhead.

'Um . . . yeah!'

'A really brilliant, lovely day.'

'Except it is a bit wet,' I can't help pointing out. 'And, you know, grey.'

'Wet! Grey!' Ken waves his hands as though to dismiss such minor considerations. 'That's March, innit? That's the seasons. You got to love the seasons.'

I stare at him. What's going on? Ken is usually as miserable as Eeyore on a particularly gloomy day.

'Oh, Lucy, it's good to see you.' He gets up and comes over, and before I know it I am being enfolded in a hug.

Well. This is auspicious. My fairy godmother has obviously woken up after a particularly long sleep and is in wish-granting mode.

I seize the opportunity. 'Ken, I wonder if we could talk about the future?'

I'm proud of that. Non-confrontational, you see. Easing him into it.

'The future!' he cries joyfully. 'Oh yes, we can talk about the future. In fact you'll be the first to know!'

'Know what?'

Ken sits down and beams at me.

'I,' he says slowly, 'have sold the magazine.'

'What?' I say.

'I've sold the mag.'

I plop down heavily onto the nearest chair. 'You've sold *PC Games Universe*?'

'Sure have. To Associated Magazines.'

'But we've no circulation.'

'Apparently we had just enough to annoy them,' Ken says gleefully. 'Just enough for them to want us out. They're pushing their title.'

'PC Games Galaxy.'

'Yeppers.'

We hate *PC Games Galaxy* and all it stands for. It is the puppet mouthpiece of corporate computer journalism and never slags off games by the big houses.

'But we hate—'

Ken holds up a hand. 'I know what you're going to say, Lucy. But you can't think like that when you've got a business to run. Associated—'

'They are The Man, you know.'

'Associated made me a handsome offer,' Ken says. 'Just to pack it in. We couldn't go on like this forever, Lucy.'

'But—'

'It's time to grow up,' he says, rather sternly. 'Act mature. Be your age.'

I look meaningfully at his sweatshirt, which says WHO FARTED in huge red letters.

Then something occurs to me.

'What do you mean just pack it in? Aren't we selling the magazine to them? Getting . . .' I don't know, 'merged, or something?'

'Ah.' His face falls slightly. 'Not as such.'

'Not as such?'

'We're more being sort of . . . eliminated.'

I glance round the offices. 'But . . .'

'Apparently they have all the input they want on *PC Games Galaxy*.'

'But our columns . . .'

'They don't like them.'

'Our graphics . . .'

He shakes his head. A further nasty thought occurs to me.

'My reviews?'

'I tried, mate, I really did,' Ken says apologetically. 'I sent them clippings even. Look.' He hands me a slim grey paper file which is indeed full of cut-outs of some of my best reviews.

Somebody has crossed them out with blue marker pen. My review of *Empire Earth* flutters to the floor. It has CRAP written on it in the same blue pen.

'Don't mind that,' he says. 'They don't appreciate you like I do.'

But I do bloody mind!

'Look, don't despair, Lucy,' he says. 'I've written you two really great references.'

'Two?' I'm numb.

He hands me two envelopes.

'This one talks about what a brilliant reviewer you are and how you always get your copy in on time.'

'OK.' I take it.

'And this one,' Ken blushes slightly, 'this one says what a brilliant secretary you are, talks about your typing and computer skills and your pleasant and . . .' he hesitates, 'ladylike attitude.'

'Fuck that!' I burst out. 'I'm not a secretary, Ken! Never have been!'

'Yes, but I thought you might consider it.'

'You what?'

'Lucy, I asked around,' he says earnestly. 'Contacts. You know. They said most of the computer gaming mags are staffed up to their eyeballs. They use freelancers and pay them next to nothing, and they're laying people off instead of taking them on.' He smiles weakly. 'I thought you'd have a better chance of a job as a secretary. If I made up something really nice.' Ken nods at the envelope I'm clutching between my thumb and forefinger as though it were toxic. 'I did say great things about you.'

'Yeah. Thanks.' I stare at him. 'So what you're basically saying is I'm out of a job.'

'No,' he corrects me. 'You're out of *this* job. I'm sure you'll find something. Land on your feet.'

I smack my hand to my head.

'Oh, thank God.' I laugh with relief.

'What?' Ken demands.

'You're joking, aren't you? 'Good one, too. You really had me going there, you bastard.'

'Lucy—'

'I thought, look at this selfish fuckwit, he's sold his soul to The Man and he's kicking me onto the street.' I shake my head. 'Just when I really need a raise, too.'

'But it's not—'

'You know, you may be a fat ugly bastard with all the personal charms of a drunk baboon, but you're a funny fucker. I'll give you that,' I say.

'It's not a joke!' he shouts.

I deflate. 'It's not?'

'No. It's not.'

'But how can you do this to us?' To my horror tears have started to prickle in the corner of my eyes and I dash them away angrily. 'Just dump us?'

'I'm married, remember? I do have a family. I poured my heart and soul into this magazine for six years and I think I deserve a bit of reward,' Ken says, with an aggravating amount of reasonableness.

'What about Tim and Richard and Iain?' My fellow reviewers. 'Did you give them letters saying what great *secretaries* they were?'

Ken's not a bad person and I shouldn't be bitter. But I am. I'm feeling as bitter as a bitter lemon laced with sloe juice.

'They don't need them. Richard's a qualified accountant. He was going to leave anyway. Iain's father runs a successful distillery in Glasgow. And Tim's got a maths degree from Bristol, first class, it's not going to be hard for him to find a job.' Ken looks at me sympathetically. 'I only meant to help you with the secretary letter, Lucy.'

I swallow hard. 'I know. Thanks, Ken,' I mutter ungratefully.

'I mean, it's not like you have a degree or anything.'

'Yeah.'

'And you're not really qualified to do anything.'

'Mmm.'

'You should take a course, learn to type.' I do my reviews with three fingers. 'You've already got computer skills. A good secretary always makes money.'

'But I don't *want* to be a secretary. I want to play games for a living.'

'You've got to think of alternatives, Lucy.'

'I could join a band,' I suggest hopefully.

He gives me a look. 'You're twenty-four. You're too old to be in a band. That's for students. And anyway, without your salary here, what are you going to do for money?'

I have absolutely no idea.

'I'll be fine,' I lie brightly. 'Enjoy your . . .' I want to say 'thirty pieces of silver' but stop myself. '. . . money,' I finish.

'Lucy.' Ken lumbers to his feet again, offers me a solemn handshake. 'This is a blessing in disguise. You'll see.'

Well, I think as I stumble down the narrow stairs to the alley and step into what has become full-blown rain, all I can say is it's a bloody good one.

For want of anything better to do I go home. First I mope for a couple of hours. I've got some great music for moping. Pearl Jam, Creed, they're king whiners. But then I can't take it, so I switch off the stereo and go round to our newsagents.

I was looking for a Walnut Whip which always cheers me up. I can still remember being a little girl and Dad said I could have one sweetie and I had to choose between a Walnut Whip and a Creme Egg. Oh, the agony of decision. I plumped for the Creme Egg. It was the wrong choice, of course, and after I'd scoffed it I sat mournfully in my bedroom dreaming of that chocolatey nutty crunch . . .

But I digress. They didn't have any Walnut Whips. They didn't really have any good sweets at all. I had to make do with a Drifter. It was turning into the shittiest day ever, so I suppose I wasn't all that surprised.

But then I saw the rack of papers.

Ah!

Light dawned. It was Monday, right? *Media Guardian* comes out on a Monday. I know this because I had an actor boyfriend for about five minutes and he always used to comb through it, looking for open calls and stuff.

I fished through my pockets and found a couple of pound coins. Cool. I would take the paper home, read through the ads and get a new job. I mean, I'd got the last one without looking very hard, hadn't I?

My mood lifted fractionally. Maybe it would all be all right.

Three hours later I was starting to get a headache.

They don't want much for the money, do they, these jobs? Only stuff like 'at least three years' experience on a broadcast radio network'. Or 'must have editorial experience in major regional publishers'. And then they offer you sixteen grand.

It was very depressing. And even though I'm a sunny girl, I was starting to feel maybe just *slightly* worried.

What Ken said. You know. About the lads all having family money or great qualifications. And me, not. I had a copy of last week's *Loot* somewhere and in between wondering about making up a lying CV I checked the rent prices.

It's insane. You have to be a millionaire to live somewhere nice in London, or at least making about thirty grand. I'd have to treble my salary just to stand still.

What am I going to do?

The key turns in the lock. I freeze. It's Annoying Victoria, come to show me the engagement ring she bought herself and triumph over turning me out. And I can't even be nasty to her! She's marrying Ollie.

'Oh, hey there.'

It's not her. It's Ollie. I smile at his sandy hair with relief.

'How's it going?' he says with a guilty half-smile.

'Oh, fine,' I say. My voice has done a weird little-girl cheerleader breathy thing. 'Fine,' I repeat, sounding like a strangled kitten.

'Lucy.' Ollie looks concerned. He puts down his briefcase and comes over to me. 'Is something the matter?'

The matter? No, why would it be? Except you're marrying Martha Stewart and kicking me out of my home.

'No, I'm fine.'

'Are you sure? It's just that you keep saying you're fine.'

'Well, apart from the fact I got fired today. But I'm fine with it,' I tell him, and then unfortunately ruin the effect by bursting into tears.

Ollie stands around looking awkward, then fishes out a white linen handkerchief from his breast pocket. He's never seen me cry before. I don't think he's got any idea what to do.

'Come on,' he says after a moment. 'I'm taking you out for an Indian.'

'I can't, I don't have any money.' I drip tears into his handkerchief.

'I do. Absolutely my treat, all night. Drinks too.'

'Well . . .' I am hungry. But if you run you're always hungry.

'We can even get a taxi.'

Now he's talked me into it. And anyway, I'm officially poor. I can't turn down free food. Who knows if I'll ever eat again, I think mournfully.

I cheer up over the naan bread. Ollie takes me to the Calcutta Sapphire, which is a very posh Indian on the King's Road. So posh, in fact, that they look askance at my Bon Jovi T-shirt and leather biker jacket, and for a minute I think they won't let me in. But Ollie tips the maître d' twenty quid and then they're all smiles.

Mmm. I am *starving*. They have everything I like here. I order some naan and some poppadums and some Bombay duck, I absolutely love Bombay duck.

'Should I get the prawn korma or the lamb roghan josh?' It's just like the Creme Egg vs. Walnut Whip dilemma all over again. I am haunted by the idea of making the wrong choice.

Ollie grins at me. 'We'll get both and share.'

'Ah.' I smile at him, relieved. 'And maybe some chicken tikka masala?'

'Of course we'll get that.'

'And some dal?'

'No problem.'

I wind up excitedly ordering about six different dishes.

'You and your appetite.' He shakes his head.

'What? You think I'm a greedy pig?'

'Not in the slightest. You'll never meet a man who doesn't like a woman to enjoy her food.'

'Does Vicky eat like a normal person, then?' I'm curious; I've never seen her eating anything. Once she let on that she carried around celery to snack on.

'Yes,' he says. 'Like a normal girl. You know, not much. Picks at everything, mainly.'

I put down the Bombay duck from which I've just taken a huge bite.

'I like you how you are, mate,' says Ollie. His blue eyes are twinkling; he's got a great smile, I must say. It sort of crinkles up his face. He has a kind of crumply look to him in general which I've always loved. Victoria will probably make him change it. No more of those rumpled suits and slightly too long blond hair.

'You're the second man today that's called me mate.'

Ollie lifts a brow. 'We are mates, aren't we?'

I'm being silly. 'Course we are. I'm sorry, I'm just having a rough day.'

'Marriage isn't going to change me,' Ollie says. 'We're still going to be friends, you know.'

I wish I could believe that.

'I know,' I lie.

This is crazy. I can't believe I'm starting to get jealous of Victoria. I bet nobody calls her 'mate' or tells her she isn't qualified to do anything. She eats like a 'normal girl'. Unlike me.

Unlike me in every way. And she's winding up with my friend. Not to mention my flat. And a great career. While I'm going to get . . .

Oh no, not tears again.

I grab the nearest thing to hand and blow my nose. Unfortunately it's my napkin. Ollie stares at me in fascinated horror.

I tuck it into my sleeve.

'Don't worry. I'll slip off to the loo and stuff it in the bin,' I reassure him.

'Um . . . right.' Ollie gives himself a little shake. 'Listen. I think I can help you.'

'How's that?'

I suppose he doesn't mean 'dump Victoria and go back to how we were'.

'Job-wise,' he says.

'I don't want to be a secretary.'

'A secretary? Can you type?'

I shake my head.

'Thought not,' Ollie says. 'It's not as important as a secretary. But it would pay OK, enough for you to find another flat share.'

Not as important as a secretary, eh? I'm about to make a face but then our main dishes arrive and they smell so heavenly, I don't bother.

'And it's got prospects,' he says, temptingly.

'Prospects?'

'You could learn the industry. Get promoted. Make a real executive salary. Eventually the good ones wind up making six figures. Or being millionaires.'

My forkful of chicken tikka halts on its way to my mouth.

'Well, I'm listening,' I tell him graciously.

'Property,' he says.

'Like an estate agent?' I shudder.

'Lucy.' Oh no, Ollie's going to tell me off again. He's got that cross look on his face, like when I leave a grimy ring round the bath. 'Sweetie, you are almost twenty-five. In five years you'll be thirty. And what will you have to show for it, eh?'

I try to think.

'A complete collection of *Kerrang!* back issues,' he says, 'and some used copies of *Duke Nukem*.'

'My *Kerrang!* are worth quite a bit of money, actually,' I say with dignity.

'You know what I mean.' His cross look softens. 'It's fun to live wild while you're young. I always admired that about you. Your sense of adventure.'

'You did?'

'But when you just keep going, that's when it gets stupid. It's no fun being old and poor. You don't want to wind up sixty-five and in a high-rise council flat.'

'Living on cat food,' I add helpfully.

'Exactly. Now, you're a clever girl. I can tell. You just need a little application. If you go to work for Todd, you can learn a big business. You can get onto a professional track. Get better pay, wind up on commission. Even get a mortgage and a place of your own.'

'Mmm,' I say. Sounds thrilling. But alas, a small and sulky part of me knows he's right.

'When you go to rock gigs, aren't you the oldest person there?'

I wince. 'Ouch.'

Ollie grins. 'Sorry. But it's for your own good.'

The waiter arrives with my much-needed bottle of beer; I take a good swig while Ollie sips his Merlot.

'Who's Todd?' I try to muster some enthusiasm.

'American guy I met at college. I did some work for him for free when he was just starting out. He was in real estate in New York, but he moved here a couple of years ago to get a slice of the UK market. As it's so hot.' Ollie eats a couple of prawns. 'Anyway, he relocates foreign businessmen into smart London flats. Very high-end rentals. His company's taken off, and his receptionist is on maternity leave. So there's a slot open.'

'OK.'

'He'll give you the job, but you'll have to make a couple of changes.' Ollie pauses. 'To tell the truth, more than just a couple.'

'Like what?' I ask suspiciously.

'Well, these are Americans and Japanese mostly. Some Swiss. They have lots of money and they want the Rolls-Royce, real English treatment. As Todd's a Yank, it's very important to him that his receptionist is a proper English rose.'

'Ah.' Light dawns. 'So you want to make me over?'

'You don't need a makeover,' Ollie says. 'You're pretty enough how you are.'

I blush. 'Thanks.'

'But you must change,' he pauses, 'just about everything else, I'm afraid.'

'What do you mean?'

'How you dress. How you act. Your grooming, if you can call it that.' He chuckles and I hastily hide my fingers with their stubby, ripped-off nails under the table. 'No more drinking beer. No more swearing. No more clomping around in Doc Martens. No more mess. No rock gigs. No action movie posters. No more trying to get other people to be interested in *Star Wars Galaxies*.' He takes a breath. 'No more football. No more rugby. No more sweatshirts. No more tatty jeans. No more set lists.'

'No more fun,' I say mournfully. 'You're asking me to change my whole life!'

31

'Not really,' he says. 'Just at work. Be a bit more presentable, sweetheart. You know. Ladylike. *Graceful.* I know you can do it,' he adds encouragingly. 'And Victoria will give you some tips.'

Oh great!

'Very nice of her,' I mutter.

'Let's start now.' What is he, some kind of style Moonie? He summons the waiter over with a discreet nod of his head. Ollie's got that way about him. He's quiet, but when he wants something people jump to it.

'Yes, sir?'

'Can you take away the Heineken? And bring the young lady a glass of Chardonnay.'

'But I don't really like . . .' I take a look at Ollie's face and my voice trails off. 'I mean, that will be lovely.' I swallow. 'Thank you.'

'See?' He smiles proudly at me. 'You're already getting the hang of it.'

'You can't be sure this Todd person will hire me.'

'Oh, I can,' he says. 'As long as you turn up looking decent. Like I said, think English rose.'

English rose. Right.

'I'll pull some strings for you,' he says. 'But I'm using up a major favour. So just promise me you won't let me down.'

The waiter returns with my Chardonnay. I am about to take a huge fortifying gulp, but remind myself just in time. English rose. I take a tiny sip. Ollie beams.

'I won't,' I say. I give him a big smile to cover up the fact that I feel weepy again. 'It's really nice of you to help me, Ollie. I would never let you down.'

3

I spend the next day clearing my room. Depression hangs over me like a big fog, but I can't let it stop me. I mean, Ollie's right, isn't he? The world doesn't care about you having fun. No, you have to squeeze into its little boxes to get anywhere. Why should I be any different?

I try to be glad my good time lasted this far. But I can't. Big tears keep welling up and plopping down my cheeks at regular intervals. Thankfully, though, nobody is here to see them.

I try to keep busy. Ollie *will* be proud of me. I lovingly peel off the Oasis set list and my *Die Hard* poster from the walls and put them into some cardboard boxes I picked up at Safeway's. Same goes for my *Kerrang!* collection, my Metallica drumstick that Lars Ulrich personally threw in my direction, all my games, and most of my clothes. On Friday I'll call my dad to come down from Kent with the car. I can store them all in my parents' attic.

It takes all day and finally there's nothing in my bedroom except my computer and a few plain Gap T-shirts and 501s. I even find the vacuum cleaner, and once I've discovered how it works, I hoover all over the room. Actually, when I'm finished, the carpet looks different.

I can definitely do this. I walk out of the flat and head for the broken-down everything for 99p shop on the corner of the next road. They have a poster of a fluffy kitten in a patch of daisies. Perfect! I take the fluffy kitten home, carefully re-allocate some Blu Tack from my Oasis set list and stick it up over my bed.

After that there's nothing to do but wait.

The key turns in the lock at five twenty and Ollie bustles in, followed by Victoria. He's carrying several grocery bags from Marks & Spencer, full of expensive ready-meals stuff and bottles. Victoria gives me a sour look before twisting her features into a smile.

'Hi, you guys,' I say. And then, because I have to, 'Victoria, congratulations! I haven't seen you since I heard the news. It's brilliant! Well done.' I swallow. 'I know you two will be incredibly happy.'

'Of course we will.' Victoria smiles briskly to cover up her bitchiness. 'But I think it's Ollie who deserves the congratulations, don't you? For winning my hand,' she explains.

'I thought you won his hand?'

Ollie chuckles, but Victoria looks as if she's swallowed a wasp.

'It's not like that. It's very traditional for the bride to propose on February the twenty-ninth. Ollie had to be on his best behaviour to make sure I'd do it,' she says. 'You planned it all, didn't you?' She squeezes his hand possessively. 'He's so passive-aggressive,' she purrs.

'I've cleaned out my room,' I say as cheerfully as I can. 'All ready to move out.'

'*Have* you?' Victoria sounds slightly mollified. 'Well, that's good news, Lucy. I thought you were never going to leave! Quite frankly.'

'Let's have a look,' Ollie says. He walks into my room with Victoria behind him.

'Very good,' Victoria says, sounding surprised. 'Lovely poster, actually.'

Ollie glances at the new poster and snorts with amusement.

'The carpet's gone a funny colour,' I say anxiously. 'It's

not burgundy any more. It's more red. I hope I didn't damage it.'

'I don't think so,' he says gently. 'I think that was just the dirt.'

'Oh.'

'Anyway, great job.' He kisses me on the cheek. Victoria looks askance at us. 'We're all going to stay in tonight and celebrate.'

'Celebrate?'

'Definitely.' Ollie removes two bottles of champagne from one of his carrier bags. 'We're celebrating your new career, Lucy. Todd said it would be fine for you to have the job. You can start on Monday.'

'Oh! Well, that's great.' I force another smile. 'Thanks very much.'

'You'll be able to get some new clothes by then, right?' he asks, suddenly anxious. 'I mean, dresses and stuff?'

'Oh yes. My dad's going to take me home for the weekend. I'm sure my sisters have left some clothes behind I can have.'

I'm the youngest girl of five, and all my elder sisters are like Victoria, without being complete bitches. You know, they wear skirts and their handbags match their shoes.

I anticipate returning to the flat minus all my treasures, and plus several boxes of utterly dull, girlie clothes.

'That's brilliant,' Ollie says, relieved. 'And Victoria, love. Maybe tomorrow you can take Lucy and get her nails done?'

Victoria smirks insincerely at Ollie. 'Anything for your friends, darling,' she says. She shoots me a meaningful look. 'It'll be nice to have a real heart-to-heart with Lucy.'

Oh please, no!

'The champagne's a lovely idea,' I say desperately. 'But why don't I have a quick glass with you and then pop out to the pub or something. I'm sure you two want to be romantic.'

'Well—' starts Victoria, but Ollie cuts her off.

'Certainly not,' he says indignantly. 'We're all going to have a nice dinner together. Victoria's going to whip something up. She's a brilliant cook.'

So she can cook, too. She can't eat, but she can cook.

'Not *brilliant*,' Victoria says modestly.

'And you're the guest of honour, Lucy. We're not the only ones starting a new life.' He gives Victoria's bony waist a squeeze. 'You're beginning a whole new phase yourself.'

Victoria minces into the kitchen in her strappy high heels, produces a pink, frilly apron from somewhere, removes several packets of fish from the shopping, and before I know it the kitchen is resounding to the quick, efficient sounds of a knife chopping on Ollie's granite counter top. I watch as Ollie fills a champagne flute and takes it through to her, giving her a quick peck on the cheek. She smiles radiantly at him; a nonbitchy, exquisite smile. Next to her, all the ingredients, fish, spices, vegetables, are arranged neatly in perfect little piles, like a cooking show on TV. The pot simmers and it smells delicious.

I sigh. Victoria is obviously Woman as she is meant to be. Can I ever catch up? No wonder Ollie never wanted to go out with me. I would no sooner buy a pink frilly apron than I would think of using it. I mean, my idea of cooking is a microwave pizza.

'So are you excited?' Ollie comes back and flops next to me on the couch. I'm sprawling on it like I usually do, but I pull myself upright, try to imagine I have piles and am wearing painful shoes. That's better. Now I'm perched uncomfortably on the edge like Victoria.

'Oh, yes.' I try for full wattage on my smile. 'I'm thrilled. Totally.'

'I understand.' He nudges me in the ribs. 'It's all going too fast. Bit of a culture shock for you.'

I sip my champagne. 'Maybe a bit,' I admit.

'You'll be fine. We've all got to grow up sometime. It won't be as bad as you think.' Ollie eyes me. 'You know, I bet you'll look good when you put on a dress.'

I glance back at Victoria. Under the pink apron she's wearing a little cashmere skirt suit in palest eggshell blue. It looks very delicate and feminine. I just can't imagine myself like that.

But if I were, would I keep a boyfriend?

I mean I never cared about it before. Never gave a toss, one way or the other. Dated a bloke, it went wrong. Dated a bloke, it went wrong. Lost a couple of mates, dusted myself off. I think I could always cheer myself up by slaughtering a few aliens. Or eating a Strawberry Mivvi. It just wasn't something I felt bad about. I was happy enough without a man, so why rock the boat?

And now . . . I don't know. I am starting to care. Just a little bit. Everything's come crashing down and I suddenly wish I *did* have a boyfriend. At least then I'd have someone to talk to about it.

'Victoria's got lots of style, hasn't she?' I say wistfully.

He looks admiringly at his fiancée. 'She sure does. I don't think I've ever met a woman so pulled-together. No matter where we go she always dresses perfectly. She seems to have, you know, this inner radar.' He laughs. 'Unlike me I must say. Although I'm going to let her buy all my clothes from now on, so maybe things will improve.'

I knew it!

'I like you how you are,' I venture.

'Yes, but,' he punches me lightly in the shoulder, 'you're not exactly an expert on the well-groomed man, are you?'

I suppose he's referring to my past dates. The last one, Mike, was a club bouncer. He was built like a Sherman tank and liked T-shirts featuring horror movies.

'I think it's one reason Vicky does so well at work,' he muses. 'Everybody respects somebody who carries themselves properly. Maybe if she gives me a hand, I'll get promoted. It's all about looking the part.'

'OK, OK,' I say sulkily. 'I get it.'

He bows his head. 'I know. I'm subtle as a brick. But cheer up, is what I'm trying to say. There are good things about the situation.'

'Like what?'

'The pay, for one.' He fishes into his jacket pocket and hands over an envelope.

'What's this?' I rip it out of his hands.

'Open it up.'

I do.

It is a contract of employment and it says I will be earning £18,000 p.a.

I stare at it. I can't believe it. I'll be rich!

'Wow.' I swallow, hard.

Ollie nudges me. 'See? Growing up's not all that bad.'

'No,' I say thoughtfully. 'I suppose I can give it a try.'

'Supper's ready!' sings out Victoria.

We go through to the kitchen. She's set the table, really neatly, with water and wine glasses for everybody, and napkins folded into little fans. I didn't know we even *had* napkins. Plus there is a vase of pale pink roses and baby's breath on a doily. There's a plate heaped with slices of hot crusty bread, the stuff you bake yourself from ready-made dough, and our bowls are full of the most amazing-smelling fish stew.

Ollie is looking at the table with pride. He goes over to squeeze Victoria and kiss her on the cheek, but she turns her face to him so it lands on her lips.

'Kiss for the cook!' she trills, sounding pleased.

'This is magic,' Ollie sighs.

Better than the turkey burger and chips I made him on his birthday, I suppose. Come to think of it, I did burn the chips.

'Yes,' I agree heartily, sitting down so I don't have to watch them kissing. I try a spoonful. 'The fish stew's delish. Thanks, Victoria.'

'Fish stew?' She wrinkles her tiny nose. 'That's *bouillabaisse*, Lucy.'

'Booly-base then.' I smile bravely. 'Anyway, it's yummy.'

Victoria sniggers at my pronunciation. I flush red and take another spoonful to hide it.

'*Bouillabaisse* is really French for fish stew,' Ollie says kindly. 'You weren't far off.'

Victoria glares at him and Ollie winces. He gives a tiny sigh which tugs at my heart. Poor Ollie. Come on, Lucy, you mustn't make this difficult for him. Right, I tell myself. Operation Be Nice to Victoria starts right now.

'So can I see the ring?' I ask ingratiatingly. Victoria extends her hand to me, like the Queen. There is a modest diamond sitting on her left hand.

'This is just temporary,' she says. 'It's the one I got for the twenty-ninth.'

'I told Vicks I wanted to buy her ring myself,' Ollie says. 'I want to be the one to give it to her.'

Victoria softens, smiles warmly at him. 'I'm taking this back to the shop.' She doesn't stop looking in his eyes.

'And I'll choose her new ring on my own. Something secret,' Ollie says.

'How romantic,' I say. Although I needn't have bothered, they don't even seem to know I'm there. Ugh! This is awful. I wish I were still going out with Paul. Or John. Anyone, really. Then I could gaze soulfully at *my* date and not feel like an utter lemon.

'So,' Ollie says after a second. 'Lucy got her contract of employment today, Vicky.' He's determined to bring me back into the conversation.

'Yes. It's really great. I'll be earning eighteen grand,' I say.

'Oh, well,' says Victoria sympathetically. She puts out

39

her manicured nails with their palest-pink polish and presses lightly on my arm. 'We all have to start somewhere, Lucy. I'm sure if you work hard, and apply yourself, it will get better.'

'But eighteen grand's a lot of money.'

'To whom?' She laughs. 'My dear, you have an awful lot to learn. To some people, perhaps, eighteen thousand a year is a lot. To the *successful* in life, it doesn't even get you out of the starting gate.'

'But like you said, Lucy has to start somewhere,' Ollie says evenly.

Vicky's eyebrows lift. 'Sweetheart, yes. And she's so lucky you would do this for her.'

'Yes, thanks, Ollie,' I mutter.

'But I'm trying to lift her sights,' Victoria goes on. 'To give her *goals*. To give her *ambition*. You want Lucy to get on, don't you? And to be successful?'

'Course,' Ollie says. 'It's nice of you to think of her like that.'

Hello? I am sitting here!

'And to be successful she'll need to *change*.'

'Oh, yes.'

'Including her attitude about money. But don't worry, Lucy, dear,' Victoria says, finally turning to me with a sweet smile. 'I'll take you out tomorrow and give you a few pointers.'

'That's really nice of you, Vicky,' I say through gritted teeth. 'Looking forward to it.'

'Of course you are.'

'This *bouillabaisse* is fantastic,' Ollie says. He's finished his. 'Any more?'

'Here, darling.' Victoria puts another dollop in his bowl.

'And fresh-baked bread.' He reaches for a chunk. 'You're just amazing, sweetheart. How you manage it I don't know. You look great, you make my place beautiful, you've got a great career, *and* you can cook! You're Superwoman, you know that?'

'Oh, Ollie.' Victoria hits him playfully on the arm, but she has gone pink with pleasure.

'I don't know how I got so lucky,' Ollie says to her. Adoration is glittering in his eyes.

'Gosh. Is that the time?' I say. 'I forgot, I have to meet someone. A friend. From work.'

'I thought you didn't have any colleagues any more,' Vicky points out. 'You know, since you've been fired.'

'That's right. Um . . . ex-colleague. He got fired too. We're supposed to be going out to drown our sorrows. I have to go, but thanks, Ollie, for the champagne,' I was going to kiss him but think better of it, 'and you, Victoria, for the lovely booly-base.'

'Oh dear,' she says, with a mock smile. 'Perhaps you'd better stick to "fish stew" after all.'

I grin weakly and head for the door. If I had a boyfriend I'd have some place to go right now. But instead my options are sit in a pub on my own or sit in a restaurant on my own.

I turn the corner and there's the Odeon. Oh joy. They're showing an Audrey Hepburn marathon. I hate Audrey Hepburn. I sigh and wander over there. That should kill four hours and with any luck they'll have finished shagging by the time I get home . . .

The movies don't finish until 1 a.m. and I'm shaken awake by an irate cleaner telling me to 'bugger off'. I stumble back to the flat in the freezing cold, let myself in, and collapse onto my bed.

And now somebody else is shaking me.

'Oh, Ollie, fuck off and die,' I moan.

'It's not Ollie.' I open one bleary eye to see Victoria perched bird-like on the end of my bed, as though trying not to be contaminated by my rumpled duvet. 'It's me.'

She's wearing a flippy, layered chiffon skirt in a floral print. The green leaves are picked out by her mint silk cardigan; her skinny, muscle-free legs taper off in a pair of narrow, pinched-looking heels, and she has dangling freshwater pearl earrings that are swaying prettily under her elegant chignon of a hairdo.

'It's already eight,' she says. 'Go and get in the shower and get dressed as fast as you can. We have an appointment at Mimi's for nine fifteen sharp.'

'Huh?'

'Oh, for God's sake, Lucy,' Victoria snaps. 'Mimi's. The nail specialists. I promised Ollie to give you some basic grooming. And I don't have all day, so let's go.' She twitches back my duvet, exposing my ancient but comfy man's pyjamas I nicked off my dad. It's freezing.

'What charming lingerie,' she says. 'Up! Up!'

I can't tell her to fuck off and die. Although I'd love to. So I swing my legs out of bed and head off to the shower, which I haven't been in for five minutes without her yelling through the door at me to 'stop wasting time'.

I towel off as fast as I can, pull on my jeans and DMs and a West Point sweatshirt I got in the States, scarf a brush through my hair, and I'm all done.

'Ready!' I say obligingly.

Victoria stares at me.

'Oh my *God*,' she says, disgusted. 'Oh well, it can't be helped. Let's just go, shall we?'

I bite my cheeks hard. Operation Be Nice to Victoria. Remember! Remember!

'This is going to be fun,' I offer.

'For you, perhaps.' She checks her watch. 'I'm a busy woman.'

'Ah, yes. Well, don't feel obliged,' I say. 'Give me the address of this Mimi's place and I'll sort it out myself.'

'I can imagine,' she says, ushering me out of the flat.

'Black nails with little white skulls on them and a five-pound chop from Supercuts. Let's face it, Lucy, you can't survive in the world of *real women*. Besides, I promised Ollie,' she gives herself a little shake, 'and whatever my darling man asks me to do I will do.' She stares at me intently.

'You two seem well suited,' I say, as some remark seems called for.

'Oh, we're more than well suited. We're soul mates.' She eyes me. 'In fact, I think you and I need to have a little chat about that. But we'll do it over lunch. First things first. Your hands are an emergency.'

She steps out fractionally onto the kerb, makes a tiny waving motion with her hand, and suddenly a taxi materializes from nowhere and swoops obediently to pick us up.

'Wow.' I'm impressed. Not that I can afford taxis, but on the rare occasions I've tried to flag one down it's always taken at least fifteen minutes. 'How did you do that?'

She sighs. 'It's called *class*, Lucy. I wouldn't expect you to understand.'

BITCH!

Mimi's is just as I expected. Tiresome. Bunch of pretentious cows wearing black and sneering, standing around clucking over my fingernails.

'What *happened*?' one of them says. 'Were you in an *accident*?'

'You go on like this and you'll damage the cuticle.'

'Maybe she's just under a lot of stress,' says one blonde dubiously.

'Ahem.' I have had enough. 'I don't *like* fingernails, actually. Long ones scratch me too much. And they're not good for holding a joystick. They get in the way of the buttons.'

They stare at me as if I'm from another planet.

'What's she saying?' asks the blonde, appealing to Victoria for a translation. She just shrugs.

'Do what you can,' she says wearily. 'Fakes. Just give her the absolute basics. Short and French. She can't handle polish.'

They sniff elegantly and, in resentful silence, take my hands and start poking at my fingernails with little sticks, and fetching pots of glue. Then they get some fake nails and meticulously cut them to fit and stick them on. It takes *ages*. And I can't flick through a magazine. Not that they've got anything good. I'd even read *PC Games Galaxy* but they don't have it.

I have to stare at my reflection for an hour and a half. To add insult to injury, the radio station is easy listening.

Victoria sits across the room from me. She's in my line of sight but attempts no conversation, studiously ignoring me. The manicurists are fluttering around her like butterflies, chatty and pleasant, fiddling with her delicate hands and high-arched feet.

She's having a great time. I console myself with the thought that the longer this takes, the less time I'll have to talk to her.

'Isn't that better?' Victoria says when we emerge from the salon. She grabs my hand and holds it up to the light. Realistic and very uncomfy nails are now stuck to my fingers.

'Oh, absolutely.'

'You're not such a ragamuffin. Now for a haircut.'

She pours me into another taxi.

'Where are we going?'

'Vidal Sassoon,' she says. 'I want something classic and maintenance-free – you're obviously not going to *do* anything with it.'

'But I can't afford that.' Until my lovely new salary hits the bank I can hardly afford the Supercuts she was sneering at. And to be honest that was my plan. Little trim at Supercuts. What's wrong with that?

'It's free,' Vicky says. 'As a fashion editor I get accommodated.'

'Hey, that's really cool.'

'Yes,' Vicky agrees, bored.

I have to make her like me, I tell myself. So far I'm obviously not doing too well. If I can't get her to like me I won't be able to keep being mates with Ollie. And that's a horrible, horrible idea.

'I'm so envious of how successful you are,' I lie gushingly. 'Ollie's always talking about it. He worships the ground you walk on.'

Victoria preens. 'Well, yes. I am pretty successful. I make sixty thousand,' she says, tossing her dark hair.

Sixty grand?

I blink. I was lying before. Who cares what Annoying Victoria does in her career? But *sixty thousand pounds*? I had no idea. No wonder she carries a Louis Vuitton bag. I shake my head, feeling down. She's the ultimate nightmare, of course. But she's also perfect. She and Ollie, with her colour-coordinated outfits, her well-dressed table, her fat salary, and her sodding booly-base.

I swallow, desperate not to get red-eyed. I'm starting to feel a bit like a joke. Victoria so clearly despises me. And she has everything, whereas all I have is a job I don't particularly want because my best friend pulled strings.

But I must suck it up. Victoria is the perfect woman. I must realize this and not just keep telling myself she's a stupid vicious old cow.

'That's wonderful,' I say humbly.

'Actually I think I'm underpaid,' she replies coolly. 'I'll be asking for a lot more next bonus round. Here we are.'

We disembark at Sloane Square and she shoves me before her into the chrome and marble sanctuary, smelling of shampoo and money.

'Victoria, darling.' A plumpish redhead with a fabulous crop comes over and kisses the side of her cheeks. 'Right on time.'

'Bernice, this is the charity case,' she says, herding me towards her with a push. 'Just chop it all off and give her your standard bob.'

'No!' I cry.

Too loud, I realize too late. Everybody has turned round and is staring at me. Victoria looks daggers.

'Stop making a *scene*,' she hisses. 'You're getting this done for free. It costs *hundreds* of pounds. Who's the expert here, me or you?'

'But I like my hair long,' I protest.

'So what? You don't know anything. A short bob, Bernice,' she snaps. 'She looks like she's been dragged through a hedge right now. I'll be back in an hour. I'm popping round to Peter Jones.'

She marches outside, her back rigid with annoyance. I turn to the stylist with a lump in my throat.

'Look, please . . .'

'Relax,' she says. She winks at me. 'It's your hair, innit? Not hers.'

Bernice takes me over to a black leather chair and washes my hair in the sink. It's actually not bad. Like getting a scratched back.

'You've got lovely hair,' she says.

'But Victoria thinks it's too long.'

'She probably wishes hers was like yours. You can practically sit on it. How come you grew it so long?'

'Well.' I decide to be honest. 'I hate the hairdressers. And also I like to headbang at gigs.'

She laughs, delighted. 'That's a new one. Anyway, I'll take off about three inches, you'll never notice, and that'll get rid of all the split ends. You don't need any colour. Never let anyone colour your hair.'

'No?' I ask, perking up.

'Natural blonde. Don't get too many of them. Honey, but you're still blonde. D'you style it much?'

'Not as such.'

'Naw, thought not. Not to worry, I'll feather it a bit. Then what you do is you use a bit of hairspray and stop using the scrunchies. It'll flow down your back. Look really good. Use spray-in conditioner.'

'OK.' I'm taking mental notes.

'Your hair's very feminine,' she says, and I laugh. 'What is it?'

'I don't get called that much,' I say.

'Dunno why not,' she says, seriously. 'Pretty girl like you. Anyway, just wait till I'm done. Want a mag?'

'Do you have anything with computer games?'

She shakes her head. 'Not interested in fashion?'

'Not really.'

'I've got *Heat*.'

I perk up. 'Great. *Heat*'s brilliant. It's the new *Just Seventeen*.'

Vidal Sassoon is cool. For a start Bernice is kind and funny. She says she's jealous of my hair. She told me the trouble with being a hairdresser is that you always want to try out new cuts and so your own hair gets shorter and shorter all the time. She gives me loads of compliments, too, but I think she's just being nice. I don't even notice the time, and when she's finished, she spins me round to face the mirror.

'Tah-dah!' she says proudly.

'Ooh.' I smile. My hair's a bit shorter but it's still long, at least four inches past my shoulders. It sort of flips out at an angle down the sides, and then the ends are carefully chopped in a neat, elegant line.

'Toss it about,' Bernice says. I give my head a couple of Metallica-worthy bangs. She laughs, but my hair sort of flies everywhere and then, miraculously, settles back into the same smooth shape.

'Fuck me. That *rocks*,' I say. 'Thanks a million.'

'Any time. Just keep it trimmed. Once a month.'

I turn to the doorway to find Victoria standing in it. She's weighed down by plastic bags and she looks cross.

'Victoria.' Bernice pushes me towards her. 'I decided not to go for the bob. She looks better like this, don't you think?'

Victoria's mouth makes a little moue of annoyance. 'I don't think it's practical. Given Lucy's disposition.'

Given my what?

'But so elegant,' Bernice says. 'I was actually inspired by you.'

'By me?' Victoria preens a little and flicks her own shiny chestnut mane.

'Yes. We'd all like to carry off that ultra-femme thing you've got going on,' says Bernice. Is it just me, or is there a hint of mockery there? I glance uncertainly at Victoria. But perhaps I'm wrong, because she doesn't seem angry any more. On the contrary, she's simpering.

'Oh? Me?' She gives a tinkling little laugh. 'Well, Bernie, if you say so . . . Come on, Lucy,' she adds, shoving me towards the door. 'You mustn't take up any more of Bernie's valuable time.'

'Thank you,' I manage, as I'm hustled towards the exit.

Bernice winks at me and mouths, 'Come back any time.' She doesn't say it aloud, though. Like me, she is clearly terrified of Victoria.

'Lunch,' Victoria says when we're outside. It's more of a flat statement than a friendly suggestion. 'We don't need to go anywhere special. The Bluebird is fine. Taxi!'

Another cab screeches to a halt.

'The Bluebird? But that's a Conran restaurant. They're really expensive.'

'Yes, well.' Victoria stares out of the window. I smooth down my new, neat hair hopefully but she's not going to offer any compliments. 'I suppose so, if you're used to meals that come in brown paper bags.'

I sigh. This is hard going.

'You know, it was wonderful of you to sort out my nails and hair.'

She shrugs.

'But there's no need to give me lunch as well. I'm sure you've got loads of really important things to do at the magazine.'

'Of course I do.' Victoria turns to me and fixes me with a dark stare that lets me know I'm not getting out of this. 'But you and I need to have a little talk, don't we, Lucy?'

'Do we?'

Victoria smiles meanly. 'I think so,' she says.

Ho-hum. Better get it over with, then.

We are ushered to a table right away, even though the place is packed; Victoria moves with arrogant assurance through the throng, delicately folds her legs under the table, and indicates that I should sit down.

'Can I get you anything to drink?' the waiter says.

'I'll have a be— um, a glass of wine.'

'What kind of wine?'

'White,' I say decisively. There, that wasn't so hard. I can do this!

Victoria sighs. 'She'll have a Pinot Grigio.'

'And for you, miss?'

'Just seltzer.' Vicky smiles dazzlingly at him. 'Got to watch my figure!'

The waiter leers as if he'd like to watch it, wrinkles his nose at me, and melts away.

'Decided what you want yet?'

'The fish and chips.'

She says, 'Of course you do. I'm having the rocket and parmesan salad.'

'And then what?'

'Oh, that's all,' Victoria says. 'In fact, it's a special treat to have the parmesan. All that salt and fat. I don't usually eat at lunch,' she informs me. 'Looking good takes work.'

The waiter returns with our drinks, and takes our order. I sip the Pinot Grigio; it's slightly bitter and I don't really like it, but at least it's alcoholic. And I think I might be going to need it.

'We need to talk,' Victoria pronounces.

'Yes, so you said.'

She glares at me. 'About Ollie.'

'Oh?' I affect innocence.

'Lucy,' she says with heavy emphasis and a pitying tone, 'it's over.'

I sit upright. 'It's what? Already?'

'Not me.' She scowls. 'You. You and Ollie. It's over. Done. Finished.'

'Of course it is, I'm moving out.'

'That's not what I mean. I mean this little crush you've got on him. This sort of moony love you keep showing, trailing around after him.'

I blink. 'Trailing after him?'

'You know.' She waves her talons dismissively. 'Following him to rugby matches, tagging behind him to the pub. It's pathetic, Lucy. Really.'

I open my mouth. 'I *like* rugby matches.'

'Oh, sure,' she says. 'It's very convenient, isn't it? How you like everything Ollie does?'

Is she mental?

'That's why we're friends,' I explain. 'Why he asked me to move in. We're mates.'

'Men and women aren't friends,' she says flatly. 'Didn't you see *When Harry Met Sally*?'

'I prefer films with explosions. Or zombies, you know . . .'

'Lucy, Lucy, Lucy,' Victoria says sadly. 'You're almost twenty-five years old. This schoolgirl infatuation has got to end. Ollie's in love with me. He's marrying me. You're only making yourself look pathetic.'

'Victoria, I haven't got a crush on Ollie.'

'Oh, please, Lucy,' says Victoria. 'Everybody he knows

50

has noticed it. They all talk about you, you know. All his colleagues, everyone.'

I find myself getting angry. I can feel my cheeks burning.

'What everyone, who everyone?' I snap. 'There's nothing to talk about.'

'Isn't there?' she asks me, patronizingly. 'Penniless college dropout meets Scottish landed gentleman on holiday, moves into his place for a peppercorn rent, goes nowhere in her career, and is seen with him everywhere? Shadowing his girlfriends' every move? Well, not me, Lucy,' she says heavily. 'I'm wise to it.'

I've gone red. 'Ollie's not a landed gentleman.'

'No, but he will be. His father owns a hundred acres in Banffshire and a gorgeous Georgian manor house.' Her eyes narrow. 'Don't tell me you didn't know.'

I didn't. The only thing Ollie has ever said to me is that he hates his dad.

For a second I think about those sad nights. Ollie's stories about his family made me want to cry. Imagine feeling so lonely and unloved. I worship my father. And all I'd ever said to Ollie was how my family was so kind and nice.

'Look, we just got on,' I tell her. 'And now he's met you, I'm moving out. I'm really happy for you both,' I lie.

'Yes, well.' Victoria stares at me as the waiter puts down our food. 'I give you fair warning, I won't take kindly to any flirting with my fiancé. Ollie doesn't like girls like you, Lucy,' she says. 'Not romantically. Men don't, you know. Not men with class. He wants somebody elegant, somebody with poise and style. A little femininity. That's all he asks.'

'Then there's no need to feel threatened by me,' I say. I can't help it.

'Oh, I know that. I'm not telling you this for me. I'm doing it for Ollie. He got you this job – well, a chance at this job. And he wants you to *move on*.'

'Ollie does?'

'Naturally we've discussed it.'

'You've discussed me?'

'Yes. The awkward situation with you.'

I can't believe it. My forkful of chips stops on the way to my mouth. Ollie has discussed me and my non-existent crush with bitch Victoria?

I'm so embarrassed I want to cry. Is that what he thought? That I was following him around like a little puppy, trying to mess up his relationships?

I'm totally humiliated. And furious. I force myself to remember everything Ollie's done for me, what a good friend he's been.

'Well, if Ollie thinks I'm in love with him he's mistaken,' I say, and my voice sounds all distant. 'As far as I'm concerned we were only ever friends. And that's all we'll ever be.'

'The "friends" thing again. Oh yes.' She sighs. 'Well, I daresay he'll invite you to the wedding.'

I blink.

'And maybe see you occasionally. A couple of times a year at parties perhaps. No harm in that.' She smiles serenely at my aghast expression. 'But otherwise . . . well, now we've had this little chat, I'm sure you understand. Ollie already has plenty of friends. Men friends. People from his own background. And of course a man's *best* friend is always his wife.' She smiles at me with that condescending tilt of her head. 'I hope you get that, Lucy?'

'Thank you, Victoria. Yes, I get it.' The food is crispy and tasty but I'm choking on it. 'And thank you for everything you've done for me this morning. I hope you and Ollie will be very happy. And now I have to go,' I say because my eyes are becoming blurry with tears from the shame of it all. I fish around madly in my bag but there's only ten quid and my crumpled Travelcard. I put the ten quid on the table; it probably doesn't even cover the glass of wine but it's all I've got.

'Oh dear,' Victoria sighs. 'And I so hoped we weren't going to have another scene.'

I pretend I haven't heard her. 'Enjoy your lunch!' I say brightly. 'Got to go,' and I blunder my way out of the restaurant.

But I'm sure she saw that fat, treacherous tear trickle down my cheek.

I find a Barclays and take out forty quid. I've only got eighty-seven pounds forty left in there now, and I'll have to give Ollie some money for the electricity and the gas. And the internet connection.

It would be lovely to rip up the contract of employment in a grand gesture. Tell Ollie I've never thought twice about him and I don't want any of his charity. Unfortunately I don't have too many other options.

I stand there in the chilly afternoon. Hmmm. No way can I go back to the flat. I'd rather gnaw off my toes and eat them with a pickle than see Victoria again.

I take out my battered Travelcard and head for Charing Cross. I'm going home.

4

By the time I get on the train I'm feeling a lot better. For a start I've got one of those long tubes of salt 'n' vinegar Pringles and two cans of orange Tango, and that would cheer anybody up. My appetite's come back – it's never gone for very long. Not even when I feel down. And it's hard to concentrate on being depressed when all you can think about is a cheddar and tomato baguette they warm up for you in one of those rotating ovens in the little station cafes. Yum!

Anyway, I'm going *home*. And that's brilliant. OK, so I have to borrow some stupid uncomfortable clothes from my sisters and everybody's going to laugh at the hair and nails. But so what? At least I'll get to see them. Anne's not there, she's with her husband making yet more babies. There are rabbits with more family planning nous than Anne and Joe. And Laura's in the States, doing something glamorous in Chicago; she's been trying to break into TV for years now, and a local station gave her a ten-minute slot on 'European Elegance'. Why Chicago I have no idea, but at least it makes her happy.

But Mum mentioned that Catherine and Emily were both home, I think. Staying with them for a month, or two weeks, or something.

That's my family; can't stay away. It's not natural, really. Whenever we get free time we tend to go home. I used to think that everybody's family was close like ours. Now I know how lucky I am.

Of course it's not very fashionable, is it? You're meant to have a tortured childhood and poetically miserable adolescence. Not just sit there being happy.

I wonder what Victoria's family is like?

Dad honks the horn when he sees me at Tunbridge Wells station. I don't know why, as if I wouldn't recognize his old brown Volvo. He's had the same car since 1986. I think if I magically got rich and gave him a turbo Porsche it would just rot in the garage.

I climb into the front seat and give him a big kiss.

'Darling!' He hugs me. 'Lovely to see you.' Dad draws back. 'The hair, what is it?'

I finger it nervously. 'Don't you like it?'

'Is it a wig?' Dad says.

'No . . .'

'Or some of those extensions? Your mother saw that on a television show. Fake hair,' Dad says. 'Jolly good idea! Is it that?'

'It's my hair, Dad,' I say.

Dad puts the car into gear and we head out to Groombridge. 'I like it,' he says heartily. 'It just doesn't look like you, that's all.'

This means he hates it. I fish out my scrunchie from my jeans pocket and hastily tie it back. There, now I look almost normal.

'Seen any good games, darling?' Dad asks. 'Wasps played London Irish, that was a thriller. Did you go with Oliver?'

Dad always calls him Oliver.

'I – no,' I say. 'He was too busy.'

Dad goes on into a long rant about the Wasps backs. He doesn't rate them, and I like to argue with him. But today my heart's not in it. Hope he doesn't notice.

'So who else is home?'

'Ah.' Dad's face lights up again. 'Well, Emily was going to pop back to London at lunchtime, but when you called she changed her mind, so she's here for the night.'

'Brilliant.'

'And then Catherine's staying for the month. You must be nice to her, poppet.'

'I'm always nice to Catherine,' I say, aggrieved. She's the second youngest and we're very close, even though we're so different.

'I know that, sweetheart. But she's split up with her boyfriend. You know, Percy.'

'Peter?'

'Whatever his name was,' says Dad with profound contempt. Dad is great. He has nothing but enthusiasm for all our boyfriends, and will find endless good things to say about Joe, since he actually made it to the altar, even though Joe is the dullest thing this side of a local newspaper bridge column. But if we split up from them or, worse, they leave us, then they become the most useless wastes of skin for a hundred miles in any direction.

'He was a fool,' Dad says. 'A complete berk. An utter loser.'

'Oh – yes,' I agree.

Peter was, in fact, the youngest-ever partner at his City headhunting firm and made over half a million pounds a year. He also drove a Ferrari and sent Catherine dozens of roses almost every week 'just because'.

'She was right to dump him,' Dad says. 'The pillock.'

'So . . . she dumped him?' I'm amazed, I thought it was wedding bells for sure. It's been four years.

'Oh yes, kicked him right out,' Dad says stoutly. 'Didn't want a useless sack of lard like him hanging about.'

Peter's a tall, handsome bloke, without an ounce of spare fat anywhere.

'Right.'

'But,' Dad shakes his head, 'she is taking it quite hard.

She mopes around a bit. Maybe you can cheer her up,' he says hopefully.

'I'll try.'

'You could teach her to play computer games,' he suggests brightly. You're so good at that, darling. Maybe she could get a new job . . .'

Catherine works in Peter's firm.

'They haven't fired her?'

'No, but I don't think she wants to stay. That's no career for my Catherine. Asking stupid overpaid young men to move about to new firms.'

Previously, Dad had thought that headhunting was the wave of the future.

'She could review computer games, like you, darling. You do so well at that,' Dad says. 'And you have a wonderful time, don't you? No stress at all.'

'Ah, well. About that,' I begin, then see the expectant look on my dad's face. I've always been the adventurous one, you see. The tomboy, the son he never had. It'll devastate him if I let him down. He always told me that of all his children, he thought I was the truly successful one. Because I was always happy.

'It's been great,' I say carefully. 'But I've decided to give . . . other fields a go.'

'Other fields?' Dad asks. 'But why? You love computer games. Donkey Kong!'

What is it with people and Donkey Kong?

'Space Invaders!' Dad says helpfully. 'Ms Pac-Man! All good stuff.'

'Ah, yes. But, you know, a bit childish,' I say.

'Childish? Nonsense. It's big business, you know. People don't buy LPs any more, they buy Donkey Kong,' Dad says knowledgeably.

'Yes, well. I want to try new things.'

'They can't pin you down, can they, Lucy?' Dad asks, 'What are you going to do next?'

'I'm going to try estate agency,' I say.

Dad stares at me anxiously.

'Here's the turn, Dad!' I say. And thank God he has to swerve to avoid an oncoming lorry. Phew, that was close. And I don't just mean the lorry.

He makes the turn into our village and I ask how Mum's doing. Anything to get off the subject. There will be the bustle of arriving and finding my bedroom and walking down to the shop to buy a toothbrush. Whatever will help me not to have to go over this. It's been a hard day, and I don't think I can take that look of disappointment on Dad's face. I love him so much, you see.

'Lucy! Oh, it's Lucy!' Mum says. She sounds overjoyed. She comes out of the kitchen, all covered in flour and red-faced; I suppose she's been standing over the oven again. Mum has this habit of compulsively opening the oven to check whatever's in there hasn't burned. I suppose that's why all our meals are only ever half-cooked.

I give her a hug. 'What are you making?'

'Sausage rolls.' She makes a face. 'But I burned them.'

'Can I have some?' Yum, I love sausage rolls. And this probably means they aren't all pink and raw in the middle.

'Oh, well, if you want.' Mum looks pleased and emerges with a big tray of sausage rolls, golden-brown and perfect. 'They're burned to a crisp, of course.'

I take one and demolish it.

'Is it burned?' Mum asks anxiously.

'No. It's wonderful. Can I have another one?'

'Have as many as you like,' says Mum, going pink with pleasure.

'That's my girl,' Dad says admiringly. 'Eats like a man, don't you, Lucy?'

There's the sound of cluttering from upstairs and Catherine comes down.

'Catherine!' I stand up and give her a hug.

She looks terrible.

Not as in shabby terrible. There are no baggy sweatpants or shapeless tops, no unwashed, greasy hair. That's just not Catherine, like it's not any of my sisters. If I saw Catherine in a pair of jogging pants I'd think she'd been possessed. She's wearing a navy-blue scoop-neck jersey dress with a flippy skirt and a smart pair of flats. In her world, this probably counts as comfort dressing. She's made up, too, just barely, but then Catherine has not been seen without make-up in daylight since she was seven. She's wearing what I think is tinted moisturizer and a brown sort of blusher, with some neutral shadow on her eyelids and just a bit of mascara.

Obviously waterproof mascara. Because she's been crying. That's what I mean when I say she looks terrible. Her eyes are bloodshot and there are massive dark circles under them that concealer can do nothing to hide. Her skin, beneath the tint, is pale. She looks gaunt, as if she hasn't slept for a week.

'Hey, baby bro.' That's her nickname for me, ever since I started rejecting dolls to play with toy forts. 'It's so good to see you!' She hugs me back and I can feel her ribcage. I want to drag her off immediately for a heart-to-heart but now's not the time.

'Where is she?' Emily comes in from the garden. She's just as groomed as Catherine, but more urban chic; Catherine calls her the fashion victim. I beam when I see her. Em's wearing exactly what she always does. Isn't it great how some things never change? She has on these narrow black trousers with a Gucci crocodile belt, a black cashmere T-shirt, and dangling earrings, some kind of green stone set in black gold. Her hair, which is naturally mouse, is now rich chestnut shot through with raven black strands. It's cut into an angled bob that starts way above the nape of her neck, and tapers down diagonally to her chin. I feel proud. Victoria could never look this good.

Em rushes over and hugs me. I grab her right hand. 'What's this?'

'Do you like it?' she asks modestly. It's a knuckleduster of a ring in deeply orange gold set with some sort of misshapen pink pearl.

'Yes. It's cool.'

Emily's a jewellery designer. She makes a living selling her one-off pieces to a small but fanatically loyal customer base of rich girls she meets in nightclubs. It doesn't pay that well, but her boyfriend, George, is something important in surveying and likes to shower her with gifts, so she does all right.

'But never mind about that, what's this?' Emily retorts. She grabs my own hand and examines the new fake nails. Even Catherine comes over with a spark of interest.

'Are they real?' Catherine asks.

I shake my head.

'Wow. Good fakes,' she says admiringly.

Emily puts her hand on my forehead. 'Feeling ill? A bit peaky?'

'What's happened to your hand?' says Mum, sounding worried.

I laugh it off, a bit awkwardly. The nails feel stupid to me too.

'I've got a new job. I thought they'd help.'

'What kind of new job?' asks Mum. 'What was wrong with the old one?'

I sigh. 'I'll tell you all about it at supper.'

'Where are your cases?' says Dad, having just noticed I don't have any.

'Not with me. It was a spur of the moment thing. I'll borrow some pyjamas off you.'

It has to be Dad because the girls don't have pyjamas. Not one pair between them. Little frilly nighties and sexy slips with lace, or teddies like Victoria. And who can sleep in those? Itchy as hell if you ask me. An oversize pair of Dad's old cotton pyjamas will do me fine.

'And I've got to go down to the shop to get a toothbrush.' I fix Catherine with a stare. 'Catherine, come with me?'

She looks as if she's going to say no, but then sighs and says, 'I'll get my coat.'

She's got the same look on her face I had this morning. Best get it over with.

'Are you OK to talk?' I ask her when we're walking down the High Street towards the shop.

'Fine,' she says. 'It's good, anyway; if I'm outside I can't start crying.'

I squeeze her waist. 'So what happened?'

'A conversation.'

'Must have been a real dinger.'

She sighs; it's half a wince.

'It was this girl in the office. Esther. She's from New York. She's Jewish and really gorgeous, as well as really clever.'

'You're not exactly ugly and thick, Catherine.'

She smiles at me with tears beading her lashes. 'Thanks. Well, anyway, she spends a lot of time at his desk. More than she needs to. And I was just teasing him about it, you know. His new girlfriend and all that.'

'And he was having an affair with her?'

She shakes her head. 'He just smiled and said there was no harm in looking, all men did that. And I said, you know, there is some harm in looking, it kind of depends. Like if your wife were pregnant and fat and she caught you staring at other girls all day. That would be really depressing. Don't you think, Lucy?'

'Oh, definitely,' I say supportively. 'Of course it would be. Why, didn't he agree?'

'Not just that. He then got all serious and said men are biologically programmed not to be monogamous . . .'

'That old chestnut again.'

'Yeah, well. He said that in Europe everybody has these little affairs and nobody gets their knickers in a twist over it.'

'What did you say?'

'That I thought that was an urban legend. What, French girls don't care if their husbands cheat? That's bollocks.'

I watch her carefully. Catherine never swears. Her cheeks have these tiny heightened red dots of pink on them. She looks almost feverish.

'Women still have hearts wherever they come from,' she says. 'Then he said I was being naive and bourgeois.'

'And . . .'

'I asked him if he'd ever had an affair. And he said no. But he looked me right in the eye and said he didn't know if he could always say the same. He said he *wanted* to be faithful to me. But he wasn't sure if he could manage to do it, for his whole life.'

'Oh, Catherine.'

'And then he saw the look on my face and told me he did want to marry me. Someday. But that he had to be honest with me. He said,' the tears are threatening, and she swallows them back, 'he said that sexual fidelity wasn't as important as companionship and real love . . . and that we needed to be grown-up about these things.'

'I see.' My heart's in the pit of my stomach. I haven't spent a lot of time with Peter; the few times I met him I thought he was just about all right. But I know, only too well, how my sister feels about him. She's been in love, so in love, from the first moments. Almost sick in love with him.

'What did you do?' I whisper.

'I told him that I was going to be very grown-up about it and that I'd be out of the house by that night. He said not to play silly buggers. I told him to just fuck off.'

I gasp. Catherine, using the f-word?

'Then I went and saw the MD and asked for a month's vacation effective immediately. Peter had a meeting, he couldn't get out of it, so he went off to that, and I took a taxi home.'

'But you had so much stuff there.'

'I can move fast when I want to,' she says drily. 'I found a luxury flat rental in the West End, that afternoon; paid by credit card, then got a firm of movers round. When he came back that night I was gone,' she said proudly. 'Nothing left, not a trace. Not even a packet of tampons in the bathroom cupboard.'

'Wow.'

'At least I found out before I married him,' she says miserably. 'Four years, and that's the first time he ever brought up marriage. To tell me that if we did, he'd have affairs.'

'And that's it? You haven't heard from him since?'

'How could I? He doesn't know where I live. And he'd hardly dare call here.' She smiles thinly. 'Can you imagine if he got Dad on the phone?'

I laugh. 'That would be ugly.'

We're at the shop. I go in and buy a toothbrush, a Walnut Whip, a copy of *Heat*, and the *Kent and Sussex Courier*.

'Oh brilliant, the *Courier*,' Cathy says. And I know just what she means. It is impossible to dwell on yourself, the Middle East, global warming or anything dreadful when you are reading headlines like 'FETE TOMBOLA RAISES RECORD SUM'.

Once I've paid, and commiserated with Mrs Hadham, the owner, about people letting their dogs poo right next to her welcome mat and not cleaning it up, I steer Cathy back outside.

'And so what will you do when the month is up?'

'Go back to work,' she says.

'But Peter's there.'

'It pays great. And he works on a different floor.' Cathy

64

shrugs. 'I'm not giving it up just so he can feel less awkward.' She looks at me, red-eyed. 'I need to take a leaf out of your book, Lucy. I need to be independent and not live with a man, not be supported by a man, and just enjoy myself.'

'It's not all it's cracked up to be,' I say, thinking of Victoria and Ollie, and my total lack of a love life. 'There's no money. And no men.'

'The second is a bonus,' Catherine says, bitterly.

I give her a hug, but I'm thinking: at least you had a love life to go wrong.

When we get back, there's another car in the driveway. I make a face. I was looking forward to a nice, gentle evening alone with my family. Who is it? It's a Jaguar, all shiny and sleek. I run through my parents' friends. They mostly drive the same battered old hulks Dad does.

'Oh no,' Catherine says.

'Whose car is it?'

'That's George's car.'

'Oh, no,' I echo.

Neither one of us really likes George. He seems smarmy and too conventional for Emily. I think his habit of buying her expensive gifts, including a car, is suspicious. He likes to take her to all his boring corporate parties and show her off, you know, look at my chic, hip girlfriend. *I* may be dull but here's my girlfriend! It's as if he's buying her.

'What's he doing here?' Catherine demands. 'Em's going up to London tomorrow anyway. He could have left her alone for one night to hang out with you.'

'Maybe he just couldn't bear to be away from her,' I suggest. It makes me cross, too, but I don't want to go into a sulk.

'Maybe he's come to give her another present.'

'Maybe he wants to take her to a chartered surveyors' conference.'

Catherine giggles. She's never got over the time when George wore a badge that said, 'In the Property Jungle, Look for the Chartered Surveyor', with a picture of a boa constrictor on it.

'Oh well,' I say. Emily loves him, so what can you do? Fuck all, basically. And I think to myself that it might not be such bad timing. Anything to distract Catherine, even the much disliked George Greene.

We link arms and go into the kitchen together.

'Hello, George,' begins Catherine with admirable fake cheeriness. He's standing there, sort of looming – he's six three – over Emily, who's perched on a chair in front of him. Wearing a smug smile on his face.

And then we both notice that Em's all red-eyed. Like Catherine, except puffy, as though from recent crying. And Mum is hovering. And Dad is standing there next to an open bottle of Veuve Cliquot holding out two glasses.

'Here they are, here they are!' says Mum. 'Darlings, Emily's got some news!'

'Guess what!' shrieks Emily, although I think we both have a pretty good idea. 'George just proposed! We're going to get married!'

She holds out her left hand. Opposite the cool, rough pink and orange ring is a very boring and uninspired one carat round solitaire diamond.

'Don't you think it's just the most beautiful ring *ever*!' says Em, with no discernible trace of irony. She does, however, cast an anxious glance at Catherine. But she needn't have worried. Catherine would never spoil Emily's day.

'I do!' Catherine lies. She rushes over and grabs Em's hand, and goes into gushing raptures about how beautiful it is. 'I'm thrilled for you, Em, I'm so pleased . . . George, it's a beautiful ring.'

'Welcome to the family, George!' I say heartily. I would give him a hug, but I think it might freak him out. So I offer him a firm, dry handshake instead. He seems to appreciate it.

'Yeah, thanks,' he mutters.

Dazzling conversation is not George's primary social skill.

'Champagne!' says Dad, beaming. 'Celebrating Emily and her wonderful young man!'

'Yes please,' say Catherine and I simultaneously. We grab the champagne glasses like drowning women and swap the tiniest of wicked glances at each other.

'Jolly good, darling,' says Dad to Emily. 'George is the best piece of property on the market. Aren't you, George?'

George shuffles his feet and grunts as Em gazes adoringly at him. Ah yes, Dad's canonization of George has now begun.

'Get it?' asks Dad helpfully. 'Chartered surveyor . . . . on the market . . . eh?'

We all muster a titter.

'I don't think I've got anything special enough for dinner,' Mum says, worried. 'I was going to do a chicken, but I think it's burnt. And there wouldn't be enough anyway . . .'

'Never mind about that,' Dad says. 'We'll all go to the pub.'

Thank God for that; best idea I've heard all day. And I'm getting a pint. The Chardonnay-sipping campaign can bloody well wait till Monday.

Pub supper is your average nightmare. George sits there like a lump of pudding, saying nothing. Emily gushes about how great George is. Dad joins in. Mum worries about catering for the wedding. Catherine asks lots of bright, lively questions to mask her inner agony. And I just sit there.

In the scheme of things, losing my job and best mate somehow seems not very important. But at least I won't be grilled over it. I take a leaf out of George's book and eat my chilli con carne in relative silence, throwing in the odd gush over George, or the ring, as called for.

It's selfish – ridiculously selfish. And I'm ashamed for thinking it. But all this emotional turmoil actually makes me jealous. Catherine's soul-destroying pain, as well as Emily's radiant happiness. My sisters, my stylish, groomed, feminine sisters, have these kind of lives; the sort where big loves, big things, happen.

And I've just been ticking along like a student who never grew up. Oh, and being laughed at behind my back by Ollie's friends.

It's all incredibly depressing. I sip my Heineken and wonder if I can change things. Maybe I can. Now I have these fake nails, and the long, angled hair. Maybe I can borrow my sisters' clothes, and that'll be all it takes; I can slip into my new job, and be a different person. A better person. The kind of girl that men like for more than matey conversation in front of Sky Sports . . .

Emily and George go off together in the morning, thank God. There are tears from Mum, and lots of hugs from me and Catherine. Dad slaps them both on the back a few times, which makes George give a pained little cough. Emily insists we both be bridesmaids.

'You're not going to make me wear some kind of gross meringue concoction, are you?' I ask.

'Please, Lucy.' Emily tosses her chic little bob. 'This is me you're talking to. You'll probably both be in a moss-green trouser suit by Chloe.'

'Who's Chloe?' I ask. 'One of your mates?'

Emily rolls her eyes good-naturedly and follows George into his Jag, and they crunch off down our gravel drive amidst lots of waving and tears and shouts.

Mum is crying her eyes out, for no good reason I can see, unless it's the thought of having to have George over for Christmas lunch for the next thirty years. But Dad puts his arm round her shoulders and shepherds her away into the drawing room.

'So.' Catherine manages a small grin for me. 'It's just us then.'

'Looks like it,' I agree.

'I want to hear what's going on with you,' she says. 'Something important,' she adds shrewdly. 'I know.'

'How do you know?'

'The nails,' she says. 'And even though you've tied it back, you've done something to your hair.' She reaches round and tugs out my scrunchie, and what do you know? My new, blonde, angled cut falls impeccably into place, just like it did in the salon.

'Ah-hah! Thought so,' says Catherine with narrowed eyes. 'You can't fool me, Lucy. What's going on?'

We have a cup of tea – if anything happens to my mother, the world price of tea will plummet. We probably consume more tea in my house than the whole of Britain in the eighteenth century – and I tell her the whole, sad story.

'Mmm,' Catherine says when I'm finished. 'To be honest, I can see the point of the image change.'

'You can?'

'Sweetie, with the best will in the world, Megadeth T-shirts and executive offices don't mix.'

'It was Metallica,' I protest sulkily. 'Megadeth suck.'

'You know what I mean.'

I nod.

'And it sounds like pretty good money,' Catherine adds, encouragingly. 'I was planning to have a word with you about that computer magazine anyway.'

'You were?'

'With what they were paying you, it was really more like a hobby.'

I scuff my DMs against the kitchen floor. 'Suppose,' I say ungraciously. I wish everybody didn't have to agree. Lucy has to move on. Lucy needs to grow up.

'I was happy, you know,' I say.

'I know.' Catherine smiles at me. 'But for how long? How much longer would you have enjoyed that kind of life?'

'Anyway.' There's no good in moping, I tell myself. I have to face the day. Wake up and smell the coffee. Etc. 'I'm looking forward to this new challenge,' I say importantly. That's how professionals speak, isn't it? 'I mean, how hard can it be, really? Wearing skirts and putting on heels.'

'And not doing all the stuff you do.'

'That too. I've got four sisters. It's not like I haven't watched you guys do it. Actually, that's the reason I came down here,' I tell her. 'I need to borrow some clothes.'

'Business wear?'

'Yeah. You've loads of that, haven't you? Skirt suits in pinstripes and stuff?' I ask vaguely.

Cathy laughs. 'Girls don't wear pinstripe suits. And men mostly don't either. Or carry umbrellas and wear bowler hats.'

'Oh.'

'You won't fit my clothes, anyway. Or Emily's.'

'Why not? I'm not fat,' I say, offended.

'No, but you are muscled. You have strong thighs. And you've got a classic hourglass figure, whereas we're both stick insects.'

That's certainly true.

'I'm afraid you'll have to wear some of Anne's old stuff,' she says, looking concerned.

'Well, what's wrong with that?'

All my sisters fit a different womanly profile. Emily's urban chic; Catherine is floral and pretty; Laura's got a kind of preppy, American thing going on; and Anne, well. Anne is mother earth. She's the oldest, twelve years older than me, and it didn't surprise anyone when she got married at twenty-five and started popping out babies.

I remember what Ollie said about this guy Todd.

'I think Anne's style is just what they're looking for.'

Anne liked Laura Ashley dresses and big Alice bands, and twinsets with fake pearls; now she has real ones. She wore lots of flats and hardly any trousers. She was the original Sloane Ranger.

'Maybe we should try to develop your own style,' says Cathy hopefully. 'I could show you some magazines. *Cosmo, Elle, InStyle, Vogue . . .*'

I hesitate.

'And *Stylish* is the hot new title these days.'

Stylish is Victoria's magazine. To my horror, Catherine has pulled out this month's copy and is flicking through it.

'You have to get this next month,' she says. 'They're doing a big feature on *What Is Femininity?* You should take a look at it.'

'Ah, thanks.' I turn away from the pile of magazines. 'I think I'll just go and raid Anne's old wardrobe.'

'Well,' Cathy says, 'as soon as you get some money, make sure to buy new clothes. I mean those things are frightful. They're twenty years old. Look, if you want I can get you some things. Why don't we take a trip into Tunbridge Wells and go to the shopping centre? They've got some good stores in Victoria Place.'

Oh please no. The hair and nails was more than enough. A vision of a tedious afternoon with Cathy, much though I love her, dances before my eyes. Trying on skirt after skirt and dying of boredom.

'That's OK. I'm sure they'll be fine. I just need a few dresses and stuff. And I can't take your money.' I hug her. 'This whole thing is about me growing up and learning to stand on my own two feet. Right?'

'I suppose so,' Catherine concedes.

My dad comes back into the kitchen. 'Mum's feeling a lot better now,' he announces. 'She's going to go off to the garden centre. Who wants to go with her?'

'Oooh, I will,' Catherine says. 'I want to get some house plants for the new flat.'

'I will too,' I say, trying to sound enthusiastic. Loads of plants, I mean who cares? I like plants. In gardens, and as long as I don't have to actually do anything with them.

'Well, if you want to, sweetie,' says Dad. 'But I'm sure Mum'll do fine with Catherine. I was thinking of going down to the river for a bit of fishing, but if you're not in the mood . . .'

'Oh! I am, I am!' I jump up. I *love* fishing. 'I am so in the mood. Have you got a spare pair of waders?'

Dad looks at me as if I've gone mad. 'Yours are still here, darling. You don't think we'd throw them away?'

We load our gear into the back of the car and Dad trundles off down to the field that borders the river. I sit there, sort of glowing. I love to spend time with Mum, of course, but me and Dad have this special bond. I love my parents equally, but Dad and I have always been close; ever since I was quite small.

'Good news about Emily,' I observe.

'Yes.' Dad beams. 'Marvellous chap, George. Perfect for her.' He glances at me. 'What about you, poppet? When is it going to be your turn?'

'Oh, I don't know.' I laugh it off. 'I'm not the romantic type.'

'Everybody's the romantic type,' Dad says. 'What about that Scottish fellow?' he asks.

'Ollie?' I blink.

'Oliver. Exactly. I thought you two would have set a date by now.'

Dad parks the car at the edge of a muddy field, opens the five-bar gate, and we stroll down to the river in our wellies. It's a slightly cloudy day; good fishing weather. Normally this would be my idea of bliss. Time alone with Dad, you know; just sitting there in companionable silence, listening to the river rush past, tying flies, trying to trap the fish; and

Kent is so beautiful. You can keep your Costa del Sol or your Swiss Alps when you have these uneven, clumpy fields thick with grass, and the knots of trees, the streams, and the hedges of the south-east.

But today, as I tramp after him, I only feel consternation.

'There wasn't anything between me and Ollie, Dad. We were just friends.'

'Oh, come on, darling.' He chuckles. 'You don't need to have secrets from me. I know you were mustard keen on him.'

Does everyone in the whole world think this?

'Why did you think that?'

'Well, you talked about him all the time. It was pretty obvious,' Dad says, reaching out and ruffling my hair as if I'm five.

I get thick-throated and busy myself with my rod and fly.

'No,' I say, crossly, to cover it. 'Ollie was just a good friend, and he never liked me in that way.'

'Oh darling,' says Dad, humouring me. 'He wasn't one of those gay fellows, was he?'

'Ollie? Hell no.'

'Then of *course* he liked you "in that way". Why wouldn't he?' Dad asks, as if this is an unanswerable point.

'He just didn't. And nor did I,' I lie hastily. 'Anyway,' since I can't bear this much longer, 'he's getting married. To his girlfriend Victoria Cobham,' I add, in case Dad assumes it's to me.

Dad looks astonished. 'Good Lord. I suppose I was barking up the wrong tree. Oh well, the chap must be mad.'

I'm slightly surprised this is the worst he has to say. For the iniquitous crime of not fancying me, Ollie should surely have been labelled the stupidest man in England or weak as water and an utter prat. Or something.

'It's not like you've met Victoria,' I say.

'Met her father,' Dad says.

I stare at him.

'Clive Cobham. Property developer. Dodgy character,' Dad says. 'I vetted some of his deals, advised the council to turn them down. They didn't. I think some brown envelopes may have changed hands. I couldn't prove anything, though.'

Before he retired, my father was a civil servant; chief executive to the local county council. Some people might call it boring, but not for Dad. Because he loves it here. He loves Kent. He even loves East Sussex. Every single day he went off to work, joyfully, in his quiet way. Because he loved the chance to make things better for people. To open libraries, to save woodland, to preserve hospitals. He lost more battles than he won, but he was always trying. And I think that's what made him so happy. I couldn't be prouder if he were a billionaire.

'How do you know it's the same Cobham?'

'He had a daughter called Victoria. And a son called Percy. He was a social climber,' Dad says. 'Straight out of darkest Essex, but despised his own kind. Gave his children upmarket names and bunged them in public schools.' Dad purses his lips. 'Nasty piece of work, Cobham.'

This cheers me up immensely, as Victoria is so snooty. Ollie was never like that in a million years, and apparently he's a real blue blood. I suppose I should call Vicky insecure. But the fact is I still think of her as just a cow, basically.

'And so you're not going to marry that Oliver fellow,' Dad muses. 'Pity. I thought he sounded all right.'

'Dad.' I cast my fly, not very well. 'You never even met him.'

'Ah, no,' he says. 'But I could tell he made you happy, sweetie. And that's what counts.'

'Oh.' I try to toss my hair like Victoria, but it just ends up flopping over my face, so I hastily tug it to one side. The new nails snag in it, but after a bit of a wrestle I get them out. Being ladylike officially sucks. 'Anyway, I am happy,'

I say with fake merriment. 'I'm getting a new look and my new job pays *loads*. And I think it's going to be fun!' I smile gaily at Dad. I can't bear the idea that he should know I'm miserable.

'Well, if you're sure, darling,' Dad says. He gives me a forced smile of his own. 'I expect it'll all work out right in the end.'

5

When I finally make it back to the flat, on Sunday night, I feel drained. Thank God Ollie and Victoria aren't there. I put my borrowed suitcase in my room and examine the contents. Dresses and skirts made of scratchy material. I pick one out, grab a pair of Anne's navy court shoes and some tights, and I'm ready to go.

I don't bother with the rest of the case. Tomorrow I'll have to find a new place, so there's no point unpacking.

Monday dawns grey and overcast. I'm wide awake, staring at the still-bare branches of the chestnut tree, by seven o'clock. This is it, then; D-day.

I feel nervous. I jump out of bed and head to the bathroom, but the shower's going; I can hear Ollie singing.

I pound on the door.

'Ollie,' I call, in a delicate, ladylike manner. 'Excuse me.'

No answer.

'Ollie,' I cry in one of Victoria's high-pitched specials. 'Yoo-hoo.'

He hums a bit louder.

'OLLIE, FUCK OFF AND GET THE FUCK OUT OF THE SHOWER!' I scream in my normal voice.

The water sluices to a halt and the door opens a crack, letting me see a pair of bright blue eyes and a cloud of steam.

'All right, all right, hold your horses,' he says.

'I've got to get in the shower. Big day at work.'

'So I heard. Me and the entire street.'

'You're bloody deaf,' I complain. 'Anyway you probably look like a prune.'

He shuts the door and emerges a second later wrapped in a towel, which does nothing to conceal a very nice pair of biceps.

I look away. 'Hope I didn't wake Victoria.'

'Ah, she's not here. I left her at her place. She needs her beauty sleep for Monday mornings. You get in there and get all tarted up.' Ollie's eyes are sparkling. 'I'll make some breakfast.'

'All right,' I say, mollified. Ollie does good breakfasts.

I wash my hair, not forgetting to condition it, spraying on something Victoria has in an expensive-looking bottle, then do my teeth. I check the coast is clear then bolt back to my room in my own ratty towel. It's greying and it's got holes in it but so what? It dries you, doesn't it? I mean what are towels *for*? I can't understand why Victoria makes such a fuss about it. Then I nuke my hair with a dryer and brush it with a Mason-Pearson that Catherine gave me. It doesn't look that bad. I think about make-up, but I don't know anything about make-up. I have a nasty feeling it could go a bit Bridget Jones on me and I could turn up with an orange-looking face and mascara streaking my forehead or something.

OK, so now it's just dress girlie time.

I examine the outfit I have selected. Surely this is perfect. I don't know what Catherine was worried about. It's obviously feminine, and it's demure. And conservative. It's a big blue Laura Ashley dress from the eighties with a little velveteen bow on the arse, a wide skirt and long sleeves. I struggle into it and then pull on the tights. Oh shit, how I hate wearing tights. Ugh! Argh! Do women do this every day? Voluntarily? I hated it as a girl and I hate it now. They manage to feel itchy and clammy simultaneously. I HATE them. I want to rip them off with my new long fingernails until they ladder into a billion itchy threads. But I bite my lip and force myself to bear it. I have to, don't I? No point in whining.

I slip my tights-clad feet into Anne's plain court-heeled shoes. There! All I need is a bouffant hairdo and I'd be a dead ringer for Nancy Reagan, probably.

I head out to the kitchen where Ollie is just slapping some plates on the table and do a twirl.

'Well?'

His eyes widen and he gives a snort of laughter, which sends coffee spurting out of his nose.

My face falls. 'What's wrong with it?'

'Oh, nothing,' he says, carefully. 'Nothing at all.'

This is clearly a lie. I place my hands on my hips. My eyes dare him to let out just one squeak of that suppressed laughter.

'It's great,' he says. 'Nearly as good as the poster of the kitten.'

'Oh bugger,' I wail, sitting down in front of my plate. The delicious scent of mushrooms, fried tomatoes and bacon wafts up towards me. 'It'll never work, Ollie! I can't pull this off.'

'Course you can,' he says seriously, sitting opposite me. He fills my big American mug I got on holiday with fragrant black coffee. My mug says DON'T MIND THIS ASS WHUPPIN' in big black type. I suppose it'll have to go in favour of a bone china cup and saucer. 'Eat your breakfast. You can't back out now.'

Morosely I dig into my lovely mushrooms. 'Top breakfast, thanks.'

'Don't tell Victoria. She wants to get me on a low-fat regime. Lose some weight for the wedding.'

'Lose some weight?' I ask, staring. Ollie doesn't have a spare ounce on him. 'But you're not fat.'

'Well. She thinks I should change my exercise routine.

Less free weights, more running. She says the muscle look is out.'

'Out?'

'She fancies Johnny Depp,' he says, a touch sadly. 'And Leonardo di Caprio.'

'But he looks like a girl.'

'It's all the rage these days.'

I daren't say anything, for example, 'Victoria is a stupid anorexic cow.' I just make a small face.

'You're no judge. You fancy Arnold Schwarzenegger,' Ollie says.

I shrug. 'Doesn't everybody?'

'Not exactly everybody,' Ollie says. 'I, for example, have never given him a second thought.'

'You're not funny, you know,' I say gloomily.

'No.' He pauses. 'That dress, on the other hand . . .'

I hit him. 'Look, it's a dress, right? It's long. It's navy. It matches my shoes. It doesn't show anything. I've got my hair down and I'm wearing tights. And low heels. And I have a manicure.' I swallow a large and supremely wonderful mouthful of bacon and tomato. 'What more do you want? Blood?' I demand, reaching for my coffee.

'No, you're right.' Ollie struggles to look serious. 'It's a great start. I daresay you'll get the hang of it soon enough.'

What does he mean by that?

'Just remember not to swear. Or do any of that other stuff.'

'Right,' I agree.

'Are you putting on make-up?'

I shake my head. 'Not quite sure about make-up yet.'

'Too much too soon,' Ollie says wisely. 'I can ask Victoria to give you some more tips.'

'Ah, no, that's OK,' I say hastily. 'I don't want to impose.'

'It'd be no trouble for her. She likes you.'

Mmm. 'Well, I have a few ideas of my own,' I say. 'Got to, uh, develop my own style. I'll be trying that out tomorrow.'

He looks dubious so I promise I will slap on some concealer and bronzer.

'Maybe that's a good idea,' he says. 'You look as if you didn't get too much sleep.'

Reassuring.

'You'll be fine,' he adds, noticing my expression. 'Just remember, this is a new adventure!'

Through the open door to my bedroom I can see my computer sitting dead and silent. In Australia my paduan Xa-Tu has probably just paid his credits to the Intergalactic Travel Commission and is about to commence many hours of gaming fun.

I sigh wistfully.

'And get there early,' Ollie tells me seriously. 'First impressions count.'

He's right, of course. I can do it. I go down to the tube and travel out to Notting Hill Gate. I've studied the A-Z, and I walk confidently in the direction of Marsham Street.

At least, I try to walk confidently. In fact I stumble quite a bit. These shoes feel weird. You can't run in them or anything. The toes are all pointed. My feet feel squashed and I keep tripping, and people are sort of staring at me.

I glance down and see there is a massive white scuff over the toe of the left shoe. Arse! Will it ruin the impression? I make a note to myself to hide it. The dress has a long skirt. Maybe if I'm careful . . .

I can see in the windows of the expensive-looking shops that I've gone a bit red-faced and flustered. That won't do. I'm on the whole 'English rose' trip here. So I duck into a newsagents and buy myself a copy of *Vogue*. That'll impress them, right? A copy of *Vogue*. I also pick up some cheese Quavers, but obviously these need hiding. There's plenty of space in Anne's old blue handbag; in fact I think I could store a lightly armed infantry regiment in there if I wanted to.

That's better. I will be serene, I tell myself. I will arrive in

Tory blue, everything matching, hair and nails done, and carrying *Vogue*. I will wow them!

Here we are. Marsham Street. Oh, this is pretty; lovely pastel-coloured houses and cherry trees frothing in spectacular white and pink. Everything looks clean and *extremely* expensive. My mood lifts fractionally; this will be better to arrive to every morning than a sweatshop in the Oval, won't it?

There's number seven. Lucky number. Ollie told me to look hard or I might miss it. And indeed at first sight it's just another pretty house with a mint-green paint job and flowery window boxes. But then I see the discreet brass plaque: MAYLE ACCOMMODATIONS and underneath, LIVING WITH DISTINCTION.

This is it. I check my watch. It's only eight forty-five. I square my shoulders and walk in the front door.

There is the softest grey carpeting under my feet, and as I enter, a tiny golden bell tinkles, like in an old-fashioned bookshop. But instead of books lining the walls, there are framed watercolour landscapes. There is an enormous sofa and several chairs, heavily padded and covered with chintz, an oak coffee table laden with copies of *Country Life* and the *Economist*, and in front of this waiting area several antique desks. The state-of-the-art computers are humming quietly, and behind them sit three girls and a man.

The man is young and clean-cut with sulky brown eyes and thick lashes. The women are all in their late twenties, I would guess, or early thirties.

I begin to feel not quite so well dressed. I mean, look at these girls! They have more than matching colour outer garments and accessories. One of them *does* have an Alice band, but everything they're wearing looks, well, elegant. Much nicer than mine. Soft little twinsets and tweedy skirts. Is that Chanel? I think Chanel does things like that, don't they? And big pearls. Real ones. I wish I hadn't worn

Anne's old glass fakes. And flat pumps and silky shirts. As well as, natch, full make-up. Nobody has their hair loose, everybody has tied it up on top of their heads. There are French plaits, a chignon, and a bun with what looks like a diamond barrette in it.

The young man looks at me without enthusiasm.

'May I help you, madam?' he asks.

He has an amazingly plummy voice. Compared to him Prince Charles sounds like David Beckham.

'Ahm, yes,' I say. Confidence! 'I'm here to see Todd Mayle.'

His face softens a touch. 'And do you have an appointment to see Mr Mayle?' he asks.

'Oh yes,' I say. My grip tightens on my *Vogue*. Nerves. 'I'm . . . Ollie McLeod sent me?' I say loudly. 'I'm here for the receptionist position?'

Why is everything coming out as a question?

He blinks. 'You?'

'The one and only,' I say, jokingly. He does not look amused. There is a tinkle, and the door opens again. A Japanese man enters. The young man instantly elbows me to one side.

'Sit there,' he hisses. 'And don't say *anything*. Mr Okinsaka, *konichi-wa*. How good to see you again, sir,' he says in his normal voice, bowing low from the waist. 'We examined several locations in our portfolio and selected . . .'

I blush further and go to sit down on the overstuffed couch. Unfortunately, my *Vogue* decides to spill open. To my horror, a little shower of glossy cards and subscription offers tumbles out of it all over the soft grey carpet. I dive towards the floor to pick them up, but my court shoes catch against the table leg, and before I know it I have stumbled forwards, banging my shin against solid wood. I land face first in the couch, my skirt raised high over my bottom, flashing a thick, reinforced tights gusset over a pair of Marks & Spencer's finest white knickers. Or once-white knickers.

And, of course, I hear my own voice floating up, muffled by a mouthful of navy blue cotton skirt.

'Oh, FUCK it,' I say.

OK, so it's not the world's most auspicious beginning. But I make a good recovery, I think. I yank down the blue skirt and perch as delicately as I can on the edge of the couch. The women and the young man are staring at me with horror.

What would Victoria do?

'Oh bother,' I say, and smile pleasantly. 'Goodness me.'

Like Wimbledon, everybody's head turns, simultaneously, towards the Japanese client. He is smiling broadly. You might even say lasciviously. He bows towards me and smiles, so I bow back towards him.

This doesn't seem to cut much ice with the nearest girl to me, a slim brunette in a cream-coloured cardigan and shirt combo over a Jaeger tweed skirt. She turns her head towards me and rolls her eyes in disgust.

'Excuse me one second, sir,' says the plummy young man. He bows low again and comes over to me, bending his ear to my head and hissing in it.

'You're obviously not going to be suitable for this office, miss. Please leave.'

Leave?

I blench. Surely they're going to give me a chance?

'Are you . . . Todd Mayle, then?'

'No. Of course I'm not Mr Mayle,' he whispers angrily. 'I'm James Fossbert-Smythe.'

'Well, I'm supposed to see Mr Mayle.'

I don't budge, even though I'm going crimson. This is horrible. Doesn't he understand? I *have* to have this job. I've got no money and no place to live.

'Mr Mayle is not here, and in his absence I'm the office manager. You are not suitable. Now leave at once.'

I think about threatening to make another scene. But how could I do anything worse than flash my knickers at a top client? I suppose that horse has already bolted. And besides, Ollie asked me not to let him down. I can't ruin his relationship with this firm of stuck-up, unforgiving gits . . .

'Very well,' I say, with as much dignity as I can muster. 'I'm leaving.'

'Try to do it decently,' he says.

Tears of humiliation prick at my eyes. OK, so I fell over. But it was an accident, wasn't it? And the swearing, it just came out. It's not like I meant to do it. Would I be wearing these itchy tights if I'd come here intending to show them all up?

I swallow firmly against the lump in my throat. 'Good day to you, then,' I reply with hauteur.

Fossbert-Smythe stands back, arms folded, waiting for me to exit the building. The three Stepford Wives all have their heads down and are tapping at their computers, pretending not to notice me, though I bet they are really just playing Hearts. I am embarrassing, and therefore invisible, like a loud-mouthed drunk on the night bus.

I grab my copy of *Vogue* – why should they have it? – and stick my chin up, putting my battered leather bag carefully over my shoulder, and gingerly thread my way past the treacherous coffee table.

The little doorbell goes again, and a tall man enters. White, this time; late thirties, and, check it out, devastatingly gorgeous. He has classic movie star features: an even nose, high cheekbones, disdainful chocolate eyes with thick black lashes, and dark, close-cropped hair, sexily sprinkled with strands of grey. He is wearing a suit that looks made to measure, dark shoes, and a huge gold Rolex. Unable to help myself, I gasp out loud.

The vision glances at me with slight amusement. I get the feeling he has had this reaction before.

'Good morning, sir,' Fossbert-Smythe says smarmily.

'Hello.' The vision has a deep, throaty American accent. This must be him, I think with a pang of despair. Todd

85

Mayle. Why did I ever think I could have worked for someone like him? He's way out of my league. Too good-looking and smooth by far. The kind of guy you see sitting reading the news on an American TV network, not the sort you bump into in real life in London. He makes me nervous. Well, more nervous than I am already.

Mayle bows to his customer and launches into fluent Japanese. The customer, bowing again (living in Japan, no wonder they all have flat abs – all the constant bowing), chuckles and says something back to him, with a nod at me.

Mayle lifts one eyebrow.

'Ah, we had a brief incident,' Fossbert-Smythe says. 'But I have explained to the young woman that she is clearly not quite the calibre we expect at Mayle Accommodations and she is leaving. It's all taken care of,' he adds hastily. He is clearly desperate Mayle should not think he has lost control of the situation.

I open my mouth but only a despairing squeak comes out. I cover it with a cough.

'Yes, I'm sorry, Mr Mayle,' I say. 'It was an accident. Please don't hold it against Oliver McCleod. I'm going now, goodbye.'

'Not so fast,' Mayle says. 'You're Miss Evans, are you?'

'Yes. Lucy Evans.'

'My office is in the back over there. Why don't you go inside and have a seat, and I'll be right with you.'

'But . . .' says Fossbert-Smythe, outraged.

Todd Mayle turns to him calmly. 'Yes, James?'

Fossbert-Smythe swallows. 'Nothing, sir. Nothing at all.'

I hesitate for a second then flee into the back office. This time, I manage to stay on my feet.

It's a beautiful room, a cross between a library and an office. There is a mahogany desk with a computer, but the walls are lined with bookshelves groaning with leather-bound volumes, and where there aren't gorgeous old books there's costly-looking wallpaper. The chairs here are burgundy leather, and there are little Moroccan side tables inlaid with mother-of-pearl. One wall is sliding glass doors that lead out to a charming little garden, blazing with tulips and daffodils; there is a manicured scrap of grass and a wall, up which various plants have been trained. Roses and wisteria, I imagine. I'm certain Mayle has it set up so it flowers all year round.

It's gorgeous, and despite my discomfiture, I feel my blood pressure dropping. Outside, I can hear Mayle and the client in a low hum of Japanese. And nothing else; the snotty girls and Fossbert-Smythe have obviously gone back to work as though nothing has happened. I breathe out. Todd Mayle has smoothed it all over. My humiliation is vanishing like a ripple in a puddle.

He comes in five minutes later.

'Sorry to keep you waiting,' he says, shutting the door. 'No, don't get up.'

'I'm tremendously sorry about tripping over like that,' I say urgently. 'It won't happen again. I mean, if you hire me, that is.'

'Hey.' He gives me a wink and a practised smile. 'Forget about it. I have. Would you like some coffee?'

'Love some.'

He presses a button on his phone.

'James, would you come in here please?'

The door opens. 'Yes, Mr Mayle?'

'Miss Evans here would like some coffee. How do you take it, Miss Evans?'

Fossbert-Smythe looks as if he's bitten into a lemon. He pastes a smile on his face but his eyes are glaring at me. I feel half triumphant, half terrified.

'Black, no sugar,' I tell him. 'Please,' I add hastily. 'And thank you.'

'No trouble at all,' he lies. 'And for you, Mr Mayle?'

'I won't.' Mayle nods at him. 'Just fetch Miss Evans' coffee, James. That will do.'

'Right away,' he says. He flashes me a quick look of loathing and leaves the room.

I wiggle uncomfortably.

'Now,' says Mayle. 'You are a friend of Oliver McCleod's?'

'That's right,' I say. My voice has gone all throaty. Very Eartha Kitt. I cough.

'And how long have you known him?'

'About five years.'

'Really?' He examines me with clinical interest. 'So are you . . .'

'His girlfriend?' I shake my head. 'Just a friend, you know. In fact, Ollie's getting married.'

'Ah, yes. I remember he mentioned something about that.' Mayle smiles impersonally at me. 'And he thought you might want our new receptionist's job.'

'Yes. Very much.'

At least that's true, I think to myself.

'So you're interested in real estate?' he says, staring at me with those stunning dark eyes.

'Oh yes. Passionately.'

'Well, it's always healthy to have a passion for the field. What is your particular area of interest, Miss Evans?'

'Houses.'

'Houses?'

'Yes. I like them better than flats. You know, more space.'

'I was thinking more of yield vs. growth, REITs, mortgage derivatives, vacancy hedging.'

'Ah,' I say slowly. I have no idea what the hell he just said. 'Well, of course, vacancies must be filled. And that's what Mayle Accommodations is there for!' I smile my most brilliant smile at him.

'I see,' he responds, unimpressed.

James comes back in with the coffee. And I'm actually glad to see him. I mean, derivatives? Aren't they something to do with stocks and shares?

Mayle is not smiling.

'You know, I love beautiful houses – like this one,' I try desperately. 'But the technical side of things I'm not so up on. Ollie told me that you're a genius, though, Mr Mayle, and he said if I worked for you I could learn things.'

'Did he?' Mayle cracks a faint grin. 'And you want to learn from me, is that it?'

'Absolutely.'

'No harm in that, I guess. You're certainly a pretty girl,' he remarks.

'Thank you.' I glow with pleasure. And congratulate myself for not saying, 'Look who's talking.'

'James did inform me that you'd used colourful language in the office. In future, that would be a dismissal matter.'

I hang my head, then realize he said 'in future'.

'Does that mean I can stay?'

'Well, let's see. I am prepared to offer you the position on a short-term trial basis.'

My face falls.

'If you can manage to perform to the highest standards with no adverse incidents for two months, then we'll review.'

'Right.'

Before I dropped out of Durham we got career counselling. I struggle to remember what they told me.

'In order to help me . . .' what would Americans say? '. . . uh, perform at an optimal level, could you outline for me your expectations for maximum performance standards?' I look at him. Result! He seems to like the gobbledgook.

'You are the public face of Mayle Accommodations, so naturally an impeccably polite manner is essential. Perfect humility to all clients, and I do mean all clients. I once heard a horror story about a letting agent who was rude to a hippie gentleman who walked into his office in sandals. That hippie gentleman was the lead singer in a rock band.'

I open my mouth to show I'm shocked.

'I know,' says Mayle. 'His net worth was over twenty mil. That agent lost some serious cheesecake for his short-sightedness. Then, of course, as well as your manner, there must be excellent grooming. No revealing clothes. Attire for ladies here is demure and feminine at all times. In future, scuffed shoes and worn purses are not acceptable.'

I flush bright red. I had no idea he'd noticed my shoes or my bag. 'Purse' is American for bag, and they call purses wallets.

'You've seen the ladies out there. My assistants, Jade, Buffy and Melissa.'

I chuckle, then realize too late he is not joking and turn it into another cough.

'You should dress like they do. But you may pick more British designers if you like,' he says. 'Catherine Walker, for example. Princess Diana wore a lot of Catherine Walker.'

Designers? With what money?

'No problem at all,' I say.

'Your accent's very cute. It's perfect to have another English voice in the office, with all us Americans. You'll be like a female James.'

I will?

'But just tone down the English eccentricity,' he says. He gestures at my dress, and shoes. 'You'll wear make-up in future. And perfume.'

'Perfume?'

'Chanel is fine,' he says, reassuringly. 'And be at the office by eight a.m. sharp. Remember, your outer appearance reflects your inner reality. Think modesty, beauty and charm. Think Princess Diana. You admired Princess Diana?'

'Oh – yes. She was my style heroine,' I say.

'Excellent. Then we should have no problems,' he says. 'Welcome aboard, Miss Evans.'

'Please call me Lucy.'

He inclines his head. 'Lucy. And you can call me Mr Mayle, or sir.'

Mayle winks at me again. But I'm not sure he's joking, so I say humbly, 'Thank you, sir.'

'That's my girl,' he says smugly. 'Sort out your appearance and I'll see you tomorrow.'

I walk out of there as fast as I can, avoiding James Fossbert-Smythe's glare, and head for home. My mind is racing. Mostly with thoughts of how scarily stunning Todd Mayle is. I can hardly believe it. I've got the job even though I bollocksed it up a bit. But still, I can leave that out when I tell Ollie.

I won't have to run home to Kent. I won't have to listen to Annoying Victoria gloat.

But my triumph is short-lived. There's everything Todd Mayle said. I feel a bit panicked. Obviously my appearance is not what I'd hoped. I haven't risen to the girlie heights like Victoria or the women in his office. Maybe Catherine was right about Anne's stuff being dated. But what can I do?

Calm down, Lucy, I tell myself. It's a problem, like a quest on a game. And you're good at quests. I always solve the quests in record time. Why not this one?

I get on the tube; the flat'll be quite safe, Ollie and Victoria are at work on their high-paying jobs. I just need to think for a few moments. I'm sure I can sort something out. I've got the bloody job, and I'm not about to lose it because of the wrong clothes.

As soon as I get in the front door, I make myself a cup of tea, and then get a piece of blank paper out of my printer. I find a Biro in Ollie's room (he won't mind) and write on it, in big blue letter's 'Lucy's Problem File'.

Then I draw a line down the middle of the paper and write PROBLEM on the left and SOLUTION on the right.

I've always done this. Victoria caught me at it one time and laughed at me.

'Problem/Solution?' she mocked. 'What is this, Lucy, more computer speak?'

'If you write down your problems, then you find you can think of the answers,' I said. 'It's a bit like giving a friend advice except you're the friend. We can always answer other people's problems, don't you think? We just get stuck on our own.'

'Well, Lucy,' she said, with a tinkling laugh for Ollie's benefit, 'just don't bother trying to solve any of *my* problems. There's a dear.'

Grrr. The memory has me gritting my teeth. Don't think about her. Think about Todd Mayle. And looking professional. It wouldn't be so hard to do girlie things like wear tights and high heels if it were in a good cause, like, I don't know, getting large cheques, and growing up. And having Ollie respect me.

OK. Here we go. In the PROBLEM column I write:

1. Don't know exactly what he wants looks-wise. Can't ask Victoria for help.
2. Don't know how to do make-up.
3. Don't have any money re: Catherine Walker, Chanel perfume.

Then I look at the SOLUTION column expectantly. Nothing happens. Take a sip of tea. Nothing happens.

Oh shit. Maybe this isn't going to be as easy as I thought.

I glance around the room for inspiration, and my gaze lands idly on my crumpled copy of *Vogue*.

Of course! That's the answer. Screw you, Victoria. Know thine enemy. Women's magazines. That's what I want. Maybe not *Vogue*, I mean they are known for kooky fashion shoots of stuff nobody actually buys. But I could look at the adverts. And there are other mags.

I make a quick foray out to the newsagent's and get all the essentials. *Heat, Marie Claire, Company, Elle* and *InStyle*. My hand hovers over *Stylish* but I let it drop. I just can't stand her. Am I being immature?

Oh well. Too bad. I lug them all home, they're heavy, all thick with adverts, and sit on the couch, studying up. They're actually really useful. *Marie Claire* has a 'Look great for your shape' feature. *Elle* has 'style at any age' (it's clear from the pictures that although I am twenty-four, Todd wants me dressed as if I'm thirty-five). *Company* has 'Best bags and shoes under forty quid', thank God. And *Heat* and *InStyle* have lots of pics of celebrities looking gorgeous in quite similar outfits.

I'm very businesslike. First I make notes of what to buy. Apparently, I need something called a 'capsule wardrobe'. Despite its name, sadly, this is not a wardrobe you put in a capsule and bury deep in your garden so you never have to wear anything so itchy and uncomfortable again. Rather, it's a collection of clothes items you can mix and match to make it look like you own more outfits than you really do.

There are five days of the week. And trousers are obviously right out at Mayle Accommodations, unless you are in fact male.

So, I make that:

Four skirts (tan, navy, floral, black) just on the knee. Something called 'pencil' which means they don't go outwards.

One dress. Floral.

Two pairs of shoes with low heels (black and navy).

Five shirts. Two cream, two navy, one floral. Note to self: all the florals must have blue in them.

One tan leather bag.

Three little cardigans: cream, navy, black.

And one navy blue jacket.

Plus one small bottle of Chanel perfume.

This is the bare minimum, it seems. But it is also quite a lot of stuff. So what I have to do is find the absolute cheapest places to get it all. Luckily the women's magazines are a help there too, they have all these great features like 'Splurge vs. Steal' where they show you a designer lipstick that costs forty pounds and then one exactly the same colour from Maybelline and it costs two fifty. I select some cheap but nice-looking clothes. It seems all a bit of a production, frankly, because I'll have to go all over the place – Warehouse, Top Shop, Zara, H&M. But when I've finished I'll have my capsule wardrobe and I'll only have spent about three hundred pounds. I'm sure the bank will let me overdraw.

I think about it. I could get all this on Oxford Street, I think. Around there anyway. I'm sure I've seen those shops on my way in to metal gigs at the Astoria.

This is going to be terminally dull. *Shopping*. I hate shopping. Unless it's for computer games. On the other hand, it's got to be done.

I pull off my dress and tights, thank God, and slip into my jeans and DMs. Then I sigh, grab my bag and head out the door.

6

I wish I could tell you it wasn't that bad. I wish I could tell you that as soon as I walked into Zara, I was overwhelmed by all the gorgeous clothes and discovered my inner Britney Spears.

No such luck. They all look the same to me, boring skirts and dresses hanging on racks. You don't know what they'll be like till you put them on, and then you might not like them. And you have to go back out there and queue for bloody ages with a bunch of fourteen year olds just to get back into the changing rooms.

I tell myself it's part of the job. I have the actual ripped pictures of the things I want, torn out of the magazines and shoved into my handbag. So at each shop I don't waste time searching for it – one tan skirt looks much like another, doesn't it? I find a shop assistant, who is usually chatting to her mates and very sniffy at being asked for help. But I fish out the right picture and ask her where it is.

One of the girls, in Weston's, the brand-new hot fashion chain (so *Elle* told me), actually refused.

I went up to where she was standing with two other girls and a bloke. They all wore chic black tees and trousers, with little mikes wired up to their ears like they were TV producers, or roadies at a Madonna gig. I'm almost at the end now, just need the floral dress and skirt. Thank God because shopping sucks. I stagger up to them, weighed down with my H&M and Zara bags and all my new make-up from Boots.

'Hi,' I say. 'Can you show me where . . .' I rummage around in my scuffed bag and triumphantly produce the photos of the floral dress and skirt. They have a print of navy flowers on them that will match my H&M navy cardigans. Or I could use the cream ones. You chart it out, you see. Like maths.

'. . . these are?'

'Dunno,' says the girl, and turns back to her conversation.

'But I really need to find them.'

They ignore me.

'Excuse me.'

The boy turns to me disdainfully. 'Dresses are over there,' he says, gesturing. 'We're in a sales conference, sorry.'

I feel myself slowly flush. 'But you're not.'

'What?' he says, hostile.

'You're not in a sales conference. You were just talking about how your mate Darren got caught smoking a joint.'

All four of them turn to stare at me, now openly hostile.

'I've told you we aren't available,' the boy says. 'Now I've told you where the dresses are. Please go over there. Otherwise we *do* have security in this store.'

I can't believe it. He's threatening to kick me out! I glance at my pile of bags, hesitating.

The boy gives me a smirk and turns back to his conversation.

'And she was, like, I'm gonna report you. And he said, no way, so she says she won't if he hands over all his stash . . .'

I stand there, feeling hot and stupid. I suppose the ladylike thing would be to accept this and not make a fuss. I don't want to. I want to scream at them. I want to threaten to find the manager. *Make* them do what I want.

But that's not what the new me is meant to do, is it? Todd told me to think Princess Diana. I doubt Princess

Diana would have the urge to land a good drop-kick right in the middle of that smug boy's balls.

So I toss my hair, say, 'Oh well, if you're too busy,' and walk over to the dresses. My face is all red and my heart is pounding. But I'm a good girl. I thread through the racks for forty-five minutes until I finally come across the dress and the matching skirt, hidden away at the back of some neon-green silk combat trousers.

Then I queue for another ten minutes, try them on, take them to the cash registry, queue for fifteen more minutes, pay and get the hell out of there.

On the way home I feel like crying. But then again, what else is new?

In my room, I hang up all my clothes so they don't get creased, then take them all back off the hangers again to try them on in front of the mirror in Ollie's bedroom.

Yeah; they all go together. You can put a navy skirt with a cream shirt and navy cardigan, the floral with a navy shirt and cream cardigan, the black with a cream shirt and tan cardigan . . . it just goes on and on. Seconds of fun for all the family!

My mood is black so I select my black skirt for this evening; a cream shirt, tan cardigan, the black heels (they bloody pinch) and the new tan bag I got from Faith. Add one pair of itchy tights, brush out my hair, and . . .

I regard myself. Yes; success, I think. I look like Buffy or Jade now. Sure, you can tell the clothes are cheap, but they go, they match. And they aren't flamboyant with bows and stuff like Anne's eighties' dress.

I stare at my reflection trying to muster some enthusiasm. Nope; none comes. I just hope Todd likes it, I think suddenly.

Todd . . . Todd. I'd forgotten about him, so much do I dislike having to wear this stuff. Suddenly it all becomes just a touch more interesting. I examine my reflection more carefully. Does it look feminine? Girlie? Professional? Does the tan of my new bag match the tan of the cardigan?

I'm not used to dressing for male approval. Particularly not for a boss's approval. Will this pass muster with somebody so terrifyingly pulled-together?

Hmmm. Maybe it'll be better with make-up. I take most of the clothes back to my room and hang them up again. Then grab my bag of Boots make-up and go back into Ollie's room. Perhaps this is the key to Princess Di-like style. Of course, I'm not stupid. Even I know the worst thing in the world is some chick with loads of warpaint on, looking like Barbara Cartland. I fetch my copy of *Company*, they have a feature on Bobby Brown, apparently she is not the male pop star married to Whitney Houston, but a make-up girl. Or should I say artist. Make-up is an art, apparently. And Bobby – no, it's Bobbi – she thinks you should look like your normal self which apparently involves 'nudes'.

Good. I bought nudes.

So here we go.

Oil of Olay. It was cheap. Concealer. I already know how to do that. No. 7 sheer foundation in Blonde.

This feels a bit weird. I am smearing what looks suspiciously like brown paint all over my face. But I stick with it. The mag says to 'blend'. Which means rub it in with your fingertips . . .

OK.

That doesn't look too bad. Nothing like brown paint. So now the bronzer used as blusher, I also know how to do this.

And a slick of waterproof mascara.

And some of this nude eye shadow on my eyelids, and then just lipgloss on my lips, because you only do one. Eyes or lips. Which is fine with me.

Gingerly I look in the mirror again. And then slowly smile.

What can I say? I don't think I look any prettier, as such. But I do look more sort of *even*. More smoothed-out. The nails and hair and the matching clothes, and the make-up. I can see it'll be a right pain in the behind to wash it all off, I'll have to be super-careful or I'll get spots. But the nice thing is, I don't look like Lucy Evans any more. I look like someone completely different. For example, Jade, Buffy, or Melissa.

And that's perfect, isn't it? I mean, Lucy Evans wasn't working, apparently. The real me doesn't cut it, so maybe the fake me can do a little better. I imagine myself sauntering into work tomorrow (I'll practise with these heels until I've mastered them, no more tripping). 'Oh, hello, James,' I'll say throatily, in my Liz Hurley voice. 'How very *good* to see you.' And he'll stare with longing at my cute little outfit. But it'll be too late for him, because he already blew it by being nasty! And then Todd will arrive. 'Wow, Lucy,' he'll say. 'You look so professional. Perhaps I should give you a promotion. You're glowing, like . . .'

Like what?

'Like an English rose,' continues imaginary Todd. 'I certainly did the right thing in hiring *you*. You've got a big future in this business . . .'

'Hello,' coos Victoria. 'Darling? You in here?'

The fantasy withers and dies as Victoria trip-trips on her strappy sandals into Ollie's room.

'Lucy,' she says coldly. 'Is Ollie here?'

I shake my head.

'What are you doing in his room without his permission?' she demands. 'Snooping about? Going through his things? Really, Lucy.' She sighs theatrically. 'I didn't expect that, even from you.'

'I'm just using the mirror,' I say, biting my lip so I don't scream at her. 'I don't have one, remember?'

'And what's wrong with the bathroom?'

'I needed it to be full-length. I've bought some new clothes, you see. And Ollie never minds if I come in here to use his mirror.'

'*You've* bought new clothes? Yeah, right,' she says.

'I have. They're for work,' I say, defensively.

'Let me see,' Victoria demands. She marches into my room (apparently my permission is not required) and glances about. 'There's nothing in here.'

I throw open the doors of the wardrobe so she can see my new purchases.

'Good Lord,' Victoria drawls. 'Whoever would have thought you'd actually hang something up. Well, let's see.' Briskly she flicks everything out on its hanger, examines it, and hangs it back up.

I feel slightly nervous despite myself. She is an expert on this stuff. Right?

'I suppose somebody bought these for you?' she asks. 'A friend? One of your sisters?'

I shake my head.

'You hired a personal shopper? With what money?'

'I picked them out myself. I mixed and matched. Like the magazines say.'

'And who did your make-up?' Victoria snaps. 'Got it done free at a counter?'

'I did,' I tell her. 'I went to Boots.'

Victoria seems nonplussed.

'You're telling me,' she says slowly, 'that you picked out these clothes and you did that make-up?'

My heart leaps. It's good, then? It must be, or she wouldn't be talking like this.

'Oh yes,' I say airily. 'I got a chart. And pictures. For the make-up, I copied the photos.' I show her *Company*. 'Bobbi Brown. Neutrals. See?'

Victoria purses her lips. Not a good idea, as they aren't exactly plump to start off with.

'I did all right then?' I ask, hoping for some approval. 'I

mean, it was boring, of course. But it's not that difficult when you get down to it.'

'Boring? *Boring?*' she half shrieks. 'It is not *boring.* Style is *life.* Style is *everything.*'

'Not to me,' I say.

'Oh, evidently.' Victoria laughs sarcastically and tosses her hair. It doesn't spray out like mine does, though. 'I suppose you think you're *awfully* clever with your little matchy-matchy outfits, Lucy. Anybody can see they look cheap. This fabric is as thin as gossamer. And so bland! I shouldn't think you'll get too far looking like that. It's a slight improvement on your normal get-up, but don't bother slapping yourself on the back, darling, will you? Real style takes years of *work* to accomplish.'

'Oh,' I say. My face falls. Cheap and bland. Is that what Todd's going to think of me? 'Do you think it looks normal, at least?'

'Normal? Oh, you mean things an actual girl would wear, as opposed to a bricklayer.' Victoria sniffs. 'Well, I suppose so. Yes, don't worry, Lucy. You've managed to pull off the average shop girl look perfectly.'

The door opens again and Victoria does a sort of instant transformation. She gives herself a little shake, smooths her pink dress close to her body, fluffs her hair, and paints on a gorgeous, open smile. In a way it's quite impressive. How to go from prissy super-bitch to welcoming, friendly babe in two seconds flat.

'Hi,' Ollie calls out. 'You home, Lucy?'

'I'm in here,' Victoria trills, although that wasn't what he asked.

'Hi, Ol,' I say.

Ollie comes into the flat, drops his briefcase, and walks into my room. He gives Victoria an absent-minded peck on the cheek, then does an exaggerated double-take as he sees me in the black-and-tan look.

'Oh my God,' he cries. 'Where's my flatmate? Did you eat her?'

'What do you think?' I ask shyly.

'I can't believe it. You look magic. Doesn't she?' he appeals to his fiancée.

'Oh yes. Magic,' says Victoria. Only I notice the sour note under her gushy tone.

'What happened to that horror of a blue frock?' he asks. 'Thought better of it?'

'No, I went to the interview in that, and I got the job,' I say, wisely leaving out all extraneous material, 'but then I thought maybe I'd better stick to more stuff that –' I was going to say 'matches' but I don't want bitch Vicky to sneer at me again – 'co-ordinates.'

'Well, it's beautiful,' Ollie says. 'Very classy indeed. I never would have recognized you. Todd's bound to be impressed. You look just like all those girls he hires, Bitsy and Mitsy and Fluffy.'

I giggle.

'Although, obviously, far prettier,' Ollie says, squeezing me round the waist. He is genuinely delighted, and all the little annoyances and humiliations of shopping sort of glide away from me. I'm thrilled he likes it. I bask in his approval.

'Thanks, mate,' I say gruffly.

Victoria clears her throat to show us she is still there.

'Come on, darling,' she says. 'Let's go out to eat. I want a decent table somewhere, so you'd better hurry.'

'Good idea,' Ollie says, turning away. 'How about Italian? I'm starving, I could murder a plate of pasta.'

She smiles at him. 'That sounds wonderful. I'll have an insalata mista. We could go to Paolo's, that's the new place in Chelsea Wharf. Michael Winner gave it a great review in the *Sunday Times* last week.'

Ollie makes a face. 'Well, if you want to go there, I'll try it anyway.'

'Naughty!' she says, hitting him playfully.

'If Lucy is happy with it,' he adds. 'Paolo's all right for you, Lucy?'

'What?' explodes Victoria. Before she can stop herself, I suspect.

'Well, we'll be taking Lucy out to dinner, of course,' Ollie says. 'Won't we? To celebrate her landing the job and everything. You are all right with that, aren't you, hon?'

'Oh.' Victoria swallows hard. 'Of course. But I shouldn't think Lucy wants to,' she adds. 'It's been a long day for her. I expect she'd rather just curl up in front of the telly with a McDonald's.' She gives me a filthy look, daring me to disagree.

I know it's storing up trouble. But I can't help it. I want Ollie to tell me again how good I look. How Todd'll love it. And there's the added bonus of really pissing off Victoria. I think I've used up today's reserves of good girl.

'Oh, you know what, Vicky?' I say sweetly. 'Actually I'd love an Italian. And Paolo's sounds *divine*,' I add, doing a passable imitation of her.

'Brilliant. That's settled then.' Ollie, who is completely oblivious to the raging torrents of hatred and jealousy seething under the surface, slips a brawny arm round both our waists. 'A lovely evening with my two favourite ladies!'

Paolo's is exactly what I would have expected from a place Victoria loves. It is immaculate, with blond woods and recessed lighting, and about as personal and charming as your local IKEA; the staff are obsequious and yet simultaneously sneering (how do they pull that off?) and the prices are astronomical.

It's also a long way from our house. Which means, in the taxi, I get another tutorial from Vicky on femininity. Apparently it is key to ask your man all about his day, gush endlessly about everything he says, flatter him ceaselessly, and shake your head and tsk-tsk over anybody who disagrees with him.

'So I told the wife she shouldn't agree to joint custody so fast. He wants it, so if she battles, he'll be terrified. Probably give her another five hundred thou,' Ollie says.

'Marvellous advice, darling.'

Ollie smiles smugly. 'Yes, well. She seemed pleased.'

'She's so lucky to have you, darling.'

'If she'd signed a pre-nup, like I told her to, she wouldn't be in this position,' he says. 'She could just have sued under American law and got some decent money. But as it is they've only been married three years. No court in England's going to give her a big slice. Not like she wants.'

Victoria's eyes sparkle with breathless admiration. 'You're so clever, sweetheart. I bet they make you senior partner soon.'

'Oh,' says Ollie modestly, brushing it aside.

I hear myself say, 'I think that's really awful.'

'What is?' He turns to me, surprised, and Victoria shoots me one of her patented death stares.

'What you're doing.'

'I'm just fighting for my client's interests, Lucy.'

'But you're encouraging her to use the children as a weapon. What kind of mum would do that?' I ask. 'That's horrible. If he's a good father, I mean. If they've only been married three years the children must be tiny.'

Ollie nods.

'Then don't you think it'll be hard enough for them without being prevented from seeing their dad?'

'It's just a delaying tactic,' he says reasonably.

'But at that age it'll be really traumatic. And why should she get a big payout? If they've only been married for three years. She sounds like a gold-digger to me.'

Ollie smiles. 'She's not a very nice woman. But it's not my job to make moral judgements, just to get her the best deal.'

'But maybe that should be your job.'

Ollie shrugs. 'I'm a divorce solicitor.'

'But you could be so much more,' I cry. 'You're better than that, Ol.'

'Oh, Lucy, do you mind?' snarls Victoria. 'Ollie is doing a wonderful job and he's serving society.'

'How?'

Victoria is stumped for a moment, but rallies. 'He helps people resolve their differences in a *civilized* manner. Not something you're exactly an expert on.'

'I don't think using children as a football is civilized,' I mutter.

'Blimey,' Ollie says. 'One day in a decent job and I'm getting career advice.'

'Exactly,' Victoria triumphs. She loves it when he tells me off.

'This is what I get for taking you to dinner,' Ollie says, with a grin.

'You're right. I'm sorry.' I back off, and Victoria, after one more withering glance at me, resumes her regularly scheduled programme of telling Ollie how fabulous he is.

'This place is so *intime*,' Victoria purrs as we're shown to our seats. 'You were so clever to think of it, darling.'

'You thought of it, Vicky,' I say.

She scowls. 'Ollie suggested Italian.'

'As far as I'm concerned that means Pizza Hut,' Ollie says, and I laugh. Victoria forces a smile.

The menu isn't as bad as I feared, I get a mini pizza of my own. Admittedly it's 'goat's cheese and sun-dried tomatoes', they don't seem to offer pepperoni and sausage. But I'm starving, and I'm sure it'll be OK. Ollie gets a lobster ravioli.

'Are you sure you want that, darling?' Victoria coos. 'All those complex carbs? They do have a grilled fish available, and we could get it without the polenta. You know you promised to start on Atkins.'

'Yes, but I'm hungry,' Ollie explains, pleasantly enough.

Victoria looks as if she's going to say something else, then glances my way and pipes down. I think it's one of her cardinal rules – 'never criticize a man in front of another woman'. I smile sweetly back at her.

'D'you want to share a starter, Ol?' I asked. 'They have some spicy fried calamari. I bet they're delicious.'

'Ollie doesn't eat batter,' Victoria says instantly.

'Just this once won't hurt, surely?' I ask innocently. 'We are celebrating, after all.'

'We are. Why not, eh?' Ollie says gratefully.

'I'll get two orders, just to be safe,' I say. 'And some of their fried liver and pancetta. And perhaps just a bit of the Italian bread with the dipping oils.'

'Wonderful,' Ollie says, his mouth watering.

Victoria would like to kill me where I sit. I resist the temptation to wink at her.

'So tell me all about the new job,' Ollie encourages me as soon as we've ordered.

'Well, I've just got hired,' I say modestly. 'There's not a lot to tell.'

'Nice office?' he asks.

'Very nice. Seems like there's a lot of money in his business.'

'There is. Todd's made himself an absolute fortune. Not that he needs it, he comes from money anyway.'

'Does he?' I ask, fascinated. 'What do you know about him?'

'Why?' Ollie asks shrewdly. 'Fancy him, do you?'

'No,' I say, going red. I mean, I do think he's gorgeous. Definitely. But there's something just too perfect about him.

'Course you do, all the girls do.' Ollie turns to Victoria, trying to draw her into the conversation. She's perching on her chair edge, sipping her still mineral water ('bubbles equal bloating', as she informed me one day) and looking as bored as she knows how. 'Todd Mayle is Lucy's new employer.'

'How fascinating,' Victoria says evenly.

'And he's one of the most eligible men in London. He came over from the States after he broke up with his fiancée. She was Lillian Astor, the heiress.'

'I know who Lily Astor is,' Victoria admits, looking a touch more interested despite herself.

'Todd's from that background,' Ollie tells me. 'You know, they call them Boston Brahmins. All the Lowells and Cabots and that. Preppy sorts, with country clubs and suchlike.'

'If he was dating Lillian Astor, I don't think Lucy will be quite his cup of tea,' Victoria says with a smile. 'No offence, Lucy dear. Lily Astor is one of the leading lights of New York society,' she explains. 'Never a hair out of place, never an inappropriate comment, let alone a swear word.' She looks at me significantly. 'She isn't the prettiest of the society ladies, but everybody says she has such *refinement*.'

Ollie says, 'Ah, but the new Lucy could give her a run for her money.'

Victoria gives one of her little tinkling laughs. 'Oh, darling, you are so funny,' she says.

'Tell me more about Todd.' I'm ignoring Victoria, and anyway, I want to learn everything I can. He could be the key to my future.

'Well, he comes from money, like I said. He's going to inherit a lot of stock, a house in New York, a big place in the Hamptons. That sort of thing.'

'But he still wanted to make his own?'

Ollie nods. 'He's like a golden boy, has to succeed, you know? He came over here, started Mayle Accommodations, and he's racked up the cash. Connected with lots of rich foreigners: Saudis, Japanese, Swiss, even the odd Yank from back home.'

'How much do you think he's made?' Victoria chimes in.

'I don't know. About five million maybe. Of course he's worth a lot more than that anyway. But I think it's really good he doesn't sit around like some trust fund brat,' Ollie says. 'I admire *that* about him.'

There's a slightly off note in his voice.

'What, you don't like him, Ol?' I ask.

'Oh, no.' Ollie shakes his head. 'I don't really know the man. His manner rubbed me up the wrong way maybe. But like I said, I hardly know him.'

'OK, then.' I smile.

'Darling,' Victoria says. 'Maybe you should *get* to know him. After all, if he's so well connected, think of all the clients he could put your way.'

Ollie shrugs. 'I can get my own clients.'

'But it's foolish to look a gift horse in the mouth,' Victoria says, smiling just a touch too brightly.

'I wouldn't engineer a meeting for that,' Ollie says. 'I don't mix business and friendships.'

'But you asked him to give Lucy a job.'

'Yeah, but he owed me a favour. That's the way it works, sweetheart.'

Vicky's not ready to give up. 'But think of all the people he mixes with! He must know the Rockefellers. And the Vanderbilts. And maybe some Arab princes even.'

Ollie kisses her hand, and I wince to see it.

'You're my princess,' he says softly. 'And that's good enough for me.'

'Very well,' Victoria says, smiling at me to check I didn't miss any of it. 'We can talk about it later.'

The food comes. I'm glad I ordered a lot, because each actual dish is tiny. My so-called pizza is the size and thickness of a bone china saucer.

It doesn't matter, though. I'm lost in my thoughts about Todd. And how much I'm going to impress him tomorrow.

Thankfully, at the end of the night, Ollie decamps to Vicky's flat. I'll be all by myself again; sole use of the shower, plus I won't have to listen to shuffling and bumping as Ollie makes love to that life-sucking vampire. But I know I can't go on like this. Tomorrow, when I get coffee breaks, or something, I'll ring round the flat share ads I've circled in *Loot*. I've got to get out of Valentine Central. Watching him with her hurts. For one thing, I know she'll make him miserably unhappy.

But I don't have time to think about that now. I set the alarm for six. Tomorrow is Todd day. No rushing, no snagged tights, no blundering. I'll need several hours to look as groomed as Lily Astor, whoever she is. And that means straight to bed for some beauty sleep.

I'll tell you this. Femininity is bloody hard work.

There are no disasters. The alarm goes off at the intended hour. Make that alarms plural, I set multiples, like *Four Weddings and a Funeral*. When I've hit them off, cursing and yelling (I think I can still be me in my off hours, right?) I slouch into the shower.

Then I go through my routine, which I worked out on the tube on the way home last night. It was a new 'Lucy's Problem File'. Problem, how to arrive at work looking refreshed and ladylike and get Todd to respect me.

Solution: fifteen minutes in the shower. Shampoo. Conditioner. Aussie Miracle Hair De-Frizzer.

Fifteen minutes to towel-dry, apply moisturizer and anti-perspirant. And spray fine mist of Chanel, step into it, etc.

Fifteen more minutes to blow-dry and brush out hair with Mason-Pearson pure-bristle brush.

Ten minutes to apply make-up and let it set. Ignore hunger pangs.

Ten minutes to eat breakfast, drink coffee. Do this wearing Victoria's towelling dressing-gown in case of any stain-related catastrophes re capsule wardrobe.

Replace Victoria's dressing gown. Remove blonde hairs. Brush teeth. Use Victoria's expensive Rembrandt Whitening Toothpaste. Carefully re-create previous dent in tube.

Dress in prettiest outfit. First put on tights. Ignore itching! This is like the Marines. Only the strong survive. Pick navy floral sprigs on cream dress from bitchy shop. Match with navy cardigan, tan bag, and black heels from Faith. NOTE: do NOT scuff black heels from Faith. Rather, walk in mincing, girlie steps as though clenching two-pound coin in bottom. ADDITIONAL NOTE: double time required to walk everywhere, to tube, from tube, etc.

Add last minute spray of Chanel. Check self in Ollie's mirror. Look like pretty, bland stranger. Result!

Exit house. Enter tube station at 7:20. Exit tube station at 7:45. Reach Mayle Accommodations by five to eight exactly.

Give self little shake, smooth dress, paste on radiant smile à la Victoria, and confidently mince in through the front door.

'Good morning, everybody!' I say in a high-pitched tone. It's meant to be a breathy trill, like Vicky's, but it comes out sort of Daffy Duck so I hastily revert to my usual voice. 'Lovely weather,' I add.

There they all are. Sat behind their oak desks on the grey carpet. The three girls are wearing identical outfits to the ones they wore yesterday; and James is in another tailored suit. Seems this 'capsule wardrobe' thing is everywhere.

Nobody looks up from their computers. They're all just tap-tapping away.

'So where's Todd?' I say, tossing my hair.

James glances up. 'You should refer to him as Mr Mayle.'

'Mr Mayle, then.'

'He's not here. He won't be in today,' says the girl nearest me. She's a pale-skinned brunette in a lilac dress and matching cardigan; her hair is twisted up into a chignon.

DAMN!

'He won't?' I say forlornly.

'No, he won't,' the middle girl replies, waspishly. She shakes her head, doing a little impersonation of me. She's also a brunette, in a mint-green cashmere T-shirt and I can't see what else. It goes nicely with the first girl's lilac. I wonder if they get together to plan these things?

'You'll be reporting to us today,' says the last girl. She's got a slightly auburn tint to her hair, and is wearing a cream silk shirt under an eggshell blue jacket, together with a whopping string of pearls. Wow. I wish I could afford to wear real pearls.

'OK,' I say, forcing a smile. 'Sounds good to me. Shall we introduce ourselves? I'm Lucy Evans. Todd – Mr Mayle – hired me as the new receptionist.'

'*Thank* you, Lucy, we did know that,' James Fossbert-Smythe says with a nasty smile. 'Though of course he didn't actually "hire" you, he put you on a temporary two-month trial to see if he'll *want* to hire you.'

'That's right,' I say. I try to sound confident but my voice is sort of trailing away.

'These ladies,' says James, 'are Jade Middleton,' the first girl inclines her head a fraction, without smiling, 'Buffy Colvert,' Buffy ignores me altogether, 'and Melissa Traubman. They are Mr Mayle's associates.'

'Jade, Buffy, Melissa,' I say. 'Good to meet you all.'

'You *may* use first names with staff other than Mr Mayle,' James says coldly, 'but please remember you are the junior person on the team, Lucy. You report to everybody. There are no free lunches at Mayle Accommodations. You are expected to be useful.'

'I'm looking forward to that,' I lie.

'Your job description is whatever we say it is, in other words,' says Buffy coolly.

'Right. Got it.'

'And you must maintain a pleasant manner at all times,' says James. Jade and Melissa go on with their typing. Apparently to them I am not even worth snubbing.

I sigh inwardly. If this is 'growing up' I know where Peter Pan was coming from.

'So, where's my desk?' I ask, going for the 'pleasant manner' bit.

'The receptionist's desk is that one.' James points towards

a huge oak desk opposite the front door. It has a computer on it, with a telephone, a small leather-bound book, and a fountain pen in a marble pen-holder. 'I assume you know the basics? How to transfer calls, type? That sort of thing?'

'I'm a great typist,' I say proudly. You can't play on the internet and type slowly, the monsters will eat you alive. I leave out the fact I do it with three fingers. 'The phone thing I'm not too sure of.'

'Heaven save us,' says Melissa theatrically. 'She's clueless!'

I suppress a mounting urge to panic. Why are they all so against me? I haven't done anything yet!

'I can pick it up, if you just show me what to do,' I say in a small voice.

Jade sighs and rises to her feet. She pads across the soft carpet and bends over me; I am almost asphyxiated in a cloud of perfume.

'We're all very busy people here, Ms Evans.'

'Please call me Lucy.'

'So I'll show you this just one time. Do you understand,' she asks slowly, as if I'm a moron.

'Perfectly.'

'Then watch. You press this to transfer. You write out all messages here, in longhand,' she pats the books. 'Our extensions are 3, 5, 6, James is on 7, and for Mr Mayle it's zero. Got it?'

'Yeah.'

'Yes,' she corrects me. 'We don't use slang at Mayle Accommodations. Our customers expect the best in service. Which includes your telephone manner.'

'I understand,' I say humbly.

'You will answer the phone as follows.' Jade clears her throat. ' "Good morning, this is Mayle Accommodations. May I help you?" Make sure to say "May" and not "Can". You *can* help the caller, the question is if you *may*,' she says seriously. 'Correct English usage is our hallmark here at Mayle Accommodations.'

I doubt that, most of you are Yanks, I think but don't say.

'Call everybody sir or madam.'

'OK – I mean, very well.'

'If in doubt, always take a number and say an associate will return their call as soon as possible. Never try to answer a query yourself. We don't need *you* trying to take the initiative,' she says, with scorn.

'I understand,' I repeat.

'And when things are quiet, there will be other work for you to take care of,' Jade says.

'You can start,' James adds with a nasty smirk, 'by making my coffee. And then there will be filing to do.'

'Oh yes,' says Jade, nodding. 'Lots of filing.'

And there you have it. That's how I pass my first day. Repeating one phrase endlessly into the telephone – they seem upset I don't cut anybody off, or patch them through to the wrong extension. Rather than give me a compliment, however, they send me out for dry-cleaning. I make about forty cups of coffee. And herbal tea. And file until I've got paper cuts. My heels are agony, my stomach is rumbling. There's no lunch break, apparently – 'Somebody has to man the fort,' James pronounces. I am allowed to go and get a sandwich, but only to the deli next door, which has a choice of 'soggy cheese and pickle' or 'tired beef and horseradish'. I eat the beef at my desk. 'Hurry up,' hisses Melissa. 'What if somebody came in and saw you stuffing yourself?'

It's a never-ending story of fun and laughter. Why do they hate me so much? I do what they say. I'm wearing tights and heels. Everything matches. I just don't get it.

I miss *PC Games Universe*. I miss my mates and my jeans and going down the pub.

Exhausted, I glance at the antique clock on the wall. It's ten to five.

'Excuse me, James,' I say deferentially.

'What is it?' he snaps.

'I was wondering if I could make some phone calls. I have to find a flat share.'

'On company equipment? Company time? Really, Lucy.' James shakes his head. 'The answer's no, and I don't know how you could even ask.'

'It's almost five p.m. And I was going to use my mobile.' I fish it out of my bag. 'I really need to find a new place.' I'm pleading with him, and my voice gets a bit thick. So I clam up. Tears would not be a great idea. If I can just make it through the day. You need this job, Lucy, remember?

He shrugs. 'I suppose so. Providing you stay late tonight.'

Late? 'I was hoping to set up a few appointments to see flats.'

'Set them up for tomorrow.' James produces a huge pile of filing from under his desk. 'These are my latest client preference data entries. I don't have time to do them,' he says airily. 'You may as well do something around here.'

'I – of course,' I say weakly. 'No problem.'

'Then once we close, you can make personal calls. On your own phone.'

'Wow, thanks,' I mutter.

He gives me a sharp glance. 'And make sure that the office is neat and tidy before you leave.'

'Where are you looking, Lucy?' Buffy asks me.

I blink. That is the first non-hostile thing she's said to me all day.

'Oh, you know. Tooting. Balham. Clapham, not the good bits, of course. Hampstead Garden Suburb . . .'

'Hampstead's not bad,' says Buffy.

'Hampstead *Garden Suburb*,' corrects James. 'Lucy is looking in Siberia,' he says with a thin smile. 'Just make sure you leave adequate time to get to work in the morning. Today, you were late.'

It's 5 p.m. Almost on the tick of the clock, the girls rise in a single slither of silk and jersey, pick up their coats (Burberrys) and head for the door.

'I wasn't late,' I say to James, my eyes prickling again.

'Well.' He sniffs. 'You weren't early, were you? Don't expect to survive here unless you give something extra. See you tomorrow morning. Goodnight.'

He takes his cashmere overcoat and walks out without a backwards glance, leaving me sitting there, clutching my mobile and a huge pile of filing.

I would cry but I'm too exhausted. For a second I just sit there, staring into space. But the filing won't take care of itself, will it? And I'm not getting out of here until I do it.

I flip open the first cerise-coloured folder. There's a neatly typed sheet of paper on a Ms Managuchi. She is looking to rent a furnished house for six months. It must have three bathrooms and a walled garden, central air, date from the eighteenth or nineteenth centuries, allow pets, and have lifts. The next is a Sam Yablons, from Texas. He wants a four-bedroom penthouse overlooking Hyde Park, preferably on one of the Crown estates. Somebody has pencilled in a note: 'Aristocratic neighbours a must.' Rents . . . I blink. They are looking to pay up to fifteen grand. That's a month. Every month!

I take in the enormous heap of files. Each one contains at least fifty sheets like this. And what is the agency's commission for placing these tenants? A month's rent? Two?

My goodness. No wonder they can all afford cashmere coats and Louis Vuitton handbags.

Of course, yours truly is delighted to be getting paid eighteen grand a year.

I give myself a little shake. That's more than I could ever get in any other job. What's the use of being jealous? I should be glad I'll be able to afford that flat share in Balham.

I sigh and start to put away the files. It has to be done properly, no mistakes. James and Melissa and that lot would love to sack me, I know. I can't give them any excuses.

7

I finally finish at seven fifteen. My knees ache, my eyes are squinty and my fingers are sore because of all the paper-cuts but at least it's done. All I want to do is drag myself out of this well-appointed little hellhole and go to the pub. Oh yes, and have a bloody great Jack and Diet Coke, a double. Two doubles. Sod sipping wine, nobody'll see me anyway.

But I can't. I have to call round the flat shares. Otherwise they'll go, the cheap ones always move the fastest.

Here's a good one. Tooting, near bus routes. Share house with three others, sixty pounds a week.

'Hi,' I say, trying not be nervous. 'I'm calling about the flat share.'

'Yeah,' a girl's voice says, sounding bored.

'Can you tell me a bit about it?'

'In the advert, innit?'

'OK, well, what are the people who live there like?'

'What is this, the third fucking degree? We don't need that,' she says with heavy scorn, and hangs up.

I sigh and go to the next one. Hampstead Garden Suburb. Sounds nice and leafy.

'Hi, I'm calling about the—'

'It's gone already. Sorry,' says a bloke. He also hangs up.

I stare at my mobile. This day is turning into a real winner. I try Balham. That's the cheapest, anyway, only fifty-three a week and sharing with three girls.

'Hi, I'm calling to enquire about the flat share.'

'Oh yes,' says a girl. 'What would you like to know?'

I smile and breathe out. 'Can you tell me a little bit about it?'

'Sure,' she says. 'Your room would be pretty small, it's six by eight, but it's got lots of shelving and one built-in cupboard. And a nice window overlooking the garden.'

'OK.' This sounds great.

'And we're about five hundred yards from the bus stop.'

Even better.

'And the girls?'

'We're all professionals. A social worker, a librarian, and an accountant.'

'And is it still available?' I ask, trying to mask my eagerness.

'Oh yes,' she says. 'We've had tons of people round to look at it but none of them have been suitable.'

'I'm sure I'd be suitable,' I say ingratiatingly.

'You *are* a Christian, right?' she says. 'And English?'

'Uh, yes . . .'

'That's all right then. We've had loads of unsuitable applicants. Immigrants, you know. And Muslims, if you can believe that. And Jews, there are just so many Jews in this area, it's incredible. When I asked the last one if she'd accepted Jesus as her personal Saviour she said—'

I gently depress the red button on my phone. The dial tone purrs invitingly at me, asking me to make another call. And perhaps I should. There are other places listed in *Loot*, after all. But I can't face it. I just want to find a convenient oven and stick my head in it.

Wearily I pick up my bag and start to tidy away all the coffee cups round the office. It has to be spotless. Isn't that what James said?

I hear fumbling at the lock and the door swings open, giving a little tinkle. I hope it's not James. I can't take another lecture.

It isn't James. It's Todd Mayle. Looking gorgeous in a black suit and sexy black greatcoat. We stare at each other.

'Lucy?' he says.

He sounds as if he's not certain. He looks me up and down, taking in my cream dress with the navy sprigs, my navy cardigan, my new shoes and bag. Self-consciously, I toss my hair. It shimmies back into place. Bless that Bernice!

'Hello, Mr Mayle,' I say. I'm nervous, and it comes out all husky.

'What are you doing here?' he asks. 'It's almost half seven.'

'Oh.' What an opportunity to impress him with my diligence! 'I wanted to finish up some filing, make sure the place was clean. I like to give that bit of extra effort. A hundred and ten per cent!' I say enthusiastically. That's how Americans talk, isn't it?

'I see,' he says. 'Did you enjoy your first day with us?'

'Absolutely. It was awesome!'

I pat myself on the back. Any minute now they'll cast me in *Dawson's Creek*. Or give me a pair of pom-poms and a rah-rah skirt.

'Good to hear,' he says absently. He goes into his own office and returns with a file, glancing down at the piece of paper on my desk with the flat share details scrawled on it.

'What's that?'

'I was just about to clear that away.'

'What is it?'

'Flat share details,' I admit. 'I'm looking for a place to live. But don't worry, I used my mobile to make the calls. And only after office hours.'

'Why did you do that?' Mayle asks, flicking through his file. His voice is a rich, deep baritone. 'Plenty of phones here. You just press nine for an outside line.'

'Well – James told me not to use company equipment.'

Mayle looks up; his chocolate-brown eyes sweep over me again.

'James is a little too conscientious,' he says. 'I don't mind the odd personal call. As long as you don't overdo it.'

'Thank you, Mr Mayle. I'll remember that.'

'Hey, it's gone seven,' he says. 'After hours, remember? Don't you think you should call me Todd?'

'Todd.' I beam seductively at him, but unfortunately my stomach decides just then to do a drum solo. It's so loud Metallica would have been proud of it.

'Excuse me,' I say, flushing scarlet. 'I-I'd better go home and have some dinner.'

'Even better, come and have some dinner with me.'

I'm so surprised I drop my bag.

'Unless you don't want to, of course,' he adds.

'Oh! No. I mean, that's fine. I want to,' I say.

'What do you like to eat?'

'Anything—' I was about to say, a burger and chips, and a pint, but suddenly remember my training. 'Any fine dining,' I say carefully. 'With nice wines, like Chardonnay.'

'Fine dining, huh?' Mayle's eyes sparkle. 'Well, I may know one or two little places. Ready to go?'

I pick up my bag again and smile at him. 'Ready.'

'I like that dress,' he says. He breathes in, just over the crown of my head. 'And your perfume.'

'Thank you,' I say graciously. I sigh with pleasure. So it was worth it, after all. Ollie was right.

Todd escorts me outside to where his car is parked. It's a low-slung, cherry-red sports car. I've never seen anything like it, actually. It's so low-slung I wonder how I'm going to get in the front door. I think it looks a bit weird.

'Like it?' he says, as I open the door and try to lower myself into the black leather seat.

'Um, yes.'

'Well of course you do,' he says. 'It's a Lamborghini. Ever ridden in one?'

It's very uncomfortable. I shake my head.

'Thought not,' he says. 'Well – enjoy.'

He puts it into gear and pulls smoothly out into the traffic. I would love to 'enjoy', but all I can see at present is the exhaust pipe from the bloody great bus in front of us. People are looking at us with envy out of their car windows, though. I try to relax. Perhaps it's something special to get a look at so many under-chassis. Only a mechanic probably sees brake lights this close up.

'I feel like fish,' Todd announces. 'Lucy?'

Actually I feel like a big hunk of roast meat. Or a plate of pasta with a thick creamy sauce. But would Lily Astor have argued with him?

'Fish would be perfect,' I say.

'Excellent. We'll go to Wilton's,' he says, in that sexy American voice. 'A real old-fashioned English restaurant. It'll be just your "cup of tea". As they say. Right?'

'Oh – right,' I confirm. Todd looks very pleased with himself.

He drives us into St James's and finds a parking spot, then leads the way into the restaurant. To my surprise, it actually *is* an old-fashioned English restaurant. It's quiet and calm, the waiters expert and discreet, the conversation a low, old-money hum.

'How nice to see you again, Mr Mayle,' says one of them. 'Your usual table, sir?'

He nods curtly. 'I come here a lot,' Todd says to me. Gosh, his eyes are stunning. Those thick lashes. 'Take mostly Americans and Swiss. The Japanese prefer Nobu or the Savoy. And the Arabs like Claridges.'

I nod understandingly.

'You can eat low-carb here, without all the saturated fat,' he says. 'Are you a low-carb girl, Lucy?'

'Mostly . . . yes.' My stomach gives another ominous growl, so I cough to cover it. I think I might die if I don't get some bread. I mean, fish could satisfy me, but only if it came battered and wrapped in newspaper with a double helping of chips.

'I thought so. With a body like that,' he says approvingly, and for a second I forget I'm starving.

What was that? About my body?

I look closer at him. Was the millionaire with the younger, darker Robert Redford looks hitting on me?

Hitting. On *me*?

But he's looked away and is staring at his menu. Maybe I was imagining it. Americans are different, aren't they? Perhaps he was just being complimentary.

I hope so. I mean, don't get me wrong. I desperately want to impress Todd Mayle. I need the job, I need the money. And also, I want him to see my potential and promote me. I'm not sure what potential, exactly. It's hard to pin down, potential. But right now I'm defining it as 'whatever will get me a more interesting job'.

But I don't want to date him. Yes, he's very gorgeous and very rich. But maybe, you know, he's just a bit *too* gorgeous. I like my men rougher around the edges and not so . . . plastic. And up for a bit of a laugh. Like, well, like Ollie.

I need to find another Ollie, not a real-life version of Barbie's Ken. Anyway, what am I like? He only said something about my body. He's a health nut, like all Yanks.

Victoria would laugh her bony ass off. Todd Mayle isn't going to be interested in an ordinary girl like me.

'May I get you something to drink?' asks the waiter.

I am about to ask for a glass of Chardonnay but Todd jumps in.

'Champagne,' he says. 'A bottle.'

'Would you care to see the wine list, sir?'

'Do you have Veuve Grande Dame?' Mayle asks.

'Yes, sir.'

'I'll take that,' he says, decisively.

'Champagne? What are we celebrating?' I ask casually.

'Celebrating?' Todd looks blank. 'I always order champagne with dinner.'

'Oh.' Of course he does, I keep forgetting how rich he is. 'I think that's wonderful,' I say encouragingly.

Doesn't hurt to be polite, after all. And I've had a

miserable day. I'm starving and my feet are killing me and these tights itch like crazy, but who cares about that, eh? No pain no gain. Some champagne would certainly help.

It arrives in a silver bucket filled with ice. Todd looks at me. I think he's checking to see that I'm impressed, or something.

'Have you decided what you want to eat?'

'I'll have the skate and mashed potatoes,' I say.

He lifts an eyebrow as the waiter fills my crystal flute. 'That's hardly low-carb.'

'Ah. Well, I do normally do low-carb, of course,' I say. 'But you know, I kind of go running a lot and I dance and lift free weights, so right now I need the calories.'

'I'll take a dozen oysters and the smoked salmon mousse with a side of buttered spinach.'

'Very good, sir,' the waiter says, melting away.

'You need to fix your routine,' Todd says, his eyes moving assessingly over my body. 'Less exercise and less carbs. You're not fat, so you want to move to yoga, or Pilates. Otherwise you might develop muscles,' he says with distaste.

But I like my muscles, I like being firm.

'Don't worry, I'm not planning on turning into Xena,' I say. But he doesn't smile, so I stop grinning and take a hasty sip of my champagne.

'Women should be slim,' Todd tells me. The dark eyes look deep into mine. 'But they should also be soft. Feminine. Especially in our business. Presentation is everything.'

'Right.'

'I'd ditch the exercise and the starches.'

'OK,' I agree gloomily.

'After all, you're very beautiful,' he says. 'I'm sure you want to stay that way.'

Me? Beautiful?

'Thanks,' I mutter.

'I really should call Ollie,' Todd drawls. 'And thank him for sending you to me.'

Oh shit, I mean bother. I think . . . I think he *is* hitting on me, after all.

I give Todd a neutral smile, polite, but not encouraging. A boss with a crush is a complication I don't need.

On the other hand, I wish Victoria could see me now.

'You'll be quite an asset,' Todd says. 'That cute accent, and now with the right sort of clothes. I think you might be wasted on desk work. How would you like to come with me on a few appointments?'

I gasp. 'I'd love that.' Thank God I didn't shoot him down! This is exactly what I'd hoped for. Fast track . . . potential . . . etc.

There's a glimmer of light. Maybe I won't have to spend endless days shackled to that desk, answering the phone. 'Good morning. This is Mayle Accommodations. May I help you?' I might shoot myself before I even get to cash my first pay cheque.

I look hopefully at Todd.

'I could show you the ropes,' he says, musingly.

His oysters arrive.

'Want one?' he says, extending a glistening shell to me. It looks like it contains a quivering lump of phlegm. I feel slightly sick.

'No thank you,' I murmur.

Todd smiles. 'I like a girl who shows moderation.'

Moderation. One more thing to remember. I take another sip of champagne. A small one.

Does he truly fancy me, I wonder, as he tosses the oysters down, smacking his lips appreciatively? Or does he just think I have the right look for his business, that whole English rose thing Ollie was talking about?

'If you'll be guided by me you could go far,' Todd says.

'I'd love to be guided by you,' I say respectfully.

'Atta girl.' He grins. 'Now of course I can't have an

employee of mine living on the wrong side of the tracks. It gives the wrong impression.'

My face falls. 'I can't afford smart areas,' I mumble. 'I'm really sorry.'

'*You* can't, sugar, but I can,' Todd says. 'The firm does corporate lets as well as placements. I've plenty of places I can stick you, as an on-site manager.'

'What does that mean?'

'You know. Supervising the cleaning staff. Admitting the meter reader.'

'So . . . no duties?'

'You'd have to be ready to move out at a moment's notice. But no, no duties.' He gives me another wolfish grin. 'You'll have plenty of those assisting me.'

'What kind of places are we talking about?'

The waiter returns with our main courses. I'm so famished I could faint, but I steel myself to eat only the skate, and a slow forkful at a time. I push aside the delicious-looking mashed potatoes, and Todd rewards me with a nod.

'Nothing fancy,' he says. 'A three-bed in Kensington, a garden flat in Notting Hill, a one-bedroom in Knightsbridge, but it does have a pretty roof terrace.'

I gasp. 'And the rent would be subsidized?'

'Rent-free,' he says. 'In fact, I can arrange to pay you a small additional stipend for the house-sitting.'

I become aware that my jaw is hanging loose in a most unladylike manner, so I close it sharply.

'No need to look at me like I'm Prince Charming,' he says, with a disarming smile. And I blush, because that's exactly what I was thinking.

'I don't know how to thank you,' I say.

'That's OK, sugar,' he drawls. 'We'll think of something.'

I swallow drily. We'll think of something?

'Look, uh, Todd. I'm so glad to be working for you. I-I really want to thank you for the opportunity. And a flat would be great.'

'But . . .?'

'But, you know. I don't want to go out with anybody right now.' I smile at him, hoping he doesn't get angry. 'I don't think I'd be very good company. I'm focused on the job.'

Mayle looks surprised. 'Why don't you let the guy figure out if you're good company? Take me, for example. I know women. I know when I'll have fun with a girl.'

Pants. I desperately want to keep him onside. But now I've said it, I can't back off.

'I'm sure you do,' I say flatteringly. 'Being so good-looking and successful and all that.'

He relaxes visibly.

'It's more just me,' I say. '*I* don't want to go out with anybody. At all. I just thought perhaps I ought to make that clear.'

'I get it,' he says suddenly, as though inspired. 'You're gay, right? That's why you didn't know how to dress and stuff.'

'Gay people know how to dress. Anyway, I'm not gay.'

'Are you sure?'

I nod.

'Then you're seeing somebody,' he says. 'Who is it? Ollie?'

'I don't have the slightest interest in Ollie,' I say sharply. Oops. That came out wrong. But I just can't take one more person trying to fix me up with Ollie McCleod.

'Who, then?' he asks. 'You got some kind of big banker on the side? Some sexy MP or something?'

'Sexy MP?' I stare at him. 'You what?'

'Politicians are sexy,' he says. 'All that power.'

'Not over here,' I say. And not in America either, I don't say. Unless you count Arnold Schwarzenegger or something.

'I'm gonna be a politician,' he says. 'One day. It's my destiny.'

Oh.

'So no MPs,' he says. Then a thought seems to strike him. He shifts in his seat and looks penetratingly at me.

'You dating a duke?' he asks. 'An earl? A marquis?' He pronounces that 'marquee'.

I try not to laugh. 'Honestly, I'm not dating anybody.'

'Prince Harry?' he asks darkly.

'No. Not Prince Harry. No Greek shipping magnates or Premier League footballers,' I say, trying to laugh it off. 'I don't have any kind of boyfriend. Or girlfriend,' I add hastily. 'I'm trying to tell you I don't want one. I just want to get on with my job and be by myself for a while.'

He digests this.

'Well, what's a while?' he asks. 'A week or something?'

'A couple of years,' I say firmly.

That's how long it will take me to meet someone as cool as Ollie and get to know them.

Todd blinks. 'You are the strangest chick,' he says slowly. 'Are you saying you don't want a boyfriend?'

I nod, pleased that he's finally getting it.

'I'm just happy by myself,' I say. 'And getting on at Mayle Accommodations is going to take lots of my time.'

'So even if *I* asked you out, you'd say no?'

'I'd say no thank you. But you could have anybody,' I add smoothly. 'It's not like you need to date *me*.'

'No,' he muses. 'Course I don't . . .'

Todd suddenly turns sharply round in his seat.

'What's the matter?' I ask.

'Well, look who it is,' he says.

'Who?' It's not bloody James, is it? Or Buffy?

'Your friend and mine,' he says.

I stare. Ollie is walking in, with Victoria. I can't believe it!

'What a coincidence,' Todd says smoothly. He gives a little wave. I suppose you don't shout 'Oi, over here!' in Wilton's.

127

Ollie starts and smiles; Victoria, following his gaze, almost jumps out of her skin. I give her a smirk. Darling Todd, I could kiss him! Well, of course, it wouldn't take this for me to kiss him. But I could double kiss him. Just to see that stunned, infuriated look on her face.

There's no helping it, she has to come over to us, trailing after Ollie, who shakes Todd's hand briskly then bends down to give me a kiss.

'What's all this then?' Ollie asks, shooting me a sly look.

'I'm just taking the newest member of my staff out to dinner,' Todd replies. 'The newest and most attractive, that is.'

Victoria's eyes widen crossly.

'Careful, Todd, Lucy could sue you for sexual harassment,' Ollie jokes. Victoria stares, like I should be so lucky. 'Do you know my fiancée, Victoria Cobham?'

'Hey,' Todd replies, without interest.

Cool. I suppress a grin.

'Todd Mayle,' Victoria says, in her patented breathy little-girl voice. 'It's a pleasure. I've heard *sooo* much about you from my darling Ollie.'

'You have?' Todd glances at Ollie. 'Nothing good, I hope.'

Victoria laughs her tinkling laugh like this was the funniest thing ever said.

'How lucky we should meet up like this,' she purrs. 'Quite the coincidence. And I hope we'll see you at the wedding, Todd?'

Ollie glances at her sharply, but Victoria pretends not to notice.

'Oh, yeah. Sure,' Todd says. 'That'd be fun.'

'Well, isn't this nice,' Victoria says. 'Tell you what, shall we join you, Todd? So much better than eating apart.'

'Vicky, they've already eaten,' says Ollie, with a touch of steel in his voice. He gestures to our empty plates.

'Oh, that doesn't matter,' Vicky says quickly. 'We can skip a starter and be on to our main course while they have dessert.'

'Well,' Todd drawls. 'That would be lovely, any other time, Veronica.'

I smother a giggle.

'Victoria,' she says, looking daggers at me.

'Right, right. But tonight I was hoping to take Lucy away and drive her round a few apartments.'

'You're not still working at this hour?' Ollie says, with a trace of disapproval. I shoot him a warning look. What is he doing? I don't want him to scare Todd off. I'm trying to make points here!

'Work? Oh, no.' Todd gazes approvingly at me, and bitch Victoria can hardly believe it. She is staring at us like it's her worst nightmare come to life.

I suddenly realize. She thinks we're on a date!

I'm not about to correct her, either. She looks from Todd to me and back to Todd again, and I can almost see the hamster wheels turning in her brain. She forces herself to smile at me.

'No, I'm setting Lucy up in an apartment. I understand she had to move out of yours, Oliver.'

'Since we're getting married,' Victoria butts in. 'Of course otherwise we'd have loved Lucy to stay as long as she liked.'

Yeah, right.

Todd spreads his hands. 'So I'm offering her a choice of places to house-sit. It's good for the firm and it suits Lucy.'

'Really? That's great,' Ollie says, smiling at me.

I can see Victoria struggling with herself, but she loses the battle. Curiosity trumps cool.

'And where would that be?' she asks.

'Wherever she wants, really,' Todd says. 'Notting Hill, South Ken, Knightsbridge, Mayfair, Hyde Park. We have places all over.'

Victoria grits her teeth.

'Well, you certainly seem to have landed on your feet, Lucy,' she says. 'Aren't you lucky!'

'Oh no,' Todd says. 'The luck is all mine.' And he gives me the most devastating smile.

Ha ha! I think. This is absolute heaven.

I smile serenely at Victoria, who seems to be having trouble breathing.

'Come on, darling,' Ollie says, tugging at her bony arm. 'We've got to get to our table.'

'Oh, yes,' Victoria says reluctantly. 'Anyway, Todd, do stay in touch. We must all go out for dinner.'

Todd gives her an impersonal smile, nods at Ollie, and turns back to his champagne, and I have the wonderful sensation of watching Victoria walk away, her back stiff with fury.

You'd have thought she'd have been happy. If she was worried about me having a crush on Ollie, what's wrong with Todd Mayle paying attention to me?

'Interruptions,' sighs my white knight. 'Don't you just hate them? I mean, say hi, sure. But then get lost already!'

'I'm sure Ollie wanted to get to his table. And Victoria was just trying to be sociable,' I add diplomatically. For Ollie's sake.

'She's a horror show,' Todd says dismissively. 'I hate pushy women. Let's get the check, and I'll take you round a couple of those apartments.' He glances at me. 'If you've got time, that is?'

'Oh yes.' I have another sip of champagne, a tiny one of course. 'I've got time.'

Tonight just keeps getting better and better. Todd escorts me to the car, waits while I get in, then drives me round London's emptying streets.

'I love the congestion charge,' he says. 'All those poor people can't afford it, so they get on the buses. Meanwhile the roads are clearer for me. It's cut fifteen per cent off my travel time.' He pats the steering wheel. 'And you can't show this baby off in traffic!'

Then he flashes me that smooth smile to show that he's

joking. At least I presume that's what it is. I smile back.

'I don't want to drown you in places,' Todd says lightly. 'You remember how I described them to you in the restaurant? Which one do you want to see first?'

'Oh. Any of them will be fine,' I say humbly. 'It's so nice of you to do this for me, Mr Mayle.'

'Todd. Out of hours,' he says. 'You've got a good attitude, Lucy. I like that in a woman. Let's see now. Which is closest to me?'

His eyes flicker towards me in the passenger seat, and I hold my breath nervously. He seems to notice.

'Just for business, you understand,' he says evenly. 'The closer you are, the sooner you can reach me.'

'Oh sure,' I say, to cover that I was thinking any differently.

'I think Knightsbridge,' he says. 'That OK for you, sugar?'

As in Harrods and Harvey Nics?

'I think that would be perfect,' I say carefully.

The car zooms westward, and turns into a maze of side streets just a few blocks from Knightsbridge tube station. He eventually pulls up outside one of the typical, gorgeous red-brick mansion blocks.

'Pelham House,' he drawls. 'This will suit you, I think.'

I think so too. About two minutes to a tube and five minutes to Harrods. Not that I can afford anything in there. But perhaps I'll visit it; study up on the kind of clothes the truly rich girls wear. Girls like, say, Lillian Astor.

'It looks great.'

'Sugar, of course it does.'

I watch him nervously when he says 'Sugar', but he's not looking at me. Maybe he just flirts with all women.

Only he wasn't flirty with Victoria, was he?

But then again maybe it's none of the above. Maybe he isn't being all business, but he doesn't fancy me either. He could just be being kind. Or friendly.

This is a brilliant job, I tell myself firmly, and you're

about to get the all-time luckiest break on a flat. So don't blow it by getting uptight! Not unless he actually does something wrong.

And so far all he's been is nice.

'What apartment are we looking at?' I ask, as he rings the doorbell.

Mayle grins. 'The penthouse,' he says. 'It's quite impressive.'

There are footsteps and a uniformed doorman opens the door.

'Mr Mayle,' he says. 'Good evening, sir.'

'Good evening, Tony,' says Todd. The old man winces slightly, but says nothing. 'This is Lucy Evans, who may be house-sitting the penthouse suite for the company.'

I peer at his nameplate; it says 'Toby Rogers'.

'How do you do, madam,' says Mr Rogers to me. His voice is professionally neutral, but I can tell he doesn't like me. And I haven't said two words to him yet!

'Please call me Lucy, Mr Rogers,' I say, extending a hand.

The old man makes no move to take it and Todd frowns.

'We don't encourage staff familiarity, Lucy,' he says coolly. 'Tony'll stick with "madam", won't you, Tony?'

'Oh, certainly, sir,' says Rogers coldly.

I blush bright red.

'And you should call him "Tony". That's the way we do things around here. Right, Tony?'

'Just as you say, sir.'

'But his name's Toby,' I point out, in a small voice.

Rogers glances my way again. He looks slightly surprised. And for a second Todd is taken aback; he doesn't look at all pleased. But then he gives another of his bright, white-toothed American smiles.

'Tony, Toby, what's the difference?' he says. 'Huh, *Toby*?'

'Indeed, sir,' says Rogers, evenly.

'Enough chit-chat,' says Todd. 'You got the penthouse key?'

'Yes, sir.' Rogers walks back to his desk and produces an old-fashioned brass key. Todd hands it to me, and I turn it over. It's intricate, lovely; like something from a fairy tale.

We ride a modern, plush-lined lift with a velvet-covered bench in it – just like that one from *Pretty Woman* – all the way up to the penthouse floor. And when Todd takes the key and lets me in, switching on the lights, I think maybe I really am in a fairy tale.

The flat is so stunning I don't know where to start. It even seems stupid calling it a 'flat'. I am staring at a sleek, ultra-modern living room, so vast you could fit three of Ollie's entire house into it. It's got dark hardwood floors, Italian designer leather couches and chairs, a huge flat-screen TV, and recessed lighting in the ceiling. In one corner is a seventies James Bond-style drinks cabinet stocked with everything you can imagine: champagnes, liqueurs, cut-glass decanters, crystal tumblers. There's a trendy cast-iron staircase leading up to a mezzanine level – 'The main bedroom,' Todd says casually – and an ensuite bathroom behind it.

He walks me up there. It's what you might expect. Round stone sinks with gleaming chrome taps. Marble floors, mirrored walls. More recessed lighting. Another flat-screen TV. An intercom system. A sleigh bed made up in expensive linens in chocolate-brown.

I'm so speechless I can hardly say a single word. It looks as if the apartment belongs to Madonna. Or, I don't know, Calvin Klein.

Todd smiles lightly; he's clearly gratified I'm so over-whelmed.

'And the kitchen,' he says, leading me downstairs through the cavernous living room.

The kitchen is big enough for its own post code. There are granite countertops, a Sub-Zero freezer, and state-of-the-art appliances carefully concealed behind mahogany doors. There's also a working fireplace outlined in fashionable slate, a sofa, a huge table, and a central sort of island for, I don't know, chopping things on and stuff.

It's all a bit confusing frankly. I hope I can find somewhere to store my own cooking supplies, such as loaves of Hovis, Flora and Marmite.

'Wow,' I manage.

'Oh, we're not done. There are four guest bedrooms.'

So there are. Miniature versions of the palatial one upstairs, each with a queen-size bed, flat-screen TV (how many are there in this place?) and ensuite luxury shower room with loo.

'And finally a little indoor-outdoor space,' Todd says, conducting me through the corridor to a wrought-iron door that matches the stairs. He opens this, and I gasp with amazement and pleasure.

I'm looking at a fantastic conservatory. It's got three solid glass sides, and doors that open out onto a terrace; it's stocked with everything from miniature lemon trees to roses and all kinds of greenery. There are gorgeous wicker sofas heaped with silk Liberty cushions.

'It's air conditioned,' Todd drawls. 'And heated for the winter. A steady seventy degrees year round. Sprinkler system for watering, and a gardener comes once a week. A great place for the tenant,' he glances slyly at me, 'or occupant to throw parties.'

I open my mouth to say something but nothing comes out beyond a high-pitched squeak.

'So, what do you say, sugar?' he drawls. 'This place good enough, or shall I take you somewhere else?'

'I – oh – this is, um, fine,' I stammer. 'It's actually paradise.'

He grins. 'Isn't it just? Worked with the designer myself. And what should be your fee for living here? How about we say five hundred a week. Plus a hundred for travel expenses.'

I stare at him open-mouthed, then remember that doing

an impression of a goldfish may not be the most ladylike thing in the world.

'But it's an amazing thing that I can stay here,' I say. 'Even for a couple of weeks, until you find a tenant. I don't need to be paid.'

'Honey,' Todd says lazily. 'First thing to learn in business. Never turn down money. Or favours.'

'I – right,' I say. My mouth feels dry.

'And I wouldn't worry about the place being rented. The rent's set a little high even for this place. The owner won't budge, though. It's been on the market for a year.'

A year! I could live here for that long?

'I have no idea how to thank you,' I say.

'Well, since you definitely don't want to go out with me . . .'

It's half a question.

'Sorry,' I say. 'I just . . .'

'You want your space. I can respect that, I can respect that,' he says. 'In that case, you can just work extra hard. And make sure to look polished. You think you can do that for me?'

'Oh yes,' I agree gratefully. 'Anything.'

'So.' He pulls back, consults his Rolex. 'You can sort everything out with Tony. Move in tomorrow.'

'Oh. Sure. Thank you,' I say.

'Meanwhile, I'll see you tomorrow at eight sharp. And don't mention tonight around the office,' he says. 'Office politics. You know how it is. The others wouldn't like me getting too friendly with somebody so new.'

'Of course. You can count on me,' I assure him.

'The tube isn't far,' he says briskly. 'Maybe you should take it home, because I've got some papers to get to before I turn in. See you tomorrow,' he says calmly. And walks towards the door. I hurry after him.

'Stay,' he says. 'Look around the place. It's all yours.'

I try for a witty remark but nothing comes to mind.

'See you tomorrow,' he repeats, and lets himself out.

* * *

Well. That wasn't so bad, was it? He didn't do anything wrong. He didn't pat my ass or anything. I told him I didn't want to go out, and he left. I feel a bit guilty now. So what if Todd's a bit plastic looking, or scarily handsome. He gave me a nice dinner, and he was the first person in that office to treat me like a human being. He can't help being a bit polished.

I look around the flat again. It's big and scary and rich, like him. To be honest, I'm not that sure I like it. It's intimidating.

I shake myself. Stop that! It's a dream flat, and Todd is a dream boss.

I get home almost an hour later. My emotions are in turmoil, I don't know what to think. I'm elated. And disappointed.

But there's no point in obsessing over it. I can hear the sounds of Ollie and Victoria in his room, suspicious slithery, huffing sounds. Yech. Ollie and *Victoria*. It's too tragic for anything. I head into the bathroom, and very carefully peel off my clothes and wash my face, then apply some of Victoria's expensive night cream. I wrap myself in my old grimy towel and creep back into my room.

I'm still totally starving. Four mouthfuls of skate and some champagne didn't do it for me. But Todd likes his women skinny, doesn't he? I want to show willing. Project the right image.

I debate with myself. But I manage to resist the temptation of the bacon butty that is calling my name. And it's not as hard as it sounds. I'm even more tired than I'm hungry; I pull on Dad's pyjamas, set the alarm for 5 a.m., and I'm asleep before I hit the pillow.

8

When the alarms go, I'm up in a second. Bolt upright, like waking from a nightmare. Only it isn't a nightmare, is it? It's move-into-fabulous-dream-penthouse day.

I hit all the clocks before they can wake Victoria, then head into the shower. I go through that whole girlie routine again. Wash. Dry. Blow-dry. Primp. Make-up. It seems less tough than yesterday; I know what I'm doing this time.

Alas, that does not make the tights any less itchy.

And, of course, I'm nervous. I don't know, the stakes seem so much higher. The navy sprig dress was my prettiest outfit, but I do what I can: the buff-coloured skirt, white shirt, buff cardigan, tan bag and tan shoes. That, a spritz of Chanel, and my Bobbi Brown neutrals make-up.

Nervously I check the mirror. But it's OK; there she is, Buffy-girl Lucy; the one with the long shimmery hair and matching everything.

I walk into the kitchen for breakfast. What I really want is porridge, actually. Does that sound weird? On freezing days like this there's nothing like a creamy bowl of porridge with Golden Syrup and a large mug of coffee with two sugars.

My stomach rumbles loudly at the very thought of it. But I can't, I can't have that. There's no time to go running these days and if I pig out without exercise . . . well.

Low-carb, in other words.

Reluctantly I go to the fridge and break out the bacon

and eggs. Three eggs and two rashers of bacon. And some coffee. It's not porridge but it'll have to do. I'll do my teeth again to get rid of the coffee stains.

At Mayle Accommodations, who knows if I'll even get lunch. Or supper, come to that. The thought is quite depressing so I add another rasher of bacon.

'Good morning, Lucy!' sings out Victoria.

I blink over the rim of my mug. Vicky has emerged, resplendent in a silk dressing gown tightly belted around her skinny frame, under which, no doubt, is a *Hello Kitty* nightdress or something. She has little pink high-heeled slippers with frou-frou feathers on the toes.

'Hello,' I say.

'Did you sleep well?'

I blink. Is she possessed or something?

'Very well, thank you. And you?'

Two can play this game.

'Oh, I slept marvellously,' says Victoria. 'Wasn't it amazing fun us bumping into each other last night?'

'Yes, amazing,' I say. Perhaps she has short-term amnesia and has forgotten her glares and death stares in my direction. 'Anyway, you won't be bothered with me here any more. I'll be moving my stuff out tonight.'

Victoria pulls a face. 'I'll be so sad to see you go,' she says. 'After all, I think we've become quite close, don't you?'

Huh?

'Where are you moving, exactly?' she asks, with a penetrating stare.

I smile triumphantly. 'Todd put me in a little place he's renting, as a caretaker.'

She asks for details. I knew she would!

'It's in Knightsbridge,' I tell her. 'Just by the tube there. Not far from Harvey Nics, you know,' I add airily.

'In Knightsbridge,' she breathes. 'And how much is he charging you? Just a token fee?'

'Oh, he's not charging me at all. He's paying me, actually. And giving me an expense account,' I say lightly.

Ollie pads in in his pyjamas, looking bleary eyed.

'Bloody hell, it's the dawn chorus,' he says. 'Can't a man get five minutes' sleep in the mornings? It's only just gone six. Pass the coffee, Lucy.'

I hand it over. Victoria focuses on me as though Ollie isn't there, the absolute reverse of what she normally does. 'I think that's wonderful,' she lies. 'You deserve it. And what is the apartment? Basement? Or should I say *lower ground floor*,' she adds with a tight smile. You see? Even on her best behaviour she can't iron out all the bitchiness. 'Isn't that what you estate agents call it?'

'Probably. But it's not the lower ground floor, it's the penthouse.'

Almost pleadingly, she says, 'And what size – is it a studio?'

'Not exactly,' I reply. 'It's the width of the whole building. Five bedrooms, five bathrooms. The living room and kitchen are pretty large. Bigger than this place – this whole place.' I can't resist, I give her a bitchy fake smile of my own. 'And there's a conservatory and terrace.'

'And how long will you be there?' Victoria almost whispers.

'I don't know. Todd says it's quite possible he might want me there a year or more.' I examine my fake nails. 'Or, you know. He might put me somewhere nicer.'

She swallows hard.

'Are you sure you want to live there, Lucy?' Ollie asks, after three large pulls of black coffee. 'Maybe you should just pay for your own place.' He looks worried.

'What, flat-sharing in some dive with a bunch of loonies?' I stare at him. 'What's wrong with a bit of luxury?'

'That's what I say,' chimes in Victoria. 'Todd certainly seems very *generous*,' she adds, giving Ollie a significant look.

'He didn't ask you for something extra?' Ollie says, looking at me.

'Like what?'

'You know like what,' he says, blushing.

'No he didn't. And I wouldn't sleep with somebody just to get a nice flat!' I say, offended.

'Sorry, mate. Course you wouldn't.'

'But you are close?' Victoria pounces. 'You and Todd? He certainly seems to like you very much.'

I soften. 'Well, he is very nice. And yes, he does seem to like me, you know. We get on. But he hasn't asked me for *anything*,' I repeat, looking at Ollie.

It's a bit close to home. I mean, at one point I thought Todd was going to, in fact. But he didn't in the end, did he? And that's what counts.

'It seems weird to me.'

'Oh, really, Ollie,' snaps Victoria. 'Todd just has a lot of money and doesn't mind sharing it. And Lucy has obviously made quite an impression,' she says, giving me the full-wattage laser-whitened smirk.

I can't believe it. This must be what it's like to be a man. But Victoria is so determined to get Todd into Ollie's social circle, she's obviously decided that she'll even suck up to me to do it.

'Why did you invite him to the wedding, sweetheart?' Ollie says. 'I hardly know the guy.'

Victoria widens her brown eyes with exaggerated innocence. 'Don't be silly, darling! For Lucy, of course.'

I half choke on my mouthful of coffee. You what?

'Yes, Lucy and Todd are getting on marvellously,' says Victoria. 'And it can only benefit Lucy to know her boss socially. Isn't that what you wanted, darling? For Lucy to climb the ladder? For the world to see the new her? I mean, doesn't she look fantastic this morning? Everything co-ordinated. She's doing so well,' she says patronizingly, as though I were a retarded person learning to ride a bike.

'Ah, well, yes. She looks grand,' Ollie admits. He pats me warmly on the shoulder. 'You're beautiful like that. Even more beautiful, perhaps, I should say.'

Victoria pretends not to mind.

'And we want Todd to see Lucy at her best. After all, darling, Lucy is one of your closest friends. If she's made a new friend in Todd, we should get to know him too. Don't you think?'

'I suppose we should,' Ollie says. A bit grudgingly.

'Bring him round before the wedding, Lucy,' says Victoria ingratiatingly. 'Bring him to dinner. It'll be fun!'

'But Victoria,' I say slowly, 'didn't you tell me it was time for me to be *less* friendly with Ollie, while you prepare for the wedding?' I can't help it. It's an open goal and the keeper is off his line. 'Should we be doing so much socializing, do you think?'

Ollie looks absolutely bewildered.

'What are you talking about?' he asks me.

'Oh Lucy,' Victoria says, with a desperate little laugh. 'How can you have got the wrong end of the stick like that? No, I only meant that Ollie and I are best friends. Not that we'd ever want to cut you out.'

'Of course we wouldn't,' says Ollie seriously. And I glow inside.

'In fact,' Victoria says, 'I've been meaning to ask you, and this is the perfect opportunity. Lucy, will you be my bridesmaid?'

I'm still chewing it over when I get to the office. Seven fifteen, on the dot. But I'm not the first person there. The lights are on in the back. I open the door, hear the tinkle of the bell.

'Hello?' I call out. 'Anybody home?'

There's a little kerfuffle from the back office, the sound of paper being shuffled around.

'Just a second,' Jade calls brightly. 'I'll be right there!'

I hover in the doorway and a minute later she emerges, looking a little red-faced and unusually crumpled. I suppose even fashion plates can have an off day. Jade is wearing one of her usual Home Counties outfits: a silk shirt in rose-pink, a burgundy short skirt, burgundy heels that look horribly uncomfortable but very sexy in a strict nanny way, the ubiquitous pearls, and a gold Cartier tank watch.

She smooths down her shirt distractedly. 'Goodness, Lucy,' she says, her tone a little cooler. 'You startled me. I was just going over some figures with Mr Mayle.'

'I did say hello.'

'Well, you could have done it a little louder.'

Todd enters the main office looking as stunning as ever in another dark suit. I guess they're all he ever wears.

'Good morning, Lucy.'

'Hi, Todd.' I give him my most winning smile, but he frowns at me. 'I-I mean Mr Mayle. Sir.'

'I think I'll have some coffee. Black, no sugar. Jade?'

'Yes, sir.' She smiles at him. 'That'd be great.'

'Tell Lucy how you like it,' Todd says evenly, and disappears back into his office. Jade looks at me with triumph.

'White, full cream, and one packet of Splenda,' she says. 'I'm doing Atkins.'

I stare at her rail-thin body. 'Why?'

'You need to maintain what you have,' she says smugly. 'Now get to it, Lucy, don't keep people waiting.'

I blush and hurry over to the expensive coffee machine, feeling humiliated. If Victoria could have watched that little scene she wouldn't be sucking up to me, would she? Obviously Todd isn't going to be that friendly.

I make the coffee and nervously take Todd's in to him. He's on the phone, jabbering away in Japanese. He doesn't even look at me or thank me, just waves where to put it on his desk. Then I wait a second, but he glances at me with irritation, so I beat a hasty retreat to the main office.

Downcast, I bring Jade her cup.

She takes a sip.

'Mmm, thanks,' she says, in that sunny Cali-girl accent. 'Hey, this coffee's, like, really good.' It comes out 'rilly'. 'When James makes it it's never the same. I don't think he gets the proportions right. How come you figured out that crazy machine?'

Well. She's certainly in a good mood today.

I look over at the coffee maker, with its eight dial settings and multiple chrome chambers.

'Oh, I like machines,' I say. 'And computers,' I add wistfully.

'Oh Lucy.' Jade gives a little laugh, not unlike Victoria's. I think they all come from the IKEA of girlie girls out there in the cosmos. 'Next thing you'll be telling me you like fixing cars. Or fishing!'

'Well . . .'

'Get out!' Jade says. 'You British girls are the craziest thing!'

I fix myself a cup of black decaf – last thing I need around here is extra jitters – and sit at my desk. Todd comes out of his office, speaks to Jade about setting up some appointments. He doesn't even glance my way, and in another minute the door opens and James arrives, closely followed by Buffy and Melissa.

'Morning, everybody,' James says. 'Lucy, did you get that filing done?'

I nod.

'All of it?' he presses.

'Everything.'

'Very well. Get me some coffee. White, no sugar,' he says.

'So, Lucy,' Buffy says. 'Did you find somewhere to live yesterday?'

Todd pauses, for just a second, in front of the filing cabinet. Almost imperceptibly, he turns to me and shakes his head.

'Yes,' I stammer. 'In the West End. At a friend's house.'

'That's lucky,' Buffy says.

'It was,' I agree, nervously. I glance at Todd, but he's already turned his back to me.

And that's it. The end of the social whirl at Mayle Accommodations. I am invisible girl once again. Almost as soon as I've finished serving snotty James and the pastel princesses their coffee, the phone starts to ring. They keep me busy; phones, filing, typing. Plus actual clients come in today. Two urbane, handsome Arabs in beautifully cut suits, a Japanese lady with a diamond ring the size of a marble, and a couple of bland Jade-clone Americans who go into raptures over my accent.

I'm busy, all day long. But I'm *doing* nothing. It's so bloody boring I'd like to chew my own fingers off just for entertainment. And yet I'm kept occupied, so I can't even daydream.

Not that I would dare. I keep thinking of Ollie. He would tell me this is the grown-up world; it's what grown-ups do. That's why it pays so much more than something fun, like reviewing games or being in bands.

I don't know. It's just a bit depressing, that's all.

I try to think of my new and fabulous flat. That's something to look forward to. But my eyes keep sliding around the room after Todd. He doesn't look bored, not a bit. He's schmoozing the clients, glued to the phone, riffling through lists of mega-expensive properties.

I suppose it gives him mystique. Being aloof and unavailable. Jade, for example, looks at him almost as much as I do. And Buffy and Melissa, when they think nobody's watching them, give him adoring little glances.

Only James is immune to the magic. He's buried in his work, cordial to the girls, nasty to me.

I wonder what Victoria will say when she discovers Todd doesn't like me, after all. Will she go back on her word? Disinvite me from being a bridesmaid? I haven't even been able to process that yet. It's just too weird. I mean, I love Ollie. I want to be there for him. And Ollie was so thrilled when she said it.

'Darling, that's brilliant,' he said, jumping up and giving Victoria a huge kiss. 'My two favourite girls!'

But on the other hand, to have to be right there, you know, actually at the altar, while Ollie throws his whole life away . . .

'Lucy.' I look up from staring blankly at my phone.

Todd is standing over me. 'You're coming with me,' he says. 'I'm showing a client around Holland Mansions and I need to have an assistant there. You just hold the files. And bring a notepad; take down anything they say.'

'Oh, yes, right,' I say.

'You don't need Lucy, Mr Mayle,' Jade says breathily. 'She can answer the phones and I'll come with you.' She fiddles with her gold watch. And of the two of us, Jade definitely looks classier. All her stuff is the real thing, I'm just wearing good fakes.

'No,' he says. 'They're Americans, I want that British accent.'

Jade's face falls.

'Fine,' she says, covering it.

'And we need you here in case Contessa Rose di Parigi calls. I can't have such important accounts going to somebody like Lucy,' he says dismissively.

Jade nods, looking slightly more cheerful. Todd walks over to her desk, bends his head, and murmurs something in her ear. Jade flushes pale pink with pleasure; Melissa and Buffy scowl, and James stares at the wall.

I hover by the doorway. I just hope he doesn't lecture me on using his first name when he gets me outside, I haven't even moved into the new place yet. I hold tightly to the files and notepad and vow to be extra professional.

'Follow me,' Todd snaps briskly at me. I exit the building, hearing the little bell ring behind me.

He marches me down the street and into the Lamborghini, puts it into gear and swings out onto the road. He doesn't say a single word to me.

Oh well. At least it's got me out of the office.

Todd turns the wheel sharply onto the main road; after a minute the street is vanishing behind us.

'Well,' he says suddenly, in that rich, sexy voice of his. 'Thank God for that. Huh, Lucy?'

I glance at him. But he's smiling at me, really smiling.

'I couldn't wait to get away,' he says. 'One more second in there and I think I'd have gone crazy. Hey.' He waves at the sunny spring day all around us; the trees are full of cherry blossom, and the sky is pale sapphire blue.

'I don't understand,' I say in a small voice.

'It's real simple,' he says with a touch of annoyance. 'I told you, you know. In the office we have to be professional. If the other staff think I'm forming friendships, things could get awkward.'

'So that's what we are, friends?'

'At least for now.' He gives me that once-over again. 'Just taking things as they come. Seeing where they lead. Tell me, are you looking forward to moving in tonight?'

'Oh, yes,' I say. Though actually I find the thought slightly disturbing. I could get lost in that apartment. 'Thanks again. But look, Todd, I—'

'Let me stop you there,' he says, lifting one hand. I sit tensely in the seat next to him. What if Ollie was right? Is he about to slide his hand up my skirt or something?

'I heard what you said the other night, and I respect that,' he says solemnly. 'It's up to you to decide who to date. But I got to tell you, Lucy, you intrigue me. There aren't many women who turn me down.'

'I—'

'Relax,' he says. 'There are no strings attached, hon. The apartment's yours to use. You don't have to give me the time of day if you don't want to. OK?'

146

'OK.'

'However, my position is that I'd like to go out with you. You're kind of . . .' he shrugs. 'Kind of unique. So I might ask you from time to time. You're perfectly free to tell me to get stuffed. That's what you Brits say, right? Get stuffed?'

'Sometimes.' The way he says it makes me grin.

Todd glances across the car at me, as if he's assessing me or something.

'In the meantime, out of hours, I thought we could be friends. But,' he says smoothly, 'I am your boss. I don't want you to be uncomfortable. If you'd rather not be friendly that's perfectly fine. I won't push it. So what do you say?'

I sit there in this incredible car with the exhaust fumes blowing gently into my face. Well, I can't really object, can I? He's asking permission. He's given me the job and a great flat. Just because there's something slightly . . . off about him . . .

What? What's off? Maybe it's just knee-jerk anti-Americanism. He can't help being handsome and polished. And he's been nothing but nice to me.

Then I flash back to what Ollie said in the restaurant, how he didn't trust him, and I blush. Am I basing my reaction on what Ollie thinks? It's almost as if I want to prove Victoria right, that I *do* have a crush on Ollie.

'That'd be absolutely fine,' I say firmly. It's bloody flattering that he wants to ask me out! 'I'd love to be friends. Especially after what you've done for me with that . . .' enormous, sterile, 'gorgeous flat.'

'It was nothing.' He waves it away. 'Now, we do have to show this house to these clients, so it's all business, got it?'

'Got it.'

'And after that we'll duck out and have some lunch. What do you feel like?'

Sausage 'n' mash? Fish and chips? One of those big baguette sandwiches I had on the train?

'I don't know,' I say casually. 'Some lean fish or meat. And some vegetables.'

'Not starchy ones.'

'Oh no, not starchy ones. Green leafy ones.'

'Good choice,' he says approvingly.

We conduct the clients round a glorious Queen Anne mews house with a walled garden. I do the whole perfect secretary bit. I shake hands and say 'Delighted to meet you' and 'How *good* of you to come', like the Queen, then I follow Todd around, briskly noting everything they want (central air; maid service five days a week; daily fresh flower delivery). I let him talk and say nothing. After he's waved them off, he smiles at me approvingly.

'You see?' he says. 'I knew you'd be great at this. You're discreet. That counts for a lot in my business.'

'I'll remember that.'

'Beauty and brains,' he comments. 'Of course,' he glances over my outfit, 'you could do with a little more style, but that's OK. Oliver warned me that you might need coaching in that area.'

I blench. But this is my very best effort! I scientifically designed this using women's magazines.

'Don't worry,' he drawls. 'I'll help you with that. Now, lunch. How about the Ivy?'

Todd is known everywhere he goes. He tips enormous tips and always gets the best seating. I order a mineral water – Americans think you're an alcoholic if you drink at lunch – and Todd does the same. And then I get a small steak with creamed spinach. Which is better than nothing, I suppose.

Todd praises my choice and I bask in it.

'You're learning, sugar. No mashed potatoes today?'

'And I didn't go for a run, either,' I say, wanting to please him.

He gives me a wink. 'Atta girl.'

Over lunch he tells me all about himself. Gosh. I never knew anybody could be so rich and successful. He's got four houses! One in Mayfair, a townhouse in Greenwich Village, New York, a place in the Hamptons, and a villa in St Tropez. He told me he has a matching Lamborghini in each place.

'What, no private jet?' I joke.

Todd shrugs. 'I looked at a Gulfstream IV but it seemed kind of passé.'

'Oooh,' I say. Todd seems pleased.

'Of course,' he sighs, 'it's kind of an empty life.'

'What do you mean?'

'Nobody to share it with,' he says.

'You haven't been able to find anybody?'

'Anybody?' he says. 'Oh yes, I've been able to find anybody. There've been millions of girls.'

Oh.

'More girls than I can count,' he says. 'Gorgeous debutantes, international models, ballerinas, socialites from the best families, playgirls from St Tropez. And with the best bodies,' he adds. 'Slim, lovely girls with feminine figures –' here he mimes a pair of boobs with his hands. 'And, you know, wonderful manners. The kind of girl that can *behave*. Which is important, don't you think?'

'Um – definitely.' Ollie seems to think so. Maybe that's the recipe for romantic success. A bit disheartening.

'Can she go into a nightclub? Can she behave in a country club? Is she the right sort of girl to take to dinner at your parents? You don't want the same act on the dance floor you want at Mom and Dad's, am I right?'

'I'm sure.'

'But all these women,' he says, dismissing the depressing parade of eight-stone beauties with big fake tits marching through my brain with a wave of his hand. 'All these women lacked one vital thing, Lucy.'

'What was that?'

He looks soulfully into my eyes.

'They weren't *the one*,' he says.

Well. If they wouldn't do, I can't imagine what he wants to date me for.

'Then what are you looking for in *the one*?' I ask, curiously.

Todd sighs. 'What's anyone looking for? Beauty of course – goes without saying.'

Of course.

'As does a perfect body.'

Natch.

'Slim but not too muscular, and feminine.' He mimes the pair of boobs again with his hands. In fact, I have quite good boobs. 'I want a woman who's independent, who lives a full life of her own.'

'I so agree,' I say quickly. I am about to tell him that I definitely want to work and have a career and make my own money, but he's still talking.

'You know, the kind of woman who fills her own day. She goes to the gym, just for yoga and stretching. She goes to the beauty parlour, makes her own appointments. Hair and nails – she takes care of it,' he says, as though this would show great initiative. 'Then maybe a little coffee with some girlfriends, a light lunch. She might take a class in the afternoon.'

'Like what? Kickboxing?' I ask.

'I was thinking of flower arranging,' he says. 'Needlepoint's becoming fashionable again. Or she could shop, of course. There's always shopping.'

'But what about working?'

'Working? You mean as in a career?'

'Well, yes.'

'Look, honey,' he says patiently. 'Some women have to work. I know that. Girls whose men can't bring home the bacon. But not *my* wife, I think.' He smiles modestly.

'I believe I've created a great life just waiting for that special someone to share. And when I find her, well, I want to give her the fairy tale. Is that so wrong?' he asks dramatically.

'Of course not,' I say hastily.

'What would be the point in her working? So we could have, you know, twenty-five million bucks *plus* her fifty thousand?' He shakes his head. 'That would just be posturing. And not to mention embarrassing. I could just see my pals at the club joshing me about it.'

Joshing?

'No, if my wife wants to occupy her time, she can volunteer for charity work. Those twenty thousand dollar a plate benefits don't organize themselves, you know,' he adds piously.

'I can see that. Or she could volunteer at a homeless shelter,' I offer.

Todd smiles humourlessly. 'I don't think that would be quite suitable. She'd obviously be the kind of lady who knows her position. It isn't kind to mix with the wrong types, you know, Lucy. No, she could do a lot more good at the more exclusive events. Anyway, you see how she'd be the kind of girl not averse to spending the fruits of my labour.' He gives me that sexy wink again. 'Believe me, there's plenty of it to go around.'

'You're very generous,' I remark. You certainly can't fault that about him. When I think of some of the blokes I actually have dated, wanting to go Dutch, frowning if I ordered an appetizer . . .

I do think men ought to pay. Ollie always does, even though we've never dated. And Todd clearly has no problem with it.

'Thank you kindly, ma'am,' he drawls. 'I try.'

'Would you like any dessert?' the waiter asks.

They have delicious-looking puddings here. Jam sponge, chocolate mousse, raspberry and lemon tart . . .

'No thank you,' I say firmly. 'I'm watching my complex carbs.'

'Sugar's a simple carb, honey,' says Todd indulgently.

'Well. I'm watching those too.'

'We'll just take the check,' Todd says. 'And then it's back to the grind.'

'Certainly, sir.' The waiter melts away.

I have a consolatory pull at my mineral water. But it doesn't do me any good. I hate dieting.

'You know, Lucy,' Todd says after he's paid. 'You seem to have an excellent grasp of things. I've really enjoyed this special time together.'

'Oh, so have I.'

It hasn't been that bad. I'm trying to be fair to him.

'And I'd like to spend more quality time with you.'

'You would?'

'Sure,' Todd says. 'After you've moved in, of course, and you have your privacy. How about dinner on Friday night? As friends only, of course.'

I can hardly say no. 'That would be lovely.'

'Great,' he says. 'I'll be over at eight.'

He makes small talk on the way back to the office – boring questions about Ollie, his family, and how long I've known him. Which is just as well, because my mind is racing.

Todd likes me.

Todd Mayle likes *me*. Likes me *and* fancies me. OK, so I don't fancy him. But I've told him upfront, and it hasn't changed anything.

He's still, well, he's actually chasing me.

And the thing is, I think I'm starting to enjoy it. Not that there could be anything between us. Todd's not my type. But I'm just enjoying the attention. Since Victoria told me that all Ollie's friends laughed about my crush on him, I've had this devastating vision of myself – tomboy Lucy, the girl no men are interested in. And it seems as if one haircut and a new wardrobe later, this rich American pin-up is chasing me for all he's worth. The man Victoria bitched would never be interested in somebody like me.

Yeah? Well, he is, I think proudly. He's putting on the full-court press. And I *like* it. I like a man pursuing me for a bloody change. It almost makes the Chardonnay-and-tights thing worth it.

Plus, he's my boss. It can't hurt to be friends. I've been straight with him about romance, I think stubbornly.

A picture of Ollie gazing lovingly at Victoria enters my mind with the familiar stab of dismay right behind it.

I'm not using Todd . . . as such. I just deserve a bit of appreciation. Why not? I'll show Victoria. I'll show Ollie, come to that. I can be as flirty and floral as the next girl.

'Remember,' Todd says suddenly, as we turn into Marsham Street. 'Don't speak of this inside the office. Discretion, you understand? It's vital in business.'

'I understand.'

'I'm going to Paris tomorrow,' he says. 'Finding a few places on the Champs Élysées. So I'll call you on Friday night.'

'Oh.' Left alone to James's tender mercies. 'No problem,' I say brightly.

'You won't miss me, will you?' he asks, chucking me under the chin with one smooth, manicured finger.

'Oh no,' I say. 'I have a full schedule. Er, hair, make-up, you know the kind of thing.'

'Exactly,' he says. 'I hate the clingy type that calls a fellow all the time, wanting to know where he is.'

'Oh, so do I. People need their space. Anyway,' I add a touch guiltily, 'I wouldn't call you. We're not dating.'

He looks at me soulfully.

'I think you and I are going to have an interesting time together, Lucy,' he says. 'I'm looking forward to it, and I hope you are also.'

I actually think I am.

We head back into the office, and Todd goes through to the back. A second later the buzzer on my desk goes, and for one wild moment I hope he's going to summon me in there and shut the door, and then give me a huge promotion.

But he only says, 'Lucy, could you send Jade in here please, with the Richman file.'

I say, 'Certainly, sir.' I can do discretion.

'Can you take Mr Mayle the Richman file,' I say to Jade. As if she didn't hear his voice on my buzzer. I mean, she's only two feet away.

'Oh yes,' she says, going bright pink. 'The Richman file. For sure. Now where is it . . .'

She opens up her desk drawer and ruffles about in it.

I see Buffy and Melissa swap nasty looks. For heaven's sake, does misplacing a file deserve that kind of death stare?

James types furiously into his computer with a hunched air that says he hates us all.

Great office. Really. I wish I could take them all aside and teach them how to have fun. But I suppose that wouldn't do any good. This is the grown-up world, and fun isn't a part of it.

'Here it is!' says Jade brightly. 'Lucy, take messages for me, OK? I may be some time working on this file.'

'Certainly, Jade,' I respond in my most ladylike voice.

Jade grabs the file, which looks pretty thin to me, and minces into Todd's office in her uncomfortable heels. They really are high. Maybe I should get a pair like that.

The rest of the day is really dull. Jade and Todd stay closeted for most of it, and he leaves early at four o'clock.

At 5 p.m. on the dot I pick up my bag.

'And where are you going?' James asks nastily.

'It's five o'clock,' I say.

'And we have filing for you to do.'

'I don't,' says Buffy, with an air of weariness.

'Well, I do,' James trumps her. 'And somebody has to take care of it.'

'Oh, not a problem,' I say airily. 'I'll just explain again to Mr Mayle why I'm here working after hours. He asked me about it before, you know.'

'He did?' James chews this over furiously. 'I see. Well, fine. I suppose you can go then,' he says. He sounds bitter.

Mmm. I wonder if they are all teetotallers. What else could explain the cloud of misery in here?

Still, you know, it's not my problem.

'Byeeee!' I say. I walk out of the door carefully, in my new high heels. And before I leave I give them all a little girlie wave, just waggling the tips of my fingers.

That'll show them!

When I get home – I practically float home, because everything's so wonderful – Ollie is already there.

'What's up?' I say, noticing his glum face. Is everybody determined to be down today? Don't they know the world is a fantastic place to live in? Even if you do need to wear heels.

'Not much.' He lapses into silence.

'Oh. Well, I'll be moving out today.' I eye my two suitcases, packed and ready to go by the door. 'D'you think you could help me get my computer into the minicab? The monitor's really heavy.'

'No problem.' He looks up. 'So you're really moving out?'

'I had to. You chucked me, remember?' I smile to show it's a joke, but it isn't, really. I still kind of resent it. 'Two's company, and all that.'

'Yes,' he says. 'And she's a pretty girl.'

'Gorgeous,' I say politely.

'Elegant and refined,' Ollie says. 'And she has to be a winner, the amount she works.'

'She's very successful,' I reassure him.

'Right.' He lapses into silence again.

I don't want to be pulled out of my Todd-fancies-me reverie, but I can't ignore Ollie's glumness. I sigh and pull up a chair.

'What's the matter?'

'I don't know. Nothing. I probably need to work a bit harder,' he says.

'Career worries?'

'Well, not mine. Victoria's.'

'I don't get it. You're both raking it in,' I say encouragingly. 'What's to worry about? And you work far too hard anyway.'

'Maybe not.'

I wait. He wants to talk, so I'll let him.

'After the wedding, Vicky isn't sure she wants to work any more,' he says. 'She's thinking about concentrating on a family.'

'But that's sweet. Lots of little Ollies running around. Aren't you ready for kids, then?'

'Oh no. I want tons of them. And I wouldn't mind supporting a family.'

'It's just for a little while. Maternity leave, you know.'

'No, she wants to quit for ever.'

'Oh.' I digest this. 'Well, it wouldn't be my choice, but I understand. It's up to you both how to handle it.' I shrug. 'Look, if she can lower her standard of living, then you two could easily survive on what you make. You already own the flat.'

'That's the problem,' Ollie says heavily. 'She won't. Lower her standard.'

'Then how can she quit?'

'Victoria thinks, you know, I should work a bit harder.' His eyes slide away from mine onto the table. 'And not have quite so many "ridiculous scruples", as she says. About my cases.'

I don't say anything.

'What do you think, Lucy?' he pleads.

Think? I think you should run away screaming. I want to yell at him to dump the bitch. But that isn't the new me, is it? And there's Victoria again, her voice in my ear, smiling nastily and telling me that Ollie discussed my 'crush' on him with her. That all his friends talk about how I try to ruin everything for all his girlfriends . . .

'Look,' he says. 'I know you don't like Vicky, OK.'

'I do!' I lie.

'You called her Annoying Victoria.'

'Pet name,' I say firmly. 'Term of endearment.'

'But you're getting on a lot better now, aren't you?' he asks me, with a wistful note to his voice. 'Ever since she took you out to fix you up?'

'Oh, absolutely.'

'And she asked you to be her bridesmaid.'

I nod furiously.

'So tell me why you like her, now, I mean,' he says.

Oh God. Think! Think!

'Well, she was so kind to me. And she helped me get the job with Todd.'

He nods.

'And, like you say, she's so elegant. Always so pulled-together.'

'She is that,' he says.

'And successful. Which shows determination.'

'Yes.'

'And obviously she loves you.'

'Yes.' For the first time, he brightens a little. 'She does love me, doesn't she? She says she always has. She's more interested in me than any woman I've ever known.' He sighs. 'It's great to have somebody who cares about you like that.'

'I understand.' Truly, in the school of sucking up, Victoria Cobham has no equal.

'When she gives me advice, it's only for my own good.'

'Right.'

'And it is sweet that her greatest wish is to stay home and look after the kids. That's the most important job in the world.'

I think of my own lovely parents. 'Of course it is.'

'Then I've no right to complain. She's got her priorities right. And men should be men.'

'Yes. On that subject . . .' I wonder if I dare, 'I think you shouldn't listen to her about losing weight.'

He grins. 'I haven't. Told her I thought it over and I decided I'd rather support England than look like Orlando Bloom.'

'Thank God,' I exclaim. The thought of Ollie without muscles is too depressing for words.

'How did she take it?'

He shrugs. 'A man's got to have some red lines. But,' his eyes slide back to me, 'I made it up to her. I told her that gobshite Todd Mayle could come to the wedding after all.'

I draw back as if I've been slapped. 'Todd's not a gobshite.'

'I think he is.'

'Based on what? Weren't you the person saying you hardly know him?'

'Lucy,' Ollie sighs. 'He's got a reputation.'

'Yeah, well.' I toss my hair in a copy of Victoria. 'I've got a "reputation" too apparently.' I think of what she said. About his friends all laughing at me. 'And that's a load of BOLLOCKS,' I yell.

Hmm. The old me rears her scruffy head. Must work on that.

'You hardly know him either. It's only been a few days.'

'Well, you've only known Victoria a few months and you're getting married!' I counter.

Ollie looks shocked. Perhaps I've gone too far.

'What I mean is, you can know somebody in a short time. I don't know if Todd's perfect, but so far he's . . . very nice,' I finish off lamely.

'Well, all right.' Ollie suddenly looks dead awkward, as if he needs to change the subject. 'There's a rugby match on Sky Sports. Fancy watching it with a takeaway? We could get in a curry. I've a couple of Heinekens in the fridge.'

Oh, do I ever!

'Don't be silly, Ollie.' I force a smile. 'I'm moving out, remember?'

'Oh.' He looks even more depressed. 'Right.'

'I'll call the cab,' I say. 'And maybe you can unhook my computer?'

'No problem. I'll come with you, take it up the stairs the other end.'

I think of Ollie walking into my new flat, seeing it in all its stunning glory. And for some reason I don't like the idea much.

'No, that's OK,' I say. 'I've got somebody there who's going to help me.'

Actually I don't think Mr Rogers'll be much good. He looks as if he might have a heart attack trying to lift even one of my suitcases.

'A friend from work?'

'That's right,' I lie.

'A new friend,' Ollie says, and then gives me a smile; a naughty smile, a flash of the old, tour-round-Europe Ollie. 'A flash git no doubt.'

'Super flash!'

'I'm jealous,' he says. 'Not sure I like my Lucy getting new friends.'

'Don't worry, mate,' I say, and give him a bear hug. 'You'll always be the oldest and crankiest.'

He enfolds me in his arms, and suddenly I want to cry. So instead I pull out my mobile and call the cab company. I'm not likely to break down arguing with Silver Star Limos (scratched seats and smells of vomit, old Ford Fiestas and Renault Fives) over the fare to Knightsbridge. I know they'll try to stick on an extra fiver for going somewhere they've likely never been before. And possibly never heard of.

So here I am then. Standing outside Pelham House with two small suitcases and a giant computer monitor. I ring the bell. Nothing to be nervous about.

The door creaks open and Toby Rogers is looking down at me.

'Good evening, madam,' he says neutrally, as though I am the Queen rather than a scruffy twenty-something in ripped jeans and my Metallica T-shirt. I wanted to stick to the tights and heels, as though I were Catherine, you know, or one of those women that seems made-up twenty-four hours a day. But they're just not practical for transporting heavy baggage.

'I have to take these upstairs,' I say unnecessarily.

He suppresses a sigh. 'May I offer you any assistance, madam?'

Toby Rogers must be seventy-five if he's a day. I can almost see the wheels ticking as to how he will lug my desktop into the lift without giving himself a hernia.

'Yes, thank you, you can. Could you hold open the door while I get these upstairs? I'll come back down for the key.'

'Are you sure, madam?' he says, slightly alarmed. But I have already staggered past him, buckling under the weight of the twenty-inch monitor. Curse Ken for refusing to get me a laptop!

I go downstairs and Rogers has my suitcases inside and my key all ready.

'Brilliant. Thanks a million, Toby,' I say.

He looks slightly bemused. 'You're welcome, madam.'

The lift pings and one of the other residents emerges. She is wearing a boxy tweed suit, huge pearl button earrings and a scowl. She stares at my Metallica T-shirt with open hostility.

'Who is that *person*, Toby?' she demands as I drag the cases into the lift.

'That's Miss Evans, Your Grace,' he replies smoothly. 'She's residing in the penthouse.'

'Oh, bloody hell!' cries Her Grace. 'Not another one. That damned Yank!'

The doors hiss shut and I begin the smooth ride upstairs. What was that all about?

Maybe it was a bad idea to come here like this. I'm starting to get nervous. Maybe I should have shopped for some camel-coloured trousers and neutral flats and worn them with one of my shirts. That woman is an actual aristo, what if she complains to Todd that I'm lowering the tone?

I think of Todd at lunch today, all those compliments he paid me. Have I already screwed things up? Ruined the corporate image?

It doesn't bear thinking about. I hurriedly open the door and drag my tatty suitcases and computer stuff inside, then shut it again. At least I was only spotted by one resident, right? I switch on the lights – they glow instantly, lighting up the cavernous living room with their chic, recessed rays – and drag all my stuff into the smallest guest bedroom, just off the conservatory.

Then I wander around again.

Funny, without Todd, the place makes me a bit uneasy. I mean it's so big. And it's so spotlessly neat! It doesn't look like a real flat at all, it looks like a photo in a decorating magazine come to life. Except without the life. It's sort of clinical, pristine as a hospital ward and about as welcoming.

I feel clammy tendrils of unease wind themselves around my heart. What if I drop some wine on this pure white carpet? Or get a scuff mark on the sofa or something? It's not my place, after all. I'm just house-sitting. And even though Todd said maybe I could stay for a year, he also said I'd have to be ready to get out at any time.

I decide to take that to heart. I retreat to the guest bedroom, which is the size of Ollie's living room, but at least it looks like a normal room and not an aircraft hangar.

Then I carefully unpack my new clothes, my toiletries, and my computer. And that's it.

The second suitcase remains unopened. That's got my posters, my Oasis set list, my *Kerrang!* collection, and my CDs. I can't have that here. No clutter. No baggage. Just things I could stuff in one suitcase and get out in ten minutes, if I had to.

OK.

I examine my new home. There's the capsule wardrobe in the cupboard. Not many clothes. I suppose I'll need to dry clean a few every day, but there have to be loads of places round here. And now I have my Pantene in the shower and some Boots shower gel, I'm good to go. Hooray!

I flop down on the bed and wonder why I don't feel very hooray-ish.

Maybe it's the clothes. I take off my beloved jeans and T-shirt and DMs and pull on the navy skirt, white shirt, and black shoes. I won't be frightening any duchesses, but I still feel kind of down.

I don't know. It's a big flat, and even though I wanted to get away from Victoria, I'm away from Ollie too, aren't I?

I think about Ol. His sandy blond hair and brawny frame and diffident manner. I had a lot of fun in that flat. And not just in the flat – at rugby matches, down the pub, you name it.

Maybe I should call him. Invite him over. Even with Annoying Victoria it'd be cool to see him.

And then, out of nowhere, her voice again:

'Well, now we've had this little chat, I'm sure you understand. Ollie already has plenty of friends. Men friends. People from his own background. And of course, a man's best friend is always his wife . . .'

My hand drifts away from the call button.

I sit on the bed and stare into space. Then I give myself a little shake, get up, and go back down to the lobby.

'Yes, madam.' The old man notes my change of clothes approvingly. I give myself a little tick in that box.

'Do you have a Yellow Pages?'

He looks at me blankly.

'You know, telephone directory?' I speak slowly. 'With adverts in it? For curry houses and takeaway places?'

'I'm afraid not, madam,' he says, looking mildly scandalized.

My stomach rumbles.

'OK. Well, do you happen to know anywhere to eat around here – anywhere cheap?' I add hastily. 'The sort of places that do takeaways.'

He sighs. 'I could recommend some restaurants, madam, but I don't believe they do takeaways. Or deliver food. And they are rather expensive, I'm afraid.'

I deflate.

'There is a McDonald's on the Horseferry Road,' he says, suddenly. 'I do know that.'

McDonald's. Did somebody say McDonald's? Burger and fries. Or chicken McNuggets. And a burger. And extra large fries and an apple pie . . .

I think of Todd on Friday and his ban on carbohydrate. Todd's eyes, McDonald's. Todd's eyes, McDonald's . . .

My stomach rumbles again. Loudly.

'That's fine,' I say. 'I wasn't hungry anyway. Thanks, Toby.'

'You're welcome, madam,' he says, with the tiniest touch of sympathy gleaming in his eyes.

My stomach complains audibly all the way back to the lift.

9

Next day at work is awful.

Todd's not there, and I just have to sit around, answering calls and taking messages. Oh, and making coffee. The girls appear not to be speaking to each other, and James likes to bark at me in a shouty voice.

And I'm too nervous even to play *Free Cell* or *Minesweeper* or anything.

I pass the time daydreaming, and at three o'clock James and Jade sweep out together on an appointment. Melissa is already in the back talking to some Texans wanting 'a darlin' lil ol' palace' somewhere in central London, and that just leaves Buffy and me.

'Would you like some coffee?' I say solicitously. This has been the extent of my office conversational skills today.

'More coffee? I'll chew my own arm off,' she says bitterly.

Buffy is once again expensively and beautifully dressed. She has on a little sprig muslin cardigan over a pink chiffon dress, lined with silk; pink mules, a silver-pink quilted Chanel bag, and a white silk scarf round her neck.

'They have decaf,' I say.

'It's never really decaffeinated,' she says morosely. 'Did you know that? They have almost the same amount of caffeine as the regular ones.'

'How do you know?'

'They did a study,' she says. 'Back home. It was on the

165

news.' Buffy sighs. 'Things are never as good as they seem,' she says. 'It's something you can count on.'

I'm encouraged. Maybe Buffy wants to be friends.

'Do you want to be friends?' I ask.

She stares at me. 'Huh?'

'Never mind.' It was a foolish thought.

But Buffy's lips have moved upwards in the slightest of gestures. Really, a very tiny twitch. Is that what passes for a smile in American society circles?

'You don't just ask like that,' she says. 'Do you want to be friends.'

'Why not?'

'You have to work it in. Imply it. Engage the other person in conversation,' she says. 'D'you have many friends, Lucy? Are all English girls like you?'

'I've loads of friends,' I say. 'But they're all men. And of course all English girls aren't like me. I mean, not all American girls are like you, are they? There's, I don't know, Courtney Love. She's nothing like you.'

'And Oprah,' Buffy adds helpfully.

'Right. And Hillary Clinton.'

'And Tina Turner.'

'And Madonna.' I shake my head. 'But maybe not, she is a bit like you these days, isn't she? Respectable.' I sigh. 'I liked the old Madonna better.'

'But she had armpit hair,' Buffy says, horrified. 'Surely you don't like armpit hair.'

'It was a small price to pay,' I say, nostalgically.

'It's not the Brits who do the armpit hair, is it?' she says. 'It's the French.'

'French women don't have armpit hair. The French get short shrift, actually.' I'm thinking of my sister's boyfriend, and his 'all French women let their husbands fuck around' line in pre-proposal discussions.

Wait! My sister. That's a brilliant idea. I can call Catherine! She should be back in London by now. Relief floods over me; at least I won't be lonely tonight.

'Not as short shrift as the Americans,' Buffy says bitterly.

'What do you mean?' I ask.

She looks at me with eyes narrowed. 'Oh, Americans are so stupid. They're all fat. They kill people for their oil. Their President's a moron. They homogenize the globe. What's the difference between an American and a yogurt? A yogurt has culture.' She sighs. 'I actually thought that was funny, the first time I heard it.'

'I'm sorry,' I say, taken aback.

'Am I George Bush?' she asks dramatically. 'And you know what, if you don't like fast food, nobody *makes* you buy it. Or go to the movies.'

'Do you get a really hard time here?'

'All Americans do.'

'Then why don't you go home?' I ask. 'If I hated a place, I wouldn't stick around.'

Buffy looks at me wearily.

'It's not that easy,' she says.

'Sure it is. Just call a travel agents. You can get excellent discounts if you know where to look.'

'I have attachments,' she whispers. 'And I'm not ready to let them go.'

'A man?' I ask sympathetically.

'Not just any man – the man,' she says. 'But I think he's cheating.'

'Can't you confront him?'

'It's not like that.'

I know better than to argue.

'Then just dump him,' I say. 'You're really pretty, Buffy, and you have that feminine thing going on . . .' I gesture at her strawberries and cream outfit. 'Girls like you can get anybody,' I say wistfully.

'But can't keep them.' She sighs. 'I should move on. But I can't because I love him too much.'

There's nothing you can say to that, is there?

167

'I understand,' I say. 'Want to go out to dinner?'

'It's only half three,' she says, shocked.

'Late lunch, then. You can say I'm assisting you on something. We could go to a wine bar and have a spritzer and some food.'

'Low-carb?' she asks suspiciously.

'Absolutely,' I say, encouraging her.

Buffy wavers.

'Better not,' she says eventually. 'He – I mean Mr Mayle – might find out. We don't want to upset him.'

I nod. 'Good thinking. I suppose we don't.'

It's OK. I'll call Catherine after hours. I hope she's there. Otherwise I might be dialling the Speaking Clock for some company.

Thank God, Catherine *is* there. And she's in London.

'I couldn't take another night of undercooked roast pork,' she said. 'It might have given me a tapeworm.'

'So how are you feeling?' I ask solicitously. And I really do care how she's feeling. It's just that I'm also hoping to have the opportunity to talk about Todd. Get some advice. Friday's just around the corner . . .

'Fine,' she says miserably. 'Want to come over? Or I could come round to Ollie's.'

'I'm not at Ollie's any more. I've moved out.'

'Where to?' she asks with a flicker of interest. 'Shall I come round?'

I look round at my luxurious, sterile room.

'I'd much rather see your place,' I temporize. 'Where are you?'

'Just off Earls Court,' she says. 'Kingston Street. Number thirty-two, flat five-A.'

'I'll be right there,' I say joyfully.

Cathy's place is exactly what I expected. A warmer version of my own; it's neat and clean, but it has colour and a sort of Cathy spirit to it. Even though it's a standard-issue London luxury rental, kitted out in chrome and blond woods, she's made it feel like her digs always do: she's got loads of mismatched roses heaped into glass vases, her framed photo of Mum and Dad, soft rose-coloured rugs, and rude joke books in the loo. Her kitchen has little bunches of dried herbs and lavender pinned up on its minimalist walls; they look out of place, which is perfect. You can't sterilize the girl in Cathy. Even when she's heartbroken.

I want to start out with Todd right away but you can't do that, can you? Not when your sister is getting over the love of her life.

We curl up on her squashy couch which is covered with a pale-blue hydrangea print slipcover, sipping diet hot chocolate out of mugs. Catherine was amazed I said yes to diet hot chocolate, but if only she knew. I haven't had anything sweet-tasting for days. It isn't even as disgusting as normal.

'So you went back to work?' I ask.

Catherine nods. 'Not going to let that git run me away from a good career,' she says bravely. 'I might have a serious bonus coming this year. And I don't want anybody to think I'm having a nervous breakdown.' She shivers. 'The cliché's true, you know; they really are like sharks. They can smell blood.'

'So did you see him?'

'Oh yes,' she says grimly. 'I saw him.'

'And?'

'And I said, "Good morning, Peter. LIBOR's up again I see." '

I can tell there's more.

'He agreed and we moved on.'

'And?' I press her.

'And,' she sighs, 'he was with his new girlfriend.'

'WHAT?' I scream.

169

'I dumped him. He's got every right to find a new girlfriend. Why should I care?' says Catherine, who obviously cares desperately.

'The new girlfriend,' I say. 'Was it . . .'

'Esther. From New York. Yes, it was.'

I reach over and give her a hug, but she responds in a sort of brittle way. I can tell she doesn't want to hug back too hard, in case she starts to cry.

'Look, maybe she isn't his girlfriend. You said they'd been working together. Maybe they're just colleagues.'

'They were holding hands.'

'Oh.'

'And he said, "Catherine, you know my girlfriend Esther, don't you?"'

'Ouch.'

'It was, rather,' she admits.

'What did you do?'

'I smiled and said, "Of course I do! How are you, Esther?" She looked really awkward.'

'I would have said, "Pretty quick to move in on my cast-offs." Or maybe, "Everybody knows Esther, most of them in the Biblical sense." Or just, "Fuck off, you pair of losers."'

'Subtle,' Cathy acknowledges. 'Maybe I'll try that next time.' She rallies, obviously trying to be brave. 'Anyway, tell me about your life.'

'Well, you know I moved out from Ollie's.'

'That must have been a wrench.'

'I suppose.' I shrug. 'With Annoying Victoria there it's not the same. Anyway, I started work at the estate agency.'

'Yes.' Cathy tries to focus. 'Actually I noticed the outfit. That's pretty good, a lot better than Anne's old clothes.'

'I still need to improve though. The other girls in the office do it better. They have silky silver shirts and stuff. Can you help me? Shop, I mean. I need something by Friday. A dress. Something feminine, with ruffles, or whatever.'

Catherine lifts an eyebrow when I blurt this out.

'What are you talking about?' she asks. 'Ruffles? That's not you, Lucy!'

'But I need to look elegant,' I wail. 'And truly feminine, and gorgeous.'

'You look gorgeous anyway.'

'You've got to help me!' I plead.

'Don't be silly, of course I'll help,' Cathy says. 'But haven't we skipped a few steps? What's happening on Friday? And as long as you got the job, who cares about what the other girls in the office wear? Don't go nuts, Lucy. You smartened up, OK, that was probably a good thing, but what you've got on is perfectly acceptable office wear.'

'It needs to be more than acceptable. It needs to be stunning,' I say desperately. 'Pulled together. And I need all different looks. The right one for a nightclub and a – a – country club.'

'A country club?' Cathy's staring at me as if I've gone mad. 'You're going to a country club? We don't have country clubs. Unless you count Groombridge Amateur Dramatics.'

'I just mean to suit all occasions,' I say.

'And what would suit, say, a rock concert?' asks Catherine suspiciously.

I toss my head. 'Oh, those,' I say scornfully. 'I'm not interested in those any more. I like . . . Covent Garden and theatre.'

'Theatre?' Catherine scoffs. 'Name one West End play.'

'*Cats*,' I say brightly.

'Not for years,' she says. 'And you've never listened to opera in your life. What's going on?'

'There is this man,' I admit.

'I knew it!' she says. 'Is it Ollie? Is he dumping Victoria?'

'No, it isn't. And he's way more handsome than Ollie,' I say. 'He's got the most gorgeous chocolate-brown eyes and he looks really great in a suit.'

'Go on.'

'He's very generous with his money. And kind. There were bullies in the office and he protected me from them.'

'It's not your boss, is it?' Catherine asks.

'Um, yes.'

She slaps her forehead. 'Sweetie, you need this job. You can't go out with your boss!'

'I'm not,' I protest. 'We're just friends. Taking it as it comes. He's asked me to dinner on Friday night, that's all. And I really want to impress him. Climb the corporate ladder.'

'Climb the corporate ladder? That's not you,' Cathy says.

'It could be,' I say mulishly. 'If Victoria can make sixty grand a year, why not me?'

'And this guy. If you're not going out, why is he taking you to dinner on a Friday night?'

'He does want to,' I admit. 'But I already told him I'm not interested. So it's just as friends.'

Cathy shakes her head. 'Sure. Come on, Lucy! You know better.' She looks at me shrewdly. 'You don't just want to make a good impression for the job, I can tell that much.'

'It is a bit flattering.' I'll admit that much. 'I mean, you should see him, Cath! He's incredibly rich and successful, and he looks like a movie star. And he wants to date *me*!'

Cathy stares at me as if I'm a loony. 'Of course he wants to date you, who wouldn't? You're something different, Lucy.'

Yeah, well. Much good that did me with Ollie.

'But he's still a colleague. It's dangerous to start flirting with them.'

'I can't help it that I work with him. You work with Peter.'

'And look what a mess that is.' She sighs.

'Well, Todd likes the new me. And he's had millions of girlfriends and I just want to look elegant, like . . . like Martha Stewart.'

'That middle-aged frump? She wound up in jail,' Cathy warns me darkly.

'You know what I mean,' I wail. 'Can you help me?'

'Of course. But Lucy, I hope he likes you for you,' she says. 'It's not all about airs and graces.'

'Two weeks ago everybody told me it *was* about airs and graces.' I smooth down my skirt. 'Anyway, he obviously likes me for me. Because I'm not rich or titled or anything. And he found me a flat to house-sit, and he's paying me loads of money. He appreciates me,' I say. 'And it's nice.'

'Well.' Cathy puts down her mug. 'As long as he's a good bloke, I suppose it can't hurt. I can take you shopping. I've wanted to buy you some clothes for ages.'

'I can buy my own clothes,' I say proudly. 'With my house-sitting money and my travel allowance, I've got loads of extra cash. I won't even have to touch my salary.'

'It won't be enough for the kind of clothes—'

'It's six hundred a week,' I say.

She blinks. 'Well, he is generous.'

Yeah. He is. And I don't see why I shouldn't at least let him be friends.

After work next evening we hit the shops. I'm a bit more interested this time. I've got motivation.

I tell Catherine exactly what I want and she picks the stuff out for me: silk shirts from Emporio Armani, a floaty mink chiffon dress from Ghost, some black strappy heels from LK Bennett, two skirts in dark green and slate blue from DKNY, a short Warehouse cocktail dress, and a gorgeous lightweight black summer coat from Joseph. It looks like nothing on the peg but makes everything you put on under it seem formal and chic.

Then we go out for dinner. Catherine gets lamb chops and new potatoes, I get a grilled chicken salad.

'Off your food?' she asks, staring. 'Where's the huge plate of pasta or the fish and chips? They do that here, you know. They gussy it up by calling it "salt cod, rough-hewn potatoes and rocket salad" but it's basically just fish and chips.'

'I'm on a low-carb diet,' I say.

Her eyebrows shoot up. 'Why?'

'I'm just making a few changes. Eating healthier.'

'But that's not healthy for somebody who never stops dancing. And who goes running!'

I sigh. 'I've given up exercise,' I say laconically. 'Can't really be bothered any more.'

Catherine reaches over and shakes me.

'Are you a demon?' she says. 'What have you done with my sister, you foul fiend?'

I giggle. 'Catherine, it's fine.'

'Let's see,' she says. She turns to the waiter. 'Bottle of Chardonnay, please. Now if you refuse to drink, I'll know you're going anorexic, and I'll be forced to call Mum.'

'Well, we can't have that,' I admit, and let the waiter pour me a glass of wine. Which slips down quite nicely, actually. So does the second one. Cathy decides against most of the second bottle, so I finish it off for her. What the hell. Todd will never know. I'm having a great time with Catherine, and when she decides to go for pudding I don't say no. It feels like I haven't eaten in a week. They do a chocolate sponge with ginger ice cream so I have one of those. And a brandy, which burns my throat but what the fuck? I'm feeling quite merry. And so's Catherine.

'This is brilliant!' I exclaim as she signs for the bill. I haven't had this much fun since before Victoria proposed. 'Lesh go to a wine bar.'

'They're crowded,' Catherine says.

'Then lesh pick up some champagne and go to my place!' I say expansively. 'Don't you want to see it?'

'Definitely,' Catherine says, picking up all my carrier bags and gently escorting me to the door. 'That might be a

174

really good idea. But let's skip the champagne. I've got work tomorrow, and so have you.'

I tumble out onto the pavement in front of Pelham House, clutching my sister.

'Wow,' Catherine says slowly. 'You live in this building?'

'Wait till you see it.' I ring the doorbell, and Toby Rogers opens the door.

'Good evening, madam,' he says.

'Evening, Toby,' I say. 'Toby, thish my sister. Catherine. Catherine, thish my mate Toby Rogers. Not Tony. Don't call him Tony 'cos that's not his name.'

'Hi, Toby. I'm Catherine,' she apologizes.

'Good evening to you, madam,' he says faintly.

'Do you have your keys with you?' Catherine asks. 'Do you remember which flat is yours?'

'Miss Evans left her key with me, madam,' Toby says smoothly, 'and she is residing in the penthouse suite on the top floor. Shall I escort you up?'

'I know where I live,' I say indignantly.

Catherine retrieves the key from Toby.

'Thank you very much.' She glances my way. 'Sorry about her.'

'Hey!' I protest.

'There is nothing to apologize for, madam,' says Toby.

'That'sh right. Absolutely right,' I say. 'Nothing at all!'

I want to be like Victoria. So I toss my hair again. Or try to. Unfortunately, it doesn't actually agree with me. At all. The motion is making me feel kind of queasy . . .

'Oh dear,' I say.

Then I lean forward and throw up all over the marble floor.

I wake up and don't know where I am.

And I don't really care. Who gives a toss about location when your head is pounding like a bass drum and your mouth has that just-shat-on-birdcage-floor feeling?

I lie there trying not to move and provoke it. But unfortunately I have a raging thirst. Groaning, I swing my legs off the bed and stagger into the bathroom, where I thrust my head under the tap and gulp it down. That helps for about a minute; then I throw up again.

Oh God!

I look at myself. My skin is as grey as Barbara Bush's hair. I have bags under my eyebrows and my eyes are bloodshot. I'm wearing my bra and panties. And a watch, which says . . . ten to ten!

Oh shit!

It all comes back to me. I groan again and hunt down my mobile. It's on my bed next to a note from Cathy. 'Amazing place! I approve. Call me later. Feel better.'

I don't know if I'll ever feel better again. I call the office and explain there's been a death in the family.

'I'm sorry to hear that,' says James suspiciously. 'Who?'

'My Uncle Jimbo,' I croak. 'A great loss.'

Well, it's true. There has been a death in the family and it was Uncle Jimbo, and he must have been a great loss to somebody. I wouldn't really know who, since he died in eighty-nine.

'When will we expect you back?'

'Tomorrow, I think,' I croak.

'Well.' Fossbert-Smythe softens a touch. 'Condolences, Lucy. You certainly don't sound well.'

And I certainly don't feel well either. But there's some relief when I press the red button. A day off work! And you know, with some more sleep and several aspirins . . .

Then I remember. The lobby. The vomit! Will Toby have reported me to the duchess already? Or, worse, to Todd?

I groan in terror. That's not the way a future partner in Mayle Accomodations would behave, is it? Would Martha Stewart stagger into the country club and do a Technicolor yawn all over the floor?

Of course she wouldn't! I'm dead.

Moaning, I flee to the shower and scrub myself down with my trusty bar of Pears; wash my hair, which probably has vomit specks, and scarf my mouth out with toothpaste and Listerine. It does nothing for the vile headache or the raging thirst, but after I've nuked my hair dry with the wall-mounted professional hairdryer, and struggled into my sprig dress and the navy cardigan, at least I look slightly respectable.

I make up hastily, using bronzer on my cheeks to get rid of that Night of the Living Dead pallor, and ride the lift downstairs to face Toby. I hope he's there.

He's there all right. He's standing talking to the duchess. Is he telling her about me? About last night?

I hover in the background.

'Yes, madam?' Toby turns an ice-cold eye on me. 'Can I do anything for you?'

'I – um, it'll wait.'

The duchess, sensing scandal, turns round and fixes me with a gimlet stare.

'Oh, don't mind me,' she says, stepping aside.

'I just wanted to talk to you about last night,' I say, blushing scarlet.

The duchess sniffs theatrically.

'There's nothing to discuss, madam,' Toby says. 'Now, Your Grace, I shall certainly call the cleaning service and inform them that their work around Mr Snuggles' basket has been unsatis—'

'I-I just wanted to apologize,' I blurt. This is so humiliating. 'It was really awful and inconsiderate of me and it won't ever happen again. My mum would kill me, you know.'

Toby Rogers regards me. His icy stare wavers a little, then he looks down.

'What? What happened?' the duchess demands. 'Did you vandalize something, young woman? Get caught with drugs? Bring home *unsuitable men*?'

'Oh, it was nothing like that, Your Grace.' Toby warns me not to say anything with his eyes. 'Miss Evans is merely referring to the fact that she arrived home a little late last night and was sorry that she had to wake me up.'

I look at him gratefully.

'I see. Well, that's all right then,' says the duchess, with an air of disappointment. 'I'm late for my appointment at the milliner's. Good day, Toby.'

'Good day, Your Grace,' he says, bowing low.

'Have a nice day!' I say, smiling at her.

The duchess sniffs and sweeps out.

I wait till the coast is clear.

'Look, I truly am sorry,' I say. 'That was disgusting. I don't normally. But they made me switch to wine and I'm only used to beers.'

'Who's they?' he asks.

'Everybody. You know. To be ladylike.'

Toby's mouth twitches upwards. 'I see.'

'I would never expect anybody to clean up my sick,' I say, blushing scarlet. 'I'd have done it myself but I passed out. I'm so sorry.'

He gives me a creaky smile. 'Miss Catherine offered to clean up, but I had finished by the time she re-emerged. It isn't the first time it's happened, madam. I daresay it won't be the last.'

'Can't you call me Lucy?' I plead.

He shakes his head. 'That wouldn't be proper, miss. And anyway,' he adds with a keen look at me, 'Mr Mayle wouldn't like it.'

Todd. Right.

'You – you haven't told him, have you?'

He grins. 'No, madam. I shall keep the details strictly confidential.'

'Phew,' I say. 'He's coming here tomorrow night. For a date,' I confide. 'I really want to make a good impression.'

'I'm sure you will.'

I turn and head back to the lifts.

'Miss Evans?'

I turn round. 'Yes, Toby?'

He looks away. 'Nothing. It doesn't matter. Have a pleasant day, madam.'

10

When Friday evening finally arrives I can hardly think straight. I've got everything ready. Catherine came over last night and ooh-ed and aaah-ed about the flat, which made me feel lovely. She suggested fresh flowers, so we went shopping together for roses. I have half a dozen white ones in a vase on the coffee table, the blooms match the carpet, and they look gorgeous with their dark, glossy leaves. I've got the chic lights on dimmer switch and some candles lit on the kitchen table, with extra-wide holders so there'll be no wax on anything. And some champagne chilling. Catherine gave me some make-up tips, and I'm in my new floaty chiffon and LK Bennett shoes. And she lent me this gorgeous Butler & Wilson fake diamond lariat, which points temptingly down towards my Wonderbra-clad boobs.

Now it's half past seven, so all I've got to do is wait. My phone goes. I dive on it.

'Todd,' I purr.

'It's not Todd, it's Ollie.'

Oh. 'Hey, Ollie.'

'What are you doing?'

'Nothing much. Sitting around.'

'Shall I come over then? And see your new place?' he suggests hopefully. 'You haven't called since you moved out.'

'I know, I'm really sorry. I've been busy.'

'Too busy for your best mate, eh?' he says. 'How quickly they forget.'

'Ha ha.'

'Anyway, shall I come round? I've nothing to do and it's so boring here.'

'Where's Victoria?'

'Out with her girlfriends. Wedding planning.'

'I'd love to see you but I can't tonight. I've got a date,' I say, feeling the thrill of it flow through me. It is kind of a date, right? At least, Todd would like it to be. And I feel good about letting Ollie know that.

I think I'll keep the just friends thing to myself. For now.

'Who with? Todd?'

'Of course with Todd,' I say. 'What, do you think I lead some kind of James Bond double life?'

'Very funny, Evans.'

'I really like Todd.' Better knock this on the head. 'You didn't ask my opinion about Victoria. Or Rhiannon. Or Fay. I accept Victoria, don't I?'

'You do.'

'Then you should make an effort to accept Todd.' I'm pushing it now, I suppose. I'm actively letting him think we're going out. But what can I say? Victoria's mean comments – they hurt. The fact that Ollie discussed me with her, that hurt more. I want them both to think I'm dating a millionaire. I could be, if I wanted to.

Todd's not the one for me. I can't imagine seriously dating anybody, at least until this stops . . . hurting.

I wince inwardly. I don't want to think about it. Ollie's taken. He loves Victoria. That's it.

'Look,' I relent. I can't play games forever. 'Victoria wanted to get together, didn't she? How about I set up dinner for the four of us? If this goes well, I mean. I might puke up all over him,' I speculate. 'Or fall over and show my knickers. And anyway,' I admit it, 'Todd and I are really only friends.'

'I've been living with you for three years and I never got so much as a flash of knickers!' says Ollie irritably.

'Well, you weren't my boyfriend, were you?'

'I suppose not,' he grumps. 'The new you is no fun, Lucy. Do you know that?'

'Yeah, well. Fun never got me very far, did it?' I say.

Suddenly the tone of the conversation has changed. I think about all my years with no real boyfriend, and no success. Why was I happy? Rejected by men and I didn't even care.

Well, that's all over now. I'm going to be like Catherine and Emily. And Victoria. The kind of girl who deserves real romance, even if it's not with Todd.

'I've got to go,' I say, annoyed with him for puncturing my mood. 'Call you later, OK?'

I hang up and sit there brooding. I wish people would stop having a go and just be happy for me.

I wish Todd would call!

There's a low, melodious sound. Ding-dong.

I look around, and then realize it's the doorbell. I jump up, heart thumping, to go and open the door, but it opens itself, and Todd walks in.

'Todd! Hi.'

I'm nervous. I'm actually trembling. Todd looks very polished, so no change there. But do I? True, I took two hours just doing my hair and make-up, and that's not counting misting my clothes with perfume, flossing, plucking out stray hairs, painting my fake nails, but it's not enough.

I mean, look at him. Look at that elegant suit, that soft cashmere overcoat. The faint tang of expensive aftershave. The huge Rolex.

I feel a bit overwhelmed. How am I supposed to present myself as an up-and-comer when his coat probably cost six months of my salary?

'Hey,' he says. 'Good to see you. Looking forward to it?'

Well, yes and no. It's a bit of an ordeal, actually. But at least Todd's smiling at me in a friendly manner.

'Would . . . would you like a drink?' I say, remembering my manners. My voice has suddenly gone all high and squeaky. 'I've got champagne,' I add with a touch of pride.

'What kind?'

'Veuve Cliquot,' I say, trying for an air of sophistication.

'Grande Dame?'

He's confusing me. 'No, Veuve Cliquot,' I explain. 'It's French.'

Todd gives a little snort. 'Honey, I was asking if it's Veuve Grande Dame. If it's vintage.'

'Um, I don't think so.'

'I only drink vintage,' he says. 'Life is too short to drink bad wine.'

Is Veuve Cliquot bad wine? I feel ashamed. I spent thirty-five quid on it.

'I'll remember next time.'

'Don't feel bad.' He flashes me a quick smile. 'Got any lines?'

'Excuse me?'

'Coke. Blow. Bolivian marching powder.'

'You mean cocaine?'

'You mean cocaine?' he says, imitating me, and I flush. 'No, huh?'

'I'm sorry,' I say. I suppose I'm totally unsophisticated. A great wave of disappointment crashes over me. I'm out of my depth, aren't I? I suppose he won't be impressed with me any more.

'Don't worry,' he says. 'I think it's cute. You're just a little English rose, all innocent and demure.' His dark eyes sweep across me. 'I think that's very attractive. You can pick up bad girls anywhere, but you wouldn't want to take them home to Momma, would you?'

I smile gratefully.

'Don't mess with drugs,' he says. 'If you really don't do them.'

'I really don't,' I admit.

'I can take care of that shit myself.' He nods approvingly, and I feel I've passed a test.

'So where are we going for dinner?'

'I thought the Escargot D'Or,' he says. 'New Michelin three star off Bond Street. Extremely discreet.'

'Sounds good.' I try for preppy American, like Buffy. Or Jade.

'And what'll you be wearing?' he asks. 'Off to slip into something more comfortable?' Todd raises his eye brows suggestively.

'I . . . I was going in this,' I say in a small voice.

'That?' He blinks. 'But that dress . . . it's a day outfit.'

I look down at my dress. My best outfit, and obviously nothing like good enough.

'I'm really sorry,' I say, rushing to apologize. 'It's just that I don't have a lot of clothes.'

'But why not?'

The shame. My cheeks burn. 'Because I don't have a lot of money,' I mutter.

'Oh, Lucy,' says Todd. 'Oh, Lucy, Lucy.' The slow smile is back, curling round his lips. 'We can't have that, can we? Not for a *friend* of Todd Mayle's. Do you know any-body that knows fashion?' he asks. 'I mean, really *knows* it.'

'Oh yes,' I say, thinking of Victoria.

'Well, call her,' he says. 'Go shopping tomorrow, and use this.'

He removes a real crocodile-skin wallet from an inside jacket pocket and fishes out a credit card.

'Don't come home till you've bought a great wardrobe,' he says. 'Everything from coats,' he looks me over, grinning, 'to lingerie. Don't come home till you've spent, let's say, ten thousand pounds?'

The room seems to spin a little. But he's dead serious. I can tell.

'Ten . . . thousand pounds?' I ask, with a little squeak.

'Sure,' he says. 'A decent purse costs five hundred. More. If you need to, fifteen K is fine too.'

'I can't spend fifteen thousand pounds of your money,' I manage.

'Sweetheart.' His hand reaches out, pats me on the butt. 'It's not *my* money, it's a corporate account. Mayle Accommodations girls have to be properly dressed. Corporate image, you know.'

'But fifteen . . .'

'If it helps us land a client worth one fifty in commission . . .' he says, reasonably.

'I – suppose so.' I can't stop staring at the platinum card.

'And don't forget the lingerie,' he says, with a little smirk.

I blush. I can't hold his eyes.

'I'm not buying lingerie with your money,' I say. 'I mean, that's not what friends do. It's what girlfriends do.'

'Mmm,' Todd says. 'You're too much. You're a real tough cookie, you know that?'

'Sorry,' I apologize. 'But I did say . . .'

'I know you did.' He's looking at me curiously. 'I guess I wasn't sure if you were serious. I suppose that's gonna sound real arrogant on my part, but what can I tell you? I'm not used to it.'

I feel a small thrill of pride.

'Maybe I shouldn't take the money at all.' I look at him. 'I mean, is it really for the corporate image? Be honest. It's more like a come-on, isn't it?'

Todd blinks, astonished. Then he bursts out laughing.

'My God,' he cries. 'I never met anyone like you. Not girls, anyway. OK, OK,' he spreads his hands. 'Perhaps a little of both. I'm not playing games. I want you to go out with me, and maybe,' he says, and his eyes get serious, 'maybe more than that. But you're old fashioned, you've got to be wooed.'

'You don't need to woo me with large amounts of cash.'

'I don't need to do anything. But I want to.' He has a rather charming smile now. 'Like I say, it's a corporate account. And we hired you especially to make a good impression, so if you buy the clothes and you still hate me, Mayle Accommodations hasn't lost anything.'

'I don't hate you,' I protest.

'Give me a chance,' he says. 'Let me treat you like a lady. It's almost like nobody ever spoiled you before.'

Well. When he puts it like that.

I think of all the boyfriends the old Lucy had. More like mates, really . . .

'They didn't,' I admit.

'So we both know where we stand,' Todd says. 'I'm just asking for a chance to change your mind. Promise me you'll do this. And then go on one proper date. Not as friends, as a date.'

I hesitate.

'It's a new experience,' he says. 'And I think you're the adventurous type.'

I can't say no, can I? I get the oddest feeling I've been spun. But I can't put my finger on it. His expression is completely sincere. And he's only asking for a shot. I mean, I've dated so many class-A losers. I honestly don't know why I'm even hesitating.

'Sure,' I say at last. 'A real date. Why not?' I try for a smile. 'We can start now, if you like.'

He smiles back. 'I would like. A lot.'

Well. This is the life.

I mean, I've never been anywhere quite like this. Not even that time when Cathy took me out for lunch at a fancy City restaurant near her building. Everything here is spectacular. They don't have lights, they have chandeliers. Even in the loo. I think the cutlery's gold-plated. And the glasses are Waterford crystal. And the food, well . . . I never knew anything could taste like that. I have tiny goose livers with braised slivers of cabbage, and forkfuls of caviar and chopped egg – no blinis, because they've got carbs. And then this amazing salad with warm lobster.

And a waiter keeps hovering and filling up my glass with champagne. This time it's vintage.

Todd tells me all about himself. His life here, and his life in America. His house in the Hamptons, his yacht, his place on Fifth Avenue. He's like Richard Gere in *Pretty Woman*. And just as well dressed.

'Todd,' I say. The champagne's making me brave. 'Are you, you know.'

'What?' he asks.

'Are you the richest man in the world? After Bill Gates, I mean.'

He chuckles. 'God, no. I'm not even a billionaire.' He shrugs. 'Well, not yet, at least.' And he winks at me.

'It sounds so wonderful.' I sigh.

What would that be like? Never to have to worry about what anything costs. Like the Queen.

'Can I ask you a little about yourself?' Todd asks.

The champagne is coursing through me. 'Fire away,' I say, slowly and deliberately, so he won't know. I look around for my water glass.

'You're a pretty girl,' he says. 'Sexy too, I bet. You had a lot of boyfriends?'

'Oh no, hardly any,' I say. 'Not real boyfriends.'

'That's good,' he says. 'Not much of a past. And you're from an old English family, right?'

I nod. Well, Mum and Dad are getting on a bit.

'You've not been in the press, made any political statements?'

I laugh. 'Who, me?'

'Attended any rallies?' he persists. 'At college, for example?'

'I just wanted to go round Europe.'

'Interested in culture!' he exclaims, as if he's ticked a box. 'That's good. That's excellent. So, there are no pictures of you out there, say, burning an American flag?'

'Um, no.'

'Or in your underwear? Do any modelling?'

I shake my head. Me, a model?

'I haven't done much, really,' I say apologetically. 'I've just sat around and played video games. And travelled. Until you gave me a chance at the estate agency. But I could,' I say proudly. 'I could be interesting and . . . political. I could go on demonstrations. Against . . . war and things like that.'

Todd shakes his dark head. 'No way. I don't want you to change a thing. I like you, Lucy Evans. I like you just as you are.'

I glow. 'And I like you.' I mean, no doubt about it. It's nice to get compliments, especially when you've been feeling a bit low because your flatmate's dating a Barbie doll.

He smiles. 'Sugar, you're cute. Now tell me, what's important to you in life?'

I think. 'Well, the usual things, I suppose.'

'Like what?'

'Love.'

'Oh, sure. Love. And what else?'

I think. 'Fun.'

'Fun.' He looks pleased. 'I like fun too. Shopping is fun, isn't it? Getting your hair and nails done? That kind of fun.'

'Ah – yes,' I lie. 'And other things. Like games.'

'Tennis? Croquet?'

More like *Doom* and *Tomb Raider*. But for some reason I don't say that.

'I expect you enjoy a game of chess, or perhaps checkers. That's less challenging, right?' Todd nods at me. 'And the ballet, and theatre?'

'Ah, absolutely.'

'And sex,' he says, lowering his voice. 'Sex is important to you?'

'I thought that went with love,' I say.

He chuckles. 'Oh, right. My, but you are sweet. With a little polishing . . .' he gazes at me. 'Anything's possible.'

I shiver, I don't know why.

'You know, Lucy,' Todd says, speaking slowly and in a new, grave tone of voice. I hastily have three big gulps of water to sober up. 'I have big plans.'

'Of course you do,' I say encouragingly.

'In a little while I'll be leaving England. Maybe another six months.'

'Oh.' My face falls. I was just starting to enjoy this.

'And I'll be looking for the right woman to take home with me.' He reaches across the table, takes my hand. 'The one, Lucy. *The* One. My wife. The future Mrs Todd Mayle Junior III.'

I sort of freeze. He actually said it! No more hints. I'm not sure how to react, so I paste a neutral smile onto my face.

'That woman will be my partner for life. She'll dress and move like a lady. She'll be cultured and refined. She'll know how to let a devoted husband spoil her rotten. To accept all the good things I have to give.'

I nod as seriously as I can.

'I plan,' says Todd portentously, 'to run for the US Senate.'

Something seems called for here, so I gasp.

He smiles modestly.

'Yes, Lucy. My bride will be a Senator's wife. And after that perhaps the First Lady of the State of New York. And after *that* . . .' His hand makes a wide circle in the air. 'Who knows?'

'Who indeed?'

'You see, Lucy, it's time. Time for me to choose. To arrive

home with the perfect woman. But this is a choice that can't be rushed.'

'Oh no,' I agree. 'You wouldn't want to do that.'

Quick, have some more water.

'Of course, it's early days,' Todd says. He glances around for the waiter and scribbles in his palm; the waiter gives a little bow. 'But I know you'll be discreet. Around the office. As we move forward on this.' He smiles gently at me. 'Seeing as how you've agreed to give me a chance.'

'But – but Todd,' I say. My head is spinning. 'This is crazy. I mean, you could have anybody.'

'I told you before, I don't want just anybody.' He lifts his champagne flute. 'I can't wait to see what you look like after you've bought a few clothes.'

Ah. Yes. I imagine calling Victoria about *that*. A slow grin spreads across my face.

'You'll hardly recognize me,' I say. And suddenly I'm really looking forward to it!

I wake up thinking that something lovely's happened. And then I remember what it is.

Todd's given me a credit card and *fifteen thousand pounds*, and he wants me to buy clothes!

He actually *wants* me to spend it.

And he wants to woo me.

I lie in my luxurious bed, trying to conjure up a picture of Todd lying next to me. It's a bit difficult to be honest, so I start thinking about the fifteen grand and where I should go. I've got no idea. Obviously I'll get some Manolos and a Prada handbag, or should it be Chanel? And where are those shops anyway?

Oh yes. I get to ask Victoria. It's such a great opportunity to get to know Ollie's fiancée better. Which is, obviously, my *only* motive . . .

'Victoria!'

'Who's this?' she snaps. Obviously my best sweetie-darling voice has cut no ice.

'It's Lucy.'

'Lucy who?'

I grit my teeth. 'You know, Vicky. Ollie's friend.'

'Yaaas,' she admits reluctantly. 'But I don't have time to talk. Goodbye.'

'Oh, what a shame,' I say quickly. 'Todd will be so disappointed.'

'Todd?' she asks instantly.

'Don't worry, you haven't got time.'

'But I can make some,' she purrs. 'For *you*, and darling Todd.'

'I need a little fashion advice.'

'What kind of advice?' Her voice falters. 'On – a wedding dress?'

Huh? Surprising that she'd jump to that conclusion. But I suppose she has weddings on the brain.

'Don't be silly, we've only just had our first date.'

'Oh.' I can hear the relief from here.

'But,' I add, enjoying myself, 'it's something we've discussed. And Todd thinks a girlfriend of his has to dress up to a certain standard . . .'

And an employee, but I don't add that.

'Oh well,' she says pityingly, good humour restored. 'That's not really possible on your salary, is it?'

'I think that's why he's given me fifteen thousand pounds,' I say lightly. 'To spend on clothes. I thought maybe you could give me some advice.'

There's a horrible pause.

'Do you know, Lucy,' she says with a little, tinkling laugh, 'I must be going mad. I thought you said he'd given you fifteen thousand to buy clothes!'

'He did.' I relish the dead air. 'Hopefully that should be enough, but he says I can have more if I need it.'

Give her credit, she rallies immediately.

192

'Well, that's fabulous,' she says. 'Of course I'll come right over.'

I glance around me smugly.

'That's right, you haven't seen the place Todd got me, have you?'

'No,' she says tremulously. 'Is it – is it fabulous?'

'Come and see,' I say, purring just like her.

'I'll be right over.' She hangs up.

I walk proudly round the flat. 'Here's the kitchen – it's rather nice – and this is one of the guest bedrooms . . .'

I don't have to say too much. With an unerring eye she zooms in on every luxury feature. Her gaze sweeps across the recessed lighting, the granite countertops and the flagstone floors. She stares at the flat-screen TV, runs her manicured fingers over the long velvet curtains.

'Very nice,' she says flatly.

'This is just a rental,' I say hastily. 'And he's got much nicer places of his own in America.'

Victoria sighs. 'And he's going out with you?'

I scowl at her.

'I mean, he's going out with you!' she says with a bright, fake smile. 'Isn't that wonderful.'

There's no specific need to answer her, is there? She can think what she wants. I fish the credit card Todd gave me out of my bag.

'Do you have any ideas?'

'Oh, tons, darling,' she says, and suddenly flashes me a friendly grin. 'And it's going to be so much fun. Shall we get a taxi?'

Victoria's not so bad. You know, perhaps I've misjudged her. She certainly knows how to spend money. And she's brilliant on dresses and things like that.

We've gone all over town. She took me to Harrods, and Selfridges, and New Bond Street, everywhere basically. I had no idea shopping could be this much fun. I've bought all these clothes. They didn't look much on the racks, but when I tried them on, they draped in all the right places. Vicky's a style genius, she really is. And I didn't have to carry them. They're going to be delivered to my flat.

'That funny little man of yours can hang them up,' she says.

'Toby.'

'Oh, you use his first name, do you?' she says, arching her brow. 'Well. You're just not used to this yet.'

'Used to what?'

'All this,' she says, giving my arm a friendly squeeze.

And it's true. I'm not.

I never knew life could be like this, actually. Where everybody is nice to you, and very respectful. Everybody calls me 'madam' and gives little bows. I always thought of these shops as really snooty, but they're not, not at all! They can't do enough for you. They bring you chairs and cups of tea, even chilled glasses of champagne. And they really listen to your opinions. Like when I said I thought blue was my colour, the man in that new French boutique L'Attaque totally agreed; he just said that maybe lilac would be even better, or possibly pink or plum.

I've gone through life being all matey and not under-standing my feminine side. At least that's what Victoria says.

'You have to express yourself, darling,' she says. 'You have to get used to being *pampered*.'

'Is it nice?' I ask, feeling a glow of anticipation.

'Oh, being pampered is my specialty,' she says.

And really, wherever we go they treat her like a goddess. They're super-polite to me, but the scraping before Victoria is fantastic. I think it's because she's got so much confidence. I would never complain about anything, especially in places that are this expensive. Some of the prices, you know. It's not like I haven't seen them in *Vogue* but I never really believed them. But apparently there are people who pay thousands of quid for a handbag. Thousands! And don't blink an eye. And although I don't think Victoria's one of them, she acts as if she does it every day. She invariably sends back the first lot of clothes they bring out with a snort.

'Oh, how could you think . . .'

'I'm afraid that's *completely* wrong . . .'

I think it's some kind of a test. Just to let them know she's no sucker. She also complains a lot about the refreshments, telling them that the champagne's not chilled enough, or that it's not vintage ('This is a blend. Surely you don't expect us to drink a blend?'). Or that it's accompanied by the wrong sort of nibbles ('Chocolate truffles? Do you want us to get seriously obese? My friend only eats fresh fruit. Do you have some wild strawberries?'). I would quite like some chocolate truffles, but they're not low-carb, are they? And I know Todd would approve of wild strawberries.

Anyway, Victoria's very imperious. And they don't tell her to sod off at all. They apologize. And promise to try to get what she wants, or do better. Then when we leave, they're all smiles.

By the end of the day, I've bought masses of stuff; dresses, shoes (including two pairs of Manolos, they bloody hurt but they miraculously make me look five pounds slimmer), bags – day and evening – lingerie, tights by Woolford, jackets, the *softest* cashmere coat . . .

'Tea,' Victoria pronounces, slipping her bony arm through mine. Or maybe I should say 'slender'. 'Shall we?'

'I don't know, I'm supposed to be calling Todd. We're having another date tonight,' I say. And, bizarrely, I can hear a note of pride creeping in.

I mean, Victoria is treating me completely differently. She respects me now. As a woman. Instead of being catty, she's sucking up to me.

In fact, everybody's sucking up to me. It's like taking a day off to go and live in an alternative universe. And what can I say? It's enjoyable.

I feel a small rush of gratitude to Todd for this experience. It still feels weird, but nice weird.

Victoria looks at me with her brown eyes wide. 'Oh, but all the more reason to go and have some tea. You must go to the date relaxed and fragrant. Do you feel relaxed?' she asks sternly.

'It is a bit tiring,' I admit.

'We'll go and have everything done,' Victoria says. 'And tea at the same time. I know a fantastic little place.'

'What do you mean, everything?'

'Hair, nails, mani-pedi. It's fantastic, they have four stylists at once blow-drying you, so it only takes fifteen minutes.'

I look a bit doubtful. I hated it the last time she took me for a manicure, though the hair was OK.

'You must,' she says. 'Todd just spent over ten thousand pounds on you, he'll want you to look your most beautiful, won't he? They can even do make-up. Just imagine,' she says temptingly. 'You turn up with your hair all glossy and bouncy, your make-up done, in one of your new outfits.'

'Which one?' I ask eagerly.

'Oh darling, that Matthew Williamson pink thing is divine. Or the Comme des Garçons silk shift dress.'

'Ooh yes,' I agree happily.

'And your nails gleaming,' she goes on. 'And your feet scrubbed and with matching palest pink toenails. You could wear your new Patrick Cox open-toed pumps in the mother-of-pearl sequins, and your Judith Lieber mirrored evening bag.'

I sigh with sheer pleasure. Todd will just flip. And, you know. I wonder what Ollie would say if he saw me. I wonder how I'll compare to Victoria when I'm all dolled up.

OK. That's not right. I didn't mean that, obviously. I give Victoria a guilty smile, but she doesn't notice.

'And while they're doing all this,' Vicky says, closing the deal, 'they give you some lovely tea, black, no sugar so it's calorie-free, and they massage your neck and shoulders.'

'OK.' I try to sound decisive. 'Let's go.'

I think I've misjudged Victoria. Definitely.

I'm sitting up in this amazing luxury salon, all kitted out in gold and white, in an ergonomic chair. I'm swathed in a soft white towelling robe. Vicky's next to me, and we've had our hair done. There are four girls in sort of blue nurses' uniforms standing behind us, combing and spritzing and blasting me with warm and cool hairdryers. It's amazing. Another assistant is bent over my nails, painting them a delicate opalescent pink, and a fifth woman is at my feet, sorting those out. And she doesn't wince at my calluses from running or anything. Although they seemed to think something was called for, so they smothered my hands and feet in a gorgeous-smelling lotion and then massaged them. It was the most amazing feeling ever, *way* better than sex. And then Victoria called for a couple of cups of tea, which arrived in wafer-thin bone china cups with little saucers with roses on them. Normally I would prefer milk and two sugars, and possibly a Kit-Kat, but this is so pleasurable I don't even want one. Not much, anyway.

'Enjoying yourself?' she asks.

'Mmm.' I nod with a blissful smile.

'Well, drink up,' she says. 'When they've finished the blow-drying, the girls will come to do our facials and make-up.'

'Wow,' I say humbly. 'Today really has been incredible. Thank you so much.'

She waves away my thanks with her newly blood-red talons.

'Anything for you,' she says. 'Oh, Lucy, I know we didn't

get off on the right foot, but I think that's just because I didn't know you. Now I understand more of the person you are. And the person you can become,' she says, with an ethereal look on her face.

'What kind of person is that?' I ask, curiously. I want to know what Vicky thinks my potential is.

'Well, you know. As the chosen companion of Todd Mayle you'll have a certain responsibility.'

'Will I?'

'Oh yes. I looked him up on the internet.' Her brown eyes slide towards me again. 'Lucy, do you have any idea just how rich he is?'

'He's told me a few things.'

'It could be as much as . . .' Vicky lowers her voice. *'Five hundred million*. Maybe more.'

The saucer trembles in my hand. 'Five hundred million dollars?' I repeat in a small voice.

'Oh yes.' Victoria sips her tea with an air of refinement. 'And he has ambitions.'

'Todd wants to—' I almost say 'be a politician' but then stop myself. 'Go into public service,' I announce, pleased that at least I know something about my potential boyfriend she hasn't already researched.

'He's a man of destiny,' Victoria nods. 'Lucy, you do understand that *this is your chance.'*

I blink.

'Your chance to get out of your mundane life. To have *influence*, to be a *player.'*

'I don't want to, um, go into public service.'

'As his wife, of course,' Victoria says, annoyed. 'On his arm. His unofficial spokeswoman, reflecting him in public. Hosting charity events. Keeping up a certain social profile. Do you know how many girls would kill for the chance?' and she sighs.

'Todd told me it was a lot,' I agree humbly. 'But he said he just hadn't met the right girl yet.'

'What an opportunity for you,' she hisses, as though the manicurists might eavesdrop and decide to steal Todd away from me. 'You can't let it slip away. You have to hook him. Reel him in.'

'I thought all those fishing lessons with Dad would come in useful,' I joke.

She looks offended. 'This is no laughing matter, Lucy. I hope you never mention *fishing* in front of Todd.'

'Well—'

'Or kickboxing, or disco dancing.'

'I miss dancing,' I say.

She rolls her eyes. 'Or so-called "heavy metal", or five-a-side football, and especially not *computer games*. These things,' she says coolly, 'have no place in Todd's world.'

I nod, trying to show I can be serious. 'You've been an amazing help today. Thanks so much.'

'Oh, don't worry.' She reaches across and gives my hand the faintest touch of pressure. I suppose this counts as a squeeze when your nail varnish is drying. 'I want to be there all the way. Shepherd you through this. Let me tell you, it's hard work.'

'Is that what it's like with Ollie?' I ask.

Victoria shrugs in a bored way. I want to ask her more, but then the facial girls arrive. Our tea things are whisked away and I'm gently leaned back in my seat for yet more beautifying.

Victoria accompanies me back to my apartment. I'm meeting Todd there at seven, and it's twenty to seven now. I have a lovely squirmy feeling in my stomach, all butter-flies.

'I'll come in and help you pick out your outfit,' Victoria says.

'Oh.' I smile at her, but it's a bit close to the time, isn't it? I want to be all alone with Todd. Get his reaction, at least. 'I thought I was going with the Comme des Garçons?'

'There are so many possibilities,' she says. 'We'll pick the best one.'

I feel awfully guilty looking at her bright, chummy smile, I mean, she did give up her entire day to help me shop.

'It'll be the crowning touch.' A wheedling note has entered her voice. 'You trust me, don't you? You do think you look good . . .'

'Oh yes,' I say gratefully. She was so right about that beauty place. The make-up girls are geniuses; I don't look like ordinary, outdoorsy Lucy Evans any more. Instead I have these big mascara-fringed eyes like Bambi's mother, nude lips with a touch of sheen, high, haughty cheekbones, and generally seem all kind of modelly. My blond hair shimmers and bounces as though I could be pouting at a camera and huskily insisting that 'I'm worth it'.

'And anyway,' Victoria adds as though she can read my mind, 'I so want to have a quick drink with Todd before you two go off somewhere fabulous and romantic. I'll get to see the lovebirds at first hand and it'll only take ten minutes.'

'But Todd wants me to be discreet.'

Her brown eyes widen. 'Sweetie, I wouldn't tell a soul. I'm super-discreet. That's my responsibility as a member of the press. I knew the release date of the new Hermès Birkins two months before anybody, and I didn't even tell our accessories editor.'

'Well—'

'It's not for me, you see,' she says nobly. 'It's for Ollie. As his future bride I have to look out for him. He doesn't really like Todd, so it's important that I make overtures. He's got to learn to like him for his own good. Todd mixes in the right circles, places where Ollie doesn't have entrée. Knowing Todd Mayle could do wonders for his career.'

'But they know each other already. Ollie's the one who put me in touch with Todd.'

'That's only business. He has to *know* know him. Socially.

That's how all serious networking is done.' She smiles. 'I know you won't say no; all four of us have to get on if we're going to keep up the friendship.'

I feel guilty. 'Of course,' I say.

'Stop!' Victoria says to the cabbie. We're outside an off-licence, so the guy waits, looking bored, while she dashes in and returns moments later with a large bottle.

'Magnum of vintage Krug,' she says. 'Nineteen ninety, exceptional vintage. I read about it in the *Sunday Times* Style section. Todd Mayle will expect no less.' She glances over at me. 'Don't worry. You look ravishing, and everything's going to be fine.'

She drags me in past a flustered Toby, snapping at him that she hopes all my bags have been unpacked, then ignoring him when he starts to reply. I want to say something, apologize perhaps, but Vicky gives me this thunderous frown and practically drags me into the lift.

'You're far too liberal with the help,' she says curtly.

My dresses and things *have* been unpacked; they're all hanging neatly in my wardrobe. Victoria sniffs to show that I should expect nothing less, even though Toby's not a hotel valet or anything. I resolve to slip downstairs and tip him twenty quid. Make that thirty. Once Todd's left and can't see me. I don't want to risk aggravating him, do I?

Victoria runs her gimlet eye down my staggering array of new outfits and rejects the Comme Des Garçons in favour of an Armani silk shirt dress in robin's-egg blue, teamed with some teetering rose Manolos and my tiny pink quilted Chanel bag.

'I'll just be in the kitchen, getting things ready,' she says. 'And freshening up.'

When I join her there, she's sitting at the table, looking . . . different. Her navy short skirt seems to have got two inches shorter, for a start. And her cream silky shirt has buttons undone, you can actually see a flash of white lace from her bra.

'I think you've missed one,' I tell her kindly.

'Oh no.' She tosses her newly coiffed bob and smiles; her teeth are incredibly white, maybe I need to book in for laser treatment. 'This is all the rage. Underwear as outwear. Have some champers, Lucy,' she adds, popping the cork. There are three crystal flutes on the table, and she expertly fills two of them, tilting them so as not to spill a drop.

'Thanks.' I take a sip as her phone vibrates. She flicks it to her ear and snaps it open in a single movement.

'Victoria Cobham. Yah. Oh hi, Ollie,' she says with a touch of disappointment. 'No, just me and Lucy. Been having a wonderful girlie day out, we're best of friends, aren't we, darling?'

'I'll speak to him,' I say eagerly.

Victoria's handing across the phone when the doorbell goes. She immediately puts it back to her ear.

'Got to go, darling. See you in a bit,' she trills. 'Byee!'

She waves at me to answer the door. 'Go, go,' she says, hanging up on Ollie. Poor Ollie, but I suppose like she says, it's for his own good. Anyway, I can't think about that now, I'm all nervous. I toss my hair like Vicky, and it works much better now; a shimmery shiny curtain of rich-girl blonde.

I open the door and there's Todd. He's sporting a big smile, an expensive suit and a briefcase.

He gasps at the sight of me. Sweet really, except my carefully made-up face is already turning an unflattering shade of tomato.

'Um, hi,' I say brightly. 'Nice to see you!'

'Great dress,' he says huskily. 'It'd look better in a crumpled heap on my floor.'

I smile, although I have actually heard that one before.

'I'm sorry,' he says. 'It's just that you look so damn good.'

'Ah – Todd. There's someone here.'

'What?' he says, scowling hugely. Damn! I *knew* I

202

shouldn't have let Victoria stay. Although I must say, I can't help but be pleased at his reaction. Maybe I do look as good as I'd hoped. Because he's looking really cross.

'Honey, I gave you a bunch of money to buy whatever you want,' he says, reasonably. 'I think a little intimate time is the least I'm entitled to.'

Intimate. That might be nice. A candlelit dinner in my new clothes, looking all beautiful. Some wine, some lovely food—

'If you felt ready,' he says meaningfully, 'I'd love for us to get *better acquainted*.'

Ah. That kind of intimacy. Well . . .

I suddenly feel grateful that Victoria's here.

'Just say hi to her for five minutes,' I plead, in a low, urgent voice. 'And then we can get on to the – intimacy.' At least to talking about it.

'Who is it?' he asks crossly.

'It's Victoria,' I apologize. 'Ollie's fiancée. And she spent the whole day helping me buy things, and she took me to the hair and make-up place and got me a, what do you call it?'

'Mani-pedi?' he suggests, glancing at my hands and toenails.

I nod proudly.

'Well, babe,' Todd drawls, 'it's certainly a good start. She seems clued-in.'

'She works for a major fashion magazine and she's quite senior,' I tell him. 'And she bought you some champagne. It's vintage,' I add hastily.

'OK.' Todd shrugs. 'Just a quick one.' He gives me a sexy grin in case I might have missed the double entendre.

'Come this way,' I say in a slightly louder voice and lead him into the kitchen.

'Todd, I think you've met my good friend Victoria Cobham.' Is she noticing what a gracious hostess I can be?

'Todd,' Victoria says. She's using that annoying kitten-voice I've heard her put on with Ollie, but it doesn't rankle any more. I expect that's just part of the deal and I didn't understand. After all, I'm painting my nails, why shouldn't she change her voice? 'So nice to see you. And what a gesture for darling Lucy. I can tell you,' she says, lowering her voice and fluttering her lashes, 'I was tremendously impressed.'

'It was nothing,' he says.

'Not a lot of men have *real style* any more,' she says. 'Will you have a glass of bubbly?'

He takes it, sips, and gives a tiny nod.

'Krug nineteen ninety,' she says instantly. 'Quite a good year, I'm told.'

Todd sits down on one of the kitchen chairs and stretches out his legs. Thank goodness, his aggravation seems to have melted away.

'You know a lot about wine, Vicky?'

She beams. 'Something,' she says. 'A little, you know. But I'd love to learn more from you some time.'

'I guess it comes in useful at all those parties in Scotland,' Todd says, examining her narrowly.

'Well,' she says. 'Ollie's not as rich as you, of course. But he has a certain position. He has very aristocratic friends. From all over Europe.'

He does? Is she talking about Sven, the drunk Swedish football fan he meets for a pint every couple of months?

'I have to be able to handle the conversation in all those areas,' Victoria says. 'Fine art, wine, grouse shooting . . .'

Grouse shooting?

'It certainly matters,' Todd agrees.

'Oh, the wife of a prominent man has a deep responsibility,' Victoria says sagely. 'She reflects him. She must always be graceful . . .'

I try to stop slouching and perch daintily on the edge of my chair.

'. . . She must have conversation and social skills, and of course know when to be silent.'

'You're so right,' Todd agrees. 'Nothing worse than a yapping wife when the guy's trying to network. Don't you think so, Lucy?'

'I'm taking notes!' I say, with a winning smile. Victoria's finished her champagne now. 'So, thanks, Victoria,' I add, trying to sound final. 'You've been a great help today and I know you have loads to do . . .'

'Not really,' she says. 'I'm all yours.'

I grit my teeth. Social graces, social graces.

'Unfortunately, I don't know if I mentioned it,' I say with heavy emphasis, 'but Todd and I are off out on a *romantic evening*, so hopefully we'll see you again next time.'

'Oh.' Victoria rises, with a tiny pout at Todd. 'Of course I wouldn't want to detain you two lovebirds for a second. What a lucky girl you are, Lucy!'

'Mmm,' I say. 'And so are you, Ollie's fantastic.'

'We should do a double date some time,' she says, eyes wide as though this thought has just occurred to her. 'Go out for dinner.'

'Sure,' Todd says, nodding. 'You fix that up with Lucy.'

And suddenly I don't mind, I actually feel happy. Me and Todd, Victoria and Ollie. Dating as couples. Him showing me off. That's a proper social life. I mean, I do understand about discretion . . .

Only maybe I don't *totally* understand, because why wouldn't you want people to know you were going out with someone. It's not illegal, is it? I expect he has his reasons, though. Something to do with business and office jealousy, wasn't it?

But anyway, this is different.

'That sounds great,' I enthuse. 'Thanks so much, Victoria. We should see more of each other.'

'Oh, don't worry, darling,' she says, getting up and giving me sixteen air kisses, eight on each cheek. 'We definitely will.'

* * *

After all that the date's, well, a tiny bit anti-climactic. Todd whisks me away to a fantastic restaurant, and we get all the bowing and scraping.

'You look hot now,' he says, nodding firmly.

Which is nice. I've never looked this good in my entire life.

And for most of the evening he sort of runs over what we talked about last time. Which is totally fascinating, it's just that it feels kind of déjà vu.

But I'm not going to complain. How could I? He's been so kind. And generous. I knew he was generous – but all that money, just for clothes! It's a fantasy, isn't it?

'What did you think of Victoria?' I ask towards the end of the night. Desperate for a new subject, I suppose.

Todd considers; he tilts his head to one side.

'Seems to know her stuff,' he says. 'Known her long?'

'A few months.' I lean forward confidingly. 'I didn't really get on with her at first, I thought she was the wrong person for—'

'What's her family?'

'I don't know anything about the Cobhams. No, actually, I do.' I think of Dad. 'Apparently her father's not very nice.'

'Low class, huh,' he says, sounding disappointed.

'No, not like that.' I'm getting confused. 'What's low class got to do with it?'

'Nothing.' He gives me a flash of those brilliant white teeth, smiling, his charisma beaming across the table, and I feel weak at the knees again. 'Go ahead, tell me.'

'Well, he's a property developer.'

'Rich?'

'Loaded,' I say. 'But my dad said maybe he got that way through bribing local politicians. He couldn't prove anything, but he thought it could be a pattern.'

'Your pop's naïve,' Todd says with a touch of scorn. 'That's just the price of doing business. That's how things work in the real world.'

I stiffen. 'My dad is *not* naïve.'

Todd looks mildly surprised. 'Relax, sugar, I meant it as a compliment.' Did he? 'When you know a bit more about commerce, you'll understand.' He winks at me. 'What am I saying? That's not exactly something you need to worry about, is it?'

'But I want to,' I say. 'I've got a – a passion for commerce.'

'Really?' He grins lazily at me.

I guess not. Not really. I feel a bit deflated. I don't care about 'commerce', same way as I don't care about politics. I can't see myself as a female Richard Branson exactly. And I wish I found renting out enormous flats a bit more interesting. It's Todd's work, after all.

But I do want to do something. Have a career. It seems to matter, a lot.

'I might like to run a small business,' I find myself saying.

'But Lucy.' He's looking at me with amusement. 'You've never had any experience, honey. Before you came to work for me, weren't you doing some crazy kind of job? Writing for a home-shopping magazine or something?'

'Computer games,' I mutter.

Todd chuckles. 'Well, that's hardly going to give Bill Gates a run for his money.'

'What if I don't want to do that, though?' I protest. But only mildly. He's still my boss. 'What if I just want to run a little business, and make a bit of money, look after myself?'

'Oh. That.' He shrugs. 'It depends, I guess. If your man's rich, what would be the point?'

I sigh.

'Marie Antoinette, the Queen of France—'

'I know who she is.'

'The one who said "let them eat cake",' he continues, ignoring me, 'she wanted to "work" too. She dressed up as a shepherdess, only the fact is she was a queen living in an enormous palace.' He gives me that sincere newscaster look. 'People were offended, Lucy. If you're one of the select few, why play around? Maybe somebody else could get the profit from that small business.' He winks at me. 'I'm making a leap here that it would be profitable. But just for the sake of the argument. Do you want to be that selfish?'

I shake my head and take a big gulp of my wine.

'Moderation,' he suggests gently. 'You know what the commercials say. "Please enjoy this wine responsibly." It's never too early to start setting an example.'

For some reason I feel a bit weepy. Maybe I have had too much.

'Listen, baby.' Todd's melted-honey voice pours over me. 'I don't want you worried about anything.' His manicured hand presses on mine. 'You want to work? There will always be a place for you in my organizations. Now, and . . . whatever happens.' He gives me a brilliant smile. 'As of Monday, you're back behind a desk, right? I'll bet you'll soon be wishing you were shopping with Victoria.'

I have to admit that is possible.

'Anyway, enough talk about boring business.' He sees a passing waiter and signals for the check. 'I think it's time to go home. Check out the hot bod under that sexy dress.'

'Todd,' I say. 'I – I just don't think I'm ready,'

He stares at me for a second, then recovers.

'I see.'

'I mean, this is only our second date.'

'Yeah,' he says. 'You're right. Only the second date.' He lifts his wine glass and toasts me. 'I keep forgetting you're an old-fashioned girl.'

I am?

'I'm glad you're not angry.'

'Why on earth would I be angry? Buying a few clothes isn't the same as buying you,' he says smoothly. 'You'll be ready in your own time. I think it's cute.'

'OK.' A wall of tension seeps slowly out of me. I breathe out. 'OK.'

Todd notices my expression.

'Relax,' he says. 'I'm prepared to take it slow. As long as you're still interested in giving me a chance?'

'Oh, yes,' I say, smiling thankfully at him. 'I am.'

11

I try to be happy for the next few weeks. It's a new time in my life. I see Todd about three nights a week, though during the day he keeps away from me. He's making a serious effort. We go to dinner a lot, sometimes the theatre. I don't really like experimental stuff, but apparently musicals are not his thing. Still, a date's a date, isn't it? And at least when he takes me to the opera (yawn) it's an opportunity to dress up. People look at me. Men, specifically. And it's flattering, even though most of them are in their fifties.

I'm living in the lap of luxury, every day I swan into work dressed immaculately. Jade, Buffy and Melissa are a bit nicer to me, but James still sneers.

And that's it. I answer the phones. I look gorgeous. I have a fake receptionist voice when clients come in. Now I'm actually dating Todd, there are no more trips together outside the office in work hours. It's one long spiral of tedium from eight to five, with no breaks.

I spend all day thinking of Todd and how I'm going to play the date that night. He comes in and out, he never so much as glances at me. So I try not to show it. Even though we're still not having sex, it sort of seems irrelevant. He's not pushing it. And in the plus column, he's so glamorous and capable, and everybody speaks about him in hushed tones. The three other girls clearly adore him.

Buffy most of all, I think. Since he stopped taking me out

during the day, and I've just sat here, she's really unbent. She obviously thinks Todd's a superstar, although she's got this kind of American good-girl reserve. I don't think she's ever watched an episode of *Sex and the City*. They aren't matey like we are, are they? American girls, real ones I mean. And they don't hang out with men. I think that's the biggest difference, in America. Men and women don't seem to be friends. Not like me and Ollie.

Oh. Wait. That's right; I wasn't meant to be big mates with Ollie. Victoria's explained it all, only not in such a snide way as before. She actually apologized for what she said to me over lunch. She's being very sweet, she comes round a couple of times a week and takes me to some chic coffee place or Moroccan bistro or tapas bar. She's trying to teach me how to live in Todd's world.

'It's different when it's couples, of course,' she said and took a sip of her iced water.

We were sitting in Café des Palmes, apparently the hippest new place in Hampstead. They serve fresh berries mixed with crushed ice, which is low-carb but refreshing. Although sometimes berries don't really do it for me, if I'm honest. I'd like to cheat and have ice cream. Vanilla, maybe with hot chocolate sauce . . .

'Don't you think?' she asked, interrupting my reverie.

'Oh. Absolutely,' I said guiltily.

'I mean you never can be *quite* sure the single girl doesn't have designs on your man.' Victoria tossed her smooth, dark hair, which she's been growing longer, she says. I think it must grow quite slowly because it looks exactly the same to me.

'But when you're part of a couple, everything's different. You can trust other women with partners. You know they're no threat.' She smiled. 'It's fantastic that the four of us can hang out together.'

Well, yes, except Ollie was never there. We tried really hard to set up dinner with him but it never seemed to work out. His diary! I mean, he must have more appointments than a top LA plastic surgeon. All this time, and he just hasn't been around.

Victoria has, though. She's been there all the time, and she often hangs out with Todd and me, if Ollie's busy. I'm glad about it, it makes everything so much more fun. Having somebody else there who doesn't really mind if he talks about the US Senate. Sometimes trying to be the perfect girlfriend is really hard work but Victoria finds everything he does totally cool. I can sit back and let her gush on my behalf. Even with the new outfit and facials and everything, she's just better at this than I am.

I would never admit it, but I still don't like heels. Or tights. Or uncomfortable scratchy lingerie.

In fact, I'm wearing one of my new best scratchy underwear combos tonight. Todd booked the restaurant, it's a hip new place in Notting Hill called the Fried Ferret. It looks dead trendy. The décor combines English country brasses and horseshoes with chrome and pink leather seats. All the staff wear these amazing cool uniforms, black trousers and white shirts with a big Union Jack flag sewn on the front.

'It's very *now*, very Jamie Oliver,' Todd remarks as we're shown to our table.

Victoria beams at him. 'You choose the greatest places, Todd. Isn't it cool, darling?' She squeezes Ollie's arm possessively.

'Very interesting,' he says neutrally, in a tone that means he thinks it's total shit but can't bring himself to be rude.

'It sure is,' says Vicky. American-style. She does that sometimes when Todd's around. It must be subconscious.

'Take a seat and your waiter will be right over,' says the hostess, melting away.

We all sit down, a bit stiffly. Todd and Victoria face each other, so do Ollie and I.

'Well,' Victoria says brightly. 'Isn't this nice!'

Ollie stares at the table, and I take refuge in a sip of water.

It is nice. Or at least it should be. Ollie's here and I haven't seen him for ages. But he looks so uncomfortable. About as uncomfortable as I feel.

It's not just the underwear (cappuccino lace thong and demi-cup bra). Or the three and a half inch heels. I just feel totally embarrassed all of a sudden. The easy time I have with Victoria has kind of evaporated.

Maybe it's the clothes. I'm wearing a sedate yet sensual Emporio Armani dress in pale grey silk covered with yellow butterflies, and my dandelion-leather strappy Manolos. My eyebrows arch, my nails are all painted in Chanel Rouge Argent, and I went off and had my make-up done professionally. But I'm a bit bloody sedate compared to Victoria. She's put on this eye-popping dress, a tight, sparkling sheath of dark red sequins. It stops just below the knee and it must have some kind of built-in Wonderbra, because her boobs are spilling luxuriantly out of the top of it like Nell Gwyn about to flog an orange to Charles II. Her hair's swept up, and she has these amazing, sexy earrings – dangly crystals. Meanwhile, her waist is just as tiny as ever.

Todd can't take his eyes off her boobs. And I don't get cross about it, because I can't, either. Her boobs! You can't stop looking. She's a bit Pam Anderson, *before* the reduction. In fact, with her talons and lips a glossy rose-red, and a contrasting, fabulous sixties-style white bag covered in tiny sea shells, she basically looks like she stepped out of *Dallas*.

Compared to her, my tasteful silk outfit is as exciting as a small grey moth beside a Monarch butterfly. I'm seeing her in a whole new light. No wonder Ollie proposed. If I were a bloke, I would, too.

Todd clears his throat.

'You're looking great tonight, Vicky,' he says.

She laughs her tinkling little laugh. 'Oh, thanks, Todd. I always have to dress up when my darling Ollie's about. A girl has to be on top form to keep a man like him.' She leans over and kisses Ollie loudly on the cheek; a real smacker. 'And Lucy looks fabulously sexy too,' she adds, which makes me feel even more invisible.

I wonder. Are those her real boobs? She was always tiny. Could you even *get* that effect from a Wonderbra? There were those five days last week when she wasn't around. What if she found some clinic and popped in so she could pop out?

'I wanted to look good for the wedding,' she says, since nobody else has made another comment.

'I said I liked you how you were.' Ollie's voice, from out of nowhere. He's looking at her strangely, and I feel a little, tiny flip in my stomach. Like butterflies. Or one butterfly anyway.

Must be because I haven't seen him for ages. That's all it is.

'I know you did, honey.' She kisses him again, trails her fingers up and down the sleeve of his jacket. 'But that's you, you'd never ask for anything. I had to take the initiative.'

She beams and turns her eyes to Todd's.

'You know, when a man's getting married he's making a commitment.'

Todd nods seriously as though this is a new insight. He even manages to lift his eyes from her cleavage, if only momentarily.

'Well, just think about what that means.' Victoria turns to me. 'Your man can only have sex with one person, *ever*, for the rest of his life.'

Both Todd and Ollie look alarmed. Humph! Boys!

'I think the least that person can do is be as *sexy* as she can possibly be,' Victoria says, breathily. 'That's the duty of the wife. To be lean yet curvy, and try new things . . .'

Ollie's staring at her. There's that flip again, that little butterfly. Why? Why butterfly?

I've got a horrid feeling that I'm *jealous*.

And that doesn't make sense. I mean, I'm coupled-up. Why would I care?

'I'm all in favour of plastic surgery,' Victoria says. 'Well,' and she smooths the glittering sequins down around her boobs, 'I suppose you can see that for yourselves!' and she laughs.

'Victoria,' Ollie says. He sounds angry.

'What?' she asks, eyelashes fluttering with exaggerated innocence. 'I'm not ashamed of my body.'

'It's not about being ashamed,' he says quietly. I glance at Vicky to see if she recognizes the warning signal. 'It's about some things being private between a man and his wife.'

'Oh, darling.' She's instantly humble. 'I'm sorry if I let out my tiny little secret. But, you know, this is just talk. Everything I have is for your touch only.'

Ollie purses his lips and beckons to a waiter, and Victoria's forced to shut up as we get the drinks in. Todd orders us all champagne, but Ollie insists he'll have a Scotch. And nobody dares to argue.

I want to say something. Anything, really. Put Ollie at his ease. Now he's here, I find I've really missed him.

Yes, that must be the reason for the butterflies. Missing my best mate.

'So.' I try for natural but my voice is coming out all fake hearty. 'How are the wedding plans going, Ol?'

'Actually, I was hoping they'd be a bit more low key,' Ollie says. He doesn't meet my gaze, but he adds, 'Maybe you can talk Victoria into it.'

'Low key?' Victoria's eyes are wide. 'Ollie, you are sweet.'

'You might have influence.' Ollie looks straight at me now. 'You two have become close friends. Right?'

My throat's gone dry. 'Right.' I try for an enthusiastic nod.

'Is low key your style, Victoria?' Todd says.

'Darling, what do you think?' Victoria laughs in a way that thrusts her new and huge bosoms towards Ollie, and I'm gripped with the desire to push them away. 'Ollie has a certain position to keep up. A wife can be an asset, and that starts with the right wedding. It's going to be a wonderful affair.'

'Family and friends on the Isle of Skye would be a wonderful affair.'

'Oh, Ollie, always with that dour Scots style,' Victoria says. 'You know we've discussed image and your career. You need to make a splash to advance in this world.'

'The right sort of splash,' Todd says.

'Absolutely.' Victoria nods. 'Everything for this wedding's going to be perfect. The ideal mix of traditional and modern, and of course the *right* suppliers.'

'By which she doesn't mean the cheapest,' Ollie says drily.

Victoria shrugs. 'There are many top-rated cake designers,' she says importantly. 'But only one's *right* this year. This year, it's Kate Appleton.'

'I've heard of her,' says Todd.

'With my position on *Stylish* I'm uniquely situated to know which artiste is the *right* one in every area of the wedding.' She sounds scarily efficient. 'All the obvious stuff like florists, bridesmaid's designers, marquee décor, and the lesser known areas too. Who did the candles for Lady Davina Windsor? Where does the Marquis of Lothlothian go when he hires a bagpiper? No detail is too small,' she says. 'Everything from the grosgrain ribbon on the invitations to the rose-petal confetti and live white doves comes under *my* supervision.'

'Very impressive,' Todd says.

'And *Stylish* will do a feature on the bash.'

'No they won't,' says Ollie.

Victoria turns and stares at him. 'But darling, we agreed—'

'We didn't agree.' Ollie's tone's quite calm, but it's also implacable. 'No press at my wedding.'

Victoria's cheeks turn a bit pinkish, but she swallows hard.

'Whatever you say, sweetheart,' she coos. 'The big strong men must have it all their own way, mustn't they, Lucy?'

'Oh. Yes,' I mutter.

Thank God, the drinks are here. We order the food. I get a salad with shrimp, and Ollie looks at me, properly looks at me, almost for the first time this evening.

'Enough about us,' he says. But as he does, Victoria links her arm through his. I feel that unpleasant squirming again.

I look at Todd, to reassure myself. Yes, he's still way more handsome than Ollie. And that's what counts! I slip my hand through his arm and give him a friendly squeeze; but he's a bit stiff.

'What about you two?' Ollie's eyes flicker over me and it hurts. They're so . . . muted. Impassive, almost. It's like he doesn't miss me at all, I think with a pang. As if all those years of friendship can just be wiped out. Like that. 'How are you getting along?'

Todd smiles. 'Just fine. Lucy's a terrific little lady.'

'Oh yes,' I find myself saying, and my voice has gone strangely high-pitched. 'We're becoming *extremely* close. Todd has taught me so many new things.'

'Yes,' Ollie says coolly. 'I can see that.'

'This dress, for example,' I bluster on, determined to impress him. 'It cost over five hundred quid. A gift from Todd. Like the shoes. They're Manolo Blahniks. New ones, not even bought second-hand on eBay. And I have six pairs!'

Todd looks smug. But Ollie says nothing, which goads me into further comment.

'Actually, he can't stop spoiling me,' I say. 'You've never seen my amazing flat. And I get my hair and nails done three times a week. And everything in my wardrobe matches.'

'You're certainly different from when you first showed up,' Todd says indulgently.

'These days I never *touch* champagne unless it's vintage,' I say. 'I can't stand that blended swill.' And I toss my hair, which is long and thick, something Victoria can't do as she's wearing hers up.

'I agree,' Ollie says evenly. 'You are different.'

'Yes, well.' I snuggle up closer to Todd and kiss him lightly on the cheek. 'You started me on this path, Ollie. You showed me how I had to change. And of course you introduced me to Todd, and for that I'll be forever grateful.'

'So,' he says, sounding strained. 'Are there any sounds of wedding bells?'

I glance at Todd.

'Oh, we aren't even thinking in those terms yet, are we, sweetie?' I ask. 'We're just ... enjoying each other's company.'

Todd smirks. 'I'm certainly *enjoying* yours,' he says with heavy emphasis and splays his fingers over my ribcage.

That should be sexy. I don't know why I don't like it. But it certainly doesn't increase my desire to go to bed with him.

'Yes. It's great being in a couple!' I say. 'Todd's a real boyfriend. He treats me like a lady. He's nothing like those losers I used to hang out with.'

'That's exactly how I feel about Ollie,' Victoria says. 'Isn't love wonderful?'

I try for a smug grin. 'Mmm.'

The waiters arrive with our food. I don't seem to have much of an appetite. Todd's enjoying his steak, chewing it the regulation thirty times; he told me this aids the digestion. He also drinks extract of parsley, for all the red meat. He's very health conscious!

Victoria, like me, toys with her lettuce leaves; and Ollie

piles into his food as though he were a starving dog. OK, I suppose he hasn't exactly been pining to see me.

'Isn't this fabulous?' Victoria says. 'We must all hang out more often.'

'Sure.' Todd nods at her.

'Actually, I think that'll have to wait,' Ollie says, swallowing a mouthful of cod and chips. 'I'm very busy at the moment. Run-up to the wedding and everything.'

I don't want to let my disappointment show so I cover it with a huge gulp of mineral water. Obviously he doesn't care about seeing me. Obviously he—

'But you must have Lucy over,' says Victoria, almost as if she can read my thoughts. 'You haven't seen her for ages.'

Ollie gives me a brisk, impersonal smile. I hate it. It's the kind of smile he probably uses on his divorcing clients.

'I'm seeing her now,' he says. 'And like I said, I'm very busy. I'm sure it's the same for her.'

'Oh yes,' I agree, my face feeling strangely hot. 'I'm rushed off my feet. At work.'

'Honey,' says Todd, smiling in an amused way. He sort of waggles his head from side to side. 'What are you talking about? We don't exactly work her fingers to the bone at Mayle Accommodations,' he reports to the table. 'She basically sits at her desk and shows people in.'

'That's not fair!' I say hotly.

'No, that's right, you also answer the phone.' He chuckles, that deep, sexy chuckle, and Victoria joins in.

'Don't worry, baby,' Todd says. He slides his manicured, tanned hand over mine. 'I'm just teasing.'

I sit there fuming. But then I realise that, to tell the truth, he's right. That is all I do. And it's as boring as hell.

'I'd never allow a girl of mine to work her butt off,' he says. 'I can provide for her. What the hell would be the point?' Todd squeezes my hand. 'You're too precious to exhaust with that stuff.'

But I'm still embarrassed. My gaze slides towards Ollie.

Ollie doesn't meet my eyes. He's gone back to his chips, as if he's really bored.

Oh dear. I've got a lump in my throat, suddenly. I was so looking forward to this, and it's just going horribly wrong.

'You know,' I say, struggling not to sound weepy, 'I feel a bit funny. I think one of the shrimps might have been off.'

'Off? This is one of the top restaurants in London,' Todd says huffily.

'I know and it's fantastic,' I lie, as a Union-Jack emblazoned waiter sweeps past us carrying a tray of hors d'oeuvres. 'But I think I just need a lie-down.'

Todd shrugs. 'Sure, babe, head on home. I'll be back soon.'

Victoria smiles, gets to her feet, and hugs me; I'm enveloped in the soft silicone of her new barrage-balloon boobs.

'Take care, sweetie, get your beauty sleep,' she says. 'Talk soon. Chin chin.'

'Chin chin,' I mutter. 'Um, bye, Ollie.'

He doesn't look up. 'See ya,' he says.

I turn round quickly and head for the doors, a fat tear brimming out of one eye and trickling down my cheek. I brush it away and stumble outside. Thank God, there's a taxi. I quickly flag it down, and it stops right away; all the taxis stop for me since Victoria selected my new clothes.

'Where to, love?' asks the driver, pretending not to notice my red eyes.

I'm about to say 'Knightsbridge' but something stops me. Maybe the thought of Todd, full of champagne, maybe horny. I get a dreadful feeling his patience might be about to run out.

And there's just no way I want to sleep with him.

Isn't that dreadful. I don't even want to have sex with my own boyfriend.

'Earl's Court,' I hear myself say. 'Kingston Street.'

I need to see Catherine. I just hope she's in.

* * *

She is. The lights are on, and she opens the door and looks all shocked to see me crying.

'Lucy! What's the matter?' She pulls me inside.

'Sorry to dump on you like this,' I sob. 'Do you have, you know, company or anything?'

She looks apologetic. 'Actually, I do.'

'Oh.' My heart sinks into my boots again. 'Well, not to worry, I'll just go home.'

'Don't be daft.' Catherine pulls me upstairs. And there, sitting on her sofa, is – Peter!

Peter. He's back! I look over at Cathy.

'Peter, you know my sister Lucy,' she says smoothly.

'Hi, Luce.' He waves at me.

I glare back at him. Fuck you, aren't you the guy that dumped my lovely sister for some flash broad from New York?

'She's taking the spare room. And you're going home,' Catherine says firmly. 'Sorry, but we need a bit of a girlie heart-to-heart.'

'Oh. Yah. Right,' says Peter, standing and looking a bit awkward. I don't say anything as he grabs his coat and shuffles off. Good, I hope he gets run over leaving the flat.

'So, sit,' she says as soon as the door shuts. 'Have some tea or something. You look awful. What happened?'

'It's my boyfriend. It's Ollie,' I blurt out.

Catherine raises her eyebrows. 'Ollie's your boyfriend now?'

'No. No, it was just – we were having dinner, the four of us—'

'Ollie and Annoying Victoria came too?'

'She's not annoying any more.' I sniff. 'She's actually OK when you get to know her.'

Catherine looks sceptical.

'Anyway, I was looking forward to seeing Ollie again and he was a real bastard,' I say.

222

'How do you mean?'

'He was just all silent. And he said he was too busy to see me. He only talked about the wedding and Victoria. The only thing he said to me was could I talk Victoria into a small reception,' I wail. 'It's like he didn't even care. He barely even glanced at me.' Catherine hands me a Kleenex and I blow loudly. 'I think it's because Victoria got her boobs done. They're really huge. I expect all he thinks about is Victoria and her new boobs.'

Catherine struggles not to smile. I can actually see her biting her lip.

'I suppose it was a bit funny,' I admit. 'Todd was staring at them too. Come to that, so was I.'

'Want some tea?' Catherine asks. She goes into the kitchen and puts the kettle on without waiting for a reply. In our family we always drink tea, even when we don't particularly want any. And it is a bit comforting.

'You do know,' she says from the kitchen, 'that you still fancy Ollie, right?'

'What?'

'You heard me.' She potters about as if she'd just said something *normal*, instead of totally mad.

'Of course I don't fancy Ollie,' I say scornfully. 'I'm with Todd. And he's way more handsome.'

'He might be, but you still fancy Ollie,' she says relentlessly. 'Otherwise you wouldn't care so much. It's not like you haven't lost touch with friends before. What about those guys you used to work with on *PC Games Galaxy*? Ever speak to them?'

'Never,' I admit.

'And you don't give a monkey's, do you?'

She returns with the tea and a McVities chocolate digestive. Bonus!

'S'pose not,' I concede.

'No, you care about Ollie because you *fancy* him. And that's fatal. Always has been. You can't care properly about two people at the same time.' She sips her own Earl Grey. 'I take it you do care about Todd?'

'Of course!' I say defensively.

'And he makes you happy?'

I nod.

'Well, then.' Cathy shrugs. 'You won't like me saying this, but I think you should forget about Ollie. His fiancée's your friend now. And you want to be with Todd – if you're *sure* about that.'

'But Ollie was different. OK, I don't keep up with all my mates, but he was my absolute *best* mate.' I plead with her to understand. 'I – I like Victoria, but she's so new, and with Ollie I was so comfortable . . .'

'You don't look comfortable now.'

'It's the heels.'

Cathy mulls it over. 'All right then, go and see him. Get what the Yanks call "closure". Just talk to him, wish him well. Maybe then you can forget about him.'

'OK.' I suddenly feel a lot more cheerful. Go and see Ol. Brilliant idea. I need to be alone with him. Then everything will be like it used to, no awkwardness. I've no intention of breaking up our friendship, just getting it back. But I don't need to tell Catherine that.

'So, Peter,' I say sternly. My turn to issue unwelcome advice. Hooray. 'What was that toad doing in your flat?'

'He's not a toad.'

'Cockroach? Woodlouse? Fat, hairy spider?'

'We're back together,' Cathy says.

I sigh. 'Based on what, Catherine?'

'He apologized.'

'Well, whoop-de-do.'

'Not just that. He dumped Esther. And he told me he was wrong to say those things about marriage, and that he really wanted to be faithful to me. And that Esther was just a fling because he was panicking.' She glances shyly at me. 'He said, you know. He kind of asked me to marry him. Properly.'

'And what did you say?' I demand.

'I told him he'll have to wait a year and then ask me again. I'll see if I feel like it.' She grins. 'Peter told me he'd wait for ever if he had to.'

'Well . . .' I try to think of something else stern to say, but that all seems quite sensible. 'In that case, congratulations.'

I go over and give her a hug. And then properly start crying.

We stay up till late, talking. Cathy promises she'll actually make him wait. 'He needs to prove himself,' she says. But her eyes shine so much when she talks about him that I wonder if she'll be able to hold out.

I do have a great excuse for crying. I mean, obviously I'm happy all my sisters are in love and getting married. That's life, isn't it? You don't just hang out at your parents' for ever.

But at the same time there's this big hole. It's partly that things will never be the same. Catherine is my favourite sister, we've always been the closest. And now I'll have to share her with Peter, like I'll have to share Emily with George. Whenever they come home to Kent, and eat Mum's half-cooked sausage rolls, the husbands will be there as well. We'll never be the girls again. We'll never be just our gang.

All of a sudden, all those in-law jokes make sense to me. Who wants in-laws? They just get in the way.

There's something else, though. Same way I felt about Emily. I want this for myself, this lovely feeling she has. *I* want to be cherished. *I* want to get married!

I suppose I owe it to myself to make a decision about Todd.

I crash at Cathy's place, shower and borrow a dress from her for work. Then I rush home. There's a message on the answer machine from Todd.

'Babes, sorry, can't make it back for a drink tonight. Get better and I'll see you in the morning.'

Yay! Result! He won't be cross I ducked out on him – doesn't even know. I grab my bag and head for the tube. I need to see Ollie. And I need to talk to Todd.

Things are going to be different around here.

Todd's already left for the day when I get in. Thank goodness. He's the second part of my plan, you see. Talk seriously to Todd. Stop mucking about. If he's really going to be my boyfriend, I have to start making plans. Think about the future. And even today, I'm just not sure.

We need to talk.

But he's second on the list. First is to see Ollie. And get him to be mates with me again. If Victoria can do it, why not him?

I look round the office casually. James is hung up on the phone as usual, shielding his face with his hands so nobody can hear what he's saying. Really, like we give a shit. James has problems. Nobody should be that hostile. Jade's on her way out, Melissa, on the appointment with Todd. It's just me and Buffy, who is sitting staring at her screen, looking miserable.

I feel a quick stab of guilt. I haven't exactly followed up with Buffy. We were starting to get friendly there for a bit, and then Todd asked me out, and what with all the clothes shopping I sort of forgot about her.

I offer James some coffee. He accepts. Surprise. I think he loves it when I have to suck up to him. But at least it gives me an excuse to go over to Buffy.

'Coffee?'

'Thanks,' she says glumly. 'Though I shouldn't, because it stains your teeth.'

'But you've got to have some pleasures,' I say, trying to cheer her up.

'I guess.' She sighs. 'Do me a favour, Lucy, never fall in love.'

'You've had a bad time?' I ask sympathetically. 'Who's the guy?'

'I don't want to talk about it.'

I nod respectfully.

'But he's a cheating bastard,' she says. 'And a bully. And the sick thing is, I still care about him. Even when I *see* him with this other woman. He thinks I don't know what's going on, but I do. Everybody does.' She gives me a bitter little smile. 'Not like she's unique. He fucks everything that moves and acts like the world owes it to him.'

I fiddle with my coffee spoon in horror. 'But why do you still fancy him?'

'No idea,' she says. 'My head's smart but my heart's dumb. That's about the size of it, I think.'

'Maybe you should see other men. Try to forget about him. You won't be able to meet anybody new until you sweep this man out of your life.' Wow, I sound almost sage. I'm impressing myself. 'He's dead wood,' I pronounce. 'Human garbage. Get rid of him. Recycle him.'

She gives me a small smile. 'Hey, I like that. Recycle him!'

'This other girl's got your recycling,' I say. 'Your cast-off. It's not like he won't break her heart too, is it?'

'No. She'll suffer,' says Buffy, with satisfaction. 'Thanks, Lucy. You're pretty cool, for a stuck-up European.'

'And you're not totally moronic, even though you are a seppo.'

'Seppo?' she asks.

'Septic tank, Yank,' I say, and feel a little thrill of rebellion. That's the kind of remark I'm not supposed to make any more. But Todd's not here, so what's the harm?

'We should go out,' she says. 'How are you fixed tonight?'

'Can't tonight.' It's my big date with Todd, although he doesn't know it yet. 'But tomorrow? Right after work?'

'Sounds good.'

I grin. It'll be nice to have another girlfriend, other than Victoria. The more the merrier, eh? Look at what you find out when you start to talk to people, even scary Americans with perfect teeth, Alice bands and anchor-woman hair.

'Listen, Buffy.' I feel a bit bad having to ask her for a favour right away, but I don't have any choice; James would hardly let me go out. 'D'you think I could take an extended lunch break? I want to meet an old friend of mine for lunch. It's kind of a surprise.'

'No problem. I'll take the calls.' She shrugs. 'Not like any gorgeous men have asked me away for lunch anyway.'

'Thanks,' I say.

I hustle back to my desk and call Ollie at work with my hand over my mouth. Even if James suspects something he won't be able to prove it, will he? Two can play that game.

'Hamilton Burns,' says the receptionist's cool voice. She does it better than me.

'Can I speak to Oliver McCleod, please? This is Lucy Evans from Mayle Accommodations.'

'Hold on,' she says. There's a long pause and for one horrible moment I fear he won't pick up. But then his voice comes on, distant and cold.

'Yes, Lucy,' he says, as though it's a terrible imposition to call him.

I refuse to be deterred. 'Ollie, I need to see you.'

'I told you, I'm very busy.'

'You're not too busy to see one of your best friends,' I insist.

He says, 'Is that what you are?'

Ouch. I *knew* there was something wrong.

'Ollie, don't be pathetic!' I say crossly, although really I'm a bit frightened. 'I'm coming over there for lunch and you'd better not pretend to have a meeting or something.'

He waits for a second, then says, 'All right.' I can almost

see his shoulders hunching up in that shrug he does. 'Be here at twelve forty-five, and I've only got an hour.'

'Fine.' I'm triumphant. 'I'll see you then.'

Only got an hour, eh?

Well. No problem. I can be resourceful. Months of sitting at a desk and saying not much besides 'Good morning, Mayle Accommodations' and 'Putting you through now, sir' hasn't *totally* fried my brain.

I'm not letting him get away with it. I'm not letting him brush aside our friendship as though it never happened. Of course, my life is so much better now. I have a fantastic wardrobe, money in the bank, a luxury flat and a rich boyfriend.

But I miss Ollie.

Victoria's great, of course. Don't get me wrong. It's just that she's not quite the same. And lately, a few things have been sticking in my mind. Like, would it be so very dreadful if I occasionally watched a rugby match on Sky Sports?

Only when Todd's not there, of course.

I wouldn't be sliding back to my old ways. Not likely. I love manicures. And I'm going to learn to love heels and tights if it bloody kills me.

I mean, if it kills me.

No swearing.

But somehow this lunch with Ollie, just the two of us, seems the most important thing that's happened to me in months. Since I moved out of his flat. Obviously that means I have things out of proportion, because in those months I've got my new job, my radical makeover, a cool man taking me out.

I'm not thinking about that, though. Too much analysis. It's driving me mental. I just want my mate back and like Todd says, I don't need to make 'a Federal case' out of it.

I duck into M&S and head for the food department. Actually, when I did live with Ollie, this was always a fantasy of mine. Imagine having so much cash you could afford to buy your lunch at M&S! They have little plastic boxes of white-flesh cherries that are four quid each, for example.

Four quid. Each!

But that's nothing to me these days, I think triumphantly. In fact, I could buy everything in the store and not think twice about it!

I get some fancy sandwiches I know he'll like, thick-cut salt 'n' vinegar crisps, a four-pack of peaches (tree-ripened) and some Diet Coke.

They do ready salads, too, so I get something that doesn't look too fattening. Spring green mix with low-cal dressing and boiled eggs. And a packet of strawberries, because berries are the lowest carb fruit around. Then I pay and get straight into a cab. I'll show him!

Ollie's offices look as if they're straight out of *Kavanagh QC*. A lovely old Georgian townhouse in Lincoln's Inn, with lots of upper-class women looking a bit scary in stiff tweed skirts and starchy white blouses, and men in suits trying to seem exceptionally busy and important.

I toss back my hair, safe in the knowledge it was professionally styled just yesterday, and straighten my shoulders. I think this looks very career girl, and will counter the two plastic M&S bags I'm dragging around.

'Oliver McLeod, please,' I say haughtily to the girl at reception. I also give her a don't-fuck-with-me look. Victoria taught me this. It's highly important to let everybody know you're the boss, otherwise they take advantage of you. Todd would expect it, she says. And she's probably right, although I can't bring myself to do it to Toby Rogers and I feel a bit embarrassed when she does.

'Third door on the left,' she says, looking askance at my plastic bags. I haven't quite mastered the haughty stare yet, obviously. 'But he has a lunch appointment.'

'It's with me,' I say triumphantly. 'We're working through.' I hoist up the bags. 'Lunch is for wimps.'

She raises an eyebrow. I ignore her and stalk magnificently off down the corridor. Unfortunately, one of my heels gives way and I trip on the soft beige carpeting. Then I get to hear her snickering at her desk.

Honestly!

I get up and dust myself off. Nothing is going to ruin today. OK, here's Ollie's office. I rap hard on the door.

'Come in,' he says. And my stomach starts doing the butterfly thing again.

This is ridiculous. It must be nerves. But why would I be nervous around Ollie? The whole point of Ollie is that I'm so comfortable with him. He's like those old trainers I had to throw out because they weren't feminine enough.

I let myself in and shut the door. Alone at last.

Ollie's office is really nice. Nothing like Todd's. It's far smaller, and has an Afghan rug on the floor that's slightly muddy, as well as a print of what looks like a stately home. There are file cabinets on the walls and papers all over his desk, and a quite grimy window.

I think it's brilliant.

The thought strikes me that Victoria can't come here much.

'Lucy,' he says. 'Hi.' And he sighs.

He sighs! Like it's such a penance to see me.

'Hi, Ollie,' I say chirpily. I will be upbeat. I will smile. No matter what. 'It's so great to see you again. Just the two of us.' I do a twirl for him. 'Do you like the dress? It's new.'

It's a Miu Miu dress in rose-pink wool with cap sleeves that ends just off the knee. Very Jackie O. And I'm wearing a cloud of Coco perfume, by Chanel. And a slim gold watch that Todd bought me, a Patek Philippe.

'I'm sure it is,' he says in that same cool tone. 'Isn't everything you have new?'

I take a seat in front of him without being asked. He has a green leather armchair, and it's very comfortable. Unlike this conversation.

'You know, Ol,' I say, with a light frown, 'you're coming across as very disapproving.'

'Oh, you picked up on that, did you?'

'Well then.' I can't keep the note of triumph out of my voice. 'What's your problem?' You *told* me to be like this. You got me my new job. You *wanted* me to move out. And now you're blaming me for taking your advice?'

He looks unhappy, and there's a pause.

'You know, you're not the only one entitled to a bit of happiness,' I lecture him. 'I'm glad things are so great for you and Victoria, but things are great for me and Todd too. Last night you acted as though you weren't even interested in our, um, relationship.'

'I'm sorry,' he says, after a bit.

'So you should be.' I do my stern schoolteacher impression. 'You were the one who kept telling me all my boyfriends were crap and I should get serious in life. And when I do, instead of being happy for me, you become totally absorbed in your own wedding, your own career!'

'Right.' He pushes away the pad he was writing on and passes a hand wearily through his hair. 'I'm sorry. You're right, of course. *If* you're in love,' he looks directly at me, 'then I'm happy for you. You deserve all the joy in the world.'

I blink. I don't know what I'd expected him to say. But I thought he'd be upbeat and chipper, not serious like this.

I think I'm getting a lump in my throat, which is stupid. Nobody is meant to be crying here. It's a fun lunch with a good friend.

'What's that?' he asks, pointing to the bags.

'Oh.' I'm glad of the distraction. 'Lunch,' I say proudly, drawing out his haul. 'Crisps. Peaches. Beef, mustard and pickle sandwiches. And Diet Coke.'

'What, no cans of Castlemaine XXXX?' he says.

My face falls.

'I'm just joking,' Ollie says. Something of the old light

has returned to his eyes. 'Diet Coke's grand. But I can't believe you brown-bagged lunch!'

'You said you only had an hour,' I explained, 'so I didn't want to lose half of it walking to a restaurant and ordering food. It's only overpriced rubbish anyway. This is much nicer.'

'Yes, it is.' He reaches eagerly for his sandwich. 'What are you having?'

'Oh, this.' I take out my package and try to look enthusiastic about it. 'A yummy boiled-egg salad . . .' My voice trails off at his expression.

'Lucy, what are you doing?' he asks.

'What do you mean?' I ask defensively.

'Eating this rabbit food. You didn't have anything last night either. Just a couple of crappy prawns and some leaves.'

'And a McVities chocolate biscuit!' I protest.

'When?'

Oh. 'I – I decided to pop into Cathy's last night. For a chat.'

'So you ate a chocolate biscuit,' he says, musingly. 'At least you're not anorexic.'

My mouth opens. 'What?'

'Have half a sandwich.' He hands it over, and I hesitate. 'Eat it,' Ollie says threateningly. 'Or I won't have anything. Not even the crisps.'

I take a bite. It's delicious. It's *delicious*. I feel a mad impulse to run out and buy a loaf of Hovis, toast the whole thing and wolf it down with a pat of butter.

'Lucy,' Ollie says as I ravenously tear the sandwich apart, 'you look awful.'

I swallow a big bite whole which brings tears to my eyes.

'Wha' you mean?' I gasp.

'Awful. You know what awful means,' he says.

'I don't look awful!' I retort, stung. 'I've got great make-up and my hair's all bouncy and . . .' I surreptitiously check my manicure, in case I've picked up some dirt under my nails without noticing it.

'Yes, but it doesn't suit you. You don't look like you,' Ollie says softly. 'You look like Barbie.'

'That's totally unfair,' I say.

'And you're way too thin. You never needed to lose an ounce, but look at you.' He leans forward. 'I'm really worried about you, Lucy. You've lost all your muscle tone and you look all grey and drained, and the best make-up in the world can't change that.'

I'm so shocked. I just sit there, and open my mouth, but I can't think of anything to say.

'Do you run any more?'

I shake my head.

'Dance? You used to love dancing.'

I still do, but, 'No. I don't dance any more.'

'This isn't healthy,' Ollie says. 'Your bloom has gone. Like the sparkle in your eyes.'

Which are now filling with tears. So much for a nice lunch with a mate.

'You're mean,' I say, crying. 'You're just being cruel.'

He jumps up out of his chair, comes round the desk and hugs me, tight. And despite everything, I cling to him. I cling on to him like the Titanic just sunk and he's a sturdy piece of driftwood.

'Lucy, Lucy,' he murmurs, stroking my hair. 'I'm only saying it because I care about you. I only want to help.'

I gather myself together and give him an angry shove.

'Well, you're not bloody helping!' I say. 'You're the one who told me I had to change. "Grow up," you said.'

'Just a little,' he pleads. 'Just a tiny bit of polishing, maybe. I didn't see this coming, what's happened to you. Nobody did.'

'Your precious Victoria approves,' I cry. 'She helped me, you know. Like *you* asked her to. And Todd likes it as well. So why should I care what you think?'

'Please,' he says helplessly. 'Just eat a bit more food.'

I feel a crushing weight of disappointment curl round my heart. I'd hoped he'd say something else. Instead, he sits back and hands me a Kleenex, when all I really want is another hug.

'So Todd's really serious about you?' he asks.

I bristle. 'Of course he's serious about me. We're serious about each other. Just like you and –' I just manage to stop saying 'precious' again in that sarcastic tone – 'Victoria. Todd bought me this watch!' I add defiantly. 'It's solid gold, you know.'

'There's more to this than just money, I hope,' he says, coldly again.

I'm really starting to get angry now.

'What are you saying?'

'Just that you mention his money quite a lot. And I didn't think you were that kind of girl.'

My mouth opens again. I really must stop doing that. I look like a trout.

'Are you,' I say icily, 'Are you calling me a gold-digger, Ollie?'

'I don't know,' he says. 'Are you one?'

'Of course I'm not. I only mentioned the watch because it shows he cares. He wouldn't give me something like that if he didn't care, would he?'

Ollie shrugs. 'He's loaded, it's neither here nor there to him. My question is, is he *serious*? Has he been to your parents? Introduced you to his? You both work in the same office, what do the others think about it?'

'His parents are in America.'

'Yours are in Kent,' Ollie points out.

'And we have to be discreet at work.'

'Why?'

I stare at him.

'Why? Why do you have to be discreet at work?'

'Office jealousy,' I explain. Duh!

235

'What's that got to do with anything?' he asks, maddeningly. 'It's not like he's made you a vice-president. You're still just a receptionist. How could they be jealous of that?'

I chew on this. I can't actually think of a good answer.

'Maybe it's time to go public,' I concede. 'Because we are very serious.'

'Are you now.'

'We're talking about marriage!' I snap, outraged. It's not strictly true, but it might be soon.

'Really.' He gives me that same smile. 'Because last night you said you were just enjoying each other's company.'

'Yes, well. I've been doing some thinking,' I reply. 'And I want what you and Victoria have. So Todd and I will be moving our relationship forward.' My eyes narrow. 'You do love Victoria, right?'

'Oh, absolutely,' he says immediately. 'She's the one for me.'

'Fine,' I reply angrily. 'That's just perfect then!'

'For both of us,' he says. 'Since you and Todd are the ideal couple.'

I've run out of things to say. So I snatch away his bag of crisps and eat all of them. That'll show him!

But Ollie doesn't object. Even though he loves salt 'n' vinegar. He sort of watches me eat. And I start feeling really bad. It's gone pear-shaped again, and I so don't want it to.

'Look, Ol,' I say, putting the bag down. 'I'm sorry.'

'I'm sorry too,' he says at once.

'Maybe you're right.'

He sits up eagerly. 'About what?'

'About what you said. Todd being serious. And eating, and running.' I blurt it out. 'I'm not actually a thousand per cent happy like this.'

'I knew it!' he says fiercely.

'I liked it better before,' I say, and as soon as the words

leave my mouth I know they're true. 'Going on runs and kickboxing.'

'And disco dancing.'

'Especially that.' I look at him. 'I didn't know you knew I danced.'

'I watched you sometimes,' he admits. 'I'd come home early and you'd have Madonna on full blast and you'd be jumping around in your bedroom. You looked mad.'

'I'm not like that any more,' I explain.

'More's the pity,' he says. And he sounds dead serious.

'You know, before,' I feel slightly weird, 'you never told me I had a bloom.'

'I thought you knew.' He's looking at me very oddly. Almost like—

No. Stop that. What am I doing? Am I proving Cathy right? That I fancy him?

I'm obviously a terrible person. Victoria's my friend. I'm her bridesmaid, for heaven's sakes!

'You must be really excited about the wedding,' I say, attempting to steer us back to safer waters.

Ollie leans back and steeples his fingers.

'I don't know,' he says.

That stops me. What did he just say?

'I don't know if I am. Victoria and I don't see eye to eye. Not like we used to.'

'Oh,' I say, lamely.

I can't help it, I feel a welling of excitement.

'I thought you just said she was the one for you,' I say probingly.

'I thought that,' he says, and then he breaks eye contact with me and looks away. Weary, again. 'Oh, I don't know,' he says, running his hand through his hair. 'It's just this conversation. It's got very strange.'

'I know.'

'You and I need to talk more,' he says. And the moment's gone. He's not going to say anything else about Victoria. I wait, but he just asks me something about Cathy. And before I know it, the hour's over, and he hugs me, and I leave. I leave in a daze, and outside his offices, the sunlight dazzles me, and I can't see clearly.

12

I can't wait for work to be over. I leave the office at five on the dot. Todd is still locked in conference with Melissa, and all I want to do is drag him back to my place. I need to *do* something, I need to feel some reassurance.

Since I left Ollie's, my emotions are all funny. It feels as if somebody's extracted all my bones and put them back in wrong, without my noticing – only now, nothing works right.

I go home to my flat and leave an urgent message on Todd's mobile to call me. That I need to see him.

Then I pace up and down the kitchen. I look at all of it, at the luxury appliances and granite countertops. I walk through the whole apartment. I examine my neatly laid out, perfect new clothes. I even sit in the plant-filled conservatory, my oasis.

Yep, it's definitely true: I'm not happy.

I can't sit still. It's as if Ollie triggered some kind of switch. I can't do this any more. Not in this way, anyway.

Todd will understand. Ollie's wrong about him, I think fiercely. Cathy too.

My phone goes. I jump out of my skin. Then I dive on it.

'Hello?'

'It's Todd.' He sounds slightly annoyed. 'What's so urgent, sugar?'

'Oh, nothing,' I say.

'Well then—'

'Actually it's not nothing,' I correct myself hastily. 'I really need to see you. To tell you something important – about us,' I add.

'Tell me now,' he says.

'Oh no, not on the phone.' I hear myself giving a Victoria-style tinkling laugh and wince. It's true, I am developing some bad habits. 'You have to come here.'

'Soon as I've finished up,' he says laconically. I hear a girl's voice giggling in the background.

'Who's that?'

'I'm in a meeting,' he says, without answering the question. 'You knew that. Anyway, I'll be over as soon as I'm done. Order something in, a steak and salad.'

'Actually I was going to have pasta,' I tell him.

Todd snorts. 'Pasta? You can't get low-carb pasta, not that doesn't taste like cardboard.'

'I know. I was going to get the ordinary kind. With cheese sauce.'

He laughs. 'Don't be ridiculous, you'll get as big as a house. Anyway, see you later.' And he hangs up.

I don't know exactly what I'm feeling. But cross is part of it. Scared is a bigger part, though. One thing at a time. I'll call Todd's gourmet delivery service and get him the stupid steak and salad. And even vintage champagne. No point being provocative, is there? We're going to have a perfectly reasonable discussion.

'Where did this come from?' he says.

Everything's nice. My chiffon dress and strappy heels, the candlelit table in the conservatory, the white linen, silver cutlery, champagne, steak and salad. A large silver bowl of chilled raspberries is standing to one side.

Everything except Todd's expression. He doesn't look happy.

'Myself,' I say. And it's mostly true. Ollie didn't make me feel like this, he just brought it to the surface.

'Well, quit being dumb.' He frowns. 'I need a girl who's gonna act serious.'

'But this *is* serious.' I gesture helplessly at my untouched steak. 'I've just had enough meat and eggs and lettuce. Sometimes I need toast. And I've got no energy—'

'You're *thin*,' he says. 'Nothing to worry about.'

'I think I'm too thin,' I say. My cheeks are reddening, but it's OK. I doubt he can tell. Candlelight makes everybody look more sexy, doesn't it? 'I've got no muscles and I only weigh eight stone now.'

'You can never be too rich or too thin,' he says. 'Jackie Kennedy.'

'Sure you can. Look at Paris Hilton.'

'If we're going to move this relationship on, I'd like a partner who's going to be socially acceptable.' He sounds aggravated.

'I can be socially acceptable and still be me, though, can't I?' I plead with him. 'I'm not going to go back to the way I was before. I like getting my hair done, I even like dresses . . .' I hate tights, but one thing at a time.

He hasn't pressured me into sex, at least. That's a bit strange, isn't it? With his insistence that I make myself into the perfect lady? How come he doesn't demand I roll into bed?

But he never has.

Anyway, I'll cross that bridge when I come to it. Which hopefully won't be any time soon. 'And isn't it time we let everybody know,' I hear myself say boldly. 'My parents. Your parents. Everybody at work.'

Todd stares at me with horror. 'We're being discreet at work.'

'But why?' I say, trotting out Ollie's argument. 'They can't be jealous because I haven't been promoted. I'm doing the most boring job in the world! Nobody could say you've shown me favouritism.'

Todd throws down his napkin dramatically; it lands on his steak, staining the white cloth.

'Lucy,' he says crossly. 'Let's get a couple things straight right now. You work for me. *I* will say what goes on in my offices. And I'm the *man* in this little romance. If I want to keep it quiet we go at my pace. I want a certain type of girl, OK? Discreet, ladylike, and skinny. For what I've given you,' he gestures at the apartment, 'that's not so much to ask.'

There's a horrible light in his eyes, one I haven't seen before.

'For what you've given me?' I say. 'I thought there was no quid pro quo. You told me it was all about business. And friendship.' I'm going pink in the face. 'You can't *buy* me, Todd. And if that's what you were thinking, you need to think again. I'm not going to be dictated to.' My heart is racing unpleasantly, but I don't back down.

He gets to his feet.

'Where are you going?'

'To my house,' he says. 'I expect to see you in the morning, Lucy. I expect you to be discreet. I expect you to behave the way we've agreed. Just remember who's paying for all this, OK? I've had enough of you stringing me along.' And he storms out.

I just sit there, wanting to die.

Of course it was too good to be true. All of it. Pretending to be something I wasn't. Someone I wasn't.

And, worse, pretending Todd was somebody he wasn't. I knew the kind of man I wanted, and it wasn't a smooth-talking American playboy, was it?

It was Ollie McCleod.

The pain of facing it makes me suck in my breath. Cath was right; so was Victoria. But I don't care about that. I'm just trying to cope with my sudden, naked sense of loss, and I don't mean the loss of Todd Mayle.

Half an hour later I've made my decision. It only took that long because there are practical things to sort out. Like how to return all the clothes. For most of it it's easy, I just lay them neatly on the bed, along with the bags, and those damn high heels. I tidy away the dishes, call the catering company to remove them. Then I go through the house, collecting all my possessions. That doesn't take long – I'm talking about *my* possessions, the ones I walked in with. Nothing that he's bought me, not a lipstick, not a pair of gold-plated tweezers. I even leave the Rembrandt toothpaste.

I work quickly, with a speed that amazes me. No crying; I'm too angry to cry, and mostly at myself. Todd's just a jerk, and not the only jerk in the world. The person who really pisses me off is *me*. I can't believe I fell for him! I accepted all these gifts. Because it didn't seem wrong. And all the time – despite what he said – he regarded them as some kind of payment, that entitled him to tell me how to live!

Fuck that, I think.

Oh, I shouldn't say 'fuck', I should say—

No. *Fuck* that. Sometimes only swearing will do.

I want to tear the clothes off my back. Everything. But I don't want to rip them, even the horribly scratchy red lace lingerie. No, these clothes I've worn, I'll have to give them back to him dry-cleaned and pressed. And besides, I need something to go to Cathy's in. I stupidly threw out all my old clothes. I've got no trainers, no jeans – nothing.

When the flat's ready, I call Victoria. I just want to deal with this now. Once I get to Cathy's, that's it. I'm going to take a long, hot shower, and scrub Todd Mayle out of my life. I'm going to want to forget all about him till I go to Mayle Accommodations tomorrow to resign.

'Yaas?'

Thank God. She's there.

'Hey, Vicky.'

'Darling . . .' She adopts that special drawly voice she

uses since we've become friends. 'How *are* you? Want to pop out to a nightclub? Bring Todd.'

'I don't think so.' My tone of voice cuts her off.

'Sweetie, what's happened?'

'I've broken up with Todd,' I say. 'At least, I'm going to. Tomorrow.'

There's a long pause.

'But why?' Victoria can't believe it. 'You were so close! He was so serious about you.'

'No, he wasn't.' I sigh. 'Anyway, I just wanted to let you know.'

'Lucy,' Victoria says, 'don't be stupid. You may never get a chance like this again!'

'It's not much of a chance,' I say. 'I can't be that girl. I can't be like you, Victoria. It's you, it's not me. I don't – I still don't like high heels.'

'Well.' Her voice has changed. 'I think you're mad. I would never do that to Ollie.'

'You wouldn't need to,' I reply, and my eyes are starting to tear. 'Because Ollie's not that kind of man.' I have to get off the phone. 'Talk to you later,' I say, and hang up.

Then I get my small bag of stuff and the case of clothes that need dry-cleaning and go downstairs. Toby Rogers is sitting at the front desk and looks at me coolly. I feel a fresh wash of shame. I deserve it, don't I? I've walked past him, with Victoria, loads of times. And let her insult him. I kidded myself it was OK if I didn't do it myself, but really I ought to have stuck up for him.

'Can I help you, madam?' he asks.

'Yes.' I take a deep breath. 'You can give this to Mr Mayle for me.' And I hand over the key.

Strangely enough, Toby doesn't seem at all surprised.

'I also want to apologize,' I mutter, embarrassed. 'I've been rude to you and I'm sorry. Just because Todd does it . . . I should know better.' It's no use, I'm going to cry.

'My mum and dad would be ashamed of me.' A tear wells up and plops on my cheek. I brush it away.

'Anyway,' I add, because he doesn't say anything. 'It's been nice knowing you and I hope you make it to your pension.' And I start to walk out.

'Miss!' he says. 'Hold on, miss.'

I turn back. 'Lucy. Please call me Lucy.'

'Lucy, then.' And the old man smiles at me. 'Look, it's not my place to say but . . .'

'Please do say.'

'You weren't the only one.' He shrugs. 'Never understood it. Pretty young ladies, some of 'em quite bright, too. What they put up with!'

I want to get out of there. Get to Cathy's as fast as possible. She has a chocolate digestive with my name on it.

But I'm rooted to the spot.

'I don't understand,' I say, although I have a sneaky feeling I do understand. Perfectly. 'Can you explain?'

Toby looks around the lobby, as though Todd might walk in any second.

'Coming back tonight, is he?' he asks warily.

I shake my head. 'Stormed off to his house in Notting Hill.'

'If you've got time,' he says, 'come in the back.'

Toby has a little office, tucked away behind reception. It has cleaning supplies, mops and brooms and stuff, but it also has a desk and a phone, and a kettle and a microwave – plus a neat stack of magazines and a comfy-looking armchair.

I sit down in the armchair.

'It's not really my concern,' he says. He looks very awkward. 'You didn't love him, Miss Lucy?'

'Just Lucy.' I shake my head. 'And no. I thought I might, but I didn't.' I blush. 'I haven't had many boyfriends, not real ones, so I was – I suppose I was kidding myself.'

'You remember old Charlotte?' he says, cryptically.

'Um, no.'

'The duchess,' he says. 'Bit sniffy when she first met you?'

'Oh, yes.'

'That was because you were the fourth girl to be in that apartment this year.'

I look blankly at him. 'But I thought it had been vacant—'

'No paying tenants. How could there be?' Toby makes a face. 'Mayle keeps sticking his fancy women in there. No offence, like.'

I sit there. Amazed.

'You mean, as in girlfriends?'

'Yes, girlfriends,' he says, after a pause. I get a nasty feeling he's trying to be polite. 'And they don't last long. Usually a month or so, then he sends 'em packing. I think you're the first one to walk out on her own.'

I can't think of anything to say.

'He did seem different with you,' Toby offers, consolingly. 'More like he was thinking it was serious. Any road, he never told me to get ready to chuck you out or anything, same as he did the others.'

I believe him. There's no way he could be making it up.

'But didn't these other girls mind being thrown out?'

'Course they did. We had tears, scenes, the works. But what could they do? They've no lease. No right to stay. And Mayle, he can be a nasty piece of work.' Toby frowns. 'Don't rightly know what he said to the girls, but they didn't fight him or anything, not after he talked to them.'

'You think he was threatening them?'

It seems impossible. Smooth Todd, using threats? And what kind of threats?

'Not for me to say,' Toby responds. This clearly means 'Yes, definitely.'

'Well.' I sigh. 'He won't have to threaten to get rid of me. I'm gone.' I stand up and give him a hug. 'Take care, Toby.'

'And you, miss,' he says. Old habits die hard, I suppose.

'These other girls,' I can't resist asking, 'who were they?'

'Nobody special,' he says. 'Until you they all kind of looked the same. And they were all Americans. Maybe that's why he thought you were different.'

Maybe. But who cares what he thought? He's a loser, and as of tomorrow I'll be rid of him. That's what counts.

I feel pretty thick when I get to Cathy's. But she's great, she doesn't rub it in, or tell me I told you so. Or complain when I turn up at eleven, for the second night in a row. Even though Peter's in the bedroom and the doorbell probably pulled her away from animal, monkey sex.

Peter has the good sense to stay where he is as she debriefs me. I'm only a bit tearful, which I think is a victory.

Anyway. The tea tastes delish, and she knows a place that does all night dry-cleaning. She offers to go out and drop it off for me, which is great. That way I can go to Todd's house first thing in the morning, drop off the clothes and tell him to stuff his job. That way I won't have to face James, or Jade or any of them, which is the last thing I want.

She gets me some pyjamas and a dressing gown, and when I'm changed runs out to the dry cleaner's. What a star! I make some hot chocolate while she's gone and feel a lot better.

'There you go,' she says when she gets back. 'Now you can get shot of him first thing.'

'Thanks. I couldn't face another day in that office.'

Cathy grins. 'Not cut out for property, were you?'

'How should I know?' I take a big gulp of hot chocolate. It's so good. I'd almost forgotten what it tasted like. Todd's sugar-free, fat-free substitutes weren't the same. 'I never got to do any deals. I just sat there.'

'You know,' Cathy says. 'I was glad when you got the job. I mean, I'd been worried about you. We all had.'

'Oh, thanks,' I say darkly.

'And it was great to see you in dresses, and looking nice. But – all the life drained out of you.'

'That's exactly what Ollie said,' I say, before I can stop myself.

'Ollie?' Cathy asks.

'I may have mentioned it to him.' My casual voice isn't working. 'You know, at dinner . . .'

'While Todd was right next to you? Give over, Lucy. You went to see him, didn't you?'

I shrug. 'He's my friend.'

'*Just* your friend?' she persists.

'Yes. Just my friend. He's getting married to Victoria. Nothing's changed there.'

Cathy holds my gaze. 'I'm sorry,' she says softly.

I wish she hadn't said that. Anything else would have done fine. Sarcasm or ridicule or a lecture, for example.

Pity, however, makes me want to cry. Cathy sees right through me. An annoying habit of sisters.

'Maybe I have some feelings for Ollie,' I admit. 'One or two. But he doesn't share them and he's marrying Victoria. So that's the end of that. Anyway, I don't want a boyfriend right now. After Todd . . .' I shudder. 'I just want to be by myself for a bit.'

'I suppose I can understand that,' Catherine says.

'Nothing's changed, you know. I don't have anything. Not even all those fancy clothes.' I look down at my nails. 'The best I've walked away with is a mani-pedi.'

'And it suits you,' Cathy says loyally.

'Yes, but they won't get me very far, will they?' I take another sip of hot chocolate, and now I'm just depressing myself. 'It's just a few months down the drain in the end. I'm right back where I started, with no place to live, no money in the bank, no job and no boyfriend.' I smile weakly. 'Apart from that, of course, everything's peachy.'

Cathy considers this for a moment.

'Well,' she says, slapping me on the back. 'At least you have a great hairdo.'

I sleep soundly and wake up early. I left the curtains open; dawn is about six a.m, and I can never sleep with bright sunlight hitting my eyes. Plus, waking up that way is less traumatic than an alarm.

Catherine has laid out some clothes for me; old jeans and a fitted T-shirt. I suppose this is as casual as she gets. They would never have fitted the old me, but now they slide on perfectly; they're even a bit loose. And the slides she's leant me are half a size too small; my toes stick out.

Still, I think Ollie's right. I'm not loving what I'm seeing in the mirror. It's a bit Kate Moss, which might be fine on a supermodel, but on me it just looks gaunt.

Never mind. A few huge breakfasts and a bit of jogging and stuff, and I should be back to my old self fast enough. But that's the least of my problems. I'm far too nervous to eat anything right now.

I tiptoe out of the apartment, no need to wake Peter up again. I've got the ticket for the clothes, and when I find the twenty-four-hour dry cleaner they are indeed open and they do have last night's clothes. Perfect. I pay (that can come out of Todd's 'living expenses'), and flag down a cab, and I'm on my way to Todd's.

I don't know why I'm nervous. I'm the one in control here, I tell myself. I'm the one who'll be waking *him* up from a dead sleep. I'm the one who's going to fling his clothes back at him in a dramatic gesture. I don't exactly need anything from Todd, so he can't threaten *me*.

And yet I'm still nervous. I think it was that look in his eyes last night. That nasty look . . .

The cab pulls up outside his elegant Queen Anne townhouse with the large walled garden. I pay the man and head inside.

Stuff this. I square my shoulders. Today, Todd can learn to deal with me.

I let myself in with the keys he gave me. The whole place is quiet, but I can see he came home last night. There's an empty champagne bottle on the kitchen table, Cristal, and a mirror with a dusty surface . . .

Oh, wait. That's not dust. That's probably cocaine.

Of course. He told me he did it, after all. So why should it shock me to see it here?

Whatever. Todd's vices are his own affair. I readjust last night's dress over my arm along with the strappy heels now dangling from my little finger, and head upstairs. I've only been here once before. Where was that master bedroom again? Oh yeah; end of the corridor, wasn't it?

Mentally, I go over what I'm going to say. It's going to be witty. It's going to be cutting. Frankly, it's going to be devastating. And he'll deserve every minute of it.

This is the one. I can hear the sound of gentle snoring.

I put my hand on the doorknob, turn and shove it open.

'WAKE UP, TODD!' I shout, as loud as I possibly can. 'I've brought back your clothes. And your keys. And you can stuff your—'

I'm cut off by a scream. And take a step back.

Of course he *deserves* it, but I didn't think I was quite that scary.

But hold on, that wasn't a male scream. That was a girl. He's got a woman in there!

I step back into his bedroom. Boldly. Prepared to confront Todd and whoever . . .

They're both there. Sitting up in bed and staring at me. Todd, looking bleary and rather orange; I never noticed that about his tan before. More importantly, next to him, with his black silk sheets pooling around her waist, enormous, melon-like boobies jutting out in front of her – Victoria.

I stand there, swaying on my heels. Victoria screams

again. I guess this means she doesn't have to actually say anything. I'm not sure what the Perfect Woman's Guide to Cheating and Shagging Your Mate's Man would advise her to say, anyway.

My dry-cleaner-wrapped clothes, the shoes, and Todd's keys slither to the ground.

I want to say something. But what? Where to start?

'It's not what you think!' Victoria shrieks.

That breaks the spell.

'What is it then?' I ask with heavy sarcasm. That's easier to do than wit, especially when you haven't had your coffee yet.

Todd recovers.

'Now, Lucy,' he says, soothingly. How can he do that? How? I just caught him in bed shagging my girlfriend – my *engaged* girlfriend – and he's acting like nothing's happened. Like I'm a client that needs to be managed.

'Let's all hold on here,' he says. 'We need to be adult about this.'

'Adult!' I shriek. 'What's so adult about it? You didn't even know I was dumping you and you cheat on me with – with *her*?'

It suddenly dawns on me. No wonder Todd never pressured me for sex! He was getting plenty of it elsewhere. All he cared about was a suitable wife.

Victoria squeals again. It's really getting tiresome. Then she makes a dive for Todd's pure cashmere robe, tugs it on, and gathers up her things from around the room. Without looking at me, she dives into his ensuite bathroom. And I hear the door lock.

'How could she do that to Ollie?' I demand of Todd.

'Lucy, Lucy,' he says again, as if I'm a frisky horse. 'Maybe things got out of hand . . .'

'Just slightly.'

A look of annoyance creeps over his face. 'Listen,' he says in a stronger tone. 'We're all adults here—'

'Yes, that's your favourite word this morning, isn't it?' I spit. 'Well, here are your keys. And your clothes. See you around, you loser.'

He looks at me.

'Loser?' he says, in a new, menacing voice. 'Maybe you should just remember who pays your rent. And your salary. Play nice, Lucy.'

I feel a surge of joy. 'Actually, Todd, you can't threaten me like you did those other girls. I—'

'Oh, really,' he says. 'I suppose you've been talking to them. I suppose they've told you everything.' He shrugs, casually, as if he couldn't give a damn. And all of a sudden, Todd seems truly menacing.

I can't believe I didn't see it before.

'I know what I'm offering,' he says, coolly. 'It's a pretty big prize. You don't think I'm going to audition for the part. Jade and Buffy didn't understand that. I guess you know about Melissa, too. Well, she doesn't know about *you*.' He glares at me. 'And I want to keep it that way.'

Jade. Buffy. I hang on tight to his door, because I'm feeling dizzy.

It fits, of course. It all fits.

Toby saying how the other girlfriends all looked the same.

Buffy crying and saying she was in love.

Melissa taking those closed-door 'meetings'.

I stare at Todd. My eyes are opened in a totally new way. And I feel a rage inside me that's got nothing to do with my dreams of marriage and a proper boyfriend. I can't quite believe this, but I'm actually furious *for Buffy*.

And, now I come to think of it, Buffy's scared. Scared of Todd. It's the reason she's still there.

'What happens now is up to you,' Todd says with that aggravating calm. 'Behave like an *adult* –' his eyes challenge me – 'and maybe we can work this out.'

He reaches behind him and rearranges the pillows, propping himself up. Getting comfortable.

'I'm glad you saw this,' he shrugs. 'This is my life. If you're going to be in it, Lucy, you have to understand. Play this right, and there's still a chance for you. You have a lot of what I need.'

And suddenly it hits me; exactly what I have to do.

'Yes,' I say. 'I suppose that's right. There's no point if I don't know the real you, Todd, is there? I need to understand your life. Your *needs*. Like you said, you're offering a lot.'

'Good girl.' He smiles, smugly. 'See? You're a smart cookie, Lucy. I knew you could be reasonable.' Todd's eyes flicker to my dry-cleaning and keys on the floor. 'Why don't you leave those clothes here? Then you'll have something to wear if I want you to meet me here,' he says, adding, with a touch of sadism, 'I'll get Victoria to hang them up.'

Victoria. Yes.

'What do you think about that?' he asks, reading my thoughts. 'Me considering Victoria?'

I shrug, as if I too am as hard as diamonds. 'Hey, I'm not afraid of a little competition. She hasn't got the breeding. Try her out, Todd, I know you'll come back to me.'

He laughs. 'Atta girl. We've got a lot in common. I knew that naïve little country-girl thing had to be an act.'

I bend down, pick up the dry-cleaning and lay it over a chair, surreptitiously retrieving his keys at the same time. I slip them into my pocket.

'So I guess I'll see you in the office,' I say. 'And no need to mention this to anybody. Things can go on as before.'

The bathroom door opens and Victoria comes out; she's swathed in the dressing gown, her hair is pinned up and she's in full make-up. She also appears to have recovered.

'Well,' she drawls. 'This is certainly awkward.'

'Not really,' I say. 'Todd and I are in complete agreement.'

Victoria's eyes narrow. 'I meant about me and Ollie, of course. Look, things happen. People make mistakes . . .'

I just want to get the hell out of there. I need to be alone. I need coffee, and I need to think.

'Lucy,' she says, and there's an edge of pleading to her voice, 'please don't do anything until we've had a chance to talk. Don't tell him. At least give me a chance to explain properly.'

'Well—'

'People's lives are involved!' she says dramatically. 'Surely half an hour's conversation won't make any difference?'

'All right,' I say reluctantly. 'Call me when you leave here.' I don't want to get dragged into talking to her in front of Todd. I back out of the house and get the tube to Victoria station. Appropriate, huh? A big station is the best place to be alone. Nobody will notice me, and all the little cafés are open. I find a baguette place, order a giant coffee and a cheese Danish. Perfect. I can sit by myself at a little iron table and just think.

I soon work out what has to be done. The only thing I'm not sure of is Ollie. Of course I've got to tell him. And soon. But I shrink from it. I mean, Ollie loved Victoria. God knows why, but he did. And I've no desire to present him with a second big hit of pain. First his Dad, in Scotland. And now her. He'll feel totally abandoned.

But it has to be done, even though I'm looking at it with all the enthusiasm of a Crimean war doctor who has to saw off some poor bastard's gangrenous leg.

Still, first things first. I finish my delicious breakfast and get a taxi back to Knightsbridge. There's still plenty of money in my 'living expenses' account, and I want Todd to pay for what's about to happen to him. In cash, and otherwise.

I ring the bell and wait as Toby shuffles to the door. He looks amazed to see me.

'Miss Lucy, you're back,' he says. 'But I don't understand . . .'

'Don't worry, it's just temporary,' I tell him. 'Slight change of plan.'

I change into one of my work outfits; one Todd particularly likes, a tight black Versace couture skirt that plays up the fact I now have no bottom. Oh well, I put a cheese Danish in that account. And as soon as I can, I'll buy a pair of trainers and start running again. But there's no time for that this morning.

I wait, watching the news on breakfast TV. Victoria has already left me four messages and, just as I suspected, she soon tries again. I reach over and pick up the telephone.

'Lucy,' she says breathlessly. 'Thank God you're home.'

'Victoria,' I say coldly. She's the ultimate bitch. Actually, Todd *should* marry her. Those two are well suited.

'Can I come over and see you?' she begs. 'This would be so much better face to face.'

'I've got to get to the office,' I say truthfully.

'I'm right around the corner.' I can hear the noise of traffic. 'I'm circling just in front of Harrods. Please, sweetie.'

'I suppose I can give you ten minutes,' I say, and hang up.

She arrives in two; I open the door and she attempts to envelop me in a tearful hug. I push her away.

'Come off it, Victoria,' I say. 'We're not friends. We never were, really. That was my mistake.'

'But Lucy,' she wails.

'Look, if all you want to do is stand there and feed me some bullshit, then I think we should wrap this up. What you and Todd do is up to you. But Ollie is my friend, and I'm not going to let him walk down the aisle with somebody who can't be faithful to him. He's worth more than that.' I find I'm unexpectedly emotional. 'A lot more.'

A strange expression crosses Victoria's face – more tears, then that wavers, and her eyes sort of dry up and harden. Wow! She's two people in the space of ten seconds. She's wasted in fashion, she should have been an actress. I'm almost impressed.

'Can I sit down?' she asks, in a businesslike, non-tearful voice.

I nod and flop onto the couch myself.

'Look, you're right,' she says. 'That's the first thing to say. We never were friends. I never liked you.'

I nod.

'But Ollie did, so I thought maybe we should try to get on. And when Todd started to see you, you were different. You seemed ready to change, become more feminine.'

'You know,' I say, 'I don't think this is feminine.'

'What?' she demands.

'This.' I gesture at her pink floral dress and high, shiny heels. 'Everything you wanted me to do. Heels and tights and manicures, being nasty to shop assistants and insisting on having everything top of the range.'

'Oh, that's right,' she sneers. 'I forgot. Feminine is computer games and rugby matches.'

'No,' I tell her, and as I speak, I find that this is truly what I believe. 'It is fun to get your hair styled. To wear cool clothes, I don't even mind the odd manicure.'

'What a concession. You're a regular Coco Chanel.'

'But what you do isn't feminine at all,' I say. 'Acting as if everything the man does is perfect. Doing everything to please him. Wearing damn uncomfortable clothes all the time. Never swearing. No men friends. That's not feminine. That's not how real women are. Feminine women have fun, they like men, they joke, they stand up for themselves. They're not dull wet blankets looking for a meal ticket. My sister Cathy,' I say proudly, 'she's an investment banker and a self-made millionaire, and she's more feminine than you and all those Cape Cod trophy wives put together.'

'My mistake,' she says. 'You're not Coco, you're Germaine Greer.'

'I don't agree with her politics, but Germaine Greer's

quite sexy, actually,' I say. 'For one thing, she looks like she knows how to have a laugh.' I suddenly feel a kernel of pity for Victoria. 'You could have that, you know, Vicky,' I tell her. 'You do have a good career. You don't need to regard it as a stopgap while you wait for Prince Charming to come along and pay your bills for ever. It must be pretty miserable, trying to please everybody else all the time. You know the old saying, right?'

'And what's that?' she demands.

'People who marry for money earn every cent of it.'

'Really.' I can see her struggle to contain her contempt, because she needs something from me. But it's a losing battle. Disdain is etched across every pore. 'I tell you what, Lucy. You lead your life and I'll lead mine.'

'Sounds fine to me,' I say. 'Are we done?'

'As long as you say nothing to Ollie.'

'Of course I'm going to tell him. I'm going to tell him today.'

'Are you? Have you really thought this through?' She tosses her head. 'This is his life, Lucy. His happiness. *Our* happiness.'

'You should have thought of that before you bedded my boyfriend.'

'As of last night he wasn't your boyfriend. You told me you were going to dump him, remember?'

'Were going to. You didn't give me much of a chance, did you?'

'I felt low. I've been stressed out by the wedding,' Victoria says, without embarrassment. 'I felt sorry for Todd. So I went to see him. He offered me some champers—'

'And cocaine.'

'What?' She blinks.

'I saw it.'

'All right then,' Victoria concedes defiantly. 'Some drugs too. And, OK, I got out of my head. It's not like I'm the first person in the world to do it. I wasn't thinking straight,

Lucy. Todd's very good-looking, he's a good talker. Before I knew where I was we'd ended up in bed.' She looks me right in the eye. 'It's not something I'm proud of. But I got drunk and it happens. I *love* Ollie. And he loves me,' she says defiantly. 'You might not understand that, but it's the truth. Now are you going to ruin two people's lives because you barged in and saw something you shouldn't?'

I waver for a second. She pounces.

'You've still got Todd,' she says firmly. 'He doesn't want me, he wants you. Meanwhile because I got drunk and did one dumb thing, my life has to be over. Is that what you want?'

'I can't not tell him,' I say.

'Why? Why can't you?' she demands. 'You can do whatever you want. Look, how many stag nights get out of hand, and the groom winds up in bed with a stripper? Wakes up the next day with a hangover and total regrets? Do you think his friends run and tell the bride? Of course not. Everybody forgets it ever happened, the groom goes to the church, and the bride never realizes what he did. And they have a happy marriage.'

I hesitate. I can't believe it, but I'm hesitating. Maybe it's because she's not doing the fake tears any more, but this is making a nasty kind of sense.

'I know you never read women's magazines,' she says. 'But our gossip columnist is always being asked if this wife should confess to her affair. The answer is always no. You only want to confess to make *you* feel better. The husband is better off not knowing, especially if it won't happen again.'

'And it won't?'

'Certainly not. If anything, this has woken me up to how precious Ollie is to me,' Victoria says piously.

I don't know. I don't know.

'Lucy, I can't stop you,' she says, and her voice is full of aggression and dislike. 'But ask yourself this. What are your motives?'

'What do you mean?'

'You know exactly what I mean,' she says cruelly. 'Are you truly a friend, as you claim? Or are you what I suspected all along, a sad wannabe girlfriend who'd love to ruin things for the woman Ollie really cares for? A true friend would do what's best for Ollie, not what fits their own agenda.'

She stands majestically, having made her point.

'Think about it,' she says. 'And, by the way, if you do decide not to tell him, I think we'd all better take a break from each other. I don't want you as a bridesmaid, never did. I don't even want you at the wedding. I want you to stay away from Ollie and let us get on with our lives together.'

'You're taking a risk, aren't you?' I reply, stung. 'Talking to me like that, when all I have to do is pick up the phone?'

'Not really,' she says. 'If you're such a goody two-shoes, and you honestly believe all that crap about friendship, then you won't tell him. And if you do then nothing would have stopped you. Either way, I don't want to have to pretend to like you for one more second.' And tossing her hair, she stomps out of my flat.

Well.

I don't know what I was expecting, exactly. But it wasn't that.

I have to think about this. But there's no time, no more time. I need to get to the office before Todd – before everybody. That much is crucial.

13

Too late. James is already there when I arrive. Damn. But I can't let it stop me.

'Coffee, please, Lucy,' he says in that nasty way. 'And I have some filing to do later.'

'No problem,' I smile. Bastard! Now I have to do filing, just to make everything seem normal. For this to work, everything has to be normal. Absolutely. Or Todd will suspect.

I make James the coffee, exactly how he likes it. I wish I had one of those little sugar swirlers with the crystals dried onto a toothpick. Anything to please him.

'Wonderful weather!' I say brightly.

'You're looking remarkably cheerful today,' he says, sourly. 'Any *particular* reason?'

It hits me. *He knows.* He knows about me and Todd. No wonder he's been so nasty! He's probably doing all the work. He's the only person in this office who hasn't got off with the boss!

'I am,' I say. 'James, can you keep a secret?'

'I hope you're not about to bore me to death with some little heart-to-heart,' he says flatly.

'Not exactly.' I smile at him. 'I'm going to dump my boyfriend.'

'You are?' he says, his eyes bugging out.

'Oh yes. You see, I was going out with this very rich man. Good-looking, too. The trouble is, he's an idiot. So I'm going to dump him.'

James digests this.

'It wouldn't be anybody I know, by any chance?' he asks.

'It might be,' I say. 'But I have to keep it confidential. To keep my job.'

'To . . . keep your job,' he says, slowly.

'Yes. He threatens girls, you see,' I explain. 'Not just me. I think there were others. And he threatened them, too. He's really not very nice.'

'Why are you telling me this?' James asks.

'So that you'll maybe think about things differently,' I say. 'Sometimes girls don't have a choice. Or at least, they think they don't.'

'I see,' James says. And I believe that, finally, he does.

I test the waters. 'When Buffy gets here, would it be OK if I had a few minutes' coffee break with her?' I ask. 'You see, I need to discuss some things.'

He smiles at me. 'Take all the time you want.'

Great. This might actually be easier than I thought.

She turns up a few minutes later, immaculate as ever in a camel cardigan and ivory silk blouse, with a solid gold necklace and crocodile-skin bag. I kind of understand it, too. When your heart's broken, you do want to look good.

When I next see Ollie, for example, I'm going to be looking good.

'Hey,' I say, sidling up to her. 'Got time for a coffee?'

'Sure,' she says. 'One won't hurt.'

'Not here. There's a Starbucks down the road.'

She gestures her head towards James. 'We can't take the time off, he'll notice.'

'It's still only a quarter to eight,' I persuade her. 'James said it was fine. This won't take long. We'll be back here in ten minutes.'

Which is probably the truth. It doesn't take long to have your life changed. That whole scene with Todd this morning probably took less than five minutes.

'I really shouldn't,' she demurs.

'Please, Buffy. It's very important.'

'Well, OK. Just five minutes.' She looks at me suspiciously. 'You're being very mysterious, you know.'

'Come on,' and I shepherd her out of the door. 'We'll get a decaf and I'll reveal all.'

The Starbucks is pretty full, but there's one table free, by some miracle. We sit down on the brightly coloured chairs and I wonder how to break it to her.

Maybe there's some tactful way. Maybe if I can just . . .

'Well,' she says, with a touch of impatience. 'What's this all about?'

I take a deep breath. 'Todd,' I say.

Buffy pales. I was right.

'It's Todd, isn't it? The one you're in love with.'

She nods miserably. 'How did you guess?'

'Ah – I'll get to that in a second.'

'He's in love with Melissa,' she says, looking drawn. 'I know it. That's what he's doing on all those *appointments*. He takes her everywhere.'

'And Jade?'

'He had an affair with Jade but I think it's over. He told me it was over, anyway. I don't speak to her too much.' Buffy takes a morose pull on her decaf. 'Though I was wondering, secretly, if that's where he's been going at night.'

'What?' I exclaim.

'Oh yes,' she says darkly. 'He's away from me at least five nights a week. I was wondering if he was seeing Jade again as well as Melissa. That'd be just his style,' she says.

I take a deep breath.

'Look, Buffy, this is going to hurt—'

'He *is* in love with Melissa,' she cries, agonized. 'Melissa told you!'

'No. I don't think he's in love with anyone, except

himself.' I swallow. 'You know, I had no idea you were seeing him – that anyone was seeing him. But Todd's been going out with me. And I thought I was his only girlfriend.'

Buffy just stares at me. Then she half rises from her seat, as if she's about to storm out. But her knees go all wobbly, and she crumples back down, and starts to cry.

'Buffy,' I say, alarmed. 'Don't cry. Please. He's not worth it, he's slime. I didn't know or I'd never have gone out with him. Please believe me.'

She gives a huge sniff and blows her nose. 'I do believe you,' she says.'It's just – I feel so goddamn dumb.'

'But you really did care for him,' I say, because I can see she's heartbroken. 'You loved him. Even though you knew he was cheating?'

'You don't get it,' she says, eventually. 'You'd never understand.'

I sit back in my red chair. 'Try me.'

Buffy sighs. 'I wasn't always this way,' she says, gesturing at her perfect outfit, her expensive watch. 'I wanted to be. I used to read *Town and Country* at the city library, look at *Vogue* and all that. But I was just Betsy-Ann Moss, another go-nowhere girl in a go-nowhere town in the Midwest. I dressed hokey and I wore the cheapest of everything, and the best my parents hoped for me was to get a good job as a bank teller or something.' She smiles weakly. 'I'd rather have slit my wrists, you know?'

'I bet.'

'So, anyway,' she sighs. 'My dad has a sister up in New York state, my Auntie Lou. And I got permission to go for the summer on my twentieth birthday, and of course I got a job in Manhattan and I never went back, except to visit.'

'Was it a great job?' I ask encouragingly.

'Dreadful,' she says. 'Typist in a magazine house. Paid just enough to make the rent and maybe get a coffee from the deli every morning. And I worked all hours. But it was Manhattan, you know. It was exciting. Every day you thought it could be your big break, you could get discovered.' She sips the coffee again. 'Except I never did, and one day I wake up and I'm twenty-five, poor and exhausted, and I'm thinking maybe a bank teller's a real good job, it has benefits for one thing, and on those wages back in Kansas I could get a house with a yard, instead of some dirty studio apartment with its own colony of cockroaches.'

I shudder.

'Then one day he walked into the magazine house. Had a meeting with an editor, he wanted them to do a big profile on him. I served him coffee. He asked me out.' She shrugs, trying to look brave. 'You can guess the rest.'

I nod.

'He was everything I'd ever dreamed of,' she says. 'He took me to his place in the Hamptons. He bought me clothes. It wasn't just Target and PayLess shoes any more, now I'm shopping at Saks, I have accounts all over Fifth Avenue. He promised to show me the world. And when he set up in England, he flew me over here first class. First class! Me!' Buffy blows her nose again. 'I really loved him,' she says mournfully. 'I wanted to be perfect for him. That's why I called myself Buffy. Todd Mayle couldn't date no Betsy-Ann from Wichita, Kansas. I thought I did a good job.' She examines her perfect outfit. 'Not good enough, I guess. He never really was going to marry me. He was just having fun.'

'I asked you before why you didn't quit,' I said. 'Why you didn't just go home to America.'

'Todd wouldn't let me,' she says shortly.

'What do you mean, *let* you?'

'He said first he'd fire me and kick me out of my apartment. He pays the rent. I said, no problem, I'll get another job.' She tries to look brave. 'At least I can still type, I told him. But Todd said he'd report me to the police.

He said that all the money I've been spending, which *he* gave me,' she adds, outraged, 'was company money and he'd say I stole it. "You won't go far doing time for embezzlement," he said. Then he laughed.'

I stare at her in horror. 'I knew he was some kind of bully, but I had no idea it was that bad.'

'Oh, he means it,' she says, finishing off her coffee. 'Every word. If you try to dump him he'll say it to you, too.'

'But you haven't embezzled a cent. If it's company money, he's the one doing the embezzling.'

'You think I didn't try that?' She looks bitter, and a Midwestern accent is creeping into her speech. It suits her. 'I said that to him, those very words. And he tells me he's got the money to pay for a fleet of lawyers, and he can hide anything he wants. His daddy owns a whole firm of accountants. He said if I tried any of that they'll throw the book at me. Todd said when his lawyers were done they'd be fixin' to charge me with the Kennedy assassination.' Buffy looks at me. 'You don't know him,' she says.

'Oh, I don't know. I've met people like him before.'

'Where?'

'In the playground, when I was ten. You know there's only one way to deal with bullies,' I tell her. 'Hurt them back.'

She winces. 'Hurt him?'

'You can't still love him!' I protest.

'But I do,' she says, and the accent's back now, properly back. 'I surely do.'

'You don't.' I glance at my watch. 'Todd'll be in soon, I need to make this fast. You only loved the idea of somebody rescuing you. You loved him for taking you out of the cockroach apartment. But you could have done it yourself, Buffy, and you would have done eventually. You're great with his clients!'

'You really think so?' she says.

'I do. Your phone is always ringing. I should know, I put

the calls through. You're the one they like to deal with. Any estate agent in London would hire you.'

'But what about the lawsuits?' she says mournfully. 'All his lawyers?'

'If you'll help me,' I tell her, 'there won't be any lawsuits. And everything'll work out fine. But you will have to strike back against him.'

She hesitates.

'Come on, Betsy-Ann!' I protest. 'He's just a blackmailing idiot with five women on the go at once!'

'Five? There's only us four in the office.'

I sigh. 'Long story. So are you in or out?'

She breathes in deeply and gives herself a little shake. 'I'm in,' she says.

We needn't have worried. Todd takes his time getting into the office; he isn't there till ten. I think he's trying to send me a message. Which is only fair, as I'm about to send him one!

I try to act normal. James says I don't need to do that filing, but I offer anyway. It's something to do, and it keeps me away from Buffy, who's shooting over nervous looks. I don't know if that girl's cut out for industrial espionage. Although luckily this is not a very complicated plan.

Anyway, as I slot papers into manila folders, it's a great opportunity to take a few minutes to think. Not about Todd; about Ollie. And Victoria.

I finish the filing, take a Biro and draw a line down a spare piece of A4. Don't want to give anything away so I use a code. 'Tell Ollie,' and then 'P' and 'C'. Pro and Con. Get it? Cunning, eh?

Under P I put:

1. Victoria is a total cow.
2. Victoria cheated on him.
3. He could marry her and look like a fool.

4. Victoria could be carrying Todd's baby, and Ollie will have to bring it up, unaware that it is in fact demon spawn.

Hmm. Even thinking about that last one makes me sick. But it's not likely. Todd cares too much about himself to risk a baby.

5. Ollie would be starting out his marriage based on a lie.
6. If I don't tell him, Victoria will never let me see Ollie again.

Then I chew thoughtfully on the Biro and write under C:

1. Ollie loves Victoria.

Damn. There it is.

I mean, he does love her. I wish he didn't. I wish he had better taste.

I wish . . .

OK. Let's not think through the rest of it. Does no good.

The point is, before Annoying Victoria there were Annoying Fay and Annoying Rhiannon. Ollie has a type, and the type is not me. The type is a girl who doesn't find lingerie scratchy, or regard high heels as sadistic. And I gave him every opportunity to tell me he hated her. But all he did was bring me back to the subject of the wedding.

Victoria's right. If it's a one-off, then I can't ruin Ollie's life by telling him. No matter how much I want to.

I crumple up the paper. Then I uncrumple it, and instead rip it methodically into quarters, then eighths, then tiny little pieces of confetti.

'Lucy.'

I look up to see Buffy hovering by my desk, staring at me shredding this innocent piece of paper.

'Ahm,' she says, nervously. 'I think you wanted to see Mr Mayle? Well, he's just arrived.'

I never even noticed him come in.

I buzz Todd's office.

'Yes?' he says. He sounds supremely confident. Nothing wrong in his world.

'Mr Mayle,' I say, injecting my tone with just the right mix of submission and sexiness. 'I wonder if you would like some . . . *coffee*?'

There's a pause, and he chuckles. 'Coffee,' he says. 'Sure. Bring it right in.'

I go to the machine and fix a cappuccino. Weird, my hands are trembling. It all seemed so simple over the cheese Danish at Victoria station.

Jade leaps to her feet. '*I'll* take that to Mr Mayle,' she says possessively.

Buffy tenses, and I can see James, at his desk, rolling his eyes. I keep a firm grip on the saucer.

'That's OK,' I say sweetly. 'He particularly asked for me. I think he wants to, er, hand me an assignment.'

'Buzz me as soon as you're done,' she snaps. 'I have an appointment with him outside the office in twenty minutes. So don't waste any of Mr Mayle's time.'

I smile at her. 'Jade, I can promise you I won't do that.'

Actually, she's strengthened my resolve. I manage to carry the cappuccino all the way into Todd's office without it rattling around in the saucer once, and I even shut the door behind me, one-handed.

'Todd,' I say, in my sexiest, throaty voice.

'Lucy.' He grins. 'Recovered from your little dose of reality this morning?'

'Oh yes,' I say. I put the coffee down on his oak desk. 'Here's your cappuccino, just how you like it. Non-fat milk and a whisper of cinnamon.'

'Mmm,' he says, turning round to pick it up. I slide my

hand into my bra and jiggle around. Trying to be subtle. But unfortunately he spies the movement and turns back round.

Damn!

'Well, Lucy,' he says in that throaty voice I used to think was so seductive. What was I like? It's the lamest thing ever. 'Aren't you a naughty little girl?'

'Mmm, very naughty,' I say. Trying not to panic.

He mustn't walk over here! He mustn't hug me. Or, worse, put his hand down my bra or something!

'My little tryst this morning got you going, huh?' He gets up from the desk and I'm revolted to see the not very impressive bulge down the front of his trousers. 'You've probably spent all morning wondering what Victoria was like. Hoping to get *your* try-out?'

Oh. My. God.

I smile weakly, trying not to do anything stupid. Like throw up in one of his potted topiaries.

'Come over here, babe, let's see what you've got,' he leers.

'I'm going to,' I hear myself reply. 'In just a second. I'm going to show you what I'm made of. I'm going to give you everything I've got!'

Todd laughs delightedly. 'Atta girl! I've waited a long time for this.'

'There's just one thing I was hoping you could take care of first,' I say breathily. 'I have no idea how to handle it but I'm sure you can provide the solution.'

'What is it?' he demands. 'It better not take long. Daddy wants some sugar!'

RETCH!

'It's Buffy.' I manage to keep my voice straight. 'She's threatening to make trouble for us.'

'No, you got that wrong.' He smiles smugly. 'Buffy knows better than to mess with me.'

'I thought so too,' I reply. 'But this morning she told me

she'd had enough. She knows about you and Jade – and Melissa.'

Todd shrugs. 'Not a damn thing she can do about it.'

'I know that,' I say. 'She'll just have to take her chances like the rest of us.'

'Now you're seeing sense.'

'But she went crazy when she found out about us. She told me she's going to make trouble if you don't dump everybody but her.'

Todd's eyes narrow. 'What kind of trouble?'

'She's been in London a few years now,' I explain. 'She says she knows gossip columnists. People in the press.' I lower my voice. 'She even knows things that might hurt your political career.'

That seems to do the trick. Todd's now pacing the room and the small bulge has vanished, although only a practised eye could tell the difference.

'I'm just worried about you,' I say earnestly.

'Don't be. We'll fix this.' He winks at me. 'Lucy, you're about to see Todd Mayle in action.'

He strides over to his desk and presses the buzzer on his telephone.

'This is Buffy,' she says. I'm glad to see the farm-girl accent has been replaced by the Hamptons socialite again. He mustn't suspect a thing.

'Buffy, this is Todd,' he snaps. 'Get in here!' And he slams the phone down.

Two seconds later Buffy walks in. She shuts the door behind her and I can see that she's shaking. That's OK, she would be nervous, wouldn't she?

'Buffy,' Todd snaps. 'What's this I'm hearing about you wanting to make trouble?'

'What it is, Todd, is I've had enough,' she says. Loudly. Good, that should carry.

'Don't you yell at me,' he roars. 'Just remember who pays your salary.'

'All that means is I have to do a job,' Buffy replies, tossing her hair.

'Your job is to do what you're told. I pay your rent. Forgotten that?'

'I thought you told me you paid for it with company money,' she says.

I hold my breath.

'I pay for it, that's all you need to know,' Todd says. 'I pay for those fancy clothes you're wearing and the allowance you get every week. I even paid for those pearls.'

'The same way he pays for my clothes and my flat,' I say. 'Right, honey?'

'Who gives a shit if it's company money? Do you hear Lucy bitching?' He shakes his head. 'Enough whining and threats from you, girl.'

'I don't believe you,' Buffy says.

He stares. 'What?'

'You said you could bury me,' she states. Clear as a bell. Man, I hope this works. 'You said you've got lawyers who can make it seem like *I'm* the one raiding the company cash when everybody knows you use it as a piggy bank.'

'It's my family's goddamn company.'

'But you spend all the money on yourself and your girlfriends,' Buffy cries. 'That's illegal.'

'Don't be such a hick, Betsy-Ann,' Todd says cruelly. 'Laws are there for the little people. Nobody's going to catch me with my hand in the cookie jar. But if I tell them to, they might well catch *you*.'

'I'm not gonna sleep with you any more,' Buffy says. 'You're a loser!' And her whole face goes pink with pleasure.

'Actually, Todd,' I say, moving towards the door. 'She's right. You *are* a loser.'

His whole body stiffens as this registers. He just stares at me.

'You lie, you cheat, you blackmail women. And you think having money makes it OK.'

'Fine, Lucy,' Todd snaps. 'Get your shit and get out. And keep your mouth shut, unless you want to land in the courts yourself!'

'Oh, and by the way, Buffy says you're the worst lover she's ever had,' I add. 'It's pure hell.'

'All twenty seconds of it,' says Buffy, and we glance at each other and burst out laughing.

'You little bitches!' Todd snarls.

'Now, now, Todd,' I say. I open the door to his office and look behind me, just in case he tries something physical. There's a clear path to the street door. And anyway, James is standing there, right outside the door, with his arms folded. 'You don't want to be using bad language to the police.' And I put my hand down into my bra and pull out the Dictaphone.

Everybody stares at it. Especially Todd.

'Todd?' cries Jade. 'What's going on? What have those two been saying to you, sweetheart?' She stares at us dramatically. 'I think you should both know,' she cries, tossing back her long blonde hair, 'that Todd and I are *an item.*' She gazes soulfully at Todd. 'I had to tell them. Now it's out in the open. Why should we hide our love?'

'Shut up!' Todd shrieks.

'You!' cries Melissa, staring at Jade. 'You're the one seeing *my* boyfriend? And all this time I thought it was Buffy!'

'Todd has dated everybody in this office,' I say calmly. 'And at least one girl outside of it at the same time.'

Melissa's mouth hangs open.

'More to the point, he's a blackmailing, sexually harassing jerk. And he should be in jail.' I hold up the Dictaphone triumphantly. 'I'll be making some copies for the press, and after that I'll be sending this straight to the police.'

Todd leaps forward, but James has his arm across the door.

'I don't think so,' he says.

Todd looks wildly around the room. There are five sets of hostile eyes staring at him.

'Look,' he says, after a second's pause. 'People. Nobody knows about this except us. I'm sure we can work something out.' He passes a hand through his hair, trying for composure. 'A financial settlement. In exchange for signing a binding confidentiality document—'

'Let me get this right,' James says. His cut-glass voice sounds very businesslike all of a sudden. 'You want us to sign something that says we won't reveal you've been embezzling company funds?'

'Or sexually harassing me?' Buffy chimes in.

Todd shrugs. He's amazing, really. I can't believe he thinks he can bluff his way out of this.

'Everybody has their price,' he says. 'These girls all did. So, shall we say a million pounds apiece?'

A million pounds. Each. A momentary spell seems to fall over the group. But Buffy is the first to speak up.

'I didn't have a price,' she says. 'I loved you. More fool me. But now I just want to see you in jail!'

'Wait,' Melissa says. She's gone very determined-looking. 'Wait. Buffy, maybe we all deserve some compensation. This doesn't have to go any further.'

'Oh yes it does,' says James.

Everybody turns to look at him.

'Miss Evans,' he says. 'I'll take that tape, if you please.'

I shake my head. 'This is going straight to the police.'

He reaches inside the pocket of his double-breasted suit and pulls something out. It's a little plastic wallet. He flips it open.

'James Foster,' he says. 'Serious Fraud Squad. Mr Mayle, you're under arrest.'

Melissa gives a little squeal and clutches the desk. Buffy and Jade look grimly pleased. And Todd just squares his shoulders and glares at me.

'You think you're so goddamn clever,' he snaps. 'Brilliant little Lucy Evans. Not the klutz who had to be taught how to wear a pair of heels and act like a girl. Oh no, you're Sherlock Holmes in a mini skirt, right? Well, let me tell you something. I got lawyers. And they'll get me out of this. I'll get out of this grimy little island where the goddamn sun never shines and I'll go back to the States.' His voice has turned into a high-pitched screech. He looks a little hysterical. 'And I'll be sitting in the US Senate while you're stuck as a typist in some shithole! With a *lady* by my side. It could have been you, Lucy. But Victoria told me everything. How you're about as feminine as a Russian weightlifter. How you're nothing but a tomboy, a ball-busting bitch!'

James roughly spins him round – it doesn't take much. How come I never noticed what a skinny git Todd is? In a fair fight, Victoria could probably take him.

'But I am acting like a girl, Todd,' I say sweetly. 'I was before I met you. The trouble with you is you're so effeminate you can't handle anything tougher than a Barbie. And even Barbie's an astronaut and a scientist these days. Get used to it, Todd. I never needed lessons in femininity from you. But you need to learn how to be a man.'

All the girls except Melissa applaud.

'Well, he'll have plenty of time,' James says grimly. 'About five to ten years, I reckon. We'll be in touch, Miss Evans, Miss Colvert—'

'Don't forget me!' Jade cries. 'I want to testify too!'

'Excellent,' James says. 'Detectives will call on you at your residences. Good morning, ladies,' he says cheerfully, and bodily thrusts a stumbling Todd out of the front door.

I look at Buffy. And she offers me an American high-five, which actually doesn't seem too out of place. So I slap her hand and she cheers.

'What are you going to do now?' I ask her.

She shrugs. 'No clue. Move out of his apartment. Not that I have anyplace to stay.'

I write down my mobile number. 'Call me tonight. I'll get you somewhere, at least for now. My sister's got a spare room, or my mate . . .' My voice trails away. 'Well, my sister, anyway.'

'Thanks, Lucy. You're a doll,' Buffy says.

'I can't believe you three!' comes the shriek. I look over, and Melissa has sat herself down on the reception area sofa. Her whole body is as tense as a violin string, and she's giving us all a major death stare. 'You're going to put him *in jail*? Don't you know who he *is*? He's worth—'

'Absolutely nothing,' says Jade. 'Worthless is what he is.'

Melissa tosses her carefully combed blond hair. 'Well, *I'll* speak up for him. You three obviously never had what we had together. With us it was real love. I'm going to be there for Todd. I'm going to be by his side. He can turn to me for comfort—'

'Good try, Melissa, but I don't think he wanted you more than anyone else,' Buffy said. 'He just slept with every girl in his immediate orbit. It was really a matter of location.'

'You've betrayed him!' Melissa shrieks. 'It's all just a jealous attempt to ruin our future together! You could never understand our sacred bond!'

'I don't think Todd had too good a grip on it either,' I say drily, 'judging by the brunette I caught him poking this morning, or the proposition he made to me about . . .' I check my watch, 'twenty minutes ago now.'

Melissa shrieks. 'Bitch!' she says. 'Liar!'

And on that happy note, I wave goodbye to Buffy and take a taxi back to Pelham House.

Toby's wreathed in smiles when I tell him the whole story.

'Dictaphone,' he says. 'Fucking brilliant, if you'll pardon my French.'

'Not very elaborate.'

'Best plans never are,' he says. 'Course, I suppose that's it for me. I'll lose my job, and the pension's gone . . .' His ancient face creases a bit further. 'Worth it, though,' he says after a minute.

'Certainly not. Your job's not gone.'

'They'll close the agency. Rentals and management.' He sighs. 'Nobody there to pay my wages.'

I shake my head. 'Look, Todd never did an entrepreneurial thing in his life. You can bet the whole thing was just a set-up by Mummy and Daddy back in Connecticut. Some parent company owns Mayle Accommodations, and you can sue them.'

'No money for a lawyer,' Toby says. 'The law's not for ordinary people, Miss Lucy. It's for them as can afford it, like Todd Mayle. And O.J. Simpson and that.'

He sounds so serious it's all I can do to stop laughing. But I don't want to hurt his feelings.

'I can get you a lawyer,' I say confidently. 'A . . . good friend of mine.'

I have to see Ollie at least once more. To say goodbye. And I suppose some good might as well come of it, other than me bumping up the share price of Kleenex the second I get out of his flat.

'Well,' he says doubtfully, 'that'd be nice.'

'Don't worry,' I say. 'Everything'll be sorted out. Here's my phone number.' I write it down. 'Just in case. And don't bother clearing out my flat, either. The police'll be round soon. That's all evidence.'

His face wreathes in smiles. 'You take care now, Miss Lucy,' he says.

'Bye, Toby.'

'Bye, miss,' he says. 'And miss – well done.'

* * *

277

I'm sitting in the gorgeous living room of Cathy's flat, sipping a cup of tea and trying to get my head to stop spinning.

I phoned her office and she said it was fine to come over. She'd call her building's receptionist to let me in. And she said Buffy could stay over tonight if she wanted. I don't know what I'd do without Cathy.

Go home; I'd probably go home.

And that's actually a thought.

Her sofa's big and squashy, and curled up in it with the telly on I feel quite warm and cosy. Which might be the shock. I know it won't last, though.

I can hardly believe that less than two nights ago I was still Todd's girlfriend – well, one of them, anyway. I can hardly believe I ever even *met* Todd. A few hours between now and this morning, and already it seems to be fading into the distance. Like something that happened to somebody else. I should have known from the start it was too good to be true. Who takes a totally unqualified receptionist on and suddenly gives them a luxury flat and fifteen grand to buy clothes? OK, so I was his girlfriend. Or *a* girlfriend. And as I sip my tea, the warm, safe feeling sort of fades away and I just start to feel stupid.

Sure, Todd was a jerk. But he was a damn good-looking, smooth, *rich* jerk, and they can date anybody they like. Whatever made me think he'd date somebody like me – for real?

I couldn't even get my best mate to date me.

In fact, I appear to have comprehensively bollocksed my life up, don't I?

I'm twenty-four. I've no job, no boyfriend, no flat, and no savings. If I employed Tony Blair's entire team of spin doctors, this c.v. still would not look good. To anybody.

Hmm. Sod this. I'm not going to sit around feeling sorry for myself. Even if my life *is* a complete disaster, stewing in it is not going to make it any better. I'm going to go out and buy myself some top of the range, brand-new trainers, a pair of baggy jog pants and a sports bra with some of Todd's money; I'll take it out of my last week's wages. I can send the rest to the police later. Then I'll come back here and change, and then I'm going for a run.

I get back to the flat forty-five minutes later. My hair is plastered to my head, my chest is heaving, there's sweat all over my face, my foundation's run in little streaks, and my cheeks and forehead are flushed bright scarlet.

And I feel absolutely fucking fantastic.

Oh man. It's so good. It's better than wine, better than any kind of drugs. There's nothing out there when you go running. No gorgeous best mates who prefer Annoying Fembots. No smooth, rich, lying bastards who are four-timing you with other girls. No ex-friends who really hate you and want to kick you away from their fiancés.

Nothing but me and the road and my headphones.

Everything's different when I work out. The colours are brighter. My anger sort of melts. And even Madonna seems to be quite profound. 'Papa don't preach,' she says. If only I'd listened to her when Todd started his controlling little lectures!

I peel off my sodden clothes and step into Catherine's bathroom. Wash and condition my hair, dry off. Get dressed in jeans and a T-shirt and my one pair of decent loafers. Mmm. I almost want to die with pleasure. After months of high heels it's like getting a foot massage!

Then I casually nuke my hair dry and scarf a brush through it. I head back into the bathroom to . . .

Wait a minute. What am I doing?

I halt with my hand halfway to my face. I'm making myself up. And I don't need to do that any more, do I? There's no Todd, no Ollie come to that. I can wear whatever the hell I like. I may be at the bottom again but at least I've got my freedom.

Right on!

Um, but my hand is still going, isn't it?

I'm making up. Just a bit. Stealing some of Cathy's tinted moisturizer. And maybe a *very* quick stroke of bronzer won't hurt.

There.

I stand there, almost amazed at myself. I just voluntarily put on make-up!

Hmm. Maybe I actually *do* like wearing make-up. Not the whole thing, of course; not the lingerie and heels and especially not the bloody tights. But a bit of tinted moisturizer's not going to kill me. A bit of concealer for the bags under my eyes. Even a spray of scent . . .

Looking good makes me feel better. And today, that's worth having, isn't it?

I'm going to need all the help I can get. I'm going to have to call Ollie. I need to do it while he's at work, because no way can I risk getting Victoria on the line if I call his flat.

'Oliver McLeod,' he says.

Isn't it amazing how we become totally different people at work? That voice. It's Ollie, but it's not. It's clipped and brisk and firm because he's obviously important. But it's also exhausted, and sort of drained.

'Lucy Evans,' I say. Also trying for brisk. It's better than weepy, right?

'Lucy,' Ollie says. At least he doesn't seem totally exasperated. 'How's it going?'

'I need to see you again,' I say.

He sighs. 'So soon? I'm totally snowed under here. Some of us have to work for a living, you know? We don't all have cushy grace-and-favour gigs.'

'Neither do I,' I say. 'I split up with Todd.'

'And he made you resign?' says Ollie, outraged. 'He never sacked you?'

'It's a bit worse than that,' I say. 'Actually I sort of need to talk to you about it. I might have a client for you.'

'I'm not working for Todd Mayle,' Ollie says shortly.

'Working against him,' I say. 'I know this old man that needs to sue him. But he doesn't have any money. The old man, that is, not Todd.'

There's a pause.

'Have you been drinking?' Ollie demands, in a voice that sounds refreshingly like the old him. Before Victoria. Actually, it makes my heart sort of ache.

'No. But I have watched Todd get arrested and carted off to the cells. For serious fraud.' I sigh. 'It's *very* complicated, and I need to tell you all about it. And – say goodbye.'

'What?' he says. 'What are you talking about?'

Don't cry don't cry don't cry.

'I'm leaving London,' I say, and as soon as it's out of my mouth I know it's true. 'I need to figure my life out. I'm going back to Kent. And I don't think I'll be back.'

Ollie says nothing.

'And I can't come to the wedding,' I say, and now it's getting harder not to cry. I bite the inside of my cheek, painfully. Anything for a distraction. 'This whole thing has really – upset me. Ah, Todd was cheating on me. And I don't think I can face a wedding.'

'Not even mine?'

'Not even yours,' I say, and I'm glad all those *Tomorrow's Worlds* were wrong and nobody uses videophones yet. Because he can't see the fat tear that's trickling down my cheek.

'I can fit you in at three,' he says. 'But I've only got fifteen minutes, is that OK?'

'That's fine.' The quicker the better. I don't think I could take too much more emotion today.

'You can always come round tonight,' he says. 'Victoria can cook for us. She could make her famous bouillabaisse again,' he says, and chuckles.

281

Oh God. It's amazing how much it hurts. It stabs into me like a physical pain in the chest. I shut my eyes.

'Maybe,' I say, and my voice sounds very distant. 'Anyway, see you at three.'

'Wow,' Ollie says. He shakes his head. 'Just – wow.'

I gave him the *Reader's Digest* version. That Todd was embezzling company funds to pay for his mistresses, and that he'd been three-timing me. I even told him about surprising Todd in bed this morning; I just pretended the girl was Melissa.

'And you really didn't know?' he says for the umpteenth time.

'Of course not,' I say. 'If I'd known I'd hardly have stuck around, would I?'

'I suppose not,' Ollie says, without too much conviction.

That gives me pause. Actually, I'm glad. I'd much rather be angry than weepy.

'You suppose not?' I say. 'What, you think I'd have put up with that – because he was rich?'

'I don't know,' Ollie says, and he looks at me sharply. 'What else did he have going for him, Lucy? That could get a girl like you to date him in the first place?'

'He was handsome,' I say.

Ollie shrugs dismissively. 'Skinny little nothing if you ask me.'

'Well, I didn't ask you. And he was nice to me, at the start. And I admired his achievements with the company . . .' I pause. 'What I thought were his achievements, anyway.'

'So money had absolutely nothing to do with it?'

'Not *absolutely* nothing. I mean, it is nice to be taken out to lovely restaurants and given the use of a gorgeous flat—'

'Ah-HAH!' Ollie says triumphantly. 'You can't fool me, Lucy, I know you too well. You girls pretend you don't care, but you do, all the time.'

'That's ridiculous.'

'Is it?' he asks, sadly.

'It's OK to like nice things. They're an added bonus. But it's not OK to date a man *just* because he can give you nice things. See the difference?'

Ollie chews his cheek. A bad sign.

'And,' I say, daringly, 'it's even OK to demand a man have a good career, or at least the intention of having one. He's got to at least be trying. Why should we have to date some layabout?'

'I s'pose,' he says, ungraciously. 'Although your career wasn't exactly high flying, now was it?'

'Yes, well. I was having fun,' I say. 'And I never asked my dates to pay for anything. But maybe there was,' I open my fingers about half a centimetre, '*that* much truth in what you said. It was time to get a bit more serious. Even, maybe,' I add grudgingly, 'try out a few girlie things. I just went too far.'

'Oh Lucy,' he says, sighing. 'The stupid mistakes we make, eh?'

My heart flips, slowly. 'Are you . . . are you talking about Victoria?'

'No, you're right,' he says. 'I'm just being too sensitive. It's not like I didn't know Vicky. She's not like you.'

You can say that again.

'She likes the finer things,' he says. 'She's high-maintenance. And I knew that, I liked it. It's just that . . .' He looks awkward.

'You don't have to tell me if you don't want to,' I say sympathetically. Yes you do! Tell me everything!

'It's just that when we started dating, she could afford to get them all herself. I mean, she made a healthy wage. Maybe not the same as me . . .'

'Victoria makes sixty grand,' I exclaim. 'What do you mean, not the same as you?'

'I make a lot more than that,' he says, apologetically.

'But you can't.' I blink at him. 'All your jumpers had holes in them. And you drive a Ford.'

'I don't really care about stuff,' he explains. 'I just paid off my mortgage and bought some stocks and that. Don't want to have to work for ever.'

'So . . . are you a secret millionaire, or something? You *do* have a James Bond double life, after all.'

'Don't tell Vicky,' Ollie says, sounding panicked. 'She'd want to spend it all on shoes!'

'My lips are sealed,' I say. Like my fate, eh? This day just gets better and better. Victoria *so* does not deserve him.

'Anyway . . . I kind of like the idea of a wife that works. It's not really the money, as such. It just makes her more interesting. I always loved that about Vicky, she had this drive, she was so put together. Not like me. You saw the holes in my jumpers,' he acknowledges.

'And now she doesn't want to work. Well, she said she wanted to be a mum.' I grit my teeth. This is killing me, being supportive. 'That's a full-time job. I'll bet she'll be just as interesting. More so,' I lie. Poor little bastards, having Victoria for a mum! I hope there aren't any girls, at least. She'll probably give them complexes and make them weigh in every morning.

'Yes,' Ollie says. 'Only, you know, she mentioned having a nanny.'

'Why?' I explode. 'If she's not working . . .'

'That's what I said. And she said she'll still need time to look after herself.' Ollie shoots me an anxious look. 'You're my best mate, Lucy. What do you think?'

But I can't.

I simply can't. I'm butting out. And that's the most I can do.

'I think it's something to work out between the two of you,' I say, and my voice has gone all cold and distant. 'None of my business, really.' I look at my watch. 'Anyway, we've only got five minutes left. And I need to tell you all about Toby so you can take his case. You will, right?'

'Of course I will,' Ollie says, miserably. 'I'd do anything for you.'

I quickly rattle off the details and give him Toby's phone number. Ollie writes it all down on a big yellow pad, nods, and says he has an excellent chance of an enormous settlement.

'Right, well,' I say, when we're done. 'I should go.'

'What?' he says, sounding panicked.

'Fifteen minutes is up. It's your next appointment.'

'I'll cancel it,' he says at once.

'Nah,' I say. 'I'm just going to go home. We probably won't see each other too much in the future, to be honest.' I've got a huge lump in my throat. I have to get out of here. 'So I'll just say goodbye.'

'What?' he says. 'Don't be ridiculous, Lucy! For God's sake! What are you, an Olympic sprinter? It's like you can't wait to get rid of me!'

I sigh. 'It's really complicated, Ollie,' I say. 'I just want to get out of town and – and get over Todd.'

His blue eyes narrow. 'Right. You certainly look heart-broken. I don't think you ever loved him for a second.'

I snap. 'What the hell do you know of love?' I say. 'In your rosy world where everything's perfect!'

'Nothing's perfect,' he says. 'Nothing's ever perfect.' He passes a hand through his blond hair. 'Look, come over tonight,' he says. 'Please? Just come over for dinner. I'll speak to Victoria. You can't leave like this.'

I'd rather gnaw off my own toes than sit at a table with her again.

'I don't think so, Ollie,' I say. 'I'll call you from Kent. How's that?'

He opens his mouth to protest. But there's a knock on the door and his secretary comes in, followed by a burly man in a suit with shifty-looking eyes.

'Mr Elton,' she says. 'Oh – sorry, Mr McLeod, I didn't see you had company.'

'That's quite all right,' I say, blindly grabbing my bag. 'I was just leaving. Goodbye, Ollie.' And I walk out before he can say another word.

Buffy has left a message on my mobile to say she's staying with a friend. Thank God, because I don't want to see anybody tonight. It's only 5 p.m., and I feel so drained and low. I run a bath, then write Cathy a note saying I've got a headache and I've gone to bed early. It's meant to be a lie, but when I draw the curtains and crawl into bed, feeling as if my heart will burst, I'm asleep before my head hits the pillow.

When I wake up, it's almost ten. I stumble out of bed, pull back the curtains, and the day is grimy, even though it's still the end of summer. Grey clouds to match my grey mood.

I shower and dress, and make up. That too. Then I pack up everything I have in one of Catherine's overnight cases, leave her another note, and walk to the tube. It's not very friendly staying at my sister's without saying a single word to her, but I can't stay here any longer. London's choking me. I want to go home.

I go to Charing Cross and, thank God, there's a train already waiting on the platform. I grab a ticket and a coffee and a copy of *Heat*. Not that I'm going to do any reading. But I don't want anybody talking to me, either. If you look like your nose is in the paper, they don't bother you.

I needn't have worried. It's half past ten and nobody's going to Tunbridge Wells. I have the carriage all to myself, apart from a drunk bloke who I think arrived in London asleep and is about to return to Hastings that way. I dare say the seaside air will do him good.

The train creaks out of the station, and I check my messages. One from Buffy saying to call her anytime. One from Catherine saying she hopes I'm feeling better. And five from Ollie. I delete them all without listening to them.

Thank God I have my coffee. The train windows are dirty, the sky's still grey, but the coffee's hot; and as we pass the Thames I feel as if a weight is slipping off my shoulders. No more fancy restaurants and designer kitchens, no more vintage champagne and shops you need an appointment to browse in. No cheating trust fund brats or Barbie doll girlfriends. I'm going home. And right now, I don't think I'd care if I never saw bloody London again.

14

It feels a bit odd, this.

It feels sort of other-planetary. Getting off at Tunbridge Wells at an empty station. Hoisting my tiny – OK, Cathy's tiny – overnight bag into a taxi. The taxi driver talks non-stop at me all the way home about being chairman of the neighbourhood watch, and how all his friends think he should run for Parliament. Which is great, because all I have to say is 'Mmm'.

The familiar roads and hedges slip past me. I know every turning, every house. Wow. It's amazing, coming home. It's like I never went away. Like the last few months have been this one big nightmare. And now I'm waking up.

Or I would feel that way, if not for Ollie.

But anyway. Enough of that. I can look forward to some peace and quiet. I'm not going to do *anything* for at least a month. Just sit at home and watch Sky and eat Mum's undercooked sausage rolls. Maybe do some fishing. And think, no, *meditate*. I don't do enough meditating. In fact I never have. But now would be the time to start. Just sort my head out. My only priority—

'That'll be twelve pounds, please,' the driver says.

'Oh. Right.' I fish in my bag. What's that other car doing in our driveway? Only Mum and Dad are meant to be home. 'There you go.'

He gives me change from twenty and I tip him the five-pound note because I'm not really paying attention.

'Very nice of you,' he says jovially. 'Have a nice day, as the Americans say. And remember, vote LibDem.'

'I definitely will,' I lie. 'Bye.'

'Cheery-bye!' he sings out, reaching over to close my door. He wheels the car round and lumbers off down our drive while I hesitate in front of the door.

Oh God. Is it Mrs Milton again? Mum's friend from the WI? I can't stand her. She's supposed to be all mumsy and cake-making, but she's actually a radical feminist who always bores on about Simone de Beauvoir. Or, worse, it could be Derek, our mad gardener. Derek is a top-class skiver whose work pattern appears to be five minutes, come inside for forty-minute 'tea break', another five minutes, then 'time for a bicky', and so forth. I wouldn't mind except he insists on engaging me in conversation the entire time. Asking millions of questions. My job, my love life – he should call James, they've probably got a great job for him in CID.

Maybe I'm supposed to ask him questions back, come to think of it. Only, you know, I don't want to. Because I don't care about his life. I'm sure this makes me evil.

Damn!

Honestly. I was just coming home for some comfort. To be looked after for once. Some sausage rolls and hot chocolate. And chatting to my parents and *nobody else*. Is that too much to ask? How am I supposed to think deep thoughts about my future with Mrs Minton or mad Derek there?

Oh, bloody hell, wait a minute. It's not them. I *do* recognize that car.

Our front door swings open.

'Lucy!' screams Emily. She rushes forward to envelop me in a bear hug. I clutch her to me, but there, over her shoulder, glum face, slumped shoulders, is George, my future brother-in-law, and the world's dullest person.

'Isn't it brilliant!' Em screeches. 'Have you got time off

work? Have you come down here to help me? Thank God!
I need another pair of hands. It's mad down here!
Absolutely nuts! I can't take the stress by myself.'

'The stress of what?' I ask.

She stares at me as if I'm completely mental.

'The *wedding*, Lucy,' Emily says. 'The bloody wedding!'

How could I have forgotten? I'm such a self-absorbed
cow! But much as I try, I can't stop the waves of dismay
crashing over me as Emily drags me inside into what does
indeed look like a madhouse. Or campaign HQ for the war
in Iraq or something.

Our lovely, calming house is totally unrecognizable.
There are wedding magazines everywhere. Not just strewn
on the table and heaped on the chairs; pages of them are
torn out and pinned up everywhere, along with lists and
phone numbers, recipes, and indecipherable scrawls about
cake and balloons.

And that's not everything. My mum is looking a com-
bination of thrilled and harassed to death. Far from swoop-
ing down to envelop me in motherly comfort, she gives me
a quick peck on the cheek and turns back to her phone
call.

'Well, I did say the order was provisional,' she says firmly.
'And now it won't be walnut and chocolate ganache
because one of our guests is allergic to peanuts.' A pause. 'I
am aware walnuts aren't peanuts, but we can't be too
careful, can we?' she says, triumphantly. 'And you hardly
want to see *that* headline in the *Courier*, do you? Callous
Cake-Maker Causes Choking Death Agony,' she says
dramatically. A longer pause. 'Well, I should hope so,' she
sniffs. 'So it will now be vanilla and raspberry coulis – that
right, darling?'

Emily nods.

'Did you get that? Yes, that *is* confirmed. Give me your
fax number,' Mum says, sounding awfully efficient. Fax
number? Mum's only just come to grips with the ballpoint

291

pen. 'We'll be sending through written instructions. Good day.'

She hangs up.

'That's that sorted out,' she says triumphantly.

'Imagine,' says Emily with a kind of desperation. 'Imagine if they'd insisted on walnut!'

'The order was only provisional,' says George in a monotone. 'If they'd have tried to bill us, we could have sued.'

I stare. Has everybody gone totally loony?

'Lucy, darling,' says Mum distractedly, as though just noticing I'm here. 'Would you like a cup of tea?'

'That'd be great,' I say, perking up.

'Could you make everybody one, then?' she asks. 'Only I'm a bit busy right now. We've had to sack the florist. And you can imagine what chaos that caused.'

'I take semi-skimmed milk and exactly one and a half spoons of sugar,' announces George.

'Oh, sure,' I say forlornly. 'No problem.'

'And are you planning to stay the night? asks Mum. 'Only we're a bit crammed.'

I look at her in dismay. 'Well, I was. A bit longer than a night. But if there's no room . . .'

'Of course there's room!' says Mum automatically, trying to be cheerful. 'I'll – I'll clear out a space in the box room. You used to camp in there with your little friends and play Girls' World.'

Girls' World. That's a blast from the past.

'That was Cathy,' I remind her.

'Oh. So it was. You used to play your *Donkey Kong* in there! And it had a bed. Remember?'

Yes, I do. A creaky old single with an ancient mattress whose coils dig into your spine.

'I'll change the sheets,' Mum promises, seeing my face. Oh no, I've made her even more worried now. She's starting to twist her fingers, which she only does when under extreme stress, like the time our nextdoor neighbour threatened to take us to court if we wouldn't trim back our yew hedge.

'No, that's fine,' I say hastily. 'That's absolutely terrific. It's a fantastic room. Only . . .' my voice trails away. 'I was just wondering who's in my room, and the spare room?'

'George is in your room,' Mum says. 'And the spare room is out of bounds.'

Out of bounds?

'It's the command centre,' Emily explains. With a totally straight face, I might add. 'It's where I'm doing my designs. I'm making all the bridal tiaras by hand. *And* doing the decor for the marquee.'

'And you'd better add the church flowers,' Mum says darkly. 'The vicar has a relationship with the people we sacked. They give him a discount. He might get snippy if he finds out we're going another way . . .'

She glances at me, hovering by the kitchen table with my hand on my overnight case.

'You did want that tea, darling?' she says.

I recognize the universal code for 'make the tea' in our house and morosely make my way over to the kettle. George starts to talk endlessly about the sloping ground of our lawn and the marquee's hardwood floor. He begins every other sentence with 'As a licensed surveyor . . .'

But Mum and Em are fascinated. I might as well not be here. Oh God. I can't take any more. Where's Dad?

He's out in the garden. Right down at the bottom, sitting on the old wooden bench nobody ever uses because it's covered in moss and bird poo. But even though it's a gloomy day, Dad seems quite content. He's wearing a thick sweater and reading an old copy of the *Spectator*.

'Hi, Dad,' I say. 'Brought you a cup of tea. And a chocolate HobNob.'

Dad looks up, and blinks owlishly behind his reading

glasses. For a moment I wonder if he, too, will be under-whelmed to see me. But then his face creases into a huge smile.

'Darling! When did you get here?'

'About half an hour ago.'

'This is a surprise,' he said. 'Popped back for a flying visit, eh? From your top job in the world of property? How did you get the time off?'

When Dad says 'top job in the world of property' he's not being ironic, either.

'I was only a receptionist,' I say.

'First impression. Vital to any business,' he responds instantly, taking his tea. Then pauses. 'But you said "was"?'

'I quit,' I say.

'Good for you. Dull as dishwater,' Dad pronounces. 'Or is it ditchwater? I always get that one wrong.'

'It was pretty boring,' I admit.

'Why did you pack it in?' He demolishes his chocolate HobNob and looks at me piercingly.

'Well, it was dull.'

'And?' says Dad. He may be easy-going but he's not thick.

'And,' I sigh, 'I had a disastrous relationship with my boss. At least I thought it was a relationship. In fact he had loads of girls. And he was embezzling. And now he's been arrested, and I'll probably have to testify at the trial.'

There's a pause.

'I see,' Dad says. He seems to cast about for some ray of sunshine, but my tale of woe does not give him much to work with. However –

'You weren't in love with him, though,' Dad says. 'Because you're in love with the Scottish chap.'

'No I'm not,' I say, unconvincingly. 'Anyway, it doesn't matter. Because he's still getting married to Victoria Cobham, and he obviously loves her.'

Dad looks unpersuaded, but mercifully takes refuge in his tea.

'Well, darling,' he says. 'And you've come back here for a few days to decide what to do next?'

'A few months,' I say. 'At least until I get a job. That's all right, isn't it?' I look at him anxiously.

'All right?' Dad repeats. He looks hurt. 'Poppet, this is your *home*. You can stay for ever as far as we're concerned. And you don't even need a job. You could just live here and help Mum with the cooking,' he adds, a touch wistfully. 'It'd be nice to have some properly cooked roasts for once.'

I feel my heart squeeze and I reach over to hug him. 'Dad, you're adorable. But I won't stay too long. I just – I just need to figure out where my life is going,' I say. Easier said than done.

'Up, sweetie,' Dad says stoutly. 'Your life is always going up. You're my star.'

He always used to call me that when I was tiny. It makes me want to cry. I feel like I've let him down, so badly. I was one of the brightest and bubbliest in our family, always popular at school, and now look. All my sisters are these big successes and getting married or popping out babies, while Lucy is just the loser, with no money, reduced to living with her parents.

'Not much of a star, am I?' I say, trying to keep it light, but my voice does sound a bit throaty.

Dad sets his mug down carefully against a patch of moss and looks right at me.

'Lucy,' he says. 'We didn't call you that because we wanted you to be a millionaire or a movie actress. We called you that because of all our children, you were the lightest. You had the most fun. You always smiled.' He presses my hand. 'Whatever you decide to do, darling, it's going to be fine with us. It doesn't matter what you do for a living. The only thing that matters is that you don't choose a job or a man who will suck the sparkle out of you.

You work most of your life, you know. So if your job is miserable, so's everything else.' His tone is very serious, for Dad. 'I didn't want you to go into property. I knew you'd hate it. You have to find out what you love to do, and then work in that. And as for men, well.' A big sigh. 'I don't think there's only one person for everybody. There are lots of people for everybody. It's just that when you find one that fits, you always think he is the only one. So if you're getting over that Oliver person, there will eventually be somebody else. But don't rush it. It's far better to be alone than to be with the wrong person. You can enjoy life in almost any situation if you put your mind to it.'

This is the longest speech I have ever heard Dad make.

'All right,' I say. 'All right, Dad. I won't take any more boring jobs.'

'Glad to hear it.' He picks up his mug and his *Spectator*, lecture over.

'And I said I wasn't in love with Ollie,' I can't resist adding.

Dad doesn't look up. 'I know what you said, darling.'

When I get back to the house, Mum's somehow managed to look even more frayed around the edges. Some hairs are dangling down from her bun, giving her a rather unkempt look. It suits her!

'Darling,' she says. 'Guess what?'

'What?'

'Catherine and Peter are coming down here tonight too.' She shrugs helplessly. 'Where I am going to put them? I've no room!'

'There's the attic,' I say. 'You've got lots of space in there.'

'But no bed!'

'You do. You've got that electric blow-up bed,' I say. 'And the chair in there folds out. That's two beds.'

'But it all has to be tidied!' Mum wails. 'Peter can't sleep on that. He's a high-powered executive!'

'He'll love it,' I say firmly. He'd better, I still haven't forgiven him for the Esther situation. 'And don't worry about doing the beds and tidying up. I'll do all that.'

'Are you sure?' Mum says gratefully. 'Because we were going to pop into Tunbridge Wells to look at some dresses, and Em thought you could spend a few hours trying on bridesmaids' gowns.'

Hell no. 'I can do that another time,' I say. 'You have to have somewhere for Peter and Catherine.'

'Yes, yes I do,' says Mum. 'Oh, thank you, darling. I'll tell Emily—'

There's a loud honk from the drive.

'That's George,' Mum says. 'I better be going, he hates to be late. Bye, darling,' and she rushes off, leaving nothing but the metallic tang of Yardley lavender water behind her.

Alone. At last. I never thought anything would make me look forward to tidying up, but wedding chaos will do it. Weddings are the absolute, one hundred per cent last thing I want to think about right now.

I get to the landing cupboard and take out a few pillows and sheets. Once Cathy gets here, of course, it'll be twice as bad. She'll be announcing *her* engagement, and then all the jokes about my turn next will start.

At least Emily will stop looking to me for help. She and Catherine can be mad brides-to-be together. Hey, if the worst comes to the worst at least I can grab a Jeffrey Archer novel and join Dad at the bottom of the garden. Which is the furthest away from the house he could get.

I tidy up and quite enjoy it. It's methodical work, after all, and it's brainless. Pushing the Hoover over the attic carpet, opening the windows, brushing dead insects into the dust pan. Slowly everything starts coming together and looking bright and cheerful. I sort books into piles and even find an empty milk bottle, which I fill with water and a few late roses from the garden. There. Not too bad. Actually, too good for bloody Peter.

I'm proud of myself. I'm quite good at this.

Then I clear some space in the box room, which takes longer. I lay a folded blanket on top of the ancient single mattress before I put the fitted sheet on – that should take care of my back, anyway – and try to stuff as many of our old board games onto shelves as I can, so that at least I can unpack Cathy's overnight case. I need somewhere to put my clothes, but perhaps I'll sneak into my bedroom and commandeer at least one drawer in one of the cupboards. And let's face it, that's all I'm going to need.

Hey, maybe I should become a char! Perhaps that's my future!

Or maybe not.

Although, come to think of it, I wouldn't have to stop at just *being* a char. I mean, I could get a job as a char. And do it brilliantly, so that everybody said, 'Oh, Lucy Evans is the best in the business.' And then, of course, I'd start my own franchise, 'Charming Chars' or something. We could come up with a gimmick, like, 'Our chars are guaranteed not to talk to you about their lives while cleaning your home!' That would be a winner. I could even extend that concept. 'Taciturn Taxis – Our Drivers Have Nothing to Say.' I bet we could get fifty per cent higher fees on airport trips. And anyway, once I've floated Charming Chars on the Stock Exchange I'll be famous, like that bird who started lastminute.com . . .

I stop with my feather duster in my hand. What am I like? Head in the clouds. I make one bed and already I'm the Richard Branson of bed-making.

But I do feel marginally more cheerful. Dad's right, after all. There is no point slaving away at a job you hate. I just have to find out what I want to do, and then do it. Life's very simple at times.

Ooh. Now I feel all profound.

The sound of tyres crunching on the drive blasts me out

of my reverie. They're back! Quick. I dive for my jog pants and trainers and quickly race to Dad's room to steal one of his T-shirts. No way am I ready to spend two hours listening to Emily and George on future wedded bliss. I know this makes me a candidate for worst sister of the year. And I definitely will join in when Cathy gets here. But she'll take some of the strain, and I won't have to think so much about Ollie . . .

I get my Walkman and my Madonna *Immaculate Collection* and run out of the front door, jogging gently just to warm up.

'Bye!' I call loudly to Emily and Mum.

'OFF ON A RUN, DARLING?' yells Mum. 'SEE YOU LATER!'

I haven't actually turned the music on yet. But that's fine. Headphones are as good a barrier as magazines, aren't they?

'There she goes!' says plump George. 'Always running, running, running, that one. What from, eh?' he says, and looks pleased with himself.

Emily frowns at him as I jog by them, staring straight ahead and pretending I can't hear.

'That's Lucy,' she says. 'Always so full of energy.'

Not by the time I get home, I'm not.

But I feel lifted. There's nothing like a punishing run when you're utterly low. You can hit the hills, and as you drive yourself up them, muscles screaming, sheer force of will taking you on, you feel invincible. With every pound your feet give the pavement, you imagine you're crushing your enemies into dust. I always got my aggression out this way – that, and blasting pixelated space aliens into pixelated gobbets of blood.

Everything falls away. It has to, really. You're working too hard to worry. You can't be heartbroken if you're gasping for breath.

I get back home and stagger into the kitchen. Maybe I

went a bit too hard . . . I need to get some breath, then I'll do my stretches . . .

'Ho ho ho!' says George jovially. 'That looks jolly attractive, I must say, Lucy!'

I glance at myself in Mum's age-spotted mirror. Yep, plastered hair, tomato-red face. The Lucy Evans special!

Five minutes at home and I suppose I've reverted to my unfeminine ways . . .

But actually, no.

'You know, George,' I hear myself say. 'The point is that you do this so you can look attractive.' I gesture at his pudgy belly. 'Maybe you should try it some time. Just start out with something gentle . . .'

'I say!' says George, outraged.

'Lucy!' says Mum.

I look repentantly at Emily. But she's nodding and smiling at me.

'You know, that wouldn't be a bad idea, love,' she says. 'And it's why Lucy has always eaten whatever she wanted and looked so good.'

Looked so good?

I had no idea Emily thought I looked good.

'Thanks, Em,' I mutter.

'What, are you kidding?' she says, bending over a catalogue of silk swatches. 'Cathy and Anne and me had to work so hard at it. The right clothes, the right hair. You could just throw on jeans and a T-shirt and look the prettiest of all of us.'

'Nobody's prettier than you, darling,' says George loyally. 'Although, it is true. Lucy always was a damn fine filly. Pity you can't run for a living, eh, Lucy?'

I bend into my stretches.

Hmm.

Not that George could ever speak any sense, but . . .

I think I might have an idea.

* * *

300

Cathy and Peter arrive just before six. Mum has pushed the boat out – a 'well done' roast lamb (medium rare), undercooked roast potatoes, and a couple of bottles of Sainsbury's champagne. Dad looks at me despairingly, so I quietly grab the roasting pan and slide it back into the oven while Mum's not looking.

'Lucy.'

I look up to see Catherine.

'Listen,' she says urgently. 'I got your message. But you ran out! Are you . . . are you feeling OK?'

'I feel fine,' I say. 'I didn't care for Todd anyway.'

'I know that,' she says. 'But Ollie McLeod's been calling the house. Trying to get in touch with you.'

'Oh,' My insides do a little churn. 'Well, I'll give him a call back,' I say lightly. 'I think he wants me to have a word with Victoria about the wedding. She's going completely mental.' I gesture around the kitchen, now an Aladdin's cave of wedding-related paraphernalia. 'But there's a lot of that going about.'

'Right. So there's no problem between the two of you, then?'

'Absolutely none,' I lie blithely. I'm getting really good at this. I should be in MI6 or something, like Stella Rimington,

'OK,' she says uncertainly. 'Because Peter and I were going to announce the engagement. But not if you don't feel up to it.'

I stand up from the oven and give her a huge hug, holding my hands away from her back so as not to get grease on her cashmere sweater.

'Oh, Cath,' I say. 'It's not like that. I don't want anybody else to have to feel down just because I was a bit depressed. I'm fine now. And I couldn't be happier for you two. I think you should let the whole world know. In fact, you should probably ring up Mrs Minton and—'

'Stop it!' Catherine says, and hits me on the shoulder. But she's smiling. She looks relieved. And I follow her into the drawing room, trying to look as bouncy and eager as she does herself. Seriously, I'd rather shoot my own foot off than ruin Cathy's moment. She's the best sister ever. And I do feel happy for her, and for Em. I even look at Peter and George and manage not to think of them as total fuckwits. If my lovely sisters like them, there must be *something* there, eh? No matter how cunningly hidden.

'Mum, Dad, actually, I've got some news,' Catherine says. She puts an arm around Peter. 'We're getting married too!'

Emily screams and jumps into the air, sending her champagne sloshing into George's face. So, there's something on the plus side!

'Bloody hell!' he says. But nobody's listening to him.

'Oh my God,' Mum keeps shrieking. 'Oh my God! Oh Catherine! Oh darling!'

Dad has gone up to Peter and pumped his hand in a manly way. I can hear him saying things like 'very lucky chap' and 'keeping her in the manner to which she's become accustomed'. Although perhaps when he sees his inflatable single bed and roses-in-a-milk-bottle accommodation that won't scare Peter *too* hard . . .

I curl my fingers round the stem of my champagne glass and congratulate Peter when the fuss dies down a bit.

'Look after her, won't you,' I say.

'Oh, she can look after herself.' Peter inclines his head to me. 'As I guess you heard.'

'I suppose you're allowed one total fuck-up,' I say. 'But be warned, I read a lot of mystery novels. I know many ways to kill people that are completely undetectable.'

He laughs. 'You know, Lucy, Cath was right about you.'

'Oh yes? She didn't mention that time with the pantomime horse and the itch powder, did she?' I ask. 'Because I was completely innocent.'

'No,' he says. 'She only told me that you're the happiest, funniest person she's ever met. And she says she'd give anything to be like you.'

I think my whole family is labouring under some mad delusion. But I'm going to humour them. I lift my champagne flute and toast both my sisters. It's great they're getting married. And besides, I need a drink . . .

Weddings.

Why?

That's my one-word review of the whole thing. Why? Why? When I get married, I'm sodding off to Gretna Green. Or better still, I won't get married. They're hardly lining up to ask me anyway.

Do you know, brides can spend an *entire day* shopping for stockings and garters? And expect their sisters to be interested in it?

I was right about one thing. Catherine and Emily are mostly obsessing off each other. They go everywhere together. They pore scornfully over bridal magazines, laughing at various dresses. I try not to think of Victoria doing the same thing. But at least I know she wouldn't be doing it with any sense of fun. Marriage is a job to her.

Poor Ollie.

Oh well. It was his choice.

Anyway, at least I'm at home. No bills, no romance. Just the daily joys of sneaking around the house trying to avoid being seen. That way I get dragged into the whole white lace and satin nightmare as little as possible. And I'm getting my old body back. Actually, I'm exercising like there's no tomorrow. Not only does it drive out thoughts of Ollie, it also means nobody can bother me. Exercise is the ultimate time to yourself!

Plus, I can eat Mum's sausage rolls, or four chocolate Hob-nobs at a time, without being bothered. I think I'm going to start my own line of T-shirts that say 'Life's too short for low-carb diets'.

If you can't have the occasional Strawberry Mivvi, there isn't much point, after all, is there?

And with my energy, some of the zest for life is coming back. Yes, OK, my heart's still broken. Which is monumentally unfair seeing as how I didn't even *love* Ollie before Victoria showed up – or I didn't know I loved him. And that's the same thing.

I've unpacked my old computer, and it's set up in the box room, where it sits precariously on an overloaded shelf. There's no room for a chair, so I perch on the end of my single bed and kill aliens. I've moved on from *Star Wars Galaxies* to *Doom 3*. And I'm a master at that!

'Darling.' Dad pokes his head round the door of the box room.

This is unfortunate, as I've just screamed out, 'DIE, MOTHERFUCKER, DIE!'

'Oh, er, hi, Dad,' I say, blushing. 'I, um, just stubbed my toe.'

'Yes,' he says drily. 'I heard you saying "Oh dear me".'

I smile at him. 'That's exactly what I said.'

'Or possibly it was "bother".'

'Bother's a good one,' I agree. 'I'll have to remember that.'

'You're wanted downstairs,' he says. 'George needs somebody to practise his thank-the-bridesmaids' speech on.'

I groan. 'Oh, please no.'

'Come on.'

'But I'm a bridesmaid,' I observe, hopefully. 'I mean, the speech is to me! It'll ruin it if I get to hear it in advance. Seven years' bad luck!'

Dad fixes me with one of his special stares. 'Love, show willing.'

'Oh, all right,' I say grudgingly, saving my game. And now I'm yanked out of the pixelated world in which I am a superstar to my crappy real life. 'I only wanted to come home to sort my head out,' I grumble. 'Instead I have to do my head in. With all this.'

That's quite funny. I'm just feeling smug and wondering

if I should write sitcoms when I catch sight of Dad's face. And even though he's normally indulgent, he's looking quite stern.

I feel a familiar sense of quailing as I look at him. Isn't it amazing how the second you go back to your parents, you lose about fifteen years and become a little kid again? Dad used to look at me that way when he was *really cross*. And even though I'm a grown woman who's soon going to have to testify in court, I'm a bit scared.

Dad manoeuvres himself past the door and my case and sits down heavily on the camp bed next to me.

'Lucy,' he starts.

Uh-oh. He used my name. People never do that unless they're about to tick you off.

'By "sort my head out" what you really mean is you came home to sulk.'

'That's not fair!' I say, outraged.

'Certainly it is,' he said. 'Sitting around dwelling on unhappy things, what else would you call it?'

He has a point but I'm not going to admit it.

'I'm just deciding what I want to do with my life,' I say loftily. 'Examining career options.'

'But you already agreed that a person should do what they love,' says Dad, as though I'm acting thick deliberately.

'Yes, Dad,' I say, calmly. 'But I only like rugby and fishing.'

'And exercise and computer games.'

'And heavy metal. And pop music. You're not going to suggest I go in for *Pop Idol* or something, are you? Because I'm a bit old to be Madonna now.'

'Dearest,' Dad says, in a softer voice. 'You used to make a living with your Pac-Man reviews.'

'Not really. I was subsidized.' This is uncomfortably close to my memories of Ollie. I shift on the bed.

'Well, I'm sure you can think of something. You're a clever girl.' He smiles at me. 'It's not because you need to

305

work; I told you, you can stay here for ever. It's because you need to be happy. And moping never made anybody happy. Except drugs manufacturers.'

Oh no, I don't want him to get started on big drugs companies, I'll be here all day.

'You're wearing make-up!' Dad says suddenly, as though he's just noticed.

I touch my face, worriedly. 'Don't you like it?' I ask.

'I think you look lovely. But you always do, and in any case, what does it matter what I think?'

'I don't know,' I mumble. 'You got worried when I said I was going into estate agency . . . I've always been a bit of a tomboy . . . and you liked that.'

'You didn't like estate agency.' Dad examines me more closely. 'Darling, I'd like you however you are. Why would you be worried about putting on some make-up?'

'I'm not,' I lie. But he's still giving me that look. And I hear myself say, 'You know, we've always been sort of like boys together and stuff.'

'Boys together?' says Dad, staring at me in amazement.

I try to make a joke of it. 'You know, Dad. I'm like the son you never had.'

Dad just sits there. And he looks like somebody socked him in the stomach.

'Don't look at me like that,' I say, but my voice sort of trails off. And I'm feeling a bit tearful.

'Oh Lucy,' he says. 'You are in a muddle, my duck. Aren't you?'

Dad moves closer to me and slips his big arm round me. 'Sweetheart, you weren't under the impression that I wanted a boy, were you?'

'You'd had four girls,' I blurt. 'You must have done!'

'Maybe before you were born, there was a bit of that,' he says without embarrassment. 'But when you arrived, my love, there was absolutely nobody else I'd rather have held in my arms than you. I wouldn't change a thing. I wouldn't swap you for all the boys in the world.' He kisses the top of my head.

I hug Dad back. I don't know why I'm crying, really. It seems stupid to cry when you're happy.

'You'll ruin your mascara,' he says gently.

'I'm not wearing any.'

'Oh well,' Dad says vaguely, and gets up. 'You don't get to use this as an excuse not to listen to George.'

Listening to George.

Honestly. I've just poured my heart out to my father. And I feel – a bit better about myself, actually. Can't I have some time to reflect?

Apparently I can't.

'Accustomed as I am,' George says for about the sixth time. 'D'you like that, Lucy? Accustomed as I am? It's usually *unaccustomed*, see.'

'Very funny,' I say automatically.

'I've had quite a bit of experience,' he says. 'They were riveted at the chartered surveyors' annual amateur dramatic pageant last year. I had to thank everybody after the show.'

'Mmm.' I stare into the kitchen, wildly hoping for rescue.

'And then the bit about Emily being the *jewel* in my *crown*. Because she makes jewellery!'

'Hysterical.'

'And how I hope she can use my *pearls* of wisdom!'

'Exercise!' I say suddenly.

'Pardon?' he asks, startled.

'Oh, nothing,' I say. 'Pearls of wisdom. Pearls before swine. Go on.'

'Well . . . do you think the bit about me being a diamond in the rough is too much?'

I try to concentrate. I'm going to be related to George, after all. And, like Bagpuss, Emily loves him.

'Maybe,' I say. 'To be honest, George, the best man gives the main speech. Most weddings have too many speeches,

307

don't you think? If I were you I'd just thank the bridesmaids for a wonderful job, thank Mum and Dad for the wedding, and then thank Emily for agreeing to be your wife. And spend the most time on that. She won't need jokes. In fact, the shorter the speech, the better everyone'll like it.'

He considers this.

'Suppose you're right,' he says. 'Save the longer version for the christening, eh? I'll be the only speaker then.'

The christening. Oh God, George's blood'll be in my family.

'Yes,' I agree. 'All the spotlight will be on you!' I try to sound encouraging. 'It was a really funny speech, George.' And so it was, maybe not intentionally. 'Ahm . . . you know, it's your big day. You're too much of a star anyway to concentrate on boring old speeches. Not that it was boring . . .'

Stop. Stop!

'Well done!' I end cheerfully.

He'll just hate me even more now, won't he?

'What did you mean, "exercise"?' he asks piercingly.

'I'm sorry.' Caught me. 'I just had something on my mind. I was thinking of something else, and it sort of popped into my head. But I was listening,' I say defensively. 'To all the jokes about pearls and diamonds and, um, emeralds and stuff.'

'There weren't any jokes about emeralds.' George flops down onto the sofa, which creaks under his weight. 'Oh, to hell with it. I'm not that good at speeches,' he says, as though confiding a great secret. 'I keep hoping the more I do of them the better I'll get.'

'Well, next to nobody's good at speeches,' I say. 'Except Winston Churchill and he's dead. The best speech is a short speech. Eh?'

'Oh yes. Think of the Oscars.'

'I know. I only watch them to laugh at the weird dresses. Cher does some good ones.'

'And that dead swan on Bjork!' he says, chuckling.

Good Lord, I never knew George had it in him.

'But what were you thinking about exercise? You weren't thinking I should exercise, were you?' he says pathetically. 'Em says she loves me how I am, but I do have a bit of a tummy . . .'

A bit of a tummy? You and the Fat Controller both, mate.

'Oh, no!' I protest, in horror. 'Not at all! I'd never say that. Um, think that . . .' this is getting better by the second, isn't it? 'It was about my career.'

'Your career? Didn't know you had one,' he says.

At least I'm not the only tactless person in the room.

'Thought you were a bit aimless,' he says blithely.

'Well, I've decided to do what I love. And I love exercise,' I say. 'There might not be money in computer games, but there is in exercise, isn't there? I'll get a job as an exercise instructor. Tunbridge Wells has loads of gyms and stuff, and I'm as fit as you like. I can do kickboxing and dancing and—'

'Yes, but mostly they only hire people with certificates, don't they?' he says.

That stops me for a second; just a second, though.

'Then I'll get a certificate,' I say. 'I can go on a course. I'll ace it. It'll give me something to aim for.'

'I suppose you could,' George says. He looks about as enthusiastic as I was about his speech. 'Why not?'

'You think that's dull?'

'Exercise classes are a crock of shit!' George snaps.

I'm stunned. I didn't think there was one swear word in his whole vocabulary.

'They're for thin people,' he says. 'Did you ever take classes?'

'Well, yes, and I—'

'Enjoyed them? I bet you did, looking like that,' he says. 'The whole damn industry only caters to people who are

309

already skinny and gorgeous. Like you and Em. What about the rest of us, eh?' he says plaintively. 'What about a gym where we don't have to feel embarrassed? What about somewhere we can lift weights without thirty teenage Arnolds standing around and snickering?'

'I—'

'And saying, "Get off the machine, you fat bastard,'" he adds bitterly. 'And asking if I ate all the pies?'

I smother a smile.

And then it hits me.

'George!' I say. I jump up from my chair and kiss him on the cheek. 'George, that's it. You're a bloody genius!'

He looks at me bewildered.

'I won't apply to be an ordinary instructor,' I say. 'I'll apply to teach a special class. For overweight people only. Very friendly, no judging. Taking it slow so they enjoy it. And ... we could have a kids' division, too. There are all these fat kids nowadays, and they get bullied at school ... what if I started a class for them? No skinnies allowed!'

'That's a great idea,' George says slowly. 'Stop them playing computer games, eh?'

'Computer games ... no!' I smack my forehead. 'Get them to play computer games! All the best new ones their parents won't let them have. I'll get somebody to wire some exercise bikes up with the greatest games, and the power only works if you pedal. If they want to play *Doom 3* they have to exercise! They'll have so much fun they won't even notice. That'll be my speciality. "Exercise you don't notice" ' I exclaim. 'Like ... trampolines! Kids *love* trampolines. But it's great exercise. And rollerblading ...' I pause. 'If I can find a venue with a rink. But there has to be one somewhere!' I won't be put off. 'Just think of it!'

'Lucy!' George says. He doesn't look so boring now. He's gone all animated. 'You know, I think it's a *brilliant* idea. Too good to give to somebody else.'

'But I don't exactly have the money to start my own gym,' I say.

'You could get it,' George says. 'You could borrow it.'

'I don't know anybody with a spare million quid. Do you?'

'From the bank, the bank!' he says excitedly. 'You could write a business plan. You're good at writing. Used to do all those reviews. And I could work on the financials for you. I'm not just a chartered surveyor,' he says with a touch of pride. 'I'm also a qualified accountant.'

I never thought I'd get excited by the words 'I'm also a qualified accountant'. But something's stirring in me. George looks like he actually thinks it could work. And George . . . whatever else he is, he's a conservative business-man. If George thinks it could be a success . . .

'You mean like a start-up loan.'

'We buy a piece of commercial property,' he says. 'And we outfit it as a gym. All new machines with—'

'*Doom 3.*'

'Right. And trampolines. And whatever else you said. Fun stuff.' He pauses. 'You know, the only time I ever lost weight was when I went skiing. Because I enjoyed the skiing!'

'That's it. If we could make it so people weren't embarrassed—'

'Or bored.'

'In America they have all kinds of funky stuff,' I say. 'These fake rock walls and the people climb up them. There are all these soft mattresses and cables to stop anybody getting hurt.'

'Sounds brilliant,' George says eagerly.

'And maybe an ice rink!'

'One thing at a time,' he says. 'Ice rinks are very expensive.'

'But you really think it could work?' I ask him.

'I'd join,' he says simply. 'Wouldn't you?'

Of course I would. Play *Doom* while you're biking? Bounce on trampolines? Climb rocks? Better than a stupid aerobics class!

'I'd have nice changing rooms,' I say. 'Ones with muted lights and no overhead ones, they show your cellulite. And a swimming pool with water slides. And currents!'

'Would you like a partner?' George says, and he's looking at me with, well, trepidation. George is looking nervously at *me*! Like I'm some big Richard Branson type business genius.

'Of course I would, George,' I say. 'I couldn't possibly do it without you. That is, if you're serious.'

'I'm dead serious,' he says. 'I've been thinking of taking a year off from surveying to travel the world. Backpack in Thailand. Take Em to the jewellery markets in Burma . . .'

I look at him admiringly. What a dark horse!

'But this is *way* more fun,' he says. 'I might even lose some weight!'

Dad walks in with a tray of tea and scones. They're a bit soggy in the middle still but I've learned to like them like that.

'How's the speech going, George?' he asks jovially, giving me a stern look.

'Brilliantly!' I say in a burst of enthusiasm. 'George is a genius, Dad.'

'It's Lucy who's the genius,' George says.

'We're going to go into business together, Dad!' I explode. 'We're going to be fitness entrepreneurs!'

'Wonderful, darling,' Dad says placidly. 'George, have a scone.'

'I shouldn't,' George says longingly. He pats his stomach.

'Have a scone, George,' I insist. 'Have some clotted cream, too. After tea we'll go for a bit of a walk. You can't lose weight if you think of it as giving up everything you enjoy.'

'Fitness through fun!' George says, brightening, and taking two.

'That's it,' I reply. And suddenly, even though nothing's happened yet, and we haven't had one real meeting, or drawn up one letter, I know it's going to be OK. Better than OK. It's going to be brilliant. Because this is a truly great idea. And it's doing what I love the most.

You know, my dad's the real genius. I kiss him on the cheek. Even without love, romantic love, I suppose people can be happy. If this moment's as good as it's going to get for me, well, maybe that's enough.

15

'Come on, Jody!' I yell. 'Get him! GET HIM!'

Jody twists her joystick and fires on the red button. The enemy explodes in a huge cloud of blood and gore.

'YAAAY!' she shrieks.

God, she looks bad. I'm so proud!

Jody's dripping with sweat. Her flabby chest is heaving, her cheeks are ruddy and flushed, and her mousy hair is plastered to her. But she's sitting up straight, her shoulders are back, and her fat legs are pumping away on that bike like there's no tomorrow. She's been working at the top range of her aerobic endurance for half an hour and she hasn't even noticed.

I lean across her, press a few buttons, and save her game. Then I flick a switch, and the bike slows substantially.

'Brilliant! You kicked arse,' I say. 'Cool down time, OK?'

Jody giggles. 'You said arse.'

I waggle my eyebrows. 'So I did. Don't tell your mum or I'm dead.'

Jody giggles again. I keep one eye on her heart monitor, watching it slow, hearing her breathing calm down. She's pretty seriously overweight so I'm extra careful.

Five minutes later she's completely back to normal.

'Good job,' I tell her. 'You're *fantastic* at this. A natural.'

She looks at me and her eyes are glowing. Jody's thirteen years old and eleven stone. I don't think she's ever thought of herself as 'fantastic' at anything before. But since she's

315

come to me, she's lost a stone and a half already, and she loves to do it. I think of all the kids enrolled, she's my favourite.

When I first saw her, I wasn't sure if we could do too much for her. I'd like to say that there was a hidden brilliance in the eyes concealed behind the chipmunk cheeks, or that I saw potential buried under the rolls of lard. But I didn't; I saw only a fat mass of human misery. Her parents were barrels too. A kid generally doesn't stand a chance when that happens; if Mum and Dad have chips with everything, then they reckon why can't they?

But I took her on anyway. I took her on, and I started her very slowly. The first session, we did nothing except slide down the water slides. She was the fattest girl in my fattest class, but at least none of the other kids bullied her. It's amazing, actually; they all look at each other lumbering into the room, and you can see the relief; nobody's in a position to tease.

Then I trick the lot of them.

Nothing but fun. The whole first week, we don't do any exercises at all. We go on the water slides. We go on the bouncy castle I have set up in the back, where it covers an ugly expanse of concrete. I get them on the bikes on the auto setting, the one where the pedals move automatically, and they play games. I teach them to love coming here. They associate it with nothing but fun.

The second week the exercise starts, but they don't notice it; we play games in the pool, as well as sliding. I take the bikes off auto and onto the lowest manual setting; they pedal a tiny bit. We mix up the bouncy castle with the trampolines.

Slowly, slowly, the fat starts to slide off. And I up the tempo.

It works; it always works. As long as the parents understand you need time, then we can transform any kid. Not just the body, either; they get confident, they start speaking up. I make them feel rebellious. I give them insults they can use on bullies.

And people notice. We're packed out. The worst part of the job is fielding desperate calls from parents willing to do anything to skip the waiting list. They'll bribe, they'll threaten, they'll cry sometimes. George is hiring extra staff, but still, there's only so much room in this place.

Honestly, we need to buy something else.

I can't quite believe it's happening. George is a genius. I've totally misjudged him. From day one when we wrote up the proposal and went to the bank, he's been brilliant. I sort of dazzled them with my bounce and enthusiasm, and then George plodded in with all these figures and charts – and they went for it! They all huddled in a group and said they'd call us back, and our mortgage got approved that day.

That day!

I shudder to think how much money we owe. We're not even turning a profit yet. But George promises we will be. We're booked to capacity. It's just so much cash to spend all at once.

George found the site, too. It was this rundown sports centre on the wrong end of town, with a small pool and a big, ugly gym room and an indoor track, plus an ugly yard. He negotiated the loans to get in the equipment, and we ripped up the running track, put slides on the pool, bought the videogame bikes, and did some cosmetic stuff. I persuaded him that the soft lights mattered a lot, and he persuaded me we can't afford a wave machine yet. But we did stick a rock-climbing wall on one side of the bike room, and we've got a smooth floor for rollerblades. I also bought some scooters for some of the children who can't balance.

We're busy. It's hard work. I'm in here all day. At least nobody bothers me about the wedding stuff any more. I get home around seven, Mum cooks dinner, and then I take a bath and fall into bed.

Work's my whole life. But it's *my* work and I love it. George says we're going to be very rich. I can't think about that, because I'm too tired. A good sort of tired, though.

George is looking pretty good, too. I train him when I train the instructors. He climbs the fake rock wall, and he likes to sneak out back and use the bouncy castle when the children aren't there. He's lifting weights and developing a six-pack. Emily's delighted, even though she worried when he gave up being a chartered surveyor. And when he got his ear pierced she asked me if I was involved in some kind of brainwashing cult, but I think secretly she liked it. She designed an earring, one of her own pieces; a minute square ruby in gold made to look like a jam pot.

That's what I'm calling it, by the way. Jam. We sell T-shirts (smallest size is L) with slogans: 'Jam today, Jam tomorrow' and 'I hate gym/I love Jam'. They've got a big jam pot on them with a spoon in it – I got the idea from Mum's scones. We sell loads! In fact the accessories are becoming this cult thing in Tunbridge Wells. And last week I said to George that we should start doing parties. We can rent the place out on Sundays, offer pool supervision, that sort of thing. He said it was a brilliant idea, and he also told me he's scouting out new places to buy and we have to start thinking about franchising.

Already! Even though we owe loads of money. But he tells me the bank is delighted and can't wait to lend us some more.

I feel great about myself. I honestly do. I play games, I work out, I help people who are feeling down and smothered by their bodies. Not just children, adults too. In fact these days I make it a condition, if the parents are fat too, that they join and attend. Whole families are getting fit and enjoying it.

Because, and this is what I've realized, life is just too short to have a bad time.

If you like to dance around like an idiot and sing to Madonna, you should do that.

One of my classes is called 'Dance around like an idiot'. It's extremely popular. I use the high-tech equipment of a boom-box and the kids can choose one song each and we all bounce around to it, with prizes for the kid who does the most stupid dance.

And if you like video games, you should do that. Only try to mix them up with something constructive. Our *Doom 3* bikes are getting the best press! You know who did a massive feature on Jam? *PC Games Galaxy*. Ken is features editor over there now. And after he ran that piece on my video game bikes, our phones were ringing off the hook!

It's what life is all about. Or should be. Having fun. It's what I'm all about, anyway. Make-up is nice, and I wear it, the long-lasting kind that doesn't run when you sweat. And I've even splashed out on a few nice outfits. I like Ghost and Zara. But there are no tights, no heels.

I'm happy. And nothing makes you as attractive as happiness. You know what real femininity is? It isn't wearing clothes you hate, watching your language and mincing around successful men. It's engaging with the world and being happy and having fun. You wouldn't believe how often I get asked out these days. All the divorced dads with Jam kids ask me. One of the guys from the bank even asked me. Men whistle as I'm going down the street. George says his mates are all begging him to set me up with them.

Which is nice. It feels nice. But I'm far too busy.

And anyway, I still miss Ollie.

I know, I know. It's been months. I'm not going to mope for ever.

But it's something else I've learned; you don't need to have a boyfriend if you don't want one. It's not the bloody law. I like being single. If I can't have Ollie, I need to wait for the pain to go away. I won't do things by half any more.

And even if you're mostly happy, and busy, and having fun, there can still be an ache where something's missing; there can still be part of your heart that's broken. I've learned to deal with it. Because that's reality. Nothing is perfect; life is bittersweet.

'Jodie!' I look at my watch. Quarter to four, her parents will be arriving any minute to pick her up. They've each lost two stone and are more fanatical about Jam than she is. 'Time's up, get out!'

'Awww,' she grumbles.

'You too, guys,' I yell at the swim class. There are twenty of them in there with my newest instructor Jane; she's a thickset girl who lost a stone and a half with me then asked for a job. All the kids love her. There are cries of protest, but Jane shepherds them out of the pool.

I feel a shiver of anticipation. I get a half day off today, which is to say I can leave before five. Jane and Rupa, two of my teachers, are taking the next classes, and George is in the back office. I'm so tired, all I want to do is go home and flop onto my bed with *Shopaholic and Sister*. Mum's moved me into the attic room so I have a window now, but I'm not staying there. Tomorrow at nine I'm seeing this flat I like for the second time. It's a two-bed near the Pantiles, the posh part of town. And it has its own roof garden!

I'm going to grow roses on the roof. And maybe tomatoes or something. Fresh tomatoes off the plant have this incredible scent, it's the best thing ever . . .

'Lucy.'

It's Lakshmi, my office manager. She's naturally skinny but we still hired her. George told me not to worry about the fact that I'm a disorganized slob, instead we got Lakshmi and everything's been running smoothly.

'You've got visitors waiting in the front.'

'The parents are meant to stay in the waiting room,' I say. 'The kids need ten minutes to change, they're way too early. Can't they read a copy of *Company* or something?'

'They're not parents,' she said. 'They say they're friends of yours. From London.'

I hurry towards our front office. What, has Buffy come to see me? Or even Ken, or some of the other guys from *PC Games Universe*. It's slightly embarrassing, I wasn't expecting anybody, and the offices are the dingiest bits of the complex. We use second-hand computers and haven't replaced the strip lights, and the couch in the waiting room has a couple of coffee stains on it – I got it from a small ad in the back of the *Courier* for sixty quid. I figured why spend thousands on something nobody's going to see but us? I'd rather put that money towards making our payments. Or a new video game bike, or something.

I turn into the front office and stop dead.

There, sitting together on the couch, holding hands, are Ollie and Victoria.

They're not sitting, really. More like perching. Victoria in particular has her buttocks clenched, as though she thinks the sofa might have fleas and she wants as little of her leather-clad bottom to touch its faded velvet as possible. She's not looking good, honestly. The hair and make-up are as careful as ever, but there's a drawn, pinched air about her that wasn't there before. And her expression telegraphs that this is the last place in the world she wants to be.

That's a coincidence! As she's the last person in the world I want to see.

I recover and paste a smile on my face.

'Ollie, Victoria,' I say, coming forward. 'How nice to see you here. Um, this is a surprise.'

Ollie gives me a bear hug. 'I finally spoke to your sister and she said you were down in Kent. So we thought we'd make the trip, as we can't raise you on the phone.' He looks at me severely.

'Well, I've been busy,' I say. 'New job and stuff. Sorry.'

'Your mum told me you were here,' Ollie says. 'You look great. Doesn't she, Victoria?'

I don't think by any stretch of the imagination I look great just at this particular moment. I've taught four classes in the last five hours and I haven't had time to shower yet.

'Oh yes,' says Victoria. Her voice sounds odd, and she's pasted on a bright, fake smile. 'Exactly the same. I must say, Lucy, you're very consistent,' she adds, with a musical laugh to show she's being funny, and not, in fact, a total bitch. 'Still living with your parents. And what an off-beat job. You're a gym teacher.'

'That's right,' I say. 'And—'

'You really should learn to type,' she says, with false sympathy. 'At least those jobs pay a living wage. You could rent somewhere of your own.'

'Victoria,' Ollie says sharply. 'Lucy can make her own decisions. She's never been a career girl. And if she's happy with her mum and dad, then why not, I say.' He smiles at me supportively.

'But of course!' says Victoria, widening her eyes innocently. 'I just worry about Lucy's future. But since her family's taking care of that for her . . .'

The door to the inner office opens and George comes out.

'Hi, George,' I say. 'These are my friends, Ollie McLeod and Victoria Cobham. George is my future brother-in-law,' I explain. 'Em and he are getting married at Christmas.'

'How nice,' says Victoria brightly. She extends a bony hand to George. 'I must say, this is a big complex, George!'

'You look very busy,' Ollie agrees. He gives Victoria a sideways glance, as though checking she'll behave herself.

'Rushed off our feet,' George says. 'Lucy has no time to herself. At all.'

'Maybe you should hire some extra instructors,' Victoria says. 'Though it's nice of you to give Lucy the overtime, George. She obviously needs to save her pennies.'

George blinks at her.

'She gives me overtime, more like,' he says. 'It's Lucy's company, after all. I'm just the junior partner.'

There's a stunned silence. I wouldn't be human if I said I didn't enjoy it.

'You mean . . . Lucy has something to do with the owners?' Victoria says tensely. 'Is Lucy dating the owner?'

George chuckles. 'Lucy *is* the owner, It's her gym. I should say, gyms.' He turns to me. 'Tonbridge Fitness accepted our offer on their property. We should complete in a month, and the financiers are lining up. You better start talking to your equipment suppliers.'

'I'm sorry,' I say. 'Boring business. We're expanding, we don't have enough space here.'

'Lucy!' Ollie's face lights up. 'You mean this all belongs to you?'

'George is being way too modest,' I say. 'He's got a big stake in it too.'

'But you're the majority shareholder,' George says at once. 'Not that I'm complaining. This company's the best thing that ever happened to me. Well, apart from Em, of course.'

Victoria clenches her jaw so tightly I think she might be about to start grinding her teeth.

'God, that's . . .' Ollie seems lost for words. 'That's brilliant, Lucy. Absolutely fantastic.' He slaps me on the back, just the way he used to.

'Look, I've got to take a quick shower, get changed,' I say. 'Maybe George can give you guys a quick tour or something.'

'Don't mind about us,' Victoria says at once. 'Seen one gym, seen them all.'

'Rubbish,' Ollie says. 'I can't wait to see it. And then we'll take you out for supper, Lucy. OK?'

He looks so hopeful, and obviously I can't be rude.

'Sure,' I say, accepting defeat. 'Why not?'

I take my time showering, though. I mean, I didn't ask them to come here. What the hell are they doing here?

I wash my hair and blast it dry. I'm determined to get through this, and I'm not going to do anything different from normal. I'll wear my usual clothes and go to dinner with them and that's it.

So I pull out what was already in my locker bag: a cool black trouser suit from H&M, a Zara black leather jacket, my DKNY chestnut leather tote, and my make-up – tinted moisturizer, some rose blusher and my clear lipgloss. I don't bother with mascara these days; it bothers me when I work out, and anyway, I've got dark lashes. I can look a bit Barbara Cartland if I overdo it. And then scent. I splashed out on a bottle of Hermès 64 Rue Faubourg, I really like that smell. So on it goes, I slip my feet into my Patrick Cox loafers, brush out my hair, and I'm ready.

It's not much, but it's neat and pretty and comfortable, too. Why I should I change things just because Ollie prefers the beauty queen routine?

Stop that, Lucy, I tell myself. There's no rivalry between you and Victoria. They're getting married. It's all over.

One dinner. I can do one dinner.

'Where are you guys staying?' I ask them.

I've picked the Star of Jhansi, my favourite local Indian. I know Ollie loves Indian, and I don't care what Victoria thinks.

'We've got a room in a hotel in town,' she says. 'Passable place, I suppose.'

'The Black Swan. It's lovely,' Ollie says. 'Got those fancy rooms where everything's a different shade of white, and this sunken whirlpool bath. And flat-screen TVs. It's like a hotel I stayed at in LA, once.'

'I know.' I beam at him. 'It's weird round here. You go into these ordinary-looking Victorian buildings and they're all done up ultra trendy. There are more spas here than in Chelsea.'

'I really like it,' Ollie says.

'Oh, come on, darling, it's a backwater,' Victoria says, tossing her hair. 'Provincial England, who'd live here?'

'Loads of people,' Ollie responds evenly.

'Property prices are outrageous,' I say. 'Anyway, some people like small towns, Vicky. London isn't the be-all and end-all, you know.'

'I fucking hate it,' Ollie says suddenly.

'Darling!' Victoria looks shocked.

'I do.' He grins at me. 'Wish I had the balls to be like Lucy and be an entrepreneur.'

'How are your jobs going?' I ask politely.

'Mine's going wonderfully, thanks,' says Victoria instantly.

Ollie looks at her. 'What? But they just sacked you.'

She turns bright red.

'They didn't *sack* me, as you put it,' she says acidly. 'I resigned.'

Ollie opens his mouth, then thinks better of it.

'I didn't agree with the magazine's creative direction,' she says loftily. 'And I've had loads of offers. Only I'm not sure if I want to work. Not everybody wants to be a wage slave.'

'And your firm?' I ask Ollie. Fuck it, I don't care if she wants to sulk.

'I resigned,' he says cheerfully.

'What?'

'Took your advice,' he says. 'You were right, Lucy. All along. What I was doing wasn't right. Fleecing people in divorce cases, using custody issues . . .' He shakes his head. 'No wonder I was so bloody unhappy.'

Ollie pauses for a moment, lost in himself.

'Oh, wait.' He rouses. 'There is one good thing. My last case. Your friend, Mr Rogers.'

'Toby Rogers?' I ask eagerly. 'What happened?'

'They settled.' Ollie grins at me. 'Peach of a case. We had them bang to rights. Mayle's father couldn't wait to make him go away.'

'How much did you get for him?'

'About three quarters of a mill,' says Ollie, modestly.

I gasp. 'Really?'

'I should have asked for more,' he says. 'At least we took no fee. It was pro bono, he gets the lot. He should have a very comfortable retirement.'

'That's wonderful. Thanks, Ol.'

'My pleasure.'

'So what are you going to do now?' I ask.

He shrugs. 'Absolutely no idea. Take a year off, maybe. Then some other kind of law, or something else altogether. I always liked the idea of being a teacher,' he says. 'Teaching difficult kids. The sort nobody else wants to take on.'

'I think that'd be wonderful,' I say warmly. I want to maintain some distance, but I'm so proud of him. 'That's what I do. You noticed all the kids in my gym were overweight?'

'I'd call it fat,' Victoria says nastily. 'We didn't want to say anything, of course . . .'

'I cater for people with a weight problem,' I say. 'They don't have to be scared of my gym. No hard bodies anywhere in sight.'

'Except yours,' Ollie says admiringly. 'You look great.'

'Thanks. Have some more rogan josh,' I suggest.

'I will,' he says. 'It's all delicious.'

Victoria sighs exaggeratedly. 'Do you know how many calories are in one bite of chicken tikka masala?' she asks.

'Darling,' says Ollie, with an edge to his voice. 'I thought we'd agreed. No more criticizing how the other person eats. How's your salad?'

'Delicious!' she says defiantly, looking at her few green

leaves with some plain grilled chicken that she insisted the kitchen make specially.

'Good,' Ollie says. And winks at me.

'So,' I say. 'What brought you down here, anyway?'

'I told you,' he says. 'To see you. The mountain comes to Mohammed, and all that. We weren't going to accept "I want some space", were we, Vicky? Lucy, you're one of my best mates,' he says, perfectly seriously. 'And I don't plan on cutting you out of my life. You must be over Todd by now.'

'Oh, I am,' I say, without thinking.

'Well, there you go.' He looks pleased. Damn! I just gave away my excuse. 'You must come to the wedding, and come and stay.'

Oh, sure. That would absolutely be at the top of my most-wished-for list of activities.

'Sounds great,' I lie. 'Only I'm really busy right now. As you've seen. Anyway, when is the . . . happy day?'

'October the first,' Victoria says, glaring at me. 'We've got a marvellous autumn-themed wedding. At the McLeod estates in Scotland.'

That does surprise me.

'At your dad's place?' I ask Ollie.

Ollie and his father have never been close. In fact, they've always been mortal enemies. Ollie's dad is a total son of a bitch.

'We're reconciled,' he says, without enthusiasm. 'Victoria persuaded me.'

'I'm the peacemaker,' she confirms.

'Well, that's great,' I say, uncertainly.

I'm not sure how great it really is.

'It was all over some silly misunderstanding a long time ago,' Victoria says airily. But Ollie holds up a hand.

'No it wasn't,' he says, in a very cold tone. 'I'm trying to forgive him, OK? But don't dismiss what he did.'

'You can't hold a grudge,' says Victoria angrily.

327

Ollie turns to me. 'I don't think I ever told you the full story.'

'No,' I agree. I knew his dad was an early alcoholic, who moved from hitting his mother to old-fashioned verbal abuse and coldness when he gave up the Scotch; that Ollie had spent a miserable, unloved childhood in various draughty boarding schools, after his mother died; and that a final break had come when he was seventeen.

It seemed too painful to talk about much. I never pushed him.

'Oliver,' says Victoria severely. 'This isn't a matter you should share with Lucy. It's a family thing.'

'Lucy is my closest friend,' Ollie answers her. 'And I want her to know.'

His closest friend.

His closest friend.

I don't know what I feel. Like crying. Proud. And utterly desolate. I don't say anything, maybe because I can't. Victoria tosses her hair.

'If you must,' she says distantly.

'When I was sixteen I met this girl from town. She was the daughter of our local bookie. Nice girl, redhead,' he says. 'Anyway, we were going to break up, but we hadn't been careful. I found out she was pregnant just as it was coming to an end.'

'Go on,' I say.

'I wanted to marry her. You know, support her. My dad said no way. So I told him I'd get a job and leave the house.'

'And what did he say?'

'He told me I had to see to it that she had an abortion. Pay her to have one, if necessary. He said,' and Ollie's fair face flushes, 'he said he'd have no bastard son of a common little tart making claims on the estate.'

I suck my breath in.

'And I told him it's my child. And come what may with

me and the girl, it'd still be my child. And I would always love it and be its dad, and whatever I had, I would give it, estate or no. Dad told me no son of his would act that way and he wouldn't let me throw the family land out of the window. He'd cut off my allowance, stop paying my school fees – right before A-levels.'

'So what did you do?'

'Told the girl I'd be there for her, of course. She said she didn't want to marry me but we'd raise the baby together, only after four months she miscarried.'

'I'm sorry,' I say.

'Yes.' Ollie stares into the middle distance. 'I still think about that baby at times. Anyway, Dad said I was lucky, I was "off the hook".' He sighs. 'Next morning I left the house. Got a job with the girl's father, rented a shitty bedsit in Glasgow, and asked the local comprehensive school to get me registered for A-levels. I haven't spoken to him since then. Not till a few months ago, anyway.'

'And what's it been like?'

Ollie shrugs. 'Dad said he was sorry. I suppose I'll give him a chance to prove it, at least.'

'I'm glad, if you can forgive him,' I say. 'You know, if he's truly sorry. He's the only family you've got. And family matters.'

'Excuse me.' Victoria's voice is pure ice. 'Jacob is not Ollie's only family. He'll soon have a wife and children of his own.'

'So you will.' I force a smile.

'Don't say no about coming to the wedding yet,' Ollie begs. 'You and me still get on great. I'm sorry I was such a shit to you before, Lucy. That Todd guy, he just set my teeth on edge.'

'It's fine,' I say. 'We're still friends.'

'Good, because Vicky's no fun to watch rugby with,' Ollie says with a grin.

I nod. I've missed him. Maybe more than I was allowing myself to believe.

'Victoria's been missing you too,' he says, naively. 'I'm sure you girls will want to spend some time together. Can you get an hour off tomorrow morning, Lucy? Take her out for coffee?'

I open my mouth to make an excuse.

'Please,' he says. 'I want you around, Lucy.'

What can I say?

'Sure.' I turn to Victoria, whose smile is as fake and frozen as mine. 'I'll pick you up at ten.'

She's waiting for me in the lobby. It's exactly as Ollie described, all blond woods and staff in matching white outfits. Rather like a sort of luxury dentist's office, or something. Perfect Victoria ambience, I'd have thought.

She doesn't seem to think so, though. She's standing there, all dressed in rich shades of chocolate and berry, perfect autumn colours, and made up to the nth degree; I'm in a Metallica T-shirt and jeans and my navy Miu Miu pea coat, with my Faith cowboy boots.

'There you are,' she says, although I'm a grand total of five minutes late. 'Let's get this over with, shall we?'

For Ollie's sake I wait till we're outside and walking down towards Victoria Place shopping centre. There's a Starbucks right opposite it. I reckon two coffees should do it.

Then I say, 'You know, I didn't ask you to come.'

'Not directly,' she snaps. 'But I'm sure you had something to do with it. You went to see Oliver before you left London.' Her stare is accusing.

'Yes,' I reply.

'Well, I don't know what you said to him. But you've almost ruined him!'

I blink. 'You what?'

'He left the firm. Didn't you hear him? All he did was set

330

up some damn stupid case suing Todd.' Her eyes narrow at me. 'You were a vindictive bitch, Lucy Evans! I didn't know you had it in you. You've *destroyed* Todd! You and that American bitch Buffy.'

'Oh?' I say, interested. 'Has he been tried?'

'Tried and convicted, on her testimony. His parents had to settle her harassment suit.'

I think of Toby Rogers. 'I suppose it was a big number?'

'Millions,' she says, with vicious envy. 'And they've sent him to jail for fraud!'

'Good,' I say, serenely. And good for Buffy. Betsy-Ann Moss finally taking control.

Victoria ignores this. She stares at me with hatred.

'It's been reported,' she says. 'Do you know the US press got hold of the story? They know he's in jail! Even if he does get out in six months, he'll never be a Senator now!'

We go into the coffee shop and I order two black grandes. Victoria stalks to the two-seat table all the way in the back, and when I hand her her drink she doesn't thank me. She gestures imperiously for me to sit down.

'They weren't trumped-up. He was under investigation for fraud.'

Victoria waves her hand. 'That was just a misunder-standing.'

'And he sexually harassed my friend Buffy. And me.'

'Sexually harassed?' Victoria's eyes narrow. 'Don't give me that perfect little miss innocent *bullshit*, Lucy! You couldn't believe it when he even noticed you. You couldn't wait to spend his money! I was there, remember?'

There's something quite surprising in the viciousness of her tone. I look at her carefully; she's all flushed, and there's a strange glitter in her eyes.

'Yes, you were there. Waiting for your chance. What was Todd, the bigger, better deal?'

'Don't be silly,' she snarls. 'I love Ollie.'

But this time I don't believe her.

'And he loves me.'

Unfortunately, I do believe that.

'Then why do you give a toss what happens to Todd?'

'Todd's a friend,' Victoria says loftily. 'I tried to see him when he was released on bail, but he wouldn't even talk to me.' Her eyes accuse me. 'He wants nothing to do with anybody who knows *you*.'

'Wait up,' I say slowly. 'What do you mean, he's a friend? You betrayed Ollie, Victoria. I took you at your word it was a drunken mistake. But if you're trying to see Todd now . . .'

'Yes, thank you, Vicar,' she snaps. 'I understand your pedestrian way of looking at the world.' She shrugs. 'Anyway, Todd wants nothing more to do with any of us. So I suppose you've got your way there.'

My insides are churning. Victoria tried to see Todd . . .

'It'll be all right, though,' she hisses, feverishly. 'As long as you stay the hell away from us. I don't know what you told Ollie to make him keep calling you. To make him come down here.'

'Ollie just wants us to be friends again.'

'That's not going to happen,' Victoria says. Her tone is flat. 'We're going to Scotland. And now he's reconciled with Jacob, there's nothing to stop the development. Jacob will give Ollie his share of the estate right now. I've talked to my father. We're putting something together. We're all going to get rich,' she says, as though trying to convince herself. 'Maybe not like . . . But never mind that!'

Victoria turns to me again. 'I don't want you at the wedding, she says. 'You've infected Ollie quite enough. Make some excuse. You're good at that.' She shrugs, and her voice softens slightly. 'You did one thing right. You didn't tell him about my little indiscretion, because he loves me. Now you have to follow through. Make sure he understands that we're moving on and there's no place in our married life for some desperate other woman,' she says. 'I'm sure you'll meet someone eventually, anyway. But it's really not my problem.'

She looks around, bored. Having said her piece, she apparently has no further need of me.

'Maybe I'll do some shopping. Even somewhere like this has to have a few designer stores . . .' She eyes me again. 'Why don't you go to the hotel? Ollie's having a lie-in. You can speak to him, talk him out of all this craziness. Driving down to *Kent*. He must be nuts.' She stands up. Apparently, that's it.

'You're very confident,' is all I can manage.

She looks down at me; for a second there's a flicker of doubt in her brown eyes, but then it's gone.

'You did the proper thing before, Lucy; I'll give you that. And I'm sure you'll do it again.'

'The development,' I say. 'You plan to develop his family estates? And he wants to do it?'

She grabs her bag, bored of me now.

'He will, when I've finished with him,' she says. 'Why d'you think I had him make his peace with that idiot Jacob? It's my job to know what's best for Ollie.' She extends her manicured hand with the too-long, blood-red talons. 'Goodbye, Lucy,' she says distantly. 'It's been . . . interesting.'

I walk back to the hotel very slowly.

I don't know exactly what I'm going to do. My head hurts, just thinking about it. On the one hand, I know I ought to tell him. I can't just let him marry her. She's a monster. And he's such a good bloke. If she got pregnant, he'd stay. He'd be stuck with her his whole life.

But then again, why am I doing this? When I saw them in my office they were holding hands. I mean, I don't want Ollie to marry Victoria. I don't want him to love her. I don't want him to have anything to do with her.

I want him to love me.

It's a grey day today. There's an autumn chill in the air, and out in the countryside near Mum and Dad it'll be foggy. I feel as if nothing's clear. I don't know what I'm doing. I only know I have to talk to him.

When I get to the Black Swan, I ring Ollie on my mobile. He's still in his room, thank God. I stand there in reception.

'Come up,' he says. 'I'm in 406.'

'No. You come down here. I want to take you out somewhere,' I say. Somewhere Victoria won't find us.

'All right,' he says. 'Be right there. Although you sound very mysterious.'

I ring the office, tell them I won't be in today. George asks if I'm sick; I haven't cancelled a class ever, since we started Jam. Am I sick? Maybe . . .

Oh God.

There he is. Wearing black trousers that are a bit too big, and one of his old shirts. I thought Victoria had made him throw those out. His hair's a bit rumpled. He looks, not gorgeous, maybe. But like the old Ollie, which is far better.

I take a ragged breath. My heart's pumping so hard I feel dizzy.

'Lucy!' he says. 'Are you feeling OK?'

'Yeah, fine.' I pull myself together. 'I just need to tell you something. There's a park down the road . . .'

Ollie lifts his eyebrows. 'Then let's go for a walk,' he says gently.

We get about half a mile away – just a couple of streets; I don't want to bump into Victoria coming back to the hotel. And then I stop, right there on the pavement. Kids are whizzing past us on skateboards. There's a drunk old man across the street, and he's just shouted, 'Shut up, you WANKER!' at this old lady walking to the bus stop with her shopping – not that she'd said a word.

'I have to tell you right now,' I say.

Ollie looks alarmed. 'My God, what's the matter? You don't have cancer or something?'

'Nothing like that.'

'You're pregnant? Was it that bastard Todd?'

I shake my head. 'It's not about me at all. It's about Victoria. You can't marry her.'

He looks at me strangely. 'Bit late in the day for this sort of thing, isn't it?'

'She's a total bitch,' I blurt out. 'She told me – she just told me – she wants to get her dad to do a deal with your dad. To develop property on the land in Scotland.'

Ollie looks thunderstruck.

'That's the whole reason she got you to reconcile with him,' I say. 'It wasn't because she thought you should mend fences. It was because she wants you to be rich. Ol, she's all about money. She doesn't love you, never has. She just wants a rich prestigious man to live off.'

He doesn't say anything for a few seconds, but his face goes kind of grey. Like the sky. And it makes me feel sick.

'I'll talk to her about it,' he says. 'Nobody's building anything.'

'That's not everything.' I take a deep breath. 'She cheated on you. That day I told you I found Todd in bed with Buffy, I was lying.'

'It was Vicky?'

'It was Vicky.'

Ollie opens his mouth, then shuts it again. He can't seem to find the words.

'She was playing both sides,' I say desperately. 'You were prestigious but he was worth more money. She said it was a one-time thing, not to ruin what you guys had. But just now, she told me she tried to see him again. She said it was as a friend. But if he'd have her, she'd drop you.'

He's stock still. I wish he'd say something, anything!

'I don't want to do this in the street.' He looks around. There's a Bella Pasta right opposite us, but he shakes his head. 'I'm not eating with you, Lucy.' His tone is very dreadful, very final. 'Show me this park and let's find a bench.'

Miserably, I lead him to it. Ollie doesn't say a word to me the whole way. He passes through the iron gates, casting around for somewhere to sit. And the first grimy bench he finds, he sits on.

I do the same. At the other end. The distance between us seems awfully symbolic.

'First, I suppose it's good you told me at last.' He shakes his head. 'A year out of my life, but what the fuck, eh? I never really trusted her – never could. She was always talking about money. She'd have been better off with Todd. He didn't care.'

'But if you felt like that, why were you marrying her?' I burst out.

'It's very easy to convince yourself of things,' Ollie says bitterly. 'She was very successful, put-together. I thought she'd make an interesting wife. I liked how she dressed, or thought I did. And she told me what I wanted to hear. At the beginning, that seemed important.' He shrugs. 'A shrink would say I'm always looking for approval, right? No mother, Dad was vile. Well, maybe there's something to that bollocks, after all. Victoria always made me feel like the greatest thing ever. It takes time to see that it's not real. When you want to trust somebody, you trust them.'

He looks up from the ground.

'But you,' he says. 'You – I never would have believed it. That you'd sell me out. Of all the people in the world, not you.'

'Sell you out?' I say, horrified.

'What was it?' Ollie asks. 'Were you offended because I hated seeing you with that wanker? You let a few months of coldness on my part wipe out everything that went before. We've been close for years. Years. I just . . .' His voice trails away. 'I don't know how you could do it.'

I'm shaking all over. 'You mean, not tell you? That she cheated?'

'Cheated,' he says, bitterly. 'That's a light word for such a big thing. Cheating is something you do in card games. My future *wife* was fucking another man, Lucy. Fucking him. Then you walk out of my life, you don't take my phone calls – and you'd have let me go to the altar without a clue.'

I struggle with myself. I need to tell him, to explain. But there's so much to say and suddenly, when it counts, I have no idea how to start. I'm terrified I'm going to miss my chance. My throat's all dry . . .

And he gets up from the bench.

'Well,' he says, without emotion. 'Goodbye.'

He walks away. Towards the iron gates again. And I know with every atom in my being that if I let Ollie leave now, I'll never see him again.

I get up. I've started to cry; proper, big tears are streaming down my face but I can't worry about that, or my nose getting red. I run after him, sobbing, and grab his shoulders.

'Wait! Ollie!' I say. 'Wait, wait.'

He turns round, but he doesn't take me in his arms or anything. He doesn't even offer me a tissue. He just stands there, with this frozen look, like why can't I just let him get away.

'You need to understand.'

'I think I understand perfectly well,' he says. 'Our friendship meant nothing. You betrayed me for Victoria, who you'd only known a couple of months. A bit of shopping, a couple of rich boyfriends, some girlie bonding, eh?'

'Now WAIT,' I shout. I'm angry now. 'Just WAIT because you're not LISTENING and you're being a SEXIST TWAT!'

He takes a step back – I guess he wasn't expecting that. But a relative calm comes over me. I'm just going to tell him everything. The lot. Screw feminine wiles and whatever. It's not me, in the end.

'I'm going to tell you the whole story,' I say, dashing my hand across my eyes and breathing steadily. 'Then if you want to storm off and cast me into the outer darkness or whatever, you're welcome to. But you're fucking well going to hear me out first. All right?'

'All right,' he says. And despite himself, I can see just the faintest twitch to his lips. 'Is it going to take long?'

'Five minutes.'

'Then let's go back to the bench.'

He leads me back there and sits down and looks at me expectantly.

I can't quite believe I'm doing this. My entire future, coming down to a five-minute conversation on a dirty old park bench.

But what the hell. Here goes nothing.

'We,' I start, 'were best mates.'

He inclines his head.

'And I always fancied you.'

There. That came out quite grown up. No blushing or anything. Ollie gives a little start, but he doesn't flinch. He sits quite still, listening.

'Obviously you didn't fancy me, but I didn't want to mope about it. I knew the kind of girl you went for. All like Victoria – nice clothes, loads of make-up.' I wince. 'High heels. Also, not me. Plus I'd bollocksed up all my friendships by dating them. I don't know why I couldn't have girl-friends like normal girls—'

'Maybe because you already had four sisters,' Ollie says.

Four sisters. Yeah. And we are best friends. I'd never thought of that. Maybe I'm not so weird after all.

'Anyway, I didn't want to mess it up with you, and I was basically happy—'

'So you were,' he says softly, as if to himself. 'Always happy.'

'And then Victoria proposed, and you kicked me out. And I got fired, and everybody I knew was telling me to grow up, and the job with Todd needed me to be groomed, and that—'

'You went a bit overboard,' he says.

I look at him sternly. 'Are you going to keep interrupting?'

He shakes his head. 'I'm sorry,' he says gravely. 'Go on.'

'Anyway,' I continue, 'I felt very flat and low. Because you were marrying Victoria. It's hard to tell if it was just because I hated her, or because I was in love with you.'

Now his eyes slide away from me, and he stares at his shoes. Oh God! I'm pouring out a stupid tale of unrequited love.

But no, it's not stupid to love someone. Even if they don't love you back. And it's not stupid to tell the truth.

'Anyway, I had to take a good look at myself. And maybe I was being a bit childish, back then. It's easy not to look for a good job if you don't have to. Plus, I could see how successful Victoria was – at work, too. I wanted a boyfriend. I wanted some money.' I take a deep breath. 'And Victoria told me you and she had discussed my crush on you, all your friends knew about it, and I was just making a fool of myself—'

'That wasn't true,' Ollie says instantly. 'Discuss it with her? I never knew about it.'

Well, he sure does now.

'So I wanted a boyfriend of my own. Maybe I felt insecure too. And Todd was—'

'Handsome and rich.'

I nod. 'You know what happened there. Victoria got close to me. Now I think she was just angling to get near Todd, but at the time . . .' I shrug. 'I guess I just couldn't imagine why anybody who had you would ever be interested in somebody like Todd. So it never occurred to me.'

'Oh, Lucy,' he says wearily. But I plough on. If I don't finish now I never will.

'When I found her in bed with him, I'd already had a fight with him. I was going to his house to drop off the keys. And I was going to tell you. But she promised me it was a one-off, she said she got drunk, that you and she loved each other. And that if I was really your friend, as opposed to this wishful thinking would-be girlfriend, I'd do what was right for you, not what I wanted to do.'

'What I didn't know wouldn't hurt me?'

'Something like that. I thought – I'd been to see you, and I thought maybe – but you kept talking about the wedding. I realized you did love her. Plus, since by then the whole Todd madness had evaporated, I also knew that I loved you. How could I trust my own motivation to tell you?'

I take another breath.

'I packed it in. Taped Todd so he couldn't go on bullying Buffy. Came to tell you I was leaving. Victoria told me to get out of your lives, and move on. And, basically, that's what I did.'

I'm drained.

'That's everything,' I say. 'Until, today, I finally understood that she never loved you and she was still chasing Todd. I did what I thought was right for you. Both times. If you sod off thinking I betrayed you and you never speak to me again, you're being mean,' I say, and now my voice has risen; to my horror all the grown-up calm is vanishing. And yes, here come the tears. 'Because that's not how it happened.'

Ollie reaches into his trouser pocket and offers me a hanky. I blow on it loudly. Just as well, really. A runny nose at this point would be the cherry on top of everything.

'Can I have a turn?' he says mildly. 'I think this gut-spilling thing is quite a good idea.'

I wave for him to go on.

'I dated all those girls for two reasons. No, three,' he

says. 'In order of least importance first. One, because I do like groomed girls, although they maybe overdid it. Two, because since I was a little boy I've wanted a real family. I might be the only bloke in the world who has wedding fantasies on a first date,' he says ruefully. 'Fatal. And three, because I was in love with you but there was no way you'd ever have me.'

I look at him. 'What?'

'Don't act so surprised,' he says. 'You told me so. Flat out. You said you didn't like me in that way.'

'But you weren't supposed to give up!' I cry. The injustice of it!

He spreads his hands. 'Lucy, I believed you. Of course I did. What would somebody like you want with somebody like me? Somebody boring and dull, a wage slave? A *lawyer*, for God's sake? You were this force of nature,' he says. 'This amazing ray of sunshine that everybody envied. You loved life, loved your job, loved your family, loved your body. I didn't know which was worse, the pain of living with you and not having you for my own, or the idea that we'd split up and I'd go back to my grey little life and my grey little desk. You had such zest,' he says. 'You relished every moment of being alive. That's the ideal woman,' he says slowly. 'The one who shines out like a sun, wherever you put her.'

'But you were always telling me to grow up.'

'I was jealous too,' he explains. 'And resentful, maybe. It was easy to try to tell myself maybe you weren't all *that* great. And if I couldn't get you but I could get more conventional girls, maybe conventional was what I really wanted.'

His pale blue eyes look at me under their sandy lashes; such a look of love and hope that I can't quite breathe.

'I didn't, though,' he says. 'All the time I was with them, including Vicky, I thought about you. Tried to push the thoughts away, of course. I thought I was a right bastard,

341

really. Not loyal, not true.' His eyes are sparkling now. 'Ironic, how that panned out.'

We just sit there for a moment. I pretend to be fascinated with a nearby squirrel. I have absolutely no idea what to do next.

'Well,' Ollie says. 'If I've got this right, we were in love with each other all along. We dated other people to get over ourselves. Both the other people were tossers. Is that about the size of it?'

I nod.

'Any chance,' he says slowly, 'that a successful business-woman like yourself might want to date an unemployed ex-lawyer like me?'

I suddenly feel all embarrassed.

'I'm not very good at dates,' I say. 'I think I'd be a bit shy with you.'

'I don't know why,' he says. 'You've vomited all over me on at least three occasions. Remember?'

'Are you always going to bring that up?' I demand.

'Absolutely not,' he says. 'I'll just use it as a bargaining chip next time I want to embarrass you into something.'

'Fair enough,' I say. I'm still looking at the squirrel. It seems safest.

Ollie reaches out and takes my hand.

I should tell you a bolt of electric desire pulses through my body. But it doesn't; it just feels very warm and lovely.

'Let's skip the dating bit,' he suggests. 'We know each other backwards. We can get married. I've got this elaborate wedding booked.'

'OK,' I mutter. 'But what about Victoria?'

'I'll leave a note at the hotel and pay her bill there,' he says. 'It's more than she deserves. And I'll ring her tonight. Sound good?'

'You mean it,' I breathe.

'Of course I mean it,' he says. 'My beautiful, lovely, fun, gorgeous Lucy.'

Then he reaches over with his other hand and lifts my chin, turning my head towards him. And kisses me, very lightly, on the lips. Feather-light; delicate.

Ah, now the electricity!

I'm panting. Not very . . .

Sod it. Maybe it is ladylike. After all, what's more feminine than love?